DANESBU

DANESBURY HOUSE

by Ellen Wood

Illustrations by Sydney Cowell

Edited with an Introduction by
CURT HERR

WHITLOCK PUBLISHING
ALFRED, NY

Danesbury House by Ellen Wood first published 1860

First Whitlock Publishing edition 2009

Whitlock Publishing
P.O. Box 472
Alfred, NY 14802

Editorial matter
© Curt Herr

ISBN 10: 0-9770956-6-5
ISBN 13: 978-0-9770956-6-7

This book was set in Dante on 55# acid-free paper that meets ANSI standards for archival quality.

Printed in the United States of America.

TABLE OF CONTENTS

Introduction ix

Danesbury House

I	The Mistake—The Dinner Table 3
II	The Night Journey 14
III	The Desolate House 21
IV	The Game Played Out 31
V	Evils 41
VI	Training... 56
VII	The Danesbury Operatives 64
VIII	Robert and Lionel—The Last of Glisson..................... 73
IX	Viscount Temple 80
X	Lord Temple's Folly 94
XI	The Demand 105
XII	Mrs. Danesbury—The Wedding 119
XIII	A Discovery...130
XIV	A Mad Act..142
XV	A Graceless Son, and an Evening in the Palace 154
XVI	Meeting of Old Friends...167
XVII	A Nice Young Man 177
XVIII	Evil Courses 183
XIX	An Evil Death..191
XX	Hopes and Fears—An Unexpected Event 200
XXI	Another Deathbed 209
XXII	One More Death—Anxious Thought 219
XXIII	Overcoming 229
XXIV	Arthur Danesbury—Murmurs...................................235
XXV	The Star of Hope...241
XXVI	Conclusion 246

Appendix

    Appendix A: A Chronology of Important Dates....................... 260
    Appendix B: *Introductory Preface & A Trio of Famous Women*..... 262
    Appendix C: *Father Dear Father*... 269
    Appendix D: Reviews 271
    Appendix E: Ellen Wood's Letter to Her Publisher 274

Dedication

To Sheri, Ian, and Emi Barnes, whose family bares no resemblance to the doomed Danesburys within these pages. ...well, except for the cats.

Special Thanks and Acknowledgements

I'd like to thank my research assistants Cait Turner and Rich Stockwell for their tireless skills in uncovering information used in this project. Additionally, I am extremely grateful to Norman Longmate and his fascinating cultural history of the temperance movement *The Waterdrinkers*. His material has been invaluable. I am also grateful for the Ellen Wood website and the material they have collected. Additionally, I'd like to acknowledge the students in my Victorian Sensation Fiction classes at Kutztown University. Their enthusiasm for the material was infectious. In fact, they raided every used book store in the Lehigh Valley searching for old editions of Ellen Wood's novels—a wonderful thing to see! Finally, I'd like to thank Pepper Anderson for the salads from her garden which I consumed voraciously while I worked on *Danesbury House*.

While working on this text, I have retained all colloquial spellings, and I have not corrected grammar, mechanics, or punctuation. This edition reflects the exact text as it was published in 1860.

Introduction

You are holding in your hands a prizewinner—a lost classic of Victorian literature. Its publication earned its author instant fame and within one year, would earn her countless publishing contracts, record-breaking book sales, and international success. Her name would become synonymous with best selling novels of morality and mystery, criminals and conspiracies. Her books would frequently reach multiple editions within a few months of publication; indeed, she quickly became the J.K. Rowling of her era. Upon her death in 1887, her estate was worth more than the estates of Wilkie Collins and Anthony Trollope combined. So why is this author's name so unfamiliar and the title so unknown? Overlooked and forgotten for over 150 years, *Danesbury House* was once the most popular temperance novel of the 1860s. Today, however, it has been relegated to the cobwebbed shelves of dusty, used bookstores or packed away in forgotten, dark attic trunks. Those lucky enough to stumble upon an old, tattered copy would find themselves holding a treasure chest of Victorian morality…and mid-century madness. Tracing forty years in the unfortunate lives of the Danesbury family, Ellen Wood's cautionary temperance tale is one of literature's lost guilty pleasures, for inside the thick walls of *Danesbury House* are countless rooms locking away 40 years of secrets, addictions, and insanity. What could be a better rainy-day find for lovers of old sensational books?

From the outside, Danesbury House looks elegant, formidable, and quite solid; yet one needs to approach Danesbury House (both building and novel) with caution. It is old. It creaks. The wallpaper is stained and the shingles are tattered. Like the addiction classics of the twentieth century, *Refer Madness*, *The Lost Weekend*, and *Valley of the Dolls*, its age is beginning to show and the extreme melodrama may border on camp. Yet all of these tales, whether told through prose or film, address the same societal concern: the need to repair the ills of addictions. In this introduction, I want to place *Danesbury House* in its historical context and cultural significance. I will avoid analyzing the text itself for approaching this novel so directly would reveal far too many plot spoilers. This book is best enjoyed when read as it was originally intended, chapter by chapter.

A century and a half after it was written, this novel still works. It is not high brow writing, nor does it supply the reader with deep questions of existence; it does however, sweep readers away to a time of candle-lit parlors, staircase intrigue whispered by servants, and sensational events that would make even Jacqueline Susanne proud. So, blow away the dust from the pages and step inside.

Welcome to Danesbury House.

Building *Danesbury House*

The advertisement seemed innocent enough. In 1859, the Scottish Temperance League offered a £100 award to the writer of the best work of fiction detailing the dangers of alcohol. However simple it may have appeared, this advertisement would begin the career of one of the best selling writers of the Victorian era: Mrs. Ellen Wood. By the time of her death in 1887, she left behind a legacy of over thirty full length novels, over a hundred short stories, and the honor of having written one of the best selling novels of the entire 19th century, *East Lynne* (1861).

Wood began her writing career in 1851 while living in France. Her short story, *Seven Years in the Wedded Life of a Roman Catholic*, was published in New Monthly Magazine, edited by the popular Newgate novelist William Harrison Ainsworth. Happy to see her fiction in print, she continued to submit tales and short stories on a monthly basis. Like other part-time writers and scribes, she received little to no payment for her submissions. However, this would soon change.

In 1856, her husband's glove exporting business failed. The particular circumstances appear suspicious, yet the true facts are unknown today. This business loss required the family to move back to England where they lived in rented rooms in Upper Norwood, an area located in south London. Finding her family low on funds, Wood began to approach her writing more seriously. She contacted Ainsworth, who now had two successful monthly magazines in print. She inquired if he would serialize a full length novel were she to supply one. He foolishly refused. Around this time, a valued family friend, the Vicar of Great Malvern, brought Wood's attention to a contest posted by the Scottish Temperance League. The organization offered a £100 award "for the best temperance tale illustrative of the injurious effects of intoxicating drinks, the advantages of personal abstinence, and the demoralizing operations of liquor traffic." According to her biographer son, Ellen Wood responded to the kind Vicar's suggestion by stating, "I do not like much the idea of competing for a prize. Is there not a slight want of dignity in this sort of thing?" (*Memorials of Mrs. Henry Wood* 260).[1] Pushing her dignity aside, she tackled the project with swift dedication. Unfortunately, the ad confirmed there were less than twenty-eight days left to submit a manuscript. She wrote. She entered. She won. With her first novel, Ellen Wood was on the cusp of what would become the literary phenomenon of the era: Sensation fiction. She was on her way to becoming one of England's best selling novelists of the 19th century, for within the first five years of publication, Danesbury House sold over 90,000 copies in England alone- quite an achievement for a first novel. Unfortunately for Wood, with the £100 prize award, she had to turn over the rights of her novel to the Scottish Temperance society as well- thus losing thousands in royalties.

Known for thrilling tales of mystery and melodramatic emotional content, Sensation fiction is the grandchild of 18th century's Gothic fiction. However, where the plots of Gothic novels take place in the long ago and far away, the plots of Victorian Sensation fiction occur in contemporary Victorian society and are placed within the domestic, well-mannered home. Sensation writers focused upon hidden secrets and shocking discoveries which threaten to destroy the comfortable middle-class lives contained in the pages. Thus, the Victorian domestic space becomes a place of conspiracy, criminal activity, and secret infections which threaten to destroy the home and family. No longer a refuge from a swiftly changing social landscape, the idealized Victorian domestic home became unsafe, unfamiliar, and frightening. Tales of runaway wives, lust, bigamy, arson, poisonings, insanity, and addictions filled hundreds of books which were eagerly consumed by a voracious, newly literate public whose numbers included everyone from the working class, to the landowners and middle class, to the Queen herself.

The top three Sensation novels are Wilkie Collins' *The Woman in White* (1860), Ellen Wood's *East Lynne* (1861), and Mary Elizabeth

---

[1] Though well intended, Charles William Wood's 1894 biography of his mother, *Memorials of Mrs. Henry Wood,* is questionable. He highlights and praises Ellen Wood's domestic abilities while downplaying her role as independent thinker and important writer.

Braddon's *Lady Audley's Secret* (1862). These three novels outsold all other novels of the entire century, yet they remain little known today. For decades the genre was considered trite, silly, and unworthy of serious scholarly attention. However, under current academic scrutiny, the genre is gaining solid ground in literary studies, and many universities now offer classes in the genre. Additionally, reprints such as this current novel are becoming more popular, for today Sensation fiction is an important and vital document of Victorian culture, morals, and fears. Inside the pages of these popular novels lies a wealth of important cultural concerns and social anxieties which stressed the Victorians. The world of mid-century England was shifting rapidly, and these novels offer readers insight into a wide range of changing social topics such as questions of respectability, shifting codes of class, the rise of the 'New Woman,' gender as performance, familial law, marriage reform, adultery, addictions, bigamy, crime, and anti-Semitism.

Danesbury House is rarely mentioned in academic studies of Sensation fiction. When it is mentioned, it is usually a passing thought, a mere addition used to shed more light upon Wood's breakout novel, *East Lynne*. Is this due to the fact that copies of *Danesbury House* have been nearly impossible to find? Or is this oversight due to its exaggerated melodramatic content? (Let's face it, the novel opens with an intoxicated old woman, a poisoning, and terrible death in a drunken coach crash). Whatever the oversight, *Danesbury House,* belongs in the club for it is one of the rare Sensational novels with addiction as its central theme, seconded only by Marie Corelli's 1890 potboiler novel about absinthe addiction, *Wormwood*. Where other novelists hint at addictions (Wilkie Collins' 1866 novel, *Armadale*, for example), Wood's family of alcoholics takes center stage. In fact, the very ground under Danesbury House is soaked in alcohol. It is hidden in closets, consumed at meals, drunken in bars, and nearly destroys the entire family, if not the very town they reside in.

There Goes the Neighborhood:
Danesbury House and the Temperance Movement

The Scottish Temperance League who offered the cash prize to Ellen Wood was only one of hundreds of temperance organizations which were beginning to flourish world wide in the early 19th century. It's no wonder for, according to Paul Kopperman's study, *The Cheap-*

est Pay: Alcohol Abuse in the Eighteenth Century British Army, alcoholism was "epidemic" in the British army (445). Many soldiers received their pay in rum, whiskey, or brandy. Many where given alcohol before and after battles to "heighten their belligerency and to steady their nerves." It was used by officers to create camaraderie among their troops to celebrate a birth, a victory, or other special occasions (446). Alcohol was socially sanctioned as an award, as payment, as escape, and as soother.

Additionally, the medical profession's many members actually prescribed alcohol as a cure-all for ailments. In 1839, Dr Robert Todd was popular for prescribing two pints a day of his 'brandy and port wine cure' to many of his ill patients stating, "it is far more dangerous to life to diminish or withdraw alcohol than to give too much" (qtd. in Longmate 172). Clearly these examples are not enough to be representative of the seriousness of the rampant abuse of alcohol, but they do give an idea of the ease in which alcohol was accepted as a daily part of life.

Beginning in the early nineteenth century, Ireland, New Zealand, Australia, the United States developed highly popular temperance societies urging their fellow citizens to sign pledges of total abstinence, for alcohol was destroying the social fabric and it clearly played a terrible role in the lives of the working classes. Ironically, many of the attacks against alcohol were written by common working men and women. "[P]ersons addicted to malt liquors increase enormously in bulk," warned Robert Macnish in *The Anatomy of Drunkenness* (1834). He observed, "[t]hey become loaded with fat; their chin gets double or triple, the eye prominent and the whole face bloated and stupid" (qtd. in Longmate 172). In his 1838 study, *The Curse of Britain*, The Reverend W. R. Baker observed the case of one man who was prescribed brandy to keep cholera at bay. He had "followed this advise so enthusiastically that in six months he had delirium tremens," while another unfortunate fellow who drank two bottles of brandy a day to improve digestion "died a driveller and a sot!" (173). Many of these published studies are mere conjecture and not based upon thorough medical study. They did, however, help to establish a fearful citizenry. The social reaction against alcohol reached its apex when in 1810, teetotalers spread the myth that heavy drinkers were likely to spontaneously combust. They cited a Frenchwoman addicted to alcohol who died smoldering in her chair and an Italian gentleman who had also exploded in flames. These rumors continued throughout the century and crossed continents as well. In Canada, they claimed, an alcoholic was said to have lit up in a "widely extended, silver coloured flame" and in Boston, a man exploded after burping too close to an open flame. The most extreme example in print dates to 1877 and describes a resident of San Francisco who "turned on a gas jet to light his pipe. A second later, there was a drunken moan, a flash of alcoholic flame, and he fell heavily on the floor, his head and neck veiled in smoke, while blue jets of flame were issuing from his ears, mouth, and nostrils" (175). Strong imagery indeed! Even Charles Dickens did not escape the craze over spontaneous combustion, for it kills a drunken petty junk dealer in his 1853 novel *Bleak House*. When constables arrive at the junk shop, all they find left of the poor man is a dark, oily coating on the walls and windowsill, a terrible warning to all who indulge in spirits. Even Emily Brontë's 1847 novel *Wuthering Heights* contains an explosive alcohol warning. Following a terrible fight between Heathcliff and an intoxicated Hindley, Heathcliff sarcastically comments on the dangers of letting Hindley's blood get too close to the open fire due to its high alcohol content.

These examples are only a few of the thousands of novels and literary pamphlets which were published during the temperance movement. By 1880, there were over 200 documented temperance periodicals in print, almost 900 books and novels on the subject, while some teetotaler writers where publishing an astonishing "fifty or sixty books in a few years" (Longmate 192). The marketing was so prevalent, in fact, that it became a part of the Victorian popular landscape. Temperance subjects were featured in art,[2] in literature, and on the stage as well. One of Great Britain's popular novels of working class fiction was William Harrison Ainsworth's 1839 Newgate novel[3], *Jack*

---

[2]Temperance themes are most notable in the works of George Cruikshank, whose series of eight prints titled *The Bottle* (1847) trace the destruction of a family through alcohol. His major work, *The Worship of Bacchus* (first shown in 1862), graphically illustrates the ills of Victorian society: alcohol, poverty, violence, and injustice. Its themes were considered too ugly to hang in public. Locked away for over one hundred years, the painting is gaining academic interest and was recently restored. It currently hangs in the Tate Britain Gallery.

[3]Newgate novels were potboiler, penny dreadful-like tales which followed the lives of criminals and highwaymen, and frequently recounted the histories

Sheppard, which follows the criminal career of young Jack, born to an alcoholic, working class mother. Destitute and drunk, poor Mrs. Sheppard explains her fondness for gin:

> To those who, like me, have never been able to get out of the dark and dreary paths of life, the grave is indeed a refuge, and the sooner they reach it the better. The spirit I drink may be poison, it may kill me, perhaps it is killing me: but so would hunger, cold, misery, so would my own thoughts. I should have gone mad without it. Gin is the poor man's friend, his sole set-off against the rich man's luxury. It comforts him when he is most forlorn. It may be treacherous, it may lay up a store of future woe; but it insures present happiness, and that is sufficient. When I have traversed the streets a houseless wanderer, driven with curses from every door where I have solicited alms, and with blows from every gateway where I have sought shelter, when I have crept into some deserted building, and stretched my wearied limbs upon a bulk, in the vain hope of repose, or, worse than all, when, frenzied with want, I have yielded to horrible temptation, and earned a meal in the only way I could earn one, when I have felt, at times like these, my heart sink within me, I have drank of this drink, and have at once forgotten my cares, my poverty, my guilt. Old thoughts, old feelings, old faces, and old scenes have returned to me, and I have fancied myself happy, as happy as I am now. ... It's all the happiness I have known for years ... and it's short-lived enough, as you perceive. Gin may bring ruin; but as long as poverty, vice, and ill-usage exist, it will be drunk. (Ainsworth 60)

Clearly Ainsworth saw the social problems inherent in alcohol and the plight of the working classes; however, he also capitalized upon it by using the sensationalistic qualities of the social problems to create a novel which would become synonymous with excitement, sensationalism, and ultimately, childhood corruption.

One of the most popular temperance novels was Timothy Shay Arthur's *Ten Nights in a Barroom*, written in 1854. This lurid, fast paced shocker is a first person narrative recounting the terrible effects a new bar, the 'Sickle and Sheaf,' has upon the kind town of Cedarville. Span-

---

of villains executed in the Newgate prison. *Jack Sheppard* is one of the more notoriously known Newgate novels and was blamed for corrupting minors and instigating working class crimes.

ning nearly seven years, the narration focuses on ten specific nights to document the poor town's fall from grace and contains many tragic, highly melodramatic scenes. For example, Joe Morgan, once a good citizen, becomes a frequent drinker at the Sickle and Sheaf and squanders his pay on whiskey, rather than feeding his wife and child. One terrible night, his young angelic daughter, Mary arrives at the bar and begs her drunken pa to return home:

> She was not over ten years of age; but it moved the heart to look upon the saddened expression of her young countenance, and the forced bravery therein, that scarcely overcame the native timidity so touchingly visable.
>
> "Father!" I have never heard this word spoken in a voice that sent a thrill along every nerve. It was full of sorrowful love- full of a tender concern that had its origin too deep for the heart of a child. As she spoke, the little one sprang across the room, and laying her hands upon the arm of [her father], lifted her eyes, that were ready to gush over with tears, to his face.
>
> "Come Father! Won't you come home?" I hear that low, pleading voice even now, and my heart gives a quicker throb. Poor Child! Darkly shadowed was the sky that bent gloomily over thy young life. (23)

Unfortunately for Mary, a bar fight erupts and she is dealt a fatal blow on the head by a stray bottle. In the tradition of sensational, lingering, child death-bed scenes, Mary Morgan's death is drawn out for days and climaxes with Mary cradling her guilt ridden, drunken father in her bed. Suffering terrible hallucinations from his life of alcoholism, Joe Morgan sees large toads and terrifying ghostly cats everywhere.[4] "Mary called to him, and he sprung into the bed; while she gathered her arms about him tightly, saying in a low soothing voice, "Nothing can harm you here Father" (87). Comforting her insane father in her arms, the ten year old dies. In terms of tearful lingering melodrama, Mary's death scene is rivaled only by Little Eva's from *Uncle Tom's Cabin*, written only two years earlier.

More innocent deaths follow little Mary's and the once prosperous town becomes a slum of degradation. Only a few years after the

---

[4] Terrifying cats haunting the intoxicated appears to be a temperance theme for these hellish felines also take residence inside the Danesbury estate's second floor.

Sickle and Sheaf opens, the narrator states "[a]n eating cancer was on the community, and so far as the eye could mark its destructive progress, the ravages were fearful" (153). *Ten Nights in a Barroom* became so popular, it was dramatized and became a highly popular temperance play. Poor Mary is even given a song before the fatal bottle strikes her angelic head. While the bar fight rages on, Mary stands in the tavern doorway and sings,

> Father, dear father, come home with me now,
> The clock in the steeple strikes one;
> You said you were coming right home from the shop
> As soon as your day's work was done;
> Our fire has gone out, our house is all dark,
> And mother's been watching since tea,
> With poor brother Benny so sick in her arms
> And no one to help her but me,
> Come home! come home! come home!
> Please father, dear father, come home.[5]

In 1890, Charles Bateman wrote perhaps the most baffling example of temperance literature, the uncanny *Tippling and Temperance*. His essay of 1,289 words celebrates temperance for every word in his tract begins with the letter 'T.' For example, "Thoughtless thousands turn to the tempting tap," while, "[T]hriving tradesmen taste tipple timidly...timewasters tipple tremendously...thereby turpitude thrives, turmoil triumphs." According to Bateman, the most terrible drinker of all is the "truculent tyrant throwing toast, tea cake, table knives, teacups, trays, tongs, then tearing the tablecloth" (qtd. in Longmate, 195). Clearly, Bateman's attempt at temperance literature was not a Scottish award winning entry.

Over a hundred and fifty years have passed since Ellen Wood penned her lurid tale of alcohol addiction. Whether it is read as tragic melodrama, high camp, or powerful indictment against the evils of drinking, *Danesbury House* remains an important novel. It represents the Victorian popular culture's need for shocking tales recounting the evils of drink, and it ushered in Sensation fiction, the publishing phenomenon of mid century England. More importantly, its success

---

[5] "Father Dear Father" was written by Henry Clay Work in 1864 and is reprinted in its entirety in Appendix C (269-70).

securely established the beginnings of one of Great Britain's top selling Victorian novelists, Ellen Wood.

Even though the doors of Danesbury House creak a bit and the wallpaper may be showing its age, the house retains it wonders. Open the front door and wander in. Search the rooms, climb the stairs, and listen for the secrets whispered behind the walls...

Curt Herr, Ph.D.
Autumn, 2008
Bucks County, PA

Works Cited

Ainsworth, William Harrison. Jack Sheppard. Eds. Edward Jacobs and Manuela Mourao. New York: Broadview, 2007.

Arthur, Timothy Shay. Ten Nights in a Barroom (1854). Bedford, MA: Applewood, 2000.

The Ellen Wood Website: http://www.mrshenrywood.co.uk

Kopperman, Paul E. "The Cheapest Pay: Alcohol Abuse in the Eighteenth Century British Army" The Journal of Military History, Vol. 60. No.3, (July, 1996): 445–470.

Longmate, Norman. The Waterdrinkers: A History of Temperance. London: Hamish Hamilton, 1968.

Wood, Charles William. Memorials of Mrs. Henry Wood. London: Bentley, 1894.

For Further Reading

Corelli, Marie. Wormwood. Ed. Kirsten MacLeod. New York: Broadview, 2004.

Cvetkovich, Ann. Mixed Feelings: Feminism, Mass Culture, and Victorian Sensationalism. New Brunswick: Rutgers, 1992.

Hughes, Winifred. The Maniac in the Cellar: Sensation Novels of the 1860's. Princeton: Princeton, 1980.

Jaffe, Audrey. Scenes of Sympathy: Identity and Representation in Victorian Fiction. New York: Cornell, 2000.

Picard, Liza. Victorian London: The Tale of a City, 1840-1870. New York: St. Martin's, 2005.

Pykett, Lyn. The Sensation Novel: From *The Woman in White* to *The Moonstone*. Plymouth, UK: Northcote, 1994.

Reed, John R. Victorian Conventions. Ohio: Ohio University, 1975.

Showalter, Elaine. A Literature of Their Own: British Woman Novelists from Brontë to Lessing. Princeton: Princeton, 1999.

Tromp, Marlene. The Private Rod: Marital Violence, Sensation, and the Law in Victorian Britain. Charlottesville, University Press of Virginia, 2000.

Wood, Ellen. East Lynne. Ed. Andrew Maunder. New York: Broadview, 2002.

Wynne, Deborah. The Sensation Novel and the Victorian Family Magazine. New York: Palgrave, 2001.

Danesbury House

Frontispiece.
D.H.

"Tell me the worst at once."

CHAPTER I
THE MISTAKE—THE DINNER TABLE

IT was a winter's afternoon, cold and bright, and the large nursery window of Danesbury House looked out on an extensive and beautiful prospect. Seated at it, occupied in repairing some fine lace, was a smart young woman of twenty, an upper maid, sensible and sharp-looking, with quick, dark eyes, and a healthy colour.

"There's the baby, Glisson," she suddenly exclaimed, as a child's cry was heard from the adjoining room.

Glisson, the person she addressed, was a woman of middle age, active and slender, the valued nurse in the Danesbury family. She was sitting in a low rocking chair, right in front of the fire, nodding at intervals. She half opened her eyes, and turned them on Jessy, with a somewhat dull or stupid expression.

"Did you speak?" she asked.

"The baby, Glisson. Don't you hear him?"

Glisson rose, and stepping into the night-nursery, brought forth little William Danesbury, a lovely child of nine months old. His cheeks were flushed to a crimson damask, his pretty mouth was like a rosebud, and his eyes were large and dark and brilliant. She sat down with him on the low chair: he seemed somewhat fractious, as infants will be, on awakening from sleep, and Glisson laid him flat upon her knee and rocked the chair backwards and forwards.

"The idea of your trying to hush the child off to sleep again!" exclaimed Jessy. "I'm sure he has slept long enough—all the time we were at dinner!"

"Mind your own business," cried Glisson.

Jessy was one who rather liked to have the last word. "He wants amusing, nurse; he doesn't want more sleep: and I daresay he is hungry."

Glisson made no reply. She had closed her eyes, perhaps with a view to finish her own doze, and was gently keeping the chair on the rock. The child, soothed to quiet, lay still. Jessy paused in her work, turned her head sideways, and kept her eyes fixed for the full space of a minute on Mrs. Glisson.

Presently a fit of coughing took the baby. The nurse put him to sit up, and patted his back, but he coughed violently. He had had a bad cough for more than a week past, but it was getting better. Glisson rose and looked on the mantel-piece for his cough-mixture. She could not see it.

"What have you done with the baby's medicine?" she exclaimed to Jessy.

"I have not done anything with it," was the reply. "I have not touched it."

"You must have touched it, or else it would be here," sharply retorted Mrs. Glisson.

"I tell you I have not," answered Jessy. "Where did you put it when you had used it last?"

"Where should I put it but in its place on the mantel-piece! I gave him some last night when I undressed him, and I put the bottle back. Somebody has been here, meddling," continued the nurse in an angry tone; "but I'll find out who it was. I'll let the house know that nobody shall come into my nursery with impunity. Perhaps it's carried into mistress's room."

She flung off, not in the best of tempers, the child coughing in her arms.

"Have you found it?" inquired Jessy, when she returned.

"Found it? of course I have," replied the nurse. "There shall be a stir about this: how dare anybody come and carry off my nursery things? It was in Mrs. Danesbury's closet, put amongst the spirits of camphor, and the magnesia, and the other bottles. They thought to play me a trick, I suppose, for they have been clearing the direction off: maybe they'll get one played to them, in a way they won't like, before the day is out. It's that impudent Sarah! She said, at dinner, she'd be up to pranks, now mistress was away."

Mrs. Glisson poured out a teaspoonful of the mixture, and gave it to the child. Jessy, meanwhile, was thinking how very improbable it was that any servant, even Sarah, the careless and frolicsome under-housemaid, should presume to meddle with anything belonging to the nurse and baby. All in a moment—she could not tell how or why—a doubt flashed over her. Could Mrs. Glisson have overlooked the bottle! Letting her work fall, she started up, and with one bound cleared the space between the window and the mantel-piece. Sure enough, there was the missing bottle, pushed out of sight behind a child's toy.

"Oh, nurse, what have you done?" she uttered. "Here's the baby's medicine behind Miss Isabel's doll's house! What have you given to him?"

The nurse looked confounded, and turned her gaze from the bottle in Jessy's hand to the bottle in her own. They were precisely similar in shape and size, small round bottles, each about half full, with what, to all appearance, might be taken for the same mixture. Jessy snatched the strange bottle from her, uncorked it, and smelt it. She turned deadly pale.

"Mrs. Glisson, as true as that you are alive, you have killed the baby! This is the laudanum."

"You are a fool for saying it," shrieked out Glisson, in her terror. "It can't be the laudanum bottle!"

Jessy knew that it was: she recognised it as that which was kept in Mrs. Danesbury's private closet. She laid her two hands upon the woman's shoulders, and hissed forth strange words, in her grief and excitement. *"You are not yourself, and you know it:* you are not in a state clearly to distinguish one bottle from another."

There was not a moment to be lost. She left the woman to her own reflections, to the two bottles, and the child, and tore down the stairs. In the hall she encountered a man-servant, and Jessy laid hold of him and dragged him towards the front door. The man thought she was wild.

"The baby's dying, Ralph. Fly for Mr. Pratt; don't let him lose an instant."

Ralph, after a prolonged stare of bewilderment, started off, down the steps. Jessy followed him, and was running in a different direction, when a thought struck her, and she called again to the man.

"Tell him what it is, Ralph; it may save time. The baby has had a dose of laudanum given him, in mistake for his cough-mixture."

To the right, at a distance of nearly a quarter of a mile, rose the large and extensive buildings, known by the name of the Danesbury Works. Jessy gained the spot, flew through the outer grounds and passages, and into the private room of her master. Mr. Danesbury, a tall man of commanding presence, with nobly intelligent features and earnest blue eyes, now some years past thirty, was standing by his fire, engaged with two gentlemen. To see one of his handmaids burst upon them in that unceremonious fashion astonished him considerably: he thought her wild, as Ralph had done.

"Oh, sir," she panted, "there has been a sad accident at home. Mrs. Glisson has made a mistake, and given the baby the wrong medicine."

"Wrong medicine?" uttered Mr. Danesbury.

"She missed his cough-mixture, sir, and she found it, as she thought, in my mistress's closet, and she gave him a teaspoonful. It was not his mixture, but the laudanum."

Mr. Danesbury, with a word of apology to the gentlemen, hastened from the room. "You should have sent for Mr. Pratt, Jessy," he next said.

"I have, sir, I did not lose time; Ralph is gone for him."

It was a deplorable accident, and it had happened at an unusually unfavourable moment, for Mrs. Danesbury was away from home. She had left Eastborough with her two eldest children the previous day, to pay a visit to London.

Eastborough was forthwith up in arms. To see one of the servants from Danesbury House come along, without his hat, at the pace of a steam-engine, dart into Mr. Pratt's, and to see the two, for happily the surgeon was at home, go steaming back again, caused unheard of consternation. People came out of their houses to wonder, and asked each other what had occurred, and the news soon spread to them from the works; for there Jessy's errand had been learnt by the operatives: little William Danesbury had been poisoned.

Nothing but emetics could have any counteracting effect upon so young a child, and those Mr. Pratt tried; but whether they would save him could not yet be proved. Mr. Danesbury, the first shock over, began to reflect that it might be better to send for his wife; who, whatever should be the issue, would be the more satisfied to be at home than away. He determined to despatch Thomas Harding, one of his most esteemed and faithful foremen, who had been in the works many years. "Jessy," said Mr. Danesbury to the girl, "go back to the factory, and tell your uncle to prepare for an immediate journey to London. After he is ready, he must come here to receive my instructions."

As Jessy went into the factory to do her master's bidding, she was assailed on all sides. Was the child dead? Could it be brought round? How did it happen? But she would not answer one inquiry, until she had delivered the message to Mr. Harding, and when she did explain, it was very brief. A mistake of the nurse's in taking up the wrong bottle, she said, and Mr. Pratt could give no opinion yet, one way or the other.

In those days railroads were not common, and the quickest way of general travelling was by posting. A chaise was ordered from "The Ram," and was soon at Danesbury House. Mr. Harding, equipped for the journey, was already there, had taken his orders from his master, and was now standing on the steps outside, talking with Jessy in an undertone. As the chaise rattled up, and turned round, he got inside, and just at that moment Mr. Danesbury came out again.

"Mind, Harding, how you break it to Mrs. Danesbury. Be as cautious as possible. Mr. Pratt does think there may be a little hope, tell her."

"I'll do it in the best way that ever I can, sir," he answered, the tears rising to his eyes with earnestness of feeling.

The chaise drove back at a swift pace, down the hill and through the small town, to the intense delight of the inhabitants, ever rejoicing in excitement, who flocked to their doors and windows to gaze after it as it rolled past, and at Thomas Harding, seated bolt upright in it. They would have guessed his errand, had its object not transpired.

Mr. Danesbury had turned into the house again, but Jessy stood and watched the chaise down the hill; through the town she lost sight of it, but speedily saw it again, ascending the opposite hill, for Eastborough, a very small town, deserving little more than the name of village, was situated in a valley. Jessy was the daughter of a farmer who had a large family. She had received a good plain education, was well-mannered and well-conducted, and her friends had not thought it beneath them to accept a place for her as maid at Mrs. Danesbury's, to wait upon and walk out with the two eldest children: Jessy had, at first, somewhat rebelled at it, not having thought she should be "sent out to service." Thomas Harding's wife was her father's sister.

Whilst that chaise was nearing the end of its forty-mile journey, a merry party had assembled round a well-lighted dinner table in a handsome house in Bedford Row, the metropolitan locality where so many men of the law congregate. Mr. and Mrs. Serle were its owners, and sat at either end. By the side of the former, who was an eminent solicitor, sat Mrs. Danesbury, an elegant woman of thirty years, with beautifully-refined features and dark eyes, thoughtful and expressive. Opposite to her, in a drab silk gown, sat Miss St. George, who was the sister of Mrs. Serle, and lived there because she had no other home. Next to Mrs. Serle was a young man, Walter St. George; he was in Mr. Serle's office, and had been invited to dinner to meet Mrs. Danesbury; and the middle of the table was occupied by four children, two little Serles and Arthur and Isabel Danesbury. Mrs. Danesbury was first cousin to Walter St. George, and both of them were more distantly related to Mrs. Serle and her sister. The children's dining at this late hour was unusual; but they had been out with the ladies sight-seeing, and had lost their own dinner in the middle of the day. Of course they enjoyed amazingly the dining by candle-light.

"But, sir," suddenly cried Arthur Danesbury, leaning forward that he might see Mr. St. George, "you have not told me about the Tower. Do you often go to it?"

"Well, no, I don't," smiled Mr. St. George. "But I will take you."

Mrs. Danesbury laughed. "Arthur has a book at home, describing the glories and wonders of the Tower in days gone by," she said—"lions, giants, dwarfs, soldiers in armour, and scaffolds. He cannot separate those marvels from the present Tower by any process of reasoning whatever; so I fear disappointment will be in store for him when he shall visit it."

Mr. St. George could scarcely take his eyes from the boy, who was still bending forward, so remarkably intelligent did he think his countenance. Fair, with a broad, white, intellectual forehead, his features gave promise of the same high order of beauty that distinguished his father's, and he possessed the same large, clear, earnest blue eyes. He was in his eighth year, his sister two years younger. A servant placed a glass of porter by his side, and recalled him to his dinner.

"Oh, water for me, if you please," said the child.

"Water, sir?"

"Yes," replied Arthur, "and for my sister also. We always drink water."

There was no water on the sideboard; it was a beverage not frequently called for at Mr. Serle's, and one of the servants had to go downstairs for some. Matthew and Charlotte Serle had each their small silver mug of porter.

"Your children are not going to drink water!" exclaimed Mrs. Serle, when she saw the water placed for them. "This cannot hurt them, Mrs. Danesbury; it is only porter, not stout."

"Thank you," replied Mrs. Danesbury, "they never take anything but water."

"You don't know what's good for them, I see," interposed Mr. Serle. But the subject dropped.

To be resumed, however, at dessert. In pouring out the port wine, Mr. Serle filled four glasses three parts full, and passed them to the children.

"Oh! I beg your pardon for not speaking sooner," interrupted Mrs. Danesbury; "I did not observe. Arthur and Isabel do not take it."

"Not take wine! and not take beer!" uttered Mr. Serle; "why, do you intend to make little hermits of them? I can assure you, these children, when they are indulged by dining with us, and on Sundays, look for their glasses of wine, filled 'up to the pretty,' as eagerly as we look for ours."

"I never heard of such a thing as punishing children in that way," cried Miss St. George.

"It is no punishment," was Mrs. Danesbury's reply. "They are not accustomed to it, and therefore do not wish for it."

"All moonshine!" laughed Mr. Serle. "Drink it up, children."

"No; I must repeat that I prefer they should not," returned Mrs. Danesbury. Her manner and tone, though perfectly courteous and lady-like, were unmistakably decisive, and no more was said. The little Serles drank their wine, and when the children had eaten some pears and oranges, they were all despatched to the nursery to play.

"How can you force those nice children of yours to drink water?" began Mrs. Serle, turning to her guest. "Do you do it upon principle? as people say."

"I do it because I believe it to be good for them," was Mrs. Danesbury's answer.

"But you cannot possibly think that the small portion of beer and wine which our children have just taken, can have done them any harm?"

"Whether it has done them harm, I cannot say; but I will say that water would have done them more good, even for their health's sake."

"*Even* for their health's sake!" repeated Mrs. Serle. "I scarcely follow you. There is nothing else that could be benefited by it."

"Yes," said Mrs. Danesbury, "their taste. We should be very cautious what tastes we impart to, or cultivate in a child. A child cannot dislike water naturally; it is its natural beverage, as, rely upon it, it was intended to be the natural beverage of man. A child should never be allowed to drink anything else (except at those seasons, tea and breakfast, when milk is substituted); whether at dinner, or when thirsty, let it have its appointed drink—water. Confine a child's drink to water, and he will obey the law of nature, and grow up loving the water. I believe that it is of the utmost importance that he should be allowed to do so."

"I don't see why."

"As soon as a child can sit down to table and eat dinner, how many parents give that child beer to drink with it! Take your own children, for example; have you accustomed them to drink water?"

"No," was Mrs. Serle's reply; "but, then, London water is such wretched stuff. Since the children could sit at table, they have always had a little sup of beer."

"Just so," returned Mrs. Danesbury, "you debar your children from tasting water, and in a few years' time they will have lost their relish for it—if they have not done so already. You impart to them a taste (a forced, acquired taste, mind) for stronger beverage, and indulge the taste until they learn to love it; naturally, after that, water appears insipid. Once let a child lose his liking for water, through disuse, through accustoming him to drink an artificial beverage, and you will rarely find him regain it in after life. Many grown persons will say, 'I cannot bear water; I could not drink it!' "

"I could not," interrupted Mr. St. George. "I never did drink it, and I am sure I could not begin now."

Mrs. Danesbury smiled, for she saw they all could have joined in his words, and it illustrated her theory. "Just so, Walter," she remarked; "you were not allowed to drink water when your tastes, for good or for ill, were being formed. As our tastes are trained in childhood, so will our after likings be."

"Then, it is not that you think so ill of beer and wine, as that you wish your children to grow up fond of water," observed Mr. Serle.

"That is chiefly it: they must grow up fond of one or of the other. My objection to children's taking beer or wine would be less strong, could I make sure that they would always partake of them in strict moderation; but who can answer for the future? I think," continued Mrs. Danesbury, smiling upon them pleasantly, but with deprecation, "though you must not take offence at my saying it, that when parents do not oblige their children to drink water as their common beverage, they are guilty of a positive sin."

"Oh! Mrs. Danesbury!"

"A sin against the child; and, perhaps," she added, in a lower tone, "against God, who has sent him into the world to be trained to morality and goodness."

There was a pause. It was Mr. Serle who broke it. "Are these your own sentiments chiefly, Mrs. Danesbury, or your husband's?"

"They are mine. I believe my husband thinks with me, but his hands and head are so full of business that he gives but little heed to what he would call domestic points. He has entire confidence in my management."

"Well, it is hard upon the children."

"Hard upon the children! how can you take up so mistaken an idea? It is quite the contrary. Had I said to my children at dinner just now, 'Take which you like best, beer or water,' they would have chosen water. Water, I say, assimilates itself naturally with a child's palate: beer does not. Give a glass of beer to my children, who have never had any, and they would find it salt, bitter—disagreeable as a dose of medicine."

"But, Mrs. Danesbury, if you keep your children—let us say the boy—to water, so long as you have control over him, you cannot expect that he will confine himself to water when he becomes a man."

"I do not know that," she answered: "I trust to be able to implant in him other wholesome training besides that of drinking water; I mean, touching his own responsibility of action. But, whether he shall confine himself to water or not, I shall have the comforting consciousness of knowing that I have done my duty by him, in bringing him up to like it. When Matthew and Arthur, your boy and mine, shall stand side by side in after years, the one loving water, the other despising it, the one regardless of stimulants, the other craving for them, what will have made the difference, but the opposite mode in which they were reared? You do what you can to eradicate the natural liking for water implanted in the child, I do all I can to foster it. Believe me, Mr. Serle, we should all do well to bring up our children to drink water."

"Madam," interrupted a servant, entering the room and addressing Mrs. Danesbury, "there's a gentleman below, asking to see you."

"A gentleman!" repeated Mrs. Danesbury in surprise, who had no friends in London, and thought the man must be mistaken. "For me! Are you sure?"

"He asked for Mrs. Danesbury. He has a plaid shawl round his neck, madam, and a white topcoat on. He said he came from Eastborough, and his name was Harding—Thomas Harding."

The words seemed to electrify Mrs. Danesbury, and she turned pale as death, as she started from her seat. "What can be the matter?" she uttered. "Something must be amiss with my husband or my child!"

She quitted the room, and hurried to the one where Thomas Harding had been shown. He stood in the middle of it, his hat in his hand. Mr. and Mrs. Serle caught a glimpse of a most respectable-looking man, with gray hair and an honest countenance.

"Tell me the worst at once," breathed Mrs. Danesbury. "Something is amiss with Mr. Danesbury! He has not been caught in the machinery?" she gasped, the dreadful thought occurring to her.

"Dear lady, pray don't alarm yourself: it's nothing so bad as that. Mr. Danesbury is quite well, and it was he sent me to you. Little Master William is poorly, and he thought you might like to know it."

Mrs. Danesbury sank on a chair, inexpressibly relieved. "Sit down, Mr. Harding," she said; "what is the matter with him?"

"Well, ma'am, it may sound awkward to you, in telling, but Mr. Pratt had little doubt he'd be all right," replied Thomas Harding, improving upon the hint given him by Mr. Danesbury, "and that was the last thing the master charged me to say to you. Mrs. Glisson lost his cough-mixture, and she found it, as she thought, and gave him some, but it turned out to be a bottle containing some tincture of opium. Mr. Pratt was there directly with his emetics, but the master bade me come up here and tell you, ma'am, thinking you might like to go home."

Mrs. Danesbury sat quite still for a minute, her hands pressed upon her chest. The news surprised and perplexed her—apart from the shock and grief; but she had no time to spare for superfluous questions. "How did you come?" she inquired.

"I posted up, ma'am, in one of the chaises from "The Ram." It is at the door."

"Order fresh horses to it instantly," she said, leading the way from the room. Mr. and Mrs. Serle were standing outside, not liking to intrude, and scarcely daring to inquire what had happened. She burst into tears as she gave them the news.

"Going down at once!" uttered Mr. Serle. "But how are you going?"

"Mr. Harding posted up. There is no difficulty."

She had been walking up the stairs as she replied, too anxious to lose a moment. When her things were on, she went to say farewell to her children, who, it had been hastily decided, should remain for the present. The ready tears rose to Arthur's great blue eyes.

"Why do you leave us here, mamma? it won't be nice when you are gone. When shall you come back?"

"The beginning of the week, I hope, Arthur. My darling," she added in his ear, as she held his face to hers, "Mr. and Mrs. Serle may press you to take beer and wine, but you will remember that I wish you not to do so. And tell Isabel what I say. Touch neither."

Arthur gave his head a very decided shake. His mother's word was law with him. "I will be sure to remember, mamma."

She kissed him twenty times; she kissed Isabel, breathing a blessing on them both; she bade farewell to the rest. The two children ran down to shake hands with Thomas Harding, who was in the dining-room with Mr. Serle, swallowing some hasty refreshment. The chaise, with its fresh horses, drove to the door, and Mrs. Danesbury entered it, scarcely giving time for the step to be lowered. Thomas Harding prepared to mount to the seat in front—the dicky, as it was called in those days.

"No, no, Mr. Harding," interposed Mrs. Danesbury, "you must not sit there this cold night. Come inside."

"Ma'am," he answered, in his respectful modest way, hesitating to obey, "I feel that I should be intruding."

"Not at all. Step in."

And the chaise whirled from the door, and speedily left London behind it.

CHAPTER II
THE NIGHT JOURNEY

MRS. DANESBURY naturally felt impatient for particulars, and pressed Thomas Harding to relate them, as they sped on their way. He was enabled to do so, having had them detailed over to him at length by Jessy. Mrs. Danesbury listened to the end, but she was not satisfied.

"I cannot comprehend it," she remarked. "The tincture of opium has been in the closet in my bedroom undisturbed since the night it was first brought into the house. I had the toothache badly, and sent to the chemist's for some. Sarah went for it; and, knowing I was in pain, she brought it away without giving time to label it. I placed it in my closet, and how it is possible for Glisson to have gone thither for it, and taken it, believing it was the baby's cough-mixture, which she kept in her own nursery, I cannot conceive. It is an understood thing in the house, that nobody interferes with what may be in that closet but myself. I should not be so much surprised had it been one of the other servants; but for Glisson to go to the closet, and to commit such an error, is incomprehensible. It is as though she had acted in her sleep."

Thomas Harding was silent. He was debating a question with himself. Ought he to impart to Mrs. Danesbury a rumour which had come to his ears?

"A faithful, cautious, tried old servant like Glisson!" repeated Mrs. Danesbury. "Does it not strike you as being very extraordinary, Mr. Harding?"

"Ma'am," he said, with straightforward simplicity, "I am thinking whether I ought not to tell you something which Jessy mentioned to my wife."

"If it is anything that can bear upon this case, you certainly must inform me," replied Mrs. Danesbury.

"It was the Sunday Jessy had leave to drink tea with us," he resumed. "My wife got asking her whether she should be able to reconcile herself to service, and how she liked her place; and in talking of her various duties, she said that Glisson—that Glisson—"

"Go on," interposed Mrs. Danesbury, wondering at his hesitation.

Thomas Harding leaned towards Mrs. Danesbury, and continued in a whisper, "That Glisson drank."

"That she—what?" uttered Mrs. Danesbury.

"Ma'am, that Glisson drank. Took sometimes more than was good for her."

"That Glisson drank!" repeated Mrs. Danesbury, in the very extreme of surprise. "Impossible! What could Jessy have meant by saying so?"

"My wife said it was impossible, and took Jessy to task for traducing Mrs. Glisson. But Jessy persisted that it was so—that she does drink, and is often stupid through it."

Mrs. Danesbury was silent, utterly confounded.

"Nearly every night she has one big tumbler of hot gin-and-water, sometimes more; besides drinking plenty of ale at supper, too much, in fact; Mrs. Glisson being allowed the strong ale at that meal, while most of the other servants take beer."

"Mrs. Glisson is older than most of them," interrupted Mrs. Danesbury. "And when Mr. Danesbury suggested that Glisson might drink ale with her supper, if she preferred it to table-beer, neither he nor I imagined she would take an unseemly quantity. It is incredible!"

"I fear it is true," returned Thomas Harding. "Jessy is a clear-sighted, keen girl, and is not likely to be deceived. She has seen Glisson with a black bottle to her lips in the day-time, and believed it contained gin. In speaking of this misfortune to-day, she told me Glisson was 'stupid' again, and it was in consequence of seeing she was so, that put it into her head the cough-mixture might really be on the mantel-piece, overlooked by Mrs. Glisson. Jessy says she reproached her with it, in the fright of the discovery."

"But, were it true that Glisson takes gin, how can it have escaped my detection?" urged Mrs. Danesbury. "The smell would betray her."

"Jessy thinks that it is not very often she takes it in the day-time, and you don't see her, ma'am, after she has had it at night. But she has got a trick of sucking things. Sometimes it will be a bit of camphor, sometimes a peppermint-drop: Jessy says she always knows what the nurse has been supping, when she sees her put one of these things into her mouth; and, of course, they take off the smell of anything else."

Mrs. Danesbury remembered to have smelt peppermint and camphor when the nurse had been talking; and she also remembered that Glisson had occasionally seemed stupid—bewildered—and she had wondered; but she had never suspected the cause now hinted at. "I wish Jessy had said this to me," she observed. "I should not have quitted home and left the child in her charge."

"I wish she had, ma'am, as things have turned out," responded Thomas Harding. "But very few young women, going fresh into a house, would venture to bring such a charge against an old and valued servant."

"Very true. And my perfect confidence in Glisson may have tended to blind me. The puzzle is, where can she get the gin?"

"Oh, ma'am, people who give way to drink are never at a fault to get it."

Mrs. Danesbury gathered herself into her corner of the chaise, buried in an unpleasant reverie. She was casting blame to herself. Not for having failed to detect Glisson's fault; no, blame lay not with herself there; but for having suffered the laudanum bottle to be without a label. Several times had she thought of placing a label on it, but the time had gone on and on, and this was the result. Had there been a label, Glisson was certainly not so far gone, but she might have read it. "Have you, or Mrs. Harding, mentioned this doubt of Glisson to anyone?" suddenly asked Mrs. Danesbury.

"Certainly not," was his reply. "And we cautioned Jessy not to let it escape her lips again."

"I am glad of that. I scarcely see my way clear with regard to Glisson. Mr. Danesbury thinks highly of her, and she served his mother faithfully for many years, so that I feel it would not be kind, or just, to turn her away, as I might a less valued servant. I think I must bury this in silence, even to Mr. Danesbury, and keep her on for a while, and be watchful over her, and try and recall her to what she used to be. I am convinced she cannot have taken to it long. I must question Jessy: perhaps she will tell me more than she told you."

They had been travelling at a high rate of speed all the way, and had changed horses several times, though it has not been necessary to mark their progress step by step. Now they were nearing Eastborough; and soon the lights in the town began to be visible. Had it been day, Mrs. Danesbury would have seen her husband's factory, rising on the opposite hill. It was, however, nearly midnight—a cold, frosty, starlight night. A steep hill descended to the hollow, and at the top of the hill was the turnpike gate.

The gate was closed. The postboy stopped his horses and hallooed; the door opened, and the keeper came out. Mrs. Danesbury, who was on that side, leaned forward.

"Do you happen to know, Giles, whether the child is saved?"

She received no answer. The man had gone forward, with a stumble, to open the gate; Mrs. Danesbury supposed he had tripped over a stone. He opened the gate; he did not fling it back, but kept it in his hand, and went stumbling across the road with it. The postboy urged on his horses; but Giles somehow loosed his hold of the gate, and, though he went on himself, he let the gate swing-to again. It struck the nearest horse.

The horse, a nasty-tempered animal at all times, as the postboy phrased it afterwards, began to plunge and kick; that startled his fellow, and, in spite of the efforts of the postboy, they sprang forward, and dashed madly down the hill. Mrs. Danesbury shrieked, and rose up.

"Ma'am, ma'am, don't get up, don't lean out!" implored Thomas Harding; "be still, for the love of life! Lie you down at the bottom of the chaise."

"This is certain death," she wailed. "They will inevitably dash against the bridge; and it will be certain death. Oh, my children! My Saviour, I can but commend them to Thee! Do Thou make them Thine, and keep them from the evil!"

Had it been his own wife, or one with whom he could put himself upon an equality, Thomas Harding would have forced her to the bottom of the chaise and held her there. But he did not like to act so to Mrs. Danesbury. She had leaned from the side window as she spoke the last words, probably not knowing that she did so, in her agitation and terror, and certainly not aware that they were already at the foot of the hill. But they had, as it were, flown down it; the chaise, in that same moment, struck against the lower stone abutment of the narrow, awkward bridge (which everybody in Eastborough had long said was a disgrace and a danger to the town, but which none had bestirred themselves to have altered), and the chaise was overturned. Mrs. Danesbury's head fell on the ground, and the chaise settled upon it.

How Thomas Harding extricated himself he never knew. Beyond being shaken and a little bruised, he was not hurt. The terrified horses had struggled and plunged till they freed themselves, and started off with part of the broken shafts dangling after them. The postboy was lying without motion.

Thomas Harding saw at a glance the dreadful situation of Mrs. Danesbury. To raise the chaise, or aid her of himself, he was entirely powerless. At that moment, the church clock struck out twelve, and the door of a public-house, "The Pig and Whistle," beyond the bridge, at the entrance of the town, was thrown open, and a stream of warm light and a crowd of topers came forth into the street together.

"Hilloa! help! hilloa!" shouted Thomas Harding, running towards them; "help, here!"

The group, most of whom were employed at the Danesbury Works, halted at the noise, and peered in the direction it came. They had left a room blazing with lights and fire, and could as yet distinguish no object outside. The landlord followed with a candle, perhaps believing it would render objects more distinct.

"Blest if it ain't Harding!" exclaimed one. "What's the matter, sir?" he cried, as his foreman came panting up.

Mr. Harding explained, as well as he was able for his haste and agitation. Some were capable of rendering assistance, some were not; those who were, flew with one accord to the fatal spot—the landlord still carrying the flaring candle, which soon flared out.

"I telled ye I heer'd somm'at like horses a galloping past, with shafts a'ter 'em," cried one of the men; "but ye was in such haste to abuse the landlord for saying it were twelve, that ye could not heed me."

Between them they raised the chaise, and extricated Mrs. Danesbury. She lay motionless. Harding, shocked and bewildered, and hardly knowing how to act, sped off through the town to Mr. Danesbury's, whilst others ran for the surgeon, who was not found at home, but at Danesbury House. The postboy had gathered himself up, and was sitting with his back against the side of the bridge. They gently raised him, and walked him about a few steps. No limbs were broken. He shook himself, and speech came to him.

"That there Giles ought to swing for this," were the first words that broke from him.

"What had Giles to do with it?" questioned the chorus of voices.

"He were as drunk as blazes. I saw he were when he came ducking, head over heels, to open the gate. He were so drunk, he couldn't push it back, nor hold it back, and he let it come swing agen the horses."

"Did that start 'em off?"

"It just did start 'em off: I never strode such terrified, furious brutes afore. They took, as you may say, one leap from the top of the hill to the bottom, not a bit longer it didn't seem, and the chaise caught the nasty awk'ard bridge, and we went over."

"I tell you all what," cried the landlord; "something'll be done now. The town has called out long enough about the danger of keeping such a bridge; and some folks have called out about Giles's drunkenness. It'll both be remedied now; you'll see."

"Who'll give me a arm up the hill?" cried the postboy, who was a native of Eastborough, and had driven out with Mr. Harding that afternoon, with these very horses. "I doubt if I ain't too shaky to get up it of myself. I'll go and have a word with Giles."

Two of them immediately took the postboy in tow, and they began to ascend the hill. The rest remained to keep watch over the unfortunate lady.

"Jim," cried out the landlord, "what about the horses? Where be they flown to?"

"'Taint much matter where," was the postboy's answer, "they have done mischief enough. They be off to their stables, no doubt, they be, the cantankerous brutes."

Arrived at the turnpike, they tried the house door. It was locked; but they shook it, and kicked, and shouted till Roger Giles came and opened it, very nearly pitching forward into their arms with the exertion.

"A nice state you be in!" muttered the postboy; "a sweet gentleman you be, to keep a pike! Do you know the damage you have gone and done?"

"Eh?" enunciated Giles. He was stupidly drunk, and his eye wandered uneasily to the spot where he kept his employers' cash, some vague idea hammering at his brain that the three men, now entered, might have designs upon it.

"We won't go on at him now," said the postboy to his friends: "'taint of no good. Look at the sot! But you'll both please to bear me out to my master, as to his state, so that I don't get the blame."

"This will be a bad job for you, Giles," cried one of the men. "You have took a drop once too much, my boy. Anyway it will be bad; but if Mrs. Danesbury shouldn't be got to again (and she don't look like it) I should be sorry to stand in your shoes."

They descended the hill again, and the postboy sank down as before, with his back resting against the bridge. His exertion had made him feel dizzy. Soon voices and rapid footsteps were heard, for several people were approaching. Foremost of them came Mr. Pratt, the surgeon, Thomas Harding, and Mr. Danesbury. Those keeping guard drew respectfully back, and touched their hats, even in the dark night, to Mr. Danesbury. They had brought means for a light with them, which had been thought of by Thomas Harding, and the surgeon held it to the face of Mrs. Danesbury.

"She haven't stirred, nor even moaned, sir," said the landlord of "The Pig and Whistle," who, with the others, had collected close up.

"A moment, if you please," cried out the surgeon authoritatively. "Stand back, all of you; I can do and see nothing, with you crowding round. Mr. Danesbury, will you also allow me a moment here alone? Harding, you stay and hold the torch."

Poor Mr. Pratt! He saw that Mrs. Danesbury was dead, and had so spoken to gain time for composure, and that Mr. Danesbury might not see, unprepared, that ghastly face, which told too plainly its own tale.

All had stepped back in compliance with his wishes. Mr. Danesbury's eyes fell on the postboy. "Are you hurt, Jim?" he asked kindly.

"A bit shook, sir; I don't think it's no worse. I hope it won't be no worse with nobody else, sir," he added, nodding towards where the surgeon was stooping.

"How did it happen? Mr. Harding says the gate touched the horses."

"Come swinging right agen 'em, sir; Giles were so drunk he couldn't hold it back."

"Drunk, was he?" quickly cried Mr. Danesbury.

"He were beastly drunk, sir. I have been up there to him now, some of 'em here helped me, and he can't speak, nor stand straight."

Mr. Pratt had arisen, and was at Mr. Danesbury's elbow. He passed his arm within that gentleman's, and drew him away from the crowd, halting at a certain part of the bridge, and apparently looking out, over the dark and gloomy water.

"What is it?" said Mr. Danesbury; "why do you bring me here? Have you ascertained the nature of the injury?"

"Oh, my dear friend!" cried the surgeon, "I know not how to tell you what I must tell."

Mr. Danesbury's heart sank within him: a shadow of appalling woe stole over him. But he did not speak. Perhaps he could not.

"I fear—I fear she is gone," added Mr. Pratt.

Then Mr. Danesbury clutched the surgeon's arm with a tight, nervous grasp. "The truth," he breathed, "the truth. Let me know the worst. I can bear it better than this agony of dread."

"One consolation is, that she did not suffer. She must have died instantaneously. Her neck is broken."

Mr. Danesbury let fall the surgeon's arm. He half fell, half rested on the parapet of the bridge, and a low wail of utter anguish went forth on the night air.

CHAPTER III
THE DESOLATE HOUSE

THE coroner's inquest was held on the appointed day. Thomas Harding could only depose that the gate touched the horse on his side of the chaise; he had not observed the state of the gatekeeper. But the postboy, and the men who had subsequently accompanied him to the gatehouse, testified that Giles was incapably drunk. The verdict returned was, "Manslaughter against Roger Giles, he having been, at the time of its act, in a state of drunkenness."

He was committed to prison to await his trial. The little child, William Danesbury, had recovered the effects of the laudanum, the remedies administered by the surgeon having proved successful.

Eastborough, insignificant in itself, owed what importance it did possess to its being the scene of the Danesbury Works, sometimes called the Danesbury Factory, sometimes the Iron Works. It was a concern of considerable magnitude, giving employment, in its various departments, to a large number of hands. Engineers, iron-founders, manufacturers of agricultural and divers implements, combined with other branches of trade, not essential to mention, necessarily rendered the Danesburys of a high standing in the commercial world. Not only for the extent of their operations did they bear a wide renown, but for the lofty excellence of their character, both in business matters and in private life. Just, honourable, and upright, the name of Danesbury was respected all the country round. The business had once been of small account, but the then proprietor of it, John Danesbury, raised it, by his diligence and intelligence, into importance. As his two sons, John and Philip, severally attained the age of twenty-one, they were taken into partnership with him, the firm then being altered to that of "John Danesbury & Sons." The elder of those sons, John, was the one introduced to the reader. He was now the sole proprietor, for his father and brother had both died; the latter, Philip, a young man, leaving a widow. But the appellation of the firm had not been changed: it was still known as that of "John Danesbury & Sons:" possibly Mr. Danesbury looked forward to the period when it should be so in actuality. He had married a Miss St. George, a lady every way worthy of him, and whose dreadful death was a far greater shock to him than the world suspected. Their two eldest children, Arthur and Isabel, lived and flourished, two succeeding ones had died infants, and the last had just escaped following them, as you have seen, through nurse Glisson's dose of opium.

Thomas Harding was exceedingly attached to Mr. Danesbury; and with cause. He had served his father; he now served him, and enjoyed his full confidence. There were superior clerks, as to position, in the factory, gentlemen overlookers, but they held a secondary place to Thomas Harding in the estimation of Mr. Danesbury. It was the respect due to worth, deserved, and paid to an honest, guileless man. Harding was vexed at being the depository of this secret about Glisson; but he hoped the tragical end of her mistress, caused remotely *through her,* might so tell upon her that there would no longer exist reason to betray her to Mr. Danesbury.

"Glisson took on dreadfully," said Jessy, one day that she was at the Hardings' house, about ten days subsequently to the funeral. "I was so shocked that night, when they brought the dead body into the house, that I hardly knew what I said, and did not spare her. I told her, if she had kept herself in her right senses, and given the baby the proper medicine, our poor mistress would have been alive and safe."

"What did she say?"

"I cannot tell half she said. She was like a mad woman, lying on the floor, crying out for her mistress, moaning, and wishing she had died for her. Master heard her in his room, and came in; but he thought it was all self-reproach for her mistake in having given the wrong medicine; he did not suspect she had anything worse to reproach herself with."

"Was she sober then?"

"I should think she was! The poisoning of the child had sobered her, and she had taken nothing subsequently. I do not believe she has yet. I have never noticed it, and she grieves after her mistress night and day."

"Then it has, perhaps, been such a warning to her that she'll abandon the habit altogether," returned Thomas Harding. "Jessy, girl, never suffer a word to escape you of what has been: give her a chance of redeeming herself. It is what Mrs. Danesbury would have done, had she lived: mind you, I know that."

"She's safe for me," replied Jessy. "The children are coming home to-morrow," she continued. "Some lady is bringing them, and we fancy she is going to remain—as governess, or housekeeper, or something of that. Master came to the nursery this morning, and told us that a cousin of our late mistress's would accompany the children, and the house was to take its orders from her. Glisson is uncommonly put out about it: she says those half-and-half mistresses are always more difficult to please than real ones."

"Jessy! take care to do your duty, and don't be so fond of repeating things after Mrs. Glisson," rebuked her Aunt Harding.

Danesbury House was a handsome white mansion, surrounded by fine grounds, with a smooth lawn sloping from the front, its elevated site causing it to command extensive and beautiful views of the neighbouring country.

On the morning that was to witness the return of the children, a lady approached the house, ascended the stone steps to the pillared portico, and entered a spacious hall, on either side of which were the reception chambers. It was Mrs. Philip Danesbury, the widow of Mr. Danesbury's brother. She enjoyed a handsome income from the business, and resided near; a talkative, pleasant woman, young still, possessed of good sense, and of keen penetration. She was in Yorkshire, her native place, when the recent fatal event happened, and had now been home a day or two. Mr. Danesbury had seen her the previous day, and her present visit was to Glisson and the baby. While she was in the nursery talking, she observed her brother-in-law approaching from the factory, and went downstairs to meet him.

"John," she began, as soon as they were in the sitting-room, dashing at once into some news she had just heard, "Glisson says there's a lady coming here, to be in Isabel's place."

"Not in Isabel's *place*," interrupted Mr. Danesbury, in a tone of pain. "No one can fill that. Do not say so."

"Well, you know what I meant, John. Unfortunately, no one ever can fill it, in any sense of the word. She was worth more than many of us who are left. Poor, poor Isabel!"

Mr. Danesbury sat silent, his countenance betraying a shade more of its deep sorrow. He was not a demonstrative man, and he buried his grief within him.

"But there is somebody coming to rule the household and manage the children," proceeded Mrs. Philip Danesbury. "Who is it?"

"Miss St. George, Mrs. Serle's sister. She has offered to remain here a little while."

"A 'little while!' That means an indefinite period, I suppose?"

"No time was mentioned. It was Mrs. Serle who wrote and proposed it. I thought it exceedingly kind and considerate of her, and accepted it gratefully."

"But whatever made you accept it, all in such a hurry?" continued Mrs. Philip, in her hasty way.

"I accepted it for the children's sake. Who is to overlook them? Glisson can take care of William, but Arthur and Isabel should not be left to the entire companionship of servants."

"The better plan would have been—John," she broke off, "I have been turning things over in my mind, before I knew of this Miss St. George scheme. I think Arthur should be placed at school, and I will take charge of Isabel."

"You are very kind, Maria," he sadly answered. "But the house, deprived of the two children, would be more desolate than with them. What objection do you see to Miss St. George staying here—for I think I detect that you have an objection?"

"A minute, John: answer me a question or two before I answer yours. What age is this Miss St. George?"

"I do not know. I have a general idea that she is not young. I once saw her at Mr. Serle's, but retain a very faint recollection of her. I fancy she is older than Mrs. Serle; and that she lives with her because she has no other home."

"There; that's quite enough: you have most fully answered me," impetuously returned Mrs. Philip Danesbury. "Take care of yourself, John."

"Take care of myself! In what way?"

"It will be a terrible temptation to a woman in her position, the getting herself to be the real mistress of this house. She will play her cards with the hope and view to be your second wife, John: mind she does not play them to win."

A contraction of displeasure passed across Mr. Danesbury's ample brow. He could not understand his sister-in-law, and deemed these remarks to be unworthy of her.

"John," she resumed, "I cannot help speaking out all my thoughts, but it is that I am anxious for the children's welfare and your happiness. You cannot understand these things, but I can; and rely upon it, this lady's motive in proffering a temporary sojourn here arises from a dim hope that she may improve it into a permanent one. I see also another evil—that it will cause rebellion and warfare with the servants. You look surprised, but I tell you you have had no experience in these things, and do not understand them.'

No, Mr. Danesbury did not understand it at all, and he certainly did not believe it. He asked Mrs. Philip to remain to dinner.

"I will," she replied, "and I shall let Miss St. George know, unmistakably, that I am Mrs. Philip Danesbury, the nearest kin you and the children have, and quite competent to direct the affairs of Danesbury House, where direction may be necessary, without her assistance."

Mrs. Philip untied the crape strings of her bonnet as she spoke, and ran upstairs again. She was somewhat given to be dictatorial, but she was a thoroughly sincere, good woman at heart. Glisson opened upon her grievance.

"I hope this new person's not going to take too much upon herself, ma'am, for it's what I shan't be able to put up with. I'd do anything for a Danesbury, and for my dear late mistress, who was a mistress in a thousand, but an interloper is a different sort of thing. Master said we were to take our orders from her."

"It is beginning," thought Mrs. Philip; but she did not choose to say so, she was fond of keeping servants in their places. "Miss St. George is a relative of poor Mrs. Danesbury, and every respect must be shown her, Glisson," she said, in an authoritative tone. "Jessy, I hope you hear me also. I daresay you will get on very well with her, for the time she is to remain."

Glisson made no reply. She went out for the baby, who had been laid down for his mid-day sleep, and brought him in. The sleeves of his embroidered white frock were tied up with black silk ribbon, and he wore a broad black sash.

"Poor little motherless darling!" uttered Mrs. Philip, taking the child, and clasping him to her. "I wish papa would give you to me, my little godson," she murmured, covering his sweet face, so lovely in its rosy flush, with kisses. The tears came into her eyes as she gazed on him—for the having no children had been Mrs. Philip Danesbury's great trial in life. "Glisson," she suddenly exclaimed, "how did that dreadful mistake happen? How came you to be deceived in the medicine?"

"Ma'am," said the nurse, turning round in a sort of frenzy, "I'll go down upon my knees and beg you not to ask me! I have been almost mad ever since, thinking of it; and if I have to talk of it, it will drive me quite so. I wish I had been dead before it had happened!"

She sat down in the rocking chair, threw her apron over her head, and burst into a storm of wails and sobs. Mrs. Philip walked about with the child, and considerately abstained from further allusion to it. In the midst of this, the travellers were seen approaching. It was a clear, frosty day, and they were walking up from "The Ram," where the stage-coach stopped. The two children, in their sombre black attire, were accompanied by two ladies, one of whom was in deep mourning, the other in slighter.

"Why, there's two of them!" unceremoniously uttered Glisson, who had made her way to the window.

"Miss St. George has put on deep black to be like the family, as she is to stay here," decided Mrs. Philip; "and the other must be Mrs. Serle."

She eyed Miss St. George critically as she spoke. Glisson did the same. A thin, shortish, vinegar-looking lady, with cold, light eyes, a sharp nose, and flaxen hair, Miss St. George was one of those whom black attire does not improve.

"It's a disagreeable face, if I ever saw one," cried Glisson; "as cross as two sticks. If she knew anybody was looking at her, she'd smooth it, I expect."

"Five-and-thirty, if she's a day, and a soured woman," was Mrs. Philip Danesbury's mental comment. "Won't she be having a try at John?"

The visitors were shown to the drawing-room, a spacious apartment opening to the lawn. It was fitted up with rich silk damask furniture, mirrors, ornaments, and some exquisite paintings. Mrs.

Philip Danesbury entered, and welcomed the two ladies gracefully, as though she were the mistress of the house.

"To whom have we the honour of speaking?" demanded Mrs. Serle.

"Madam, to the sister-in-law of Mr. Danesbury, the aunt of these dear children. I am Mrs. Philip Danesbury. This, I presume, is Miss St. George, who has kindly proffered us a visit."

"I proffered it for her," smiled Mrs. Serle, who appeared all complaisance. "The isolated condition of these poor children, left entirely to the servants, struck me as being so pitiable, that I suggested to Eliza to come home with them for a short period, should it be agreeable to Mr. Danesbury. I did not know of their possessing so efficient a relative near to them. From the remarks of the children, I fancied Mrs. Philip Danesbury's residence was in Yorkshire."

"I have been there for a long visit. We appreciate your kindness, and shall be happy to render Miss St. George's visit agreeable to her," was the somewhat frigid answer of Mrs. Philip.

Mr. Danesbury came in. Unusually noble he looked in his deep mourning attire, and with the saddened expression on his fine features. Ere he had well kissed his two children, he was obliged to hurry from the room: their sight brought his loss, and theirs, too painfully to his memory.

"Harriet!" exclaimed Miss St. George, the moment she was alone with her sister in the chamber to which they had been shown, "I shall go back with you; I shan't stop here. The idea of being domineered over by that sharp woman! She is mistress, and I should be no better than a temporary visitor—an interloper. I did not come down and go in mourning for that."

"You will do no such thing, Eliza. You are come, and you must remain. She is not mistress; she does not live here."

"But she comes armed with full power to do as she pleases in the house; there's no doubt of it. She'll be here for ever."

"Nonsense! Stop and feel your way. You will supersede her if you try. And if you don't, you are only where you were before."

"I hate children," cried Miss St. George. "And to assume to 'love' these will be more difficult than I thought, with her shrewd eyes upon me."

She sighed, as she turned to the glass, and began to arrange the bands of her very light hair. She had no parents, no money, and had been obliged to her sister for a home. She was not always comfortable in it; her temper was bad. Mrs. Serle would not put up with it, and at such times would make her feel that she was an intruder. To get away from it, and take the sway in such a house as Mr. Danesbury's had been a glowing prospect, and the damper cast on it by the sight and words of Mrs. Philip was a mortifying disappointment. Whether she, or Mrs. Serle for her, had cast a glance to the possibility that time and luck might transform her into Mrs. Danesbury, cannot be told.

"What an exceedingly fine man Mr. Danesbury is!" exclaimed Mrs. Serle; "I should call him one of Nature's true nobility. The child Arthur will be like him."

"And what a handsome house," returned Miss St. George. "Everything so well appointed and comfortable."

"Ay, plenty of wealth here, Eliza. If you can succeed in establishing a firm footing, you will be fortunate."

Mrs. Philip Danesbury, meanwhile, was looking about for Arthur, who had disappeared. She found him in the little room where Mrs. Danesbury used to assemble her children for the ten minutes after breakfast in the morning, to read to them their Bible stories and to talk of heaven. It was a duty she never omitted, and the children had learnt to love it. Arthur was stretched across the low sofa where his mamma used to sit, crying as if his heart would break. Mrs. Philip Danesbury closed the door, sat down, and drew him to her.

"My darling, don't sob so; be comforted."

"Aunt Philip, I shall never see her again! I never thought it could be quite true till I came home now. Oh, mamma! mamma!"

"My child, be comforted, she is better off; she is gone to heaven."

"But never to come back! never to come back!" he wailed. "Oh, mamma! if you would but come to me for one minute, only one!"

"Arthur, she cannot return to you; you know it, my darling; but you will go to her."

"But it is such a long while!"

"It will come, my child. She is one of God's angels now, and she will watch over you here, and wait for you."

His sobs nearly choked him.

"Arthur, do you know why I am sure your mamma is happy, and has gone to the rest promised to the people of God?"

"Because she was good," he sobbed.

"No, my darling. She was good—better than most people are; but she is gone because she loved Christ, and put her whole trust in Him. She had always taken God for her Guide. She taught you to do so, Arthur?"

"Yes," answered the child, and he gradually grew calmer.

"Aunt Philip," he presently said, a catching sob seizing his breath occasionally, "how could that Giles let the gate fall against the horses?"

"Because he was a wicked man," promptly answered Mrs. Philip, whose indignation was sure to break loose when she thought of the accident, and its lamentable consequences. "He had got horribly tipsy, my dear, and could not hold it back."

"Would it have happened if he had not been tipsy?"

"No, of course not. But for Giles's drinking that night, your mamma would have been alive and well now, and perhaps sitting here with us."

That set Arthur on again. "Why did he drink?" he sobbed. "Why does anybody drink?"

"Because they are beasts," said Mrs. Philip. "And they *are* nothing else," she added, as if in apology for her word, "when they drink themselves into that state."

"I never will," said Arthur.

"*You*, my dearest! Oh, no, never! Your dear mamma would be grieved in heaven, if she were to look down and see you, even once, so far forget yourself."

The child gazed upwards at the blue sky, almost as if he were looking for his mother's face there. Soon he gave his head that very decided shake, which in him, child as he was, expressed firm, inward resolve.

"No, Aunt Philip, I will *never* drink. How long is she going to stay?" he added.

"Who, my dear?"

"Miss St. George."

"I cannot tell. Don't you like her?"

"Not much," answered Arthur. "She told me she was going to be with us instead of mamma."

Mrs. Philip Danesbury wondered what there could be, or not be, in Miss St. George, that nobody seemed to like her. She only hoped her brother-in-law would fall into the general opinion.

When they assembled to sit down to dinner, Arthur was not to be found. He had made his way into the factory to Thomas Harding.

The latter shook him by the hand, and said he was glad to see him home again.

"Mr. Harding," whispered the child, struggling to hide the tears which would rise to his eyes, "could you not have helped the gate from falling on the horses?"

"Master Arthur, sir, you see this arm," said Thomas Harding, holding it out, bared to the elbow, for his coat was off, and his shirt sleeve rolled up, at his work, "well, I'd have given that freely, ay, and the other to it, to have helped it. I wish I could."

"Aunt Philip says Giles was tipsy. And that if he had not been so, mamma would have been here now."

"And that's true, Master Arthur."

"Why do they let people get tipsy?"

"Who let them, dear?"

"I don't know," said the child, puzzled himself, as he thought over his question. "Why do people get tipsy?"

"I believe they can't tell themselves why. Nobody who is worth anything does so."

"You don't; do you, Mr. Harding?"

"No; I'm thankful to say I have kept from that failing all my life," he fervently answered.

"And papa does not?"

"No, no, child. I tell you, nobody who is good does such a disgraceful thing. Only poor creatures who have no self-restraint."

"Does Giles get tipsy now?"

"No, that he does not! The jailer takes care of that. He is in prison, Master Arthur."

"For killing mamma?"

"For letting the gate swing to, and frighten the horses. He is to be tried at the March assizes."

"Is Master Danesbury here?" called out a servant-man, who had come in search of him. "Oh, there you are, sir. Dinner's waiting."

CHAPTER IV
THE GAME PLAYED OUT

THE time went on. March assizes came and passed, and Roger Giles entered upon the punishment awarded him—two years' imprisonment. Miss St. George stopped on at Danesbury House; nobody suggested to her that she should leave it, and she took care not to suggest it to herself. She behaved wonderfully well, and endeavoured to ingratiate herself with all in it, master, servants, and children. Her exertions never flagged. Her chief consideration seemed to be that of rendering herself unobtrusively agreeable to Mr. Danesbury; and, so far as he or anybody else saw of her temper, it might be that of an angel. The servants were indulged; the children were petted; it all went on as smooth as oil. Miss St. George was playing her game.

Summer came round, and with it Isabel's birthday. Some children were invited to dinner, and Mrs. Philip Danesbury was expected to preside; but she did not come, and they sat down without her, Miss St. George occupying the place opposite Mr. Danesbury; when Mrs. Philip was there, she always took it herself. At the period of dessert, Miss St. George filled glasses of wine for the children, including Arthur and Isabel.

"Why have you given wine to me and Isabel?" asked Arthur.

"It is Isabel's birthday, and you must drink her health," was Miss St. George's reply.

"But we never drink wine," repeated Arthur.

"That's no reason why you never should. On such an occasion as this it is necessary. What would Isabel say if you did not drink good wishes to her?"

"I'll drink them in water," said Arthur.

"Oh, no, that would never do," Miss St. George remonstrated; "that would not be cordial. May he not have a glass of wine to-day?" she added, appealing to Mr. Danesbury.

"If he likes," was the reply. Mr. Danesbury had never been so particular as his wife about the children's beverage being positively restricted to water. Probably he had not thought about it so much and deeply.

"There, Arthur," said Miss St. George, "your papa gives you leave."

"No," answered Arthur, passing the wine back towards Miss St. George. And, filling a wine glass with water, he wished his sister many happy returns of the day. The children followed his example, but drank their good wishes in wine.

"Now, Isabel," said Miss St. George, "thank everyone. There's your wine."

Isabel raised the wine to her lips; but before she could taste it, Arthur had risen from his seat, opposite to her, and was leaning across the table with a flushed face and kindling eye, speaking vehemently.

"Isabel! *You know!*"

His startling energy aroused Mr. Danesbury to astonishment. Isabel instantly put down her glass, blushed painfully, and likewise pushed it towards Miss St. George. "You ought to be ashamed, Isabel," continued Arthur. "If I had not spoken, you were going to drink it. You have forgotten mamma."

Isabel burst into tears. "It was Miss St. George told me," she sobbed; "I did not want to drink it."

"You have a very particular prejudice against drinking wine, Arthur," said Mr. Danesbury, smiling.

"Papa, I promised her that I never would. And Isabel knows all about it, that I never mean to, and she said she never would. Miss St. George knew it."

"Promised who?" said Mr. Danesbury.

"My dear mamma. It was the last word she said to me before she left that night; and I promised her, and she is looking down from heaven at me now."

He laid his head on the table, overcome by the remembrance of his mother, and sobbed aloud. It seemed that Mr. Danesbury was likewise overcome, for he hastily rose, and quitted the room for some minutes.

"Do not attempt to give the children wine again," he said to Miss St. George when he returned. And Miss St. George bowed her head; but she would very much have liked, just then, to give Arthur a wholesome whipping instead.

They soon heard why Mrs. Philip Danesbury had not arrived to dinner. She had received news from Yorkshire that her mother was alarmingly ill, and she had been busy making preparations to start thither on the morrow morning. She ran up at night to say good-bye. Miss St. George, lamenting outwardly, was in a state of inward rapture, fervently hoping that the visit might last six months.

Six months it did last. For Mrs. Philip Danesbury found her mother, Mrs. Heber, in a precarious state, and thought it necessary to remain. It was summer when she went, it was winter when she came back; and the very first news to greet her on her return was, that Eliza St. George was to be Mr. Danesbury's second wife.

Mrs. Philip sat down like one paralysed. "If I did not say it!" she uttered. "I wish he had chosen anybody else, for I don't like the woman; and the children will never like her. What can possess him?"

She wrapped herself up the next morning, and set off in the snow to see Mr. Danesbury. Not going to the house, but seeking him at the Works. He was in his private room.

"John," she said, when greetings had passed, and she warmed her hands over the hot blaze of the fire, "you are going to marry again, I hear."

"I believe so, Maria."

"What did I tell you? That, if you did not take care, she would play her cards and win. And she has done it!"

"It was well for me to marry again. Not that *I* cared about it," he emphatically added, "for I have not yet forgotten Isabel. But the house wanted a mistress, and the children a mother. Miss St. George is amiable, she seems a good manager; and I do believe," he added, with a comical look, "that her whole heart is wrapt up in me and the children. You should see how fond she has grown of William."

"Ah!" ejaculated Mrs. Philip Danesbury.

"What does that interjection mean?" laughed Mr. Danesbury.

"Why, it means that I do not take in what you say, John. I believe you are as completely *done* as ever man was. I do not believe in her amiability, for I think it is all put on; and I do not believe in her love for the children, no, not even for William, for I think that is put on. I cannot speak as to what it may be for you."

"Maria, you were always prejudiced against Miss St. George. You were, before you saw her."

"Admitted. Because her coming down here, in the way she did, looked to me a suspicious proceeding. Now, I am sure it was one. But when I came to see and know Miss St. George, my prejudice did not lessen. I wish you had chosen anyone else, for the children's sake. At the time I went away, I was beginning to think and hope there was another your choice would have fallen upon."

He looked at her inquiringly.

"Miss Roper."

"Ah, she is a nice girl," said Mr. Danesbury, with animation. "She would have been rather young for me."

"She is six or seven and twenty. And I am quite sure she would have made a loving mother to your children. I am astonished at your want of taste, John, in preferring Miss St. George to her."

"Now, don't call my taste in question, if you please, Maria," said he good-humouredly. "I admire Miss Roper more than I do Miss St. George, and I do not particularly care for either. I can never care for any woman as I cared for Isabel."

"You will persuade me, next, you are out of your senses," was the retort of Mrs. Phillip. "If you prefer Miss Roper, why do you marry Miss St. George?"

To tell you the truth," he answered, in a low tone, "I was, in a manner, drawn into the marriage. But, of course, this must never go beyond you."

"Drawn into it! I do not understand."

"It seems the neighbourhood got talking about my attention to Miss St. George. Which appears to me to be very strange, for I declare that I never paid her any particular attention. I certainly used to drive them out in the open carriage most evenings, herself and the two children, and she sat in the front seat with me: I could not put her in the back, you know, a relation of Isabel: and I used to give her my arm to church, and there my attention ended."

"And who says the neighbourhood made remarks?" interrupted Mrs. Philip Danesbury.

"Listen. One day Mrs. Serle arrived here in a desperate bustle. She sought an interview with me, and said Eliza had written to her that she was miserable; that after what the neighbourhood had been pleased to say, she should never hold up her head again in happiness, and that of course she must leave Danesbury House, and they might as well tear her life from her, as tear her from me and the children."

"What did you say to all this rhapsody?"

"Gave the neighbourhood a blessing, or something equivalent to it—though no rumours had reached my ears; and told Mrs. Serle that it was a mistake to suppose I had paid any particular attentions: I had paid none whatever. Mrs. Serle assured me things had been said, and asked what I could do in the dilemma; hinting that for a reproach to have been cast to Isabel's cousin—"

"About forty times removed," contemptuously interrupted Mrs. Philip Danesbury.

Mr. Danesbury smiled, as he continued: "That for a reproach to have been cast on Isabel's cousin would have proved a bitter grief to *her*, had she been in life. Then I began to think that, as I had almost determined to marry again, I might as well take Miss St. George as anybody else, and settle the neighbourhood that way. So, without giving myself time for consideration—I acknowledge that—I told Mrs. Serle that the matter had better be ended in that manner."

"And they snapped at it!"

"They accepted it," said Mr. Danesbury.

"It was all a planned trap!" vehemently spoke Mrs. Philip. "Mrs. Serle's coming down, and saying what she did, was a planned trap to draw you in, planned between her and Miss St. George. I wish I was as sure of heaven! She has played out her game."

Mr. Danesbury stood, his tall form drawn to its full height. He began pushing, with his boot, some starting bits of coal into the fire, between the bars of the grate.

"John!" said Mrs. Philip.

"Well?"

"Do not carry it out. Let her bring an action for breach of promise. She is just the one to do it."

"But, indeed, I mean to carry it out. You must not think I repent, Maria. I believe in Miss St. George's amiability, if you do not, and I think she will make me a suitable wife."

"Well—if you are satisfied, I only hope you will always find cause to be so," added Mrs. Philip earnestly. "Believe me, no one would rejoice more than I to find that I am wrong. When is it to be? I hear Miss St. George is in London."

"She returned with her sister. It is to take place immediately."

And it did so. And Eliza St. George became the second Mrs. Danesbury, to her own unequivocal self-gratulation and delight.

It was on a Tuesday afternoon, and just a week after the wedding. Glisson and Jessy were seated in their old room, the nursery; Glisson, not rocking herself in idleness, but pacing about angrily, in what Jessy called "a temper." On the carpet sat William, playing with some toys; and Jessy was trimming a cap for herself with white satin ribbon. The work seemed somewhat to puzzle her, for she pinned the ribbon on, and unpinned it, in indecision.

"Nurse, see here!" cried she, holding the cap towards the view of Mrs. Glisson, as the latter approached her in her restless wanderings. "Would this look better quilled round the crown, or put in bows at the sides? Just tell me what you think: I want it to be smart."

"It would look best this way," returned the nurse; and, taking the cap and ribbon from Jessy's hand, she dashed them to the ground. The reader, however, must not take a wrong view of Mrs. Glisson's strange action: she was perfectly sober.

"Now, then!" uttered Jessy, "what's that for?"

"I have no patience with you!" she burst forth. "Decking yourself off for a woman that's not fit to stand in your poor dead mistress's shoes; not fit to tie 'em for her, or to buckle on her garters. You are as bad as she is. Let her come and see you with the black bows in your cap, as she will me; it may show her that we sorrow after the old mistress, more than we care to welcome the new."

"Black or white won't alter it," rejoined Jessy, intent on her cap again. "It is done, and it can't be undone; and if the rest of the maids put on white ribbons, there's no reason why I should not. You are as cranky as you can be to-day."

"Cranky, ay!" ejaculated Mrs. Glisson, flinging herself on a chair with a groan, "and you'd be cranky, too, if you had the feelings of an owl. I wonder you can reconcile yourself to stop in the house after such a change! I wonder the servants downstairs can do it!"

"You are stopping yourself," said Jessy.

"Because I am forced to it. Could I go and leave that baby"—pointing to the unconscious little fellow on the carpet—"to her mercies? When I meet my poor dear mistress face to face in heaven, what would she say to me if I had abandoned her child to the dislike of a deceitful stepmother? No; if master goes and makes a fool of himself, and brings home twenty wives with two faces, one for him and t'other for other folks, *I* must stop on, and put up with it, till William's beyond my care. I told master so."

"You never did!" uttered Jessy. "When?"

"That don't matter to you. Get on with your fine wedding-cap."

There was a pause. Jessy, who was then standing at the window, broke it. "Here comes Mrs. Philip Danesbury. I suppose her cold's better, then. She has not got the children with her: I wonder how long she intends to keep them?"

"I hope she'll keep them till they are dragged from her with cords," fired Glisson. "She would, if she was of my mind. Her home will be better for them than their own now."

Mrs. Philip Danesbury came into the nursery. "Well, Glisson; well, Jessy," cried she, as the servants rose. "You have thought me lost, no doubt, but it is nine days since I stepped outside the door. Willie, what has Aunt Philip got?"

The child had risen, and ran to her. Next to Glisson, whom he dearly loved, he was fondest of Mrs. Philip Danesbury. "There," she said, giving him a pretty little toy in sugar, "sister Isabel sent that for Willie."

"When are the children coming home, ma'am?" put in Jessy.

"When their father asks for them; not before," replied Mrs. Philip, with a sharpness in her accent that seemed akin to that of Glisson. "He, and—and—his wife—will not be here before Friday."

"Oh, won't they though!" retorted Glisson, forgetting her respect in her mind's annoyance. "They are coming to-day, ma'am."

"To-day!"

"This very blessed Tuesday," returned Glisson. "Master's wanted in a hurry for some business at the works, and some of them wrote to him, and he wrote word back he would be home to-day. They got the letter at the factory this morning, and sent in and told us, by his orders. It's a black day for me, I know that."

"Jessy," said Mrs. Philip, not immediately replying to Glisson, "Miss Isabel requires a clean tucker or two: will you put them up?"

Jessy left the room. "You must try and make the best of it, Glisson," Mrs. Philip continued, when they were alone. "It would never do, you know, for you to leave William."

"That's the only thing that's keeping me: nothing else in the world. If she begins to treat him badly, I'll step between them, and ask master to uphold me for his late wife's sake."

"Hush, Glisson, she will not do that. She appears to be so very fond of him."

"Just as a certain gentleman is of holy water," irreverently snapped Glisson. "From the very first hour she set foot in this house, she has been plotting how best to catch master. I saw through her, if nobody else did. He had no more chance against her than a fly has with a spider; but just walked into the web, like a blindfolded simpleton. It's of no good, ma'am, I must speak! I am fit this day to take and hang myself. Oh, my poor dead mistress!"

Glisson bent her head in her hands, and swung backwards and forwards in her chair, after the manner of one overwhelmed with grief. In a minute she looked up again. "Ma'am! Mrs. Philip Danesbury! didn't *you* see through her?"

"I did," was the low answer.

The woman wrung her hands. "Then why, oh why, didn't you warn master, and set him on his guard? It was not for me to do such a thing, ma'am, but you might."

"I did warn him," was the rejoinder on Mrs. Philip's lips; but she checked herself, and did not speak it.

"It was a funny thing altogether," resumed Glisson. "Master did not seem fond of her—he did not seem to care about her at all. Then came that visit of Mrs. Serle. She was closeted with Miss St. George after she got here, and I'll be whipped if I didn't say to Jessy that those two were hatching mischief. After that, master was sent for from the factory, and Mrs. Serle was closeted with him. The next day the two sisters went back to London together, and we heard that there was going to be a marriage. They are deep ones, those women, if my eyes are worth anything."

"I heard that about the time of this visit of Mrs. Serle, there was a report in the neighbourhood that Mr. Danesbury's name had been gratuitously coupled with that of Miss St. George."

"There never was such a report," returned Glisson decisively, "and whoever says it, says wrong. It was just the other way. When Miss St. George came first, folks laughed and joked, and said she had come to pick up Mr. Danesbury. But at the twelvemonth's end, when she was no nearer doing it, they laughed at her for being baulked, and said Mr. Danesbury was too wise to be caught."

"Nurse, are you sure of this?"

"I am sure and certain. The servants downstairs have not had much else to do than collect news, and I'll back them for being awake to what goes on in the neighbourhood, and for what's said. Whoever told you, ma'am, that scandal was talked of master and Miss St. George, told an untruth, and knows it. It was, I say, just the opposite."

It wanted not this to confirm Mrs. Philip Danesbury's suspicions that her brother-in-law had been made the victim of a cunning plan.

"Not another hour would I have stopped but for the child," went on Glisson, "and so I told master. It was one day after Miss St. George had gone; the children were out, and master was dining alone. After dinner the bell rang for the baby, and I took him down, and master put him on his knee. 'Glisson,' said he, turning to me, 'I suppose you have heard that there is going to be a change?' 'Yes, master,' says I, 'and I'd rather have been swallowed up by an earthquake than have heard it; and I am thinking that I shan't be able to stop—it'll go against the grain.' 'What are you saying?' he interrupted, 'you must stop: you have not been in the family so many years to leave it now.' 'There's only one thing keeps me, sir,' I said, 'and that's this precious child: I must stop to put myself between him and harm, knowing that I sent his poor mother out of the world.' 'Stop with him always, Glisson,' whispered master, as he gave the child back to me, and I saw that his eyes were wet."

At this juncture in came Jessy, all excitement. "Ma'am! here they are! Glisson, they are come!"

"Who are come?" demanded Mrs. Philip, considerably startled, as she hastened to the window in the wake of Jessy. "Not Mr. and Mrs. Danesbury?"

But it was. Mr. Danesbury's chariot, with post horses, was sweeping up the gravelled drive. He was in it, and his new wife sat beside him. Mrs. Philip was at a nonplus. "I would not have had it happen so for anything!" she exclaimed. "I will not be here to receive her. Were they expected so early as this?"

"They were expected to dinner, ma'am; but not just yet," answered Jessy. "Glisson, there's my cap never finished!"

"And I hope it never will be, with those ribbons on it," retorted Glisson.

The carriage drew up, and its inmates alighted, the servants going out to receive them and to unpack the chariot. Mr. Danesbury entered but for a minute or two, and then departed to the factory, and Mrs. Danesbury was heard ascending the stairs. Her new rooms, once those of her predecessor, were on the same floor as the nursery, and it was impossible to say for which she might be making. "What on earth am I to do?" uttered Mrs. Philip.

"Step in here, to the night-nursery, ma'am," suggested Jessy, in a whisper, as she held the door open. "I do believe she's coming in here."

Mrs. Philip did so. Most particularly unpalatable was it to her to be in the new Mrs. Danesbury's house at this, the moment of her return, though she did not stay to analyse the reason. Mrs. Philip looked round the room. Glisson's bed was in it, and little William's by its side, and there she stood listening.

Mrs. Danesbury had, however, turned into her own rooms, and Mrs. Philip, after waiting a few minutes, was about to emerge from her hiding-chamber, when Mrs. Danesbury's steps were again heard. She entered the day-nursery, and Mrs. Philip, at the sound of her voice, whisked quietly inside a closet by Glisson's bed.

"How do you do, nurse?" said Mrs. Danesbury.

Glisson snatched up little William before she answered, "I'm amongst the middlings, ma'am."

"You little love!" uttered Mrs. Danesbury, making a great show of kissing the boy. "How well he looks, nurse!"

The nurse coughed. "It's to be hoped he isn't ill, ma'am."

William raised his finger, and pointed to the door of the night-nursery. "Aunt Phe-eep dere," lisped he.

Jessy felt her face flush the colour of a peony, but Glisson had her presence of mind about her.

"You silly little donkey," quoth she to the child, beginning to toss him in her arms, as if for sport, and turning his face from the door, "it's not your Aunt Philip, it's Mrs. Danesbury. He has got a trick of calling all folks Aunt Philip," added Glisson, popping out an untruth in her perplexity.

Mrs. Danesbury laughed, and returned to her own room, deeming she had accomplished her duty to the nursery in paying it a visit, and glad that it was over.

Glisson looked in at the chamber door. She could not see Mrs. Philip Danesbury. "Why, where—why, she's never gone into my closet!" breathed Glisson to herself; "but I'm the fool for leaving the key in the door!" And when Mrs. Philip emerged from it, Glisson, albeit not one of the blushing sort, turned red, as Jessy had just done.

"She's gone, is she not?" whispered Mrs. Philip.

"All safe, and shut up in her own room, ma'am. She won't come again, I'll answer for it."

"Nurse, my petticoats have knocked a bottle down, and it is either broken or else the cork has come out. It appears to have gin in it."

"Gin!" repeated nurse Glisson in a tone of remonstrance. "Gin, ma'am?"

"Well, I wondered myself what could bring gin in your closet; but it certainly is gin; there's no mistaking the smell."

"Goodness me!" cried the nurse aloud, but as though she were deliberating a question with herself, "I never can have kept that drop of gin in there since the night, ever so long ago, when I was bent double with the spasms—legs, and body, and chest, all in a cramp together!"

"How ill you must have been!" said Mrs. Philip, with sympathy.

"Oh, awful—dreadful! I remember some of 'em did run for some gin, frightened, maybe, lest I should be dying, and they drenched me with it. It must be the remains of that, forgotten all this while in my closet. Oh, yes, I can scent it here," added Glisson, sniffing; "sure enough it's gin—nasty smelling stuff! I'll see to it when you are gone, ma'am."

"Good-bye," whispered Mrs. Philip to the child; and then Glisson told what mischief he had nearly caused.

"You very treacherous little marplot!" laughed Mrs. Philip, as she gave him a shower of silent kisses. "Good-bye, nurse; good-bye, Jessy." And with a light foot she tripped along the corridor and down the stairs, and escaped, unseen by its new mistress, from Danesbury House.

CHAPTER V
EVILS

CERTAIN changes, in course of time, took place at Danesbury House. Few persons could be less alike than the late Miss St. George and the present Mrs. Danesbury: they were as two separate and distinct women, especially in the matter of temper, and Mr. Danesbury could not fail to observe that they were. The servants experienced it to their cost, and Isabel also to hers.

Isabel and her new mamma did not certainly get on well together, and yet Isabel was a sweet-tempered child, remarkably lady-like and graceful. Glisson spoke out openly, and in the hearing of her master: "It was Mrs. Danesbury's fractiousness." Mr. Danesbury knew that his wife was in delicate health, and he believed that must be the reason of her being so cross and irritable: but, so far as Isabel was concerned, he speedily set about a remedy. A gentlewoman of superior mind and manners was taken into the house as her governess, and he gave the little girl into her companionship and charge. "It will be less trouble for you," was the excuse he offered to his wife. Mrs. Danesbury seemed inclined to rebel: she did not want a governess in the house. She said Isabel might be sent to a first-class school; but Mr. Danesbury was perfectly firm upon the point, and his wife saw that he was, and submitted. Arthur was away at school, having been placed out in the spring. Strictly speaking, it could not, however, be called a school—a clergyman received half a dozen select pupils, and Arthur made one. Mr. Danesbury was one of those wise-judging fathers who deemed no money wasted that is spent upon education.

With the coming winter, a boy was born to the second Mrs. Danesbury. It was named Robert, and Glisson was constituted its nurse, the care of little Master William being turned over to Jessy. But before this could be effected, Glisson and her mistress nearly came to a battle-royal. In the first place, Glisson, though ready and willing enough to take to an infant of Mr. Danesbury, had an insuperable objection to be charged with any child of Mrs. Danesbury; and, secondly, she vowed and protested that she would not give up William. But Glisson, like her betters, found herself obliged to yield to circumstances. She was at liberty to remain in the house and attend to William, if she pleased, but not as head-nurse, for whoever took charge of the infant must fill that post. Of course, for Glisson to remain in the Danesbury nursery, and *not* be its head, was out of the question; therefore, with much outward crustiness and inward heart-burning, she did at length consent to make the change. All this unpleasantness—and in Glisson's opinion it had been nothing but unpleasantness for the past year—did not tend to improve Glisson's patience, nor yet her self-restraint.

One evening, when spring was drawing on, and the infant was three or four months old, Mr. Danesbury being absent on a journey, Mrs. Danesbury retired to her room early, not feeling well. She heard the baby cry an unusual length of time, so, throwing on a shawl, for she was partially undressed, she proceeded to the night-nursery. There sat Glisson, fast asleep. Mrs. Danesbury took up her struggling, crying child, and turned to the nurse.

"Glisson!" Glisson took no notice.

"Glisson! what is the matter with you? How dare you sleep like this, when the child's screaming? He might have been choked."

She shook the woman roughly by the arm, and Glisson opened her eyes. Alas! she had been taking something which rendered it difficult to awake readily from her state of stupidity. Mrs. Danesbury stood confounded, and in the same moment she became conscious of a strong smell of gin, and saw an empty glass and spoon on the floor. Glisson rose up from her seat, staggered, and sank down in it again. Mrs. Danesbury rang the bell violently, and Jessy came running up.

"Jessy," cried her mistress, "do you see this woman? She has been drinking. She is drunk."

Jessy made some incoherent reply. She was aware that Glisson, though horror-struck and repentant at the time of her late mistress's death, had afterwards recommenced her habit of drinking gin. But Jessy did not consider that it was her place to betray her, especially as Glisson, so far as Jessy saw, never took sufficient to render her incapable of her duties. Mrs. Danesbury, giving the infant into Jessy's hands, proceeded to rummage the room, and found the gin-bottle. Her passion rose with the sight.

"What am I to do with you, you wicked, drunken woman?"

"No more drunk than you, ma'am," hiccupped Glisson, who was just well enough to be abusive. "Who says I'm drunk?"

"Jessy," cried Mrs. Danesbury, "did you see her drinking it?"

"I saw her drink her ale at supper," replied Jessy.

"I say, did you see her drink *this?*" sharply repeated Mrs. Danesbury, touching the glass with her foot.

"No, ma'am. I have not been upstairs."

"If you had seen her, and suffered her to drink herself into this state without informing me, I would have turned you away in disgrace along with her," said Mrs. Danesbury. "This must have been a nightly habit."

"I do not come into this room at night," was Jessy's reply. "I have nothing to do here."

"You shameless creature!" continued Mrs. Danesbury, turning to Glisson. "Is not your good strong supper ale enough for you, but you must drink gin upon it? Shameful!"

"Highty tighty!" broke out Glisson, "gin upon ale? don't other folks do the same? You have your strong ale, ma'am, at supper, and you can take your spirits after it: sometimes it's gin, and sometimes it's brandy, but you don't go to bed without one of 'em. It's shameful, is it, for a poor hard-working servant? What is it for you, ma'am?

"Her passion rose with the sight."

Where's the difference? I suppose you can stand it best: more used to it, maybe."

Mrs. Danesbury was struck dumb with rage, and the more especially that she could not contradict the chief facts. For she did drink strong ale at supper, and she did, in general, take a glass of spirits and water afterwards. It was the custom to drink spirits at night at Mr. Serle's, and she had recommenced it after she became Mrs. Danesbury. The comparison was not pleasant, and she began a passionate abuse of Glisson—which might have been more temperate, but for what she had herself taken.

An unseemly quarrel ensued. Glisson was sullen and insolent, Mrs. Danesbury violent. She at length struck Glisson in her passion, and ordered her to quit the house then and there.

Glisson refused to go. She was as obstinate as her mistress, and it ended by her remaining, Jessy taking charge of the infant for the night.

Glisson was in her sober senses the next morning, penitent and low-spirited. Mrs. Danesbury, cold, sulky, and unforgiving, stood over her while she packed her boxes, and then ordered one of the men-servants to show her out of the house. This accomplished, she went into the day-nursery, where sat Jessy with William and the infant.

"I have been thinking that I would prefer you to a stranger," said Mrs. Danesbury to Jessy. "Will you take Glisson's place, and I will engage another for Master William?"

Jessy could only decline. The request gave her courage to say what she had been going to say for two or three weeks past—that she was about to leave.

"Have you any fault to find with the house?" imperiously demanded Mrs. Danesbury.

"Oh no, ma'am. But—I suppose I must tell you," stammered Jessy, "I am thinking of getting married."

"To whom, pray?"

"To Richard Gould, one of Mr. Danesbury's men. But I will stay a month or two, or even three, ma'am, if you wish, while you suit yourself."

Mrs. Danesbury, in her exasperation, thought everything was going against her, and she turned away without vouchsafing an answer.

Three or four mornings afterwards, Mr. Danesbury returned. His wife immediately gave him an account of Glisson's misconduct;

truth to say, an exaggerated one. For, now that she had had time to cool down, she doubted whether her husband would approve of so summary a mode of dealing with an old and respected servant. Mr. Danesbury was proceeding to the factory afterwards, when he met Jessy and little William. The child held out his arms, and Mr. Danesbury took him up.

"Jessy," he exclaimed, "what a strange thing this is about Glisson! How came she to get into such a state?"

"It was very unfortunate, sir."

"Did she actually strike her mistress?"

"Oh no, sir," hastily answered Jessy, "she did not do that. It was my mistress—"

"Your mistress—what?" said he, for Jessy had stopped short.

"Speak out," continued Mr. Danesbury, in his kind but commanding way, for Jessy still hesitated. "I wish to know the particulars of this affair."

"It was my mistress struck her, sir."

"Did she not strike your mistress?"

"No, indeed, sir; she did not so far forget herself as that. She was abusive, and said things which she would not have said had she been sober."

"Was it a nightly habit with her?"

"I am sure, sir, I hardly know what to say," was Jessy's rejoinder. "I'm afraid she took a little occasionally, but I should think she was never like she was that night."

"Where is she gone?"

"No one seems to know where. She has not been seen since."

Mr. Danesbury put William down again, and was walking off, but turned again.

"Jessy, I hear you are going to leave, too."

Jessy looked foolish. "Yes, sir."

"We shall be sorry to lose you, for you have done your duty; but if folks will get married, why, they will. Which of the men is it? Mrs. Danesbury forgot the name."

"It's Richard Gould, sir," answered Jessy, with downcast eyes and a crimson face.

"Richard Gould," slowly repeated Mr. Danesbury, as if pondering over the man's merits and demerits. "Well, Jessy, he is a clever workman, and may rise to a good post in the establishment. That is, if he pleases—if he will keep steady."

Scarcely had Mr. Danesbury moved away, when a good-looking young man in a workman's dress approached Jessy from an opposite direction. It was Richard Gould.

"Jessy, wasn't that the master?" he asked, before he had well reached her.

"Yes."

"I must be off into the factory, then. When the master's eyes are about, there's no skulking for anybody."

"You ought to be as diligent when he is absent as when he is present, Richard."

"Oughts don't count always, my little moraliser. I'm diligent enough."

"Richard, I saw Mr. Harding yesterday. What do you think he said?"

"Anything about me?"

"That you were getting to go out with the men to the public-houses after work. And if he saw that you continued to do it, he should write to my father to stop our wedding."

"I don't go to the public-houses," returned Richard Gould.

"He said you were there on Saturday night."

"Saturday night? Well; I believe I did go in for an hour with Foster. It did not harm me."

"And on Thursday night also," she continued.

"What an audacious—stop!" cried Richard, pulling his speech suddenly up, "don't let me tell a story. Thursday night?—that was the night I was hunting for Jackson. I had to get instructions from him about the morning's work, and found him at "The Pig and Whistle," I sat the long spell of half an hour with him at "The Pig," and drank one glass of ale, which he stood treat for. Much harm that did me, didn't it?"

"It is not the harm it does now that matters, but the getting into the habit. Uncle Harding says, if men once get into a habit of going to public-houses of a night, they are sure never to get out of it, and they don't know where it will end; and if no bad ending comes, it runs away with money that might be spent better."

"That's all true," answered the young man, "and Mr. Harding need not fear that I am going to get into it. I shall speak to him about this. Good-bye, Jessy."

Do what they would, they could not hear of Glisson. Mr. Danesbury made inquiry, but was unable to trace her, and a strong fear, a dread which he would not mention to anyone, was beginning to dawn over him—whether, in her grief and despair at the exposure which had taken place, and at being turned from her many years' home, she might not have committed suicide. In three or four weeks, however, tidings came from Glisson herself. She was in London, and now sent to draw out of Mr. Danesbury's hands a sum of money which he held for her at interest. It was £130, all she had saved, except the wages paid her by Mrs. Danesbury the morning of her departure. Mr. Danesbury wrote to her, as did Mrs. Philip Danesbury, kind letters, inquiring her plans, and so forth, but Glisson never answered.

Yes; Glisson had found her way to London. She had a brother living there, and she went to seek him. His address was somewhat vague—Daniel Low, Cow Corner, Commercial Road. Nearly a half day spent Glisson hunting out Cow Corner, and then nearly another half inquiring after Daniel Low. At last she met a man, who was hawking cauliflowers upon a flat board or barrow, and he, hearing the name, said there was a Dan Low in "his line," and he lived in Cass Court, Whitechapel. Glisson thought if his line meant crying vegetables about the streets, her brother must have considerably fallen: he used to be a respectable market gardener; or, as they call it in London, a green-grocer.

It was evening when Glisson emerged from Cow Corner and its alleys, to find out Cass Court, and the street lamps were lighted. It was the first evening she had ever spent in London; moreover, it was Saturday evening, and Glisson was thunderstruck—bewildered with the noise, the bustle, the glare, and confusion. Every tenth house or so was a flaring gin-shop—a palace, as they are called—and veritable palaces did they appear to the astounded Glisson. She stopped opposite the first she came to, and gazed in mute admiration. Its brilliant lamps were beautiful with colours and devices; and its warm, pleasant stream of light came flashing across the street every time the door opened. Glisson got jostled by the crowd at its doors; but, so intense was her entrancement, that at first she did not notice what an unhallowed crowd it was. Soon she sprang away to avoid their contact. Contact with them! Glisson shuddered, and looked at them. Could they be human beings? The rags and the tatters—the scarce-covered nakedness, were not the worst: Glisson had seen that in street beggars; but such forms and faces as these she never had seen. The ghastly squalor of the thin features, the dreadful eyes, the scarlet lips, struck upon her with awe; while the countenances gave out that look of apathy, of pallid despair, which told that the crushed, diseased spirit was fast galloping on to death. Glisson drew herself beyond their circle, and stopped again to look at them; and the sight never was erased from her memory during life. Such as had money were pouring in and out at those swinging doors; and such as had not, vented their anger and misery aloud outside. She did well to close her ears with her two fingers; for they had never yet heard such language, sin, and blasphemy so great as that crowd was shouting—and it was well that ears never should hear it, be they those of man or woman.

Glisson roused herself and continued her way. She seemed to have gazed her fill, both at the palace and its visitors. A few steps farther she came upon another. "What, another?" uttered Glisson, in her surprise. Yes, there was; it was on the opposite side of the street, and it emitted the same tempting flood of gorgeous light, and the same sort of hideous mob was blocking up its entrance. A prolonged stare, and on stepped Glisson again; but soon she came to another halt, for there was actually a third. She began to think they must be common; and she was right. They were scattered everywhere; and not only in that street, but in all the others round about, and across again, and down turnings, and up lanes, and were especially prevalent at corners—more dark misery, more raving sin; and a thought darted into the mind of Glisson (whatever her own practice had been)—upon a city, so contaminated, could the Divine blessing rest?

Intemperance is, indeed, as a very plague spot in the metropolis. It is heard of in mansions—it is seen in dens—it staggers through the streets, lurking in the alleys and the dark corners—it cries aloud from the police courts—it fills the prisons and the hospitals—and it taints with its black infection our homes and hearths. It is the curse of England's poor. Glisson saw enough of it that night, and of the facilities afforded for its indulgence. How many of that unhappy crowd might have been arrested in their downward course; nay, never have entered upon it, but for the terrible temptation thrust upon them every hour, and at every step, by these meretricious liquor shops! Numbers of them were respectable once, hard-working and contented, until the stealthy vice insinuated itself upon them. Not all at once did it come, in its full baleful aspect; but gradually and imperceptibly: moderation grew to deep drinking, deep drinking to excess, excess to an impossibility to abstain; and there they were now, crowding round—fascinated by the subtle glare—the poisonous snares of that destroying place, false as the name given to it!

Glisson, all in a maze, at length reached Cass Court, after many turnings and some misdirections, and at the entrance of Cass Court, Glisson paused, afraid to enter it. It was but one of many other such "Courts," and the same features were seen in all. The tumble-down, dirty houses nearly touched each other, so narrow was the space between them; while, from the dilapidated windows hung old cords, on which were stretched rags to dry. As Glisson went gingerly up it, her skirts lifted, and picking her way, the inhabitants flocked after her, so different was she from the natives usually seen there. A respectable-looking woman in a claret-coloured merino gown, a warm Paisley shawl, and a straw bonnet, lined and trimmed with black velvet, gloves, and an umbrella, was indeed a phenomenon for Cass Court to stare at. Men, some tolerably decent, others whose clothes hung upon them in the best way the dilapidations would permit, leaned against the walls, smoking short pipes; women, worse off still in the matter of garments, stood screaming and scolding, their hair hanging about their ears, as if they had quarrelled with combs and brushes, altogether miserable objects to look upon; and children sat about, or lay in the gutter—such children as Glisson had never seen yet. She piloted her way amidst the lot, and addressed herself to a man who wore a civil face.

"Can you tell me whether a person named Daniel Low lives here?"

"Dan Low? Yes! That's where he hangs out"—pointing to one of the houses opposite. "Front room, first pair."

Glisson looked at it in doubt: she knew her brother had not been prosperous of late years, by the many calls he had made, or tried to make, on Glisson's purse, but she could not believe he was reduced to live in this sort of plight in a Cass Court. Just then a woman put her face to a broken pane of glass in the room indicated, and the man spoke.

"Here, missus; here's a lady asking for your Dan."

"After our Dan? What's he been up to?"

"'Tain't that sort of thing. It's a stranger."

"He ain't at home yet: he's on his rounds."

"Better go up if you want 'em," concluded the man to Glisson.

She proceeded to the room indicated. It was nearly bare of furniture, save for a rude bed (or what served for one) down in a corner: a more miserable habitation it was almost impossible to conceive, and Glisson's courage died out as she gazed at it. The woman was washing some things in a tub, which things would soon be hung in the room to dry: could it really be her brother's wife? Glisson had seen her once, and then she was a pretty young woman: now all signs of prettiness were gone; her face was wrinkled, wearing a perpetual look of hard care, and her hair had turned gray—such hair! sticking out over her head, a tangled mass.

"Are you Emma Low?"

The woman fixed her eyes wonderingly on the intruder.

"Why—it's not—it's never Mrs. Glisson!"

"Yes, it's me," said Glisson. "Have you a chair, or anything I can sit down upon for a minute? I am quite overcome at finding you in this state."

Emma Low brought forward a chair from which the rush seat was gone, but she clapped a piece of board across it, and Glisson sat down. "What a dreadful place to live in!" she uttered. "I wonder the close air doesn't kill you?"

"Well, I thought it bad when we first came here," returned the wife; "but we got used to it. So you be in London?"

"How's Daniel? and how are the children?" asked Glisson.

"Middling. Dan's on his rounds: he won't be here for another hour yet. Saturday is busy nights with 'em. The young 'uns be out in the court, and about."

"What do you mean by Daniel's rounds?" questioned Glisson, puzzled at the word.

"Dan's a costermonger now; he hawks things about the streets in his hand-barrow, and we call it going his rounds. He has stuck to it ever since our business failed."

"How did it come to fail?" asked Glisson.

"Ah! how do things come to fail? Ill luck; and expenses was great."

"Is Daniel steady?"

"He's pretty well; better than some around us. He might be steadier if he would, and then we should have kept our shop on, and a good roof over our heads."

"Do you manage to get a living?" continued Glisson.

"Of course we get a living, such as it is, or else we should be on the tramp, or in the workhouse. But it's starving half the time. I'm sorry I have got nothing in the place to ask you to have," she added, "and till Dan comes home, I don't possess a single copper."

"Oh," said Glisson hastily, turning against the idea of eating in such an atmosphere, "I could not take anything, if you had your cupboard full. I went into a coffee shop, and got a cup of tea and some bread and butter, and I am tired to death, for I have been looking for you three-parts of the day."

"Have you come to London with the family?" asked Mrs. Low.

"No, I have left them."

"Left them?" was the echo. "After being there so long!"

"My mistress died," said Glisson, "and there's a second mistress now, and I did not take kindly to her, nor she to me."

The children came in, one by one, three of them, the eldest about eleven, and they were severally put to bed—after the fashion of putting to bed prevailing in that locality. Their upper garment was taken off, their rags were kept on, and they lay down.

"They have not said their prayers," cried Glisson.

"Prayers!" uttered Emma Low in an accent of much surprise, while the children stared vacantly. "Oh, law! we don't have time for those sort of things here."

"Where do you and Daniel sleep?" next asked Glisson.

"There!"

"There! on that bed, with all the three children?" returned she.

"Where else are we to sleep? 'Twasn't comfortable when we had first to do it; but it's astonishing how you get used to a thing, when there's no help against it."

"And young Dan?" continued Glisson. "And Mary? I suppose he's out with his father?"

"Indeed he's not. Young Dan has set up for himself. He has left us, and got a barrow, and goes round with winkles and herrings, and such like, or fruit when it's in. He has took up with a girl, and she goes round with him. I believe they get a living somehow."

This information afforded her considerable amazement. "Why, Dan is only sixteen!" she replied; "he's only a boy."

"There's hardly a boy of that age in our court, but what thinks himself a man," was Emma Low's answer. "As to Polly, she's out on her own account, too. It makes less mouths to feed at home; and folks, come to what we have, can't afford to be nice, and to stick at trifles."

She sighed deeply as she spoke. Glisson, full of strange doubt, but not venturing to ask questions which might solve it, sat in silence, and at that juncture a little boy came up the stairs.

"Can you lend mother a bit o' candle, please? and she'll pay it back again when father's home."

"I hav'nt got a morsel but this I'm using, Jemmy, or else, tell your mother, she might be welcome to it," replied Mrs. Low.

The boy did not go away immediately. He stood looking down at the three faces in the bed.

"He is thinking there's enough of 'em there for one bed," spoke Glisson in her ignorance.

Emma Low could not forbear a faint laugh, though she and merriment seemed to have parted company long ago. "Here, Jemmy," said she to the boy, "tell that lady how you sleep in your room."

"We all sleeps in a big bed," said he, turning up his wan face to Glisson, with a good-humoured smile; "it's as big as that."

That was about a third less large than the one Glisson had enjoyed to herself at Danesbury House.

"But tell who sleeps in it, Jemmy," persisted Mrs. Low.

"Father, and mother, and Catherine, and the babby, at the top, and me, and Neddy, and Sam, at the bottom," was the ready answer.

"So that's two more than our lot," said Emma Low to Glisson, as the boy went out.

Daniel Low came in. He was dressed pretty tidily in fustian, and was excessively astonished to see his sister. He gave her a history of his downfall, ascribing it to every cause but the right one—drink. He had brought home money, and his first thought was hospitality. One of the children was roused from the bed, and sent to the palace at the corner of Cass Court for a pint of "Old Tom," and the three sat down and discussed the gin, Emma Low providing hot water and three cracked tea-cups. Then he put Glisson into an omnibus which would take her to the inn where she had arrived late the previous night, and where she had left her boxes.

As a child's mind gradually awakens to the wonders of the world, so did Glisson's senses awake, by degrees, to the wonders of Cass Court. She was alone in London, knowing nobody; and the first shock—the first distaste—gone off, she naturally sought her relations often. Glisson's heart was good, and she was deliberating whether she could not assist them to rise out of their fallen and most undesirable position. Hence she spent many an hour in Cass Court, and its evils were progressively unfolded to her. Cass Court was not the worst of its kind; others there were, not far from it, the very hot-beds of crime—shunned even by the police, as being desperately dangerous and wicked. Take Cass Court as a whole, it was honest; and, taking it in comparison, it was respectable—in comparison, mind, with those other places hinted at. Also, it was hard-working; but the great failing of Cass Court was its dreadful poverty—and that poverty was caused by the fact that one half of what was earned was spent in drink. The occupation followed by many of the men was the same as that of Glisson's brother—they were coster-mongers in the London streets. Their social and moral state was mostly bad, and they did not care to rise from it. When the men were "off their rounds," and when those pursuing other callings had left work in the evening, their abiding place was the ale-house or the gin-shop, or some low place of amusement, where they could also get drink, or else take it with them. Too often their wives accompanied them: but Glisson understood now what the "setting up" meant. As boys and girls grew, they left their parents, other boys and girls doing the same, and set up on their own account. The parents winked at it; in Mrs. Low's sentence there was an emphatic meaning: "It's less mouths to feed at home!" The only stock-in-trade necessary to set up with was a hand-barrow, and this they contrived to get, having a few shillings in reserve to purchase the first load, whether stale fish, stale fruit, or stale vegetables. Thus they started in life, and generally obtained enough to live—or, it may be more correct to say, they obtained enough not to die. They also obtained drink; whether food was had or not, drink must be found. They also enjoyed their evening's amusements, and they would enjoy them—those amusements and the drink constituting the paradise of their lives. Once Glisson was persuaded into going; it was to a theatrical entertainment—if Her Majesty's Chamberlain will not bring an action against us for calling it such. Glisson paid for the lot—that is, for her party—a penny each, which was the price of admission to the theatre. The audience was numerous—men and women, boys and girls. Some had pewter pots of porter to regale themselves with, some had stone bottles of gin, and short pipes were plentiful. The representation began, and Glisson stopped for a whole quarter of an hour, and then struggled out of the place, her face red, and her mind indignant, for such language, such ideas, she had never dreamt of; while the rest of the company (such is use) sat on, in an ecstacy of applause and admiration; and, when it was over, left, only to look forward with feverish impatience to the performance of the next night. And that way of living, of spending the days and the nights, was a very fair specimen of the pursuits of the ladies and gentlemen of Cass Court.

But how was it that they did not strive to lift themselves out of degradation so great? Need *Glisson* have asked? It was the daily indulgence in stimulating liquors that had perverted their minds and seared their hearts. They learnt to love drink in their childhood; as soon as they could carry a pewter pot to their lips, they relished the taste of beer; as soon as they could get gin, they indulged in it: and philosophers tell us that use is second nature. The love of liquors, ere they became men, was confirmed and strong, it had grown with their growth; and if they could have overcome the inward craving for it, they never could battle with the temptations to indulge in it, which beset them all around.

Some few in Cass Court, a very few, had once been in a superior class of life, they had been gentle people. Reader! you do not believe it; but I am telling you nothing but truth. How could they have fallen from their pinnacle, to shame and misery such as this? How indeed? Ask themselves. Its bare recollection even now causes them a shudder—a sickening shudder, as they glance back at the marked features of their downward progress. It was "the drink," they will tell you. Yes, it is always the drink.

Glisson's relations had neither been gentle people nor first-class tradespeople (speaking of their grade), but they had fallen from comfort and respectability, and Glisson felt it her duty to extricate them from the contamination and distress of Cass Court. Of course, they were not backward in seconding her wishes. Indulgence in drink had been the chief cause of her brother's downfall, but they kept the fact from her. He had wasted both time and money in it, which had led to difficulties, and thence to ruin. He persuaded Glisson that if she would advance the means to set him up anew in his old trade, he should not fail to do well—perhaps realise an independence. Glisson acceded; and it was for that purpose she withdrew her money from the hands of Mr. Danesbury. A shop was taken in Hatton Garden (for in Glisson's opinion the farther they got away from Cass Court the better), and opened in the coal and green-grocery line, and Glisson was to reside with them, the best room on the first floor being assigned to her. Such was the plan entered upon, and we shall see in a little time how it prospered.

CHAPTER VI
TRAINING

IT was a fair scene. The golden gleam of summer shone upon the land, the luxuriant corn already gave token of a plentiful harvest, the grateful scent of the new-mown hay told that the grass was cut, and the cattle were lazily stretched beside the glittering pools. Especially peaceful seemed the still air, the calm landscape, as these fair country scenes do seem, on the day of rest.

Walking home from morning service was a group, amidst other groups. Mr. Danesbury, his daughter, and her governess, and his four sons, Arthur, William, Robert, and Lionel; for the time has gone by, reader, and Robert Danesbury, the young infant, is now eight years old, and his brother Lionel is seven. Two children only had the second Mrs. Danesbury.

Mrs. Danesbury did not attend church that day: she had one of her nervous headaches, and remained in bed: she often did have them; the servants declared they came on from her indulged fits of "temper"; but whatever may have been their cause, they did not tend to render the house more pleasant.

Arthur had returned from keeping his first term at Cambridge: though intended to be only what his father was before him, a commercial man, the very highest educational advantages were being afforded him. To say that Arthur was growing up good-looking, would not be saying enough: a more noble-looking youth, both in face and form, it was impossible to conceive: lofty in mind, lofty in person, lofty in countenance, was Arthur Danesbury.

Mrs. Danesbury had risen when they got home, and they sat down to dinner, which was always taken early on the Sunday. Arthur and Isabel drank water as was customary, but beer was supplied to the three younger boys—and there, for those young children, lay the error; for the first Mrs. Danesbury's theory was right. When the cloth was removed, a full glass of rich wine was poured out for them; it was the usual Sunday's treat, the accompaniment to the fruit and cakes; they were all three fond of it; they had learned to be; and they, somehow, in their little minds, connected the wine and Sunday together, and believed the wine must be a very good thing, as they always had it on that day.

Mrs. Danesbury, the present, had been positive on this point: it may be said obstinate. She *would not* bring them up to drink water. She would not let them taste it at their meals; and if they complained of thirst in the day, would order a glass of table-beer brought in for them. The fact that it had been the wish and maxim of the first Mrs. Danesbury, no doubt influenced her in thus acting; for a jealous feeling towards that lady's memory—ay, and towards her children—rankled in her heart. Mr. Danesbury did not interfere. Always a temperate man himself, sprung from a temperate family, and partaking, whether of wine or beer, only in strict moderation, he saw no harm in the children's doing so, and never cast a thought as to its bringing harm for the future.

But there is other training required from a mother to a child, besides that desirable one of confining its drink to water. Few are more deeply impressed with the responsibility resting on a mother, or more earnestly anxious for her children's welfare, than had been the first Mrs. Danesbury: few, let us hope, are more careless of it than was the second. I speak of welfare in the highest sense of the term— that they should be great and good here, and inheritors of eternal life hereafter. Isabel, Mrs. Danesbury, knew that this sort of welfare can best be attained (I had almost said, only be attained) by incessant care and watchfulness, and training of a child, from its very earliest years. She never omitted to take her child Arthur, from the time he was two years old, to herself, for ten minutes after breakfast. She would put him on her knee and read a little, and talk to him about God, and about his own childish duties—what he must do, what he must not do. She would speak in a low, persuasive, loving voice, which, of itself, was sufficient to draw the love of the child. Generally speaking, but not so invariably as in the morning, for engagements sometimes prevented her, she would take him so in the evening, and whisper pleasant words of angels loving him and watching over him in his sleep. She rarely failed to hear him his prayers herself, not trusting even to Glisson, for, as a general rule, servants do not care whether they are said reverently or irreverently. In the day-time, she had him with her a great deal, and was always striving to form his mind for *good*. One thing which she impressed fully upon him was, that this world was not his home; that at the best, he would be in it but a short period; and she taught him to live so as not to dread death. Before she was taken from him, Arthur's mind, naturally a tractable one, had been moulded *well,* and he had learned the fact that he had grave responsibilities upon him, momentous duties to fulfil, and that, as his conduct was, so would his prosperity and happiness be. These seeds never could have been eradicated from Arthur Danesbury's heart. Even had he been consigned to the charge of his stepmother, his own sense of right, so efficiently imparted to him, and the exceeding reverence, the perfect love, he had borne for his mother, would have kept him safe. But the clergyman with whom he was placed proved an admirable seconder of the principles of Mrs. Danesbury. Isabel had been taken by her mother in like manner, and her governess was a Christian gentlewoman, so that she was also fortunate. But the other children; how was it with them?

Eliza, Mrs. Danesbury, had about as much notion of this sort of training as the man in the moon. She was certainly anxious for the welfare of her children, but all in a temporal point of view. She hoped they would be grand and rich men, and rise to eminence in the world. She was very fond of them, and indulged them much; but she took no pains, except wrong ones, to correct their tempers. Pampered and indulged, they would be often passionate and naughty, Robert especially. Sometimes she did not check them at all; and sometimes, if she was in an ill-humour herself, she would punish them with inexcusable harshness, beating them with severity. She never impressed upon them that they had duties to perform to themselves and to others, children though they were. She never spoke of the necessity of self-restraint, or taught them when to exercise it. As to their religious obligations, they were taught their prayers, and would repeat them to the nurse who had succeeded Glisson, hurrying them over at railroad speed, and they were made to learn the Catechism, and were taken to church—all in a genteel, orthodox sort of way: very well for show, but very unserviceable for use. If the boys did pick up a glimmer of anything better, they got it from Mr. Danesbury, who would often gather them around him on a Sunday evening, read to them, and talk seriously to them. But the duty of imparting serious lessons lies with a mother far more than with a father, and Mrs. Danesbury did not attempt them. She was fidgety about their appearance—that their dress should be handsome, always in order; she was anxious that they should be polite in manner, and there it ended. William, of course, is included in these remarks, though he did not come in for much indulgence; but William had one advantage not enjoyed by Robert and Lionel—he was often at Mrs. Philip Danesbury's. And that lady, suspecting, or rather knowing, the state of affairs at home, strove to supply to him the part of a mother. Still, it was not like regular watchfulness, uninterrupted progress, for what was done at Mrs. Philip Danesbury's was undone at home. Mrs. Danesbury very much disliked Mrs. Philip, and would not suffer her own boys to go there, except for a formal visit now and then. You will gather from these remarks that the young Danesburys were growing up without acquiring any moral safeguard within themselves, to keep them from the evil temptations of the world, with which they must some time be brought into contact.

One day, when Arthur was at home, he took William to his room, talked to him, and told him he wished he would confine his drink to water.

"I don't like water, Arthur. Beer is nicer."

"But you are aware—you have heard—that our own mamma wished us to drink it; and you would so very much oblige me by doing so."

Truth to say, the last argument had most weight with William; for he was very fond of Arthur, and wished to do what he desired. So the next day at dinner he requested the servant to give him water, not beer. He made a face over it, however, and put it down as soon as tasted, upon which Mrs. Danesbury said some mocking words to him, which set him still more against the water; and she actually, positively, told her own two children that they might that day have a double portion of beer if they wished it, to "teach Arthur sense." After dinner, William whispered to Arthur that he was sorry, but he never should be able to drink the "nasty water" with dinner. Of course he could not; the child had never been accustomed to drink it; Mrs. Danesbury had given him the taste for stronger things.

On this Sunday, as they sat at dinner, Arthur was describing to them his University life. He appeared to have formed a close friendship there: it was with a young man of his own age, who had matriculated at the same time as himself, the Honourable Reginald Dacre.

"Those college friendships do not continue in after life, Arthur," observed Mr. Danesbury.

"Mine with Dacre will not, I daresay," replied Arthur, "for our paths will lie far apart. He will be a peer of the realm; I, but Arthur Danesbury of the iron works. But it is very pleasant while it does last. I like him excessively, and keep him out of mischief: but for me, he would be over head and ears in it."

"You keep him out of mischief!" laughed Mr. Danesbury.

Arthur laughed also. "It is true though, sir."

On the afternoon of the following day, Monday, Mr. Danesbury was walking along a somewhat unfrequented path at the back of his factory, when a woman all in rags, a beggar, apparently, came in view. He took no notice of her; he was deep in thought; but the beggar halted as he passed.

"Master!"

It was Glisson! Mr. Danesbury was shocked when he recognised her. She leaned against the wall, and broke out into wails and sobs.

"Oh, master! my dear master!"

"Glisson, what has happened? How is it that you are like this?"

"I'm just a beggar on the face of the earth, sir. I have no home and no food, and nobody in the wide world to give me shelter. I was coming to the old familiar home-place, to sit myself down in the fields and to die."

"You appear to be ill, almost helpless!"

"That's what the rheumatic fever has left me, I caught it, and the parish doctor says I shall never have the proper use of my hands and arms again, and my legs totter under me."

"What have you been doing since you left us?"

"Ah! what have I been! When Mrs. Danesbury turned me out—and most cruelly she behaved to me; ay, master, I must say it, though she is your wife, and may the Lord help the poor children when they fall under her temper!—I went to London. Not direct; for I stayed here and there upon my road; I was almost mad, what with one wretched thought or other. All at once I thought I'd go off to London, and find out my brother and his wife. Well, sir, I did; and a fine state I

"I have no home and no food."

found them in. Oh, sir, those that live in the country have need to be thankful, for they don't know what some parts of London is! It's just a hell upon earth."

"You drew out your money, Glisson."

"Yes, sir; I lent it to them to set up again—a hundred pounds of it, the odd thirty I kept myself; and he took a green-grocer's shop, and I lived with 'em. That's eight years ago. And how long did the fine shop last? Not four years; the profits were swallowed up, and they are all gone to the dogs again."

"But what have you been doing?"

"Nothing. I have just grubbed on with 'em in their vice and wretchedness; selling my clothes, and starving till I can starve no longer, so I resolved to come home here to die. I have been six days walking it, Master John."

Master John! the old familiar title of his boyhood.

"Glisson," he resumed, in a tone of deep commiseration, "have you relinquished that unfortunate habit which they tell me you took to?"

She shook her head, "No, sir."

"No!"

"The craving for drink has grown upon me. My odd pounds went in it. It's more to me now than food."

"Oh, Glisson!"

"As long as I was in your house, sir, I kept it under: I should have kept it under still, for I knew I must do it. I did drink a drop at times, but not much to harm me. What possessed me to take so much the night Mrs. Danesbury found me, I can't tell. But, up in that dreadful London, in the midst of bad example, with nothing but poverty, and ruin, and rags, and famine around me, and flaring gin-shops at every turn of a step, which make the best drink when they would not—that did for me. It does for thousands. My brother might have been sober enough, but for them enticing places, and his business would have gone on."

"Glisson, what could have been your inducement to fall into such a habit?" inquired Mr. Danesbury. "What was the commencement?"

"Do you remember a cook you once had, sir?—a fat, red-faced woman; Dolly, we used to call her in the kitchen; one of the best cooks that ever came into the house. She left just after William was born."

"Yes, I do remember her," said Mr. Danesbury, who had been casting back his thoughts.

"She taught me. She drank gin: a great deal of it. As soon as ever my mistress had been into the kitchen in a morning to give orders, she'd begin; and she never left off throughout the day. Yet she would send up her dinner properly, and do her work well, and never show it. There was no baby then, for little John had died, and I took to steal downstairs at night, and sit with her in the kitchen, after the servants had gone to bed, and drink some with her. I got a liking for it, Master John, and it stuck to me: and I could not leave it off."

"Glisson," he uttered, after a pause, a sharp pang striking him like a dart, "could it be that this was the cause of your giving the child the laudanum—and so leading to the death of your mistress?"

"Too true: too true!" she shrieked. "And I have had my dear mistress's face before me ever since, and I have drank worse to drown it. Fare ye well, sir; fare ye well for ever!"

She turned off, sobbing and moaning; and Mr. Danesbury saw her sink down behind a tree at some distance.

What should he do with her? He could not let her starve. Painful as had been the last revelation to him, he yet felt that he must give her succour. He was a considerate, benevolent man, and he would have been so to an enemy. Thomas Harding approached, and Mr. Danesbury informed him of what had occurred.

"It never was that object I saw pass round, as I was waiting at the gate to give the signal for the bell!" he exclaimed. "A bundle of rags, sir; bent as if with age, with a stick in her hand to lean upon?"

"The same," answered Mr. Danesbury; "that was Glisson. Harding, I must get somebody to take her in. Do you think any will be found to have her?"

"Plenty, sir, if only from the respect they owed your late mother, whose servant she was. Let it once be known that it is your wish, and twenty will come forward."

"I will pay a weekly sum for her support. Do you arrange it for me. Let her be comfortable."

"I'll see about it at once, sir."

"Ay; she must be got in somewhere: look at her there, under that tree."

Before an hour had elapsed, a home was found for Glisson, and she was conveyed to it, sobbing bitterly.

CHAPTER VII
THE DANESBURY OPERATIVES

HOW got on Jessy Gould? We had better see. She would have got on very well but for the public-houses; but Richard had learnt to like them much. When her friends consented to her marrying Richard Gould, they looked forward to the prospect of his rising to a good position in the establishment of Mr. Danesbury, otherwise they would not have considered him a suitable match for her. And as yet, Richard, though more comfortably off than many, was not advancing as quickly as he might have done. They had four or five children, who were kept as clean and neat as their mother.

It was half-past seven o'clock and Saturday night, and the bell rang at the Danesbury works for the men to go in and be paid. Though so large a number of them, the arrangements were well ordered and systematic, and by eight o'clock most of them were ready to depart.

They passed into the yard, out at the great iron gates. A few proceeded to their homes, but the greater portion were hastening to the public-houses and beer-shops. A group of eight or ten, Richard Gould being one, halted in consultation as to which house should be favoured with their company, and finally it was decided to honour "The Pig and Whistle," down by the new bridge.

"Ay; let's. Jones said, last night, as they had got a famous tap on at 'The Pig.' Come along, Gould, what be you stopping for?

Richard Gould was hesitating. It occurred to his memory that he had promised Jessy to bring his wages home the minute he received them, for she said she wanted a few shillings for something particular, and told him what it was.

"I must step home first," said he. "I'll come after ye. My wife's waiting for some money."

"That's a shuffle, Gould. Your wife gets her marketings on credit on the Saturday mornings."

"It isn't marketings: it's something else. I promised I'd be home."

"Bother! you don't go for to think as she'll trapes out to-night. It's a pelting cats and dogs. No woman won't leave her fireside to-night, except them as can't help it, and your wife ain't one. Come along."

Richard Gould yielded—an easy, good-natured soul he was, swayed with the wind—and away the lot went, through the rain and mud, to "The Pig and Whistle."

"The Pig and Whistle" received them with due respect. It had got a blazing fire and a warm, light room to welcome them; and once ensconced in it with their pipes and drink, they were as oblivious of homes, wives, children, and weekly marketings, as if such things existed not. A few, who "used" the house regularly, called for their scores on entering, and settled up for the past seven days. "The Pig and Whistle" was a flourishing house now, for the workmen, who had for a long while been engaged erecting the new bridge in place of the dangerous old one, had patronised it extensively.

Meanwhile Richard Gould's wife was sitting at home, in all hope. They occupied one of the cottages in Prospect Row, neat dwellings of three rooms and a detached back kitchen; or, as it was called, in local phraseology, a brew-house. The men inhabiting these cottages were all employed at the works: but there was a wide difference in their conduct, and, consequently, in their homes. Some drank their wages away, and then huddled with their wives and families into the downstairs room and the brew-house, letting the two upper rooms. Some of the wives were slatternly, some tidy; but, as a general rule, though it did not apply in every instance, the slatternly wife and the drinking husband went together. Some made of these cottages complete, pleasant dwellings, converting the brew-house into a kitchen for the rough work—the washing and cooking—and the front room into a parlour. Jessy Gould, smart and nice in all things, was one who had done the last, fitting it up with a carpet and glass, and pretty ornaments. Richard spent a great deal more in drink than he could afford, and this kept them poor; but Mrs. Gould's friends often helped them, so that they were better off than most of the workmen of his grade.

She sat at home in the parlour, busy at work finishing a child's frock, and expecting Richard. Her children were in bed, and a small saucepan stood on the hob by the fire, containing some Irish stew for his supper. She had bought her marketings in the day—it was her custom to do so, and to pay on the Monday. Too many a poor wife could not obtain even this short credit, and had to get in everything on the Saturday night, *if* her husband and his wages came home in time.

The clock struck nine, and Jessy Gould laid down her work with a sigh of despair.

"He is off with the men again! I am certain of it! He might have come home this night, when he knew what I wanted with the money." And her work went on again, but more heavily.

In the next cottage to theirs lived a man of the name of Reed, an inferior workman. Mrs. Reed was in tribulation more dire than Jessy's, and was audibly lamenting that this was Saturday night, and that Reed had gone a-drinking again. She knew to her cost the propensity he had to "go a-drinking," not only on Saturday nights, but on others. The first step was to go after him, and try to get him home before he was too far gone, and half his week's money spent. She threw a shawl over her gown, put on her bonnet, blew out the candle, left the bit of fire safe, and opened the door. But she hesitated on the threshold, for the wind and the rain came beating against her, threatening to wet her through and through. Turning her thin cotton shawl over her arms, bared to the elbows, for she had been hard at work, she locked the door, took out the key, and knocked at Richard Gould's.

"Come in."

"Good evening, Mrs. Gould. I'm come to ask you to let me leave my key here."

She left her pattens at the door, and went in. "Ain't it a shame?" she began. "Here's that drunken brute of mine never come home again! He's off, as usual, with the rest; and he knows I have not got bit or drop in the house for to-morrow, neither candles, nor coals, nor even a bit of soap, I hadn't, to wash the poor children with—so I had to put 'em to bed dirty."

"Ay; it is a shame," said Mrs. Gould. "They are all alike, I think. My husband promised to come home, and he has never come. We are invited to Mr. Harding's to dinner to-morrow, the children and all, and I wanted to buy new shoes for the two eldest, for I'm not going to take them there in their shabby old ones, which are off their feet, and Richard knows the new shoe-shop won't give an hour's credit. The men are all alike."

"No, they are not all alike: I wish they were, if it was like your Gould. If he do go out of a night, he don't get drunk, and drink all his money away, as that sot of a Reed of mine do."

Jessy thought to herself that he drank away far more than he ought of it, but she did not say so.

"Won't you sit down, Mrs. Reed?"

"Law, no! I'm off to find him out, and get some money from him. It's hard lines with us at the best, since our lodgers left, and it's harder when he gets drunk on wages night, for then the money melts like butter. Not but what I'm loth to leave your fire, and turn out into it; so comfortable as you be here to be sure!"

The woman moved to the door as she spoke. The rain was coming down in torrents.

"You will get a dreadful soaking," exclaimed Mrs. Gould. "Have you an umbrella?"

"A crazy old thing, bent and broke. But no umbrella won't be of much good to-night. Good evening, for the present."

Away she clanked in her pattens, through the garden gate and along the road. The first thing the wind did was take the "crazy old umbrella," and turn it inside out. She went on in the rain, not knowing at which of the public-houses she might find him, and with something very like a malediction in her heart on all of them. They were numerous, and she tried several unsuccessfully. It was a weary search, and she grew disheartened; she was wet to the skin, and returned to Prospect Row, hoping he had gone home.

"Has he been for the key?" she asked, putting her head inside Mrs. Gould's door.

"No; here it is. Have you seen anything of my husband?"

"I have seen nothing of either of them. I wish the beer-houses were burnt!" added Mrs. Reed in exasperation. "What a life is mine to be tied to such a sot!"

Back again to the search. She must have money for her marketings, and she must try and prevent him getting intoxicated. Just before eleven o'clock, the hour when the shops closed, she heard where he was. An acquaintance, bent on the same errand as herself, gave her the information that he, and about fifteen others, were at that noted public, "The Pig and Whistle," "a-toping theirselves stupid."

"All that way!" exclaimed poor Mrs. Reed. She went splashing wearily on, till she arrived at it, and she asked to see him. He came sullenly out of the tap-room, pipe in mouth, chafing at the jokes of his companions, who asked him if he was in leading strings that his missis must come after him. He was fresh, not yet worse, and in a shocking humour; for drink always put him in one, though he was a civil man when quite sober.

"What do you want, a-coming hunting after me?" he exclaimed, with a scowl.

"What do I want?" she retorted, "why, money for one thing. You know the house is empty. Coals, and candles, and bread, and tea, and potatoes, and soap, and salt, and meat—"

He stopped her with an oath, threw down five shillings, and told her to go along and get the things.

"What is the use of five shillings?" she asked, pushing it back. But he buttoned up his breeches pockets, and told her she might take that or none.

"Won't you come home with me?" she resumed, not choosing to argue the matter then.

Home with her! was the answer. A pretty piece of impudence she must be, to ask that!

He went back to the company and the tap-room as he spoke, and she, in a tone between scolding and crying, called out that he must be a good-for-nothing brute to keep her trapesing about after him on such a cruel night.

Before she had time to quit the hospitable door of "The Pig and Whistle," a slatternly woman, with a red face and bold aspect, dashed into it, the rain dripping off her.

"Is he here?" she demanded, her breath redolent of spirits, and her voice unsteady.

The landlord's answer was a movement of his thumb in the direction of the tap-room. She was passing towards it with a fierce step, but he interposed and stopped her.

"None of that, dame Tailor. You can't go in there to make a row—we know you of old. If you want him, I'll fetch him out."

"Fetch him out, then, and be quick about it."

This woman and her husband lived in a room in the town—one room. They might have done so well, for he was a clever workman; but drink was his bane—always had been, from a young man—and drink was now hers. She was a smart, well-conducted, tidy young woman once, and she made him a well-conducted wife. Yes, she was; even that virago, with her offensive words, and her black hair hanging about her face. But his confirmed ill courses soured her temper and broke her spirit. Her children, born to rags and wretchedness, died off as they came, dying principally of hunger. Cold, weary, and sick at heart, she used to go hunting after him, as Mrs. Reed had just done after her husband, and he would meet her with abuse, insult, and at last with blows. All the good that was in her was thrown back upon her heart. Maddened and despairing, she learned to fly to the same source to drown her sorrow, and soon she became as confirmed a drinker as he was.

Tailor came out staggering—a black-looking fellow, six feet high—and a scene of disturbance ensued. She was come for money to get more drink, and he would not give it her. He told her she was top-heavy already; she retorted that he was. Threats poured from the man, screams of rage from the woman, and oaths from both. The landlord put a summary end to it; he expelled her from the door, threatened her with the lock-up if she returned, and Tailor went staggering and muttering back to the tap-room.

Mrs. Tailor flew up the street, scolding and raving, with all the rage of a violent and half-crazy woman. "The Brown Bear" was the first public-house she passed; it stood invitingly open, and she turned into it, and called for gin-and-water, promising to pay on the following Monday.

"Who's to know whether I may trust you?" cried the landlady.

"I'll pay you, if I pawn the coat off Tailor's back. I swear it. There!"

The gin-and-water was supplied, and more after it; for landladies know that these drinking debts generally *are* settled—whether by the pledging of coats, or of any other article, is of no moment to them.

Mrs. Reed went forth from the public-house with the five shillings in her hand; but the clocks had then struck eleven, and the shops were closed. On her way up the street, she encountered many women going on the same errand that she had been. Some, now it was too late to buy what they wanted, were returning home; others were pacing before the public-house doors on that pitiless night, humbly waiting for their inhuman husbands, not daring to leave them to get home alone in the state in which they knew they would be. Inhuman *then;* kind and civil if they would but keep sober.

Jessy had finished her work, and she sat with the Bible before her, when Mrs. Reed once more entered. She closed the book.

"Well," said she, "have you found him?"

"Yes; when eleven o'clock had gone. He's down at 'The Pig and Whistle,' there's a tap-room full of 'em; and he'll come home drunk, for he's pretty far gone towards it now. Look here!"

She stretched out her hand, and exhibited the five shillings.

"He gave me *that*—and we want everything! I wonder a judgment don't overtake the beer-houses, I do. Look at the state I'm in!"

Poor thing! she was indeed in a comfortless state. Wet, as if she had been in a pool of water.

"There's that unfortunate Nance Tailor bad again. She came after Tailor to 'The Pig,' and a fine row there was, for both of 'em was in for it. The landlord put her out, and she went screeching and blaspheming up to 'The Brown Bear'; and there she'll stop till it shuts up."

"She'll drink herself to death, that woman will."

"She has had enough to drive her on to it, like some of the rest of us. Your husband's not come home, for I saw him in the tap-room down there at 'The Pig.' I'm sure it's all enough to wear the life's hope out of one. It's well that you can sit there so calm, and read that good book. I'm never in the frame of mind for it."

"The more crosses we have, the more we ought to go to it, for it is in trouble that we find its comfort," murmured Mrs. Gould. "I have taught Richard to care for it a little. He did not when we married; and I think it is that which has kept him steadier than some."

The woman looked into the fire. The expression of her face seemed to say there was no comfort for her anywhere.

"That was kind of Mr. Danesbury, having the men before him yesterday," resumed Mrs. Gould.

"Did he have them? What for?"

"He had them all before him in the long room, and said it had come to his knowledge that their habit of frequenting the public-houses at night was growing much more common than it used to be. He told them that it ruined their energies, wasted their means, and brought discomfort on their families; and he begged them to be more thoughtful, and to put a check upon their love for drink. He said he would rather raise the wages of every man who would undertake to keep from the public-house, than that they should go on drinking worse and worse, as they were doing."

"There! Now look at Reed! He wouldn't tell me, 'cause he knowed he should not take the advice. No more will any of 'em; they'll go to the public, in spite of the master. Good-night, Mrs. Gould. I wish we was all in heaven together; 'twould be better for us."

Scarcely had Mrs. Reed left, when Richard Gould came in. Not quite gone—only half so. His wife put the supper before him without speaking; he did not eat it, but went off to bed. The next morning he awoke, got up early, and went out to get the shoes for the children; for it had become a custom with some of the inferior shops in Eastborough to open for an hour or two on the Sunday morning. Perhaps the necessities of the workmen's wives had originated it. His head was aching; his wife was grieved; his wages were sensibly diminished. He begged her to say nothing at Mr. Harding's, and protested he never would be tempted out on a Saturday night again—as he had protested many and many a time before.

Poor Mrs. Reed had gone into her comfortless home, shivering and miserable. Yet she did not dare to crack up the fire, for the lump of coal on it was the last bit she had in the house, and she must keep it to boil the kettle in the morning, while she went out. A bitter feeling, a mixture of indignation and despair, stole over her heart, as she sat there waiting for her husband—despair at her unhappy misery, and indignation against public-houses in general, and her husband in particular. Her thoughts flew back to the time when she was a pretty young woman, the child of respectable, industrious parents, without a care upon her, and looking forward to a hopeful future. "Oh, that I had never married!" she aspirated; "that I could again be as I once have been!"

The tower clock tolled twelve, and those agents of much misery, the public-houses, closed for the night. Other nights the closing hour was eleven; Saturday, twelve. Why so? That the men, when they had money in their pockets, might enjoy increased facility of spending it? Let those answer who made the law. At three-quarters past twelve—it took him that time to reel home—Reed tumbled in, awfully abusive, especially at there being no fire and no supper; and, in spite of his wife's remonstrances, he managed to steady himself so as to crack up the coal, and start it into a blaze. In vain she tried to get him to bed; he lighted his pipe, and savagely ordered her to go out and buy beer, being with difficulty made to understand that the taps were closed for the night. He would sit on, and he did; now dozing, now taking a few whiffs at the pipe, and now breaking out into half-connected sentences of abuse. She, poor weary woman, was obliged to sit with him; left to himself, he might get burnt, or set the house on fire. Not only for that—he would not permit her to go; he never did when he was in that state. At four o'clock he condescended to retire, she undressing him.

Before she seemed to have closed her eyes, the children were awake and noisy, as children like to be. Fatigued and unrefreshed, she got up, he lying on like a clod; and, telling her children to be still in bed, for their father was not well, she prepared to go out. But, first of all, she looked into her husband's pockets, painfully anxious as to the amount she might find there. His wages were fifteen shillings a week—it has been said that he was only an inferior workman—and she hunted out six-and-sevenpence-halfpenny. With a sensation of despair she examined on, but there was no more. Three-and-fourpence-halfpenny gone in one night! She put it back, and wrung her hands.

"Father got drunk last night, I know," whispered the eldest child to the rest, as soon as his mother's back was turned; "it was pay night." He was beginning, child though he was, to be wise in such matters.

Mrs. Reed laid out her five shillings, eking it out to the best advantage, returned, made the fire, got up the children, and gave them their breakfast. Towards dinner-time her husband came shivering down, looking miserably cold and uncomfortable, and very angry with himself; for he was not a bad or unfeeling man, except when under the influence of drink. His wife was sullen, and would not notice him; but at last she asked him, giving way to the burden that was lying at her heart, however he came to spend so much as three-and-sevenpence-halfpenny. He didn't know how, he answered; he couldn't recollect. Somebody called for spirits, and then others called for spirits: there was a good deal drunk amongst 'em, one way or t'other. Ninepence of it was an old score which he owed. What was to be done about the landlord? was her next ominous question. He must let her have all that he had got remaining. Oh, yes! he would let her have it, he returned, full of contrition, and they sat down to dinner pretty peacefully. Of course, ale was wanted to drink with that, and the eldest child was despatched to the nearest tap for it.

After dinner, while Mrs. Reed was putting the place to rights and washing up, he took his hat and sallied out. The public-houses were open, and, in passing "The Leopard," he saw some of his acquaintance sitting at its window. He went in "only just to speak with them," for his pricking conscience was whispering a warning; but they looked so comfortable and cosy with their pipes and jugs, that his old, unhappy failing seized irresistibly hold of him, and down he sat, and called for a pipe o' bacca and a pint o' mild ale. Others dropped in, one by one, till at length the room was pretty full. He sat there till nine at night—he was unable to tear himself away—and then went home. He had not toped himself into the state of the previous evening, by no means, and he would have asserted that he was perfectly sober; but he had further diminished his scanty stock of money. His wife, in towering indignation, had been fretting and scolding away her Sunday evening in a most unhappy frame of mind, and a loud and bitter quarrel closed it, which the children woke up to hear. And thus it went on; and that man, who ought to have kept his family in comfort, sunk them, week by week, into deeper poverty. Such were the existing circumstances with the majority of the working men of Eastborough.

CHAPTER VIII
ROBERT AND LIONEL—THE LAST OF GLISSON

SEVERAL years again went by after the date of the last chapter, for over the early part of this history we cannot afford to linger.

Arthur was now in partnership with his father, receiving a small share of the profits. The promise he had given of high excellence in earlier years had not been frustrated now that he had arrived at manhood. He was indeed all that the most anxious father could wish. Upon one point Mr. Danesbury's opinion proved a correct one—the fleeting nature of college friendships. Arthur's intimacy with Mr. Dacre had ended with his college life. They both quitted Cambridge at the same period. A letter or two had passed between them, and there it appeared to close, for Mr. Dacre went abroad, and Arthur heard no more of him. William was in London, articled to an eminent firm in Parliament Street—Civil Engineers. His future destination was likewise to be the Danesbury Works, where he would take the head of the engineering department. The younger children, Robert and Lionel, had left school this midsummer, and their callings in life were to be decided on.

Mrs. Danesbury was seated in her drawing-room, waiting tea, and getting cross. Nobody seemed to be remembering the tea hour, or her own exhausting patience, of which she had not a great stock. Her two sons were off somewhere; they had grown into fine youths, almost young men, and they had wills of their own. Their taste for wine had grown also: the Sunday glass of wine was now a daily one, and they had begun to say it was not enough—they should like two.

Mr. Danesbury was surprised and hurt; he rarely took more than one himself, and he said, No! But as soon as his back was turned, they helped themselves to the extra one, and Mrs. Danesbury sanctioned it: what harm, thought she, could two glasses of wine do strong, growing lads?

The first to enter the room, and encounter Mrs. Danesbury's impatience, was Isabel. No longer a girl, but an elegant young woman, with a refined countenance and winning manner.

"Where have *you* been?" sharply began Mrs. Danesbury.

"Is it late? Oh; but the others have not come in, I see. I have been with Aunt Philip."

A displeasing announcement for Mrs. Danesbury, considering that Mrs. Philip Danesbury was her especial aversion: she would have barred all intercourse with her, had she dared.

"Aunt Philip has had bad news, mamma," continued Isabel. "Her brother is dead, the Rev. Mr. Heber. He caught a fever after visiting some of his poor parishioners, and died. He was only ill a week."

"What is to become of his family?" cried Mrs. Danesbury. "That clergyman was as poor as a church mouse."

"It is a serious question. He has left no money behind him. Aunt Philip is going to invite the two daughters here."

"With her! To stop?" sharply questioned Mrs. Danesbury.

"I suppose they will stop," replied Isabel. "They will have no other home now. Their mamma died more than a year ago. Aunt Philip says they are admirable girls; everything that could be desired."

"Shameful!" ejaculated Mrs. Danesbury. "She will saddle the Danesbury money with the cost of their maintenance. She will make it an excuse for her income being augmented. I think she is helped pretty well as it is, with her eight hundred a year."

"Mamma!" exclaimed Isabel, in a tone of remonstrance, the crimson of shame for her stepmother mounting to her forehead, "how can you speak so? Mrs. Philip Danesbury's husband was papa's brother, and she has as much right to her income from the business as papa has to his. Had my Uncle Philip lived he would have enjoyed a half share, not the small portion of eight hundred a year."

"Eight hundred, clear and sure, for Philip Danesbury's widow, is more, in proportion, than we enjoy. She is one, and we are seven."

"Oh, mamma! you ought not to look at it in that light."

"If you presume to tell me what I ought, or 'ought not' to do," she retorted, "I will send you to your room, Miss Danesbury."

Isabel's heart beat high: she leaned out of the open window to still it. Her stepmother's fits of passion and injustice sometimes told heavily upon her.

"She is the bane of the family, is Mrs. Philip Danesbury!"

Isabel thought that the family had a greater bane, so far as its peace was concerned; but she did not say so. She leaned farther from the window, and watched for her father.

Mr. Danesbury was being detained by more things than one. He had been waited upon by a tenant of his, with a complaint against his younger sons. Just as the man was being dismissed, there arrived a messenger to say that Glisson was dying. She had been ill a few days with an affection of the chest, and Mr. Danesbury had been to see her. Arthur had been that very morning; but no immediate danger was apprehended. In the afternoon, a change had taken place.

Mr. Danesbury hastened to the cottage. There lay Glisson in bed, her eyes anxiously cast towards the door, looking for him. She was almost past speaking; almost past breathing; she feebly put out her hand as he approached, and took his. Her lips moved, and he bent his ear down to catch the sound—

"Master! bless you!—and forgive!"

It was all she said. Whether the effort had been too much for her, or whether the minute for death had come, Glisson gasped twice, and died.

"I thought you were not coming in to-day," was Mrs. Danesbury's fractious salutation when her husband entered. "Where's Arthur?"

"He has gone to Mrs. Philip Danesbury's," was the reply; "and I have been detained. Glisson is dead."

"Dead!" interrupted Isabel. "Is it not sudden, papa?"

"My dear, I thought yesterday that she would not get over it. She is gone, poor thing."

"Poor thing!" sarcastically echoed Mrs. Danesbury, "I am sure it is a happy release, for herself and for other people. The death of a drunkard always is."

"She was not that at last, mamma," said Isabel: "not since she came back to Eastborough."

"She took care to have her beer at meals, and your papa's money going out to pay for it."

"Be more charitable, Eliza," spoke up Mr. Danesbury. "Animosity may surely cease, now she is dead."

"Are you going to defend what she did here?" demanded Mrs. Danesbury, who was in one of her most contentious humours.

"Oh, no. Glisson's fate should prove a warning to all who may be acquiring a love for intoxicating liquors. For the sake of a little self-indulgence she forfeited her good home here, lost her self-respect and her fair name, and died in obscurity, an object of charity."

"Isabel says that brother of Mrs. Philip Danesbury's is dead. Of course, all his children are unprovided for?"

"The two daughters entirely so; but the sons are in a way to get their own living, or soon will be. The eldest is keeping his last term at Oxford, and will be in orders immediately. I saw Mrs. Philip Danesbury this afternoon. She is going to invite her nieces to live with her. It is fortunate she is able and willing to receive them."

"And to tax your purse for it, I conclude," broke forth Mrs. Danesbury. "It is lucky for her family that she married a Danesbury."

The colour mounted to Mr. Danesbury's temples, as it had previously mounted to Isabel's. "No," he replied, after a pause of self-control, "Mrs. Philip Danesbury's means are quite equal to her receiving this addition to her household, without her requiring me to provide for it."

"Have you seen the boys?" again began Mrs. Danesbury.

"No. But I am sorry to say that I have heard of them. Fox has been to me to complain. They have been over there this afternoon, damaging his hedge, spoiling some linen spread there to dry, and giving him insolence and abuse."

"I am sure they did not," fired Mrs. Danesbury. "Abuse and insolence, indeed! Who is Fox that he should dare to come to you with such a complaint?"

"He made a worse complaint than that," returned Mr. Danesbury. "He says Robert was not sober."

"Absurd!" retorted Mrs. Danesbury. "I daresay Fox was not sober himself."

"I should like to know where they are lingering: they are aware of the tea hour. They shall no longer be in idleness: it is the root of all mischief. They seem to have set themselves against coming into the works: and you uphold them, Eliza."

"Yes," answered Mrs. Danesbury. "I wish them to choose professions: not business. Robert has decided upon his: he wants a commission purchased for him."

Mr. Danesbury looked up, not only surprised, but mortified. "A commission!" he uttered, "whatever put that in his head? I cannot sanction it. I very much disapprove of it."

"He says he will be nothing else," said Mrs. Danesbury carelessly. "Why should you object to it?"

"I wish all my children to choose a peaceful employment. I am not reflecting on the brave defenders of our country," he hastened to add, "but I prefer that my sons should not fix on the army as their profession. They must turn their thoughts to something useful, in which their time and their talents can be honourably employed; something that will give them an opportunity of saying when they come to their death-bed, 'I have led a useful life; I have improved the time and powers which it pleased God to intrust to me.'"

"And you believe this cannot be, if they enter the army?"

"We are at peace," said Mr. Danesbury, "as we have been for many years, and as we seem likely to continue for many years more. An officer of the present day passes his time in idleness: my sons must not so pass theirs."

As Mr. Danesbury spoke, Robert and Lionel entered. Good-looking youths both, but as yet less noble in form and feature than their brothers, Arthur and William. Mr. Danesbury informed them of the complaint of Fox, the nurseryman. "He says you, in particular, behaved shamefully, Robert."

"The vile old sinner! It's a lie. Papa—"

"Sir!" reproved Mr. Danesbury; "you forget yourself. No ill language before me. Tell me what really happened. The truth, mind; for I shall investigate this. In the first place, what had you been taking?"

"Taking?" echoed Robert, who had inherited his mother's crabbed temper.

"To drink? Fox says you were not sober."

"I'll wring Fox's neck, if he comes to you again with tales about us. If anybody was not sober it was himself," hastily added Robert, for Mr. Danesbury had raised his hand in displeasure. "Fox was in such a passion he could neither see nor hear."

"As I said," interposed Mrs. Danesbury.

"You took beer with your dinner, and your glass of wine after it." Mr. Danesbury might have said two glasses.

"What else did you take?"

"Only a drop of cider."

"Where did you get that?"

Robert was silent. He would have preferred not to say where. But he knew there might be no trifling when thus brought face to face with his father.

"I was dreadfully thirsty; I suppose it was the fish at dinner; and I got a drop."

"Where did you get it?" repeated Mr. Danesbury.

"In a beer shop."

"Beer, wine, and cider! no wonder Fox had the complaint to make," said Mr. Danesbury, in a severe tone, whilst Isabel had looked up startled. "I will speak to you about this when we are alone, Robert. Go on to what you did at Fox's."

"We did nothing. I just got over his hedge, and there was a big tablecloth, or something, spread out there, like a sail, and it got torn. Fox said we should pay for it; and I said I should not, for his insolence."

"But what brought you getting over his hedge at all?"

"It was in our way," haughtily answered Robert, "and we were in a hurry."

"What is that you are saying?" interrupted Mr. Danesbury. "Whatever may be your hurry, you have no right to go, broadcast, over other people's land and hedges."

"The land is ours, papa."

"No, sir, it is his. So long as he hires it from me, and pays me rent for it, it is his. I have always found Fox a civil, respectful man, and I know you must have provoked him most unjustifiably to induce him to be otherwise. The fact is, as I have been telling your mamma, you must be idle no longer. Now that it is decided you do not go to school again, you must choose what you will be. I should prefer you both coming to the works; there is room for all of you: yes," added Mr. Danesbury, with emphasis, "room for all four of my sons, and an ample and increasing income."

Robert Danesbury turned up his nose. The two boys had been to a noted aristocratic private school, where they had learnt thoroughly to despise "business." Robert had told his mamma that he should never "soil his hands with it," and she upheld him.

"I intend to go into the army, papa."

"And I want to be a doctor," cried Lionel, who was a good-natured, pleasant, nice lad.

"Anything but that, Robert," said Mr. Danesbury. "Choose anything but that."

The question was not settled that evening; no, nor for several evenings after it. Robert Danesbury was thoroughly obstinate over it; he laughed contemptuously in his sleeve at his father's arguments about leading a useful life; he was bent on obtaining his own will, and at last he said—ay, and told Mr. Danesbury—that if he could not have a commission bought, he would enlist, for go into the army he would.

Mrs. Danesbury's system of training had begun to tell. It was working already in Robert Danesbury's undutifully refusing to yield his wishes to his father's, in his persistency in embracing the one only calling that was especially distasteful to Mr. Danesbury. Why was Robert Danesbury so eager to enter the army? That he might serve his country? Not at all: but he had acquired a passion for a red coat, and for a life of pleasure and idleness.

One day he ran up to his eldest brother. "Arthur, I wish you would persuade papa about my commission. He will listen to you. Mamma says she has teased him till she is tired. He consented readily to Lionel's being a physician, and just because I want my commission, he won't give it me. Will you persuade him?"

"No, I cannot, Robert. I do not like the army for you, any more than he does. Choose something else. Would you like to be a barrister, as Tom Serle is going to be?"

"I will not be anything but an officer," returned Robert, sullenly; "my mind is made up, and nothing shall turn it. You are as unkind as you can be, Arthur."

Arthur laughed, and looked full in his face, and the cloud passed away from Robert's as he met the kindly gaze. He knew there were not many brothers in the world so good and affectionate as Arthur had ever been.

"*Won't* you persuade papa?"

"No, my boy; I could only do so against my conscience and my judgment: for I do not believe a commission would conduce to your happiness or welfare."

But Robert Danesbury, helped by his mother, carried his point, and Mr. Danesbury, under sore protest, at length consented to apply to the Horse Guards for the purchase of a commission. Lionel was placed with Mr. Pratt, the surgeon at Eastborough, to go through the necessary steps and grades towards becoming eventually a physician. It was arranged that he should pass his evenings and nights at home. Mr. Danesbury and Mr. Pratt were close friends, and the latter was pleased to receive Lionel. He was a man of sorrow, though he maintained outward cheerfulness. It arose from the conduct of his son: he had but one, who was turning out as badly as he could well do. He was never now seen at Eastborough, but was sometimes heard of in London.

Mrs. Philip Danesbury's nieces arrived, Mary and Anna Heber, the one grown up, the other several years younger. They were refined, gentle, good girls: Mrs. Philip Danesbury had said "admirable," and she had not said too much. Their beauty was the least part of them, though that was rare, and their calm, open, expressive countenances were an index to the well-disciplined mind within. They were the well-trained daughters of a sincere minister of religion. Danesbury House fell in love with them at first sight, with the exception of its mistress.

CHAPTER IX
VISCOUNT TEMPLE

GAY doings were expected in Bedford Row, in the house of Mr. Serle, for his eldest daughter, Charlotte, was about to be married to Walter St. George. The latter was now a partner, the firm being Serle & St. George. There were several years' difference between his age and Charlotte's; but the attachment had begun in her childhood. Miss Danesbury was there on a visit: she was to be one of the bridesmaids.

It was the evening of a grand dinner-party. The young ladies were upstairs dressing, and Mrs. Serle was about to go up for the same purpose. She was a bustling manager, liked looking into things herself, had been very busy, and put off dressing till the last minute. She had a lot of silver forks in her hands, which she was about to take to the servants in the dining-parlour, but had stepped into the drawing-room first, for something she wanted there. Mr. Serle came running up from the office, all in a hurry.

"Harriet, can you make room for another at dinner?"

"What an unreasonable question!" ejaculated Mrs. Serle, after a pause of surprise. "Of course I cannot."

"It must be done somehow," returned her husband.

"It can't be done. I never heard of such a thing. We are just a dozen. Who wants to come?"

"One of our best clients: Lord Temple."

Mrs. Serle was considerably mollified. Lords were not common articles on her visiting list.

"He has been getting into a scrape," proceeded Mr. Serle. "He is always getting into scrapes, like his father before him. And he has come to me to get him out of it."

"But is that any reason why you should ask him to dinner to-day? The table will only hold twelve comfortably."

"There are writs out against him," said Mr. Serle, dropping his voice to a whisper, "and he dare not show his face in the street. The house is being watched now for him, and if he stirs out he'll be arrested. Here he is safely housed, and here he must stop until the thing is settled. I have told him we will give him a bed: and to-morrow he must remain quietly upstairs with you and the girls, and not come in view of the office. It will be utter ruin to him if he gets taken, and not much less so if these Jews scent his hiding-place."

"It is very awkward about the table," remonstrated Mrs. Serle, returning to the practical part of the affair; "otherwise, I should be proud to have him. The sets of glasses are only for twelve, and the dessert knives and forks—"

"Who looks at the pattern of a glass?" interrupted the lawyer: "and I'm sure you need not put me a dessert knife and fork, for I never use them."

"The table will be so crowded, and—oh! we should be thirteen! It is the unlucky number."

"Unlucky fiddlestick!" retorted Mr. Serle, who was growing provoked. "Just tell me what I am to do, will you? There's Lord Temple downstairs, shut up in my private room, and in the house he must remain. Would you keep him there while we dine, and send him a mutton chop? Is that how you would treat a British nobleman?"

"Well, then, he must dine with us," concluded Mrs. Serle, balancing her exultation at showing off a real live lord to her guests, against the inconveniences it would cause, and her dread of the popular superstition. "Is he old or young?"

"Young. What has that to do with it?"

"I wonder whether I could coax Louisa not to come in till dessert?" continued Mrs. Serle.

"Of course you can," returned he. "That will do. Wait a minute."

"She is not so easily coaxed though, and she has been wild over this dinner-party. Oh, Matthew!"

"What now?" asked he, turning back.

"I declare we have but twelve finger glasses!"

"The dickens take the finger glasses," cried the vexed lawyer; "put me a slop basin. Wait there, I say."

"Slop basin, indeed! That's just said to aggravate me. And what am I to wait here for? I shall have the people arrive before I am ready. If I don't believe he is bringing the lord up now, and I this figure! Well, of all the idiots—"

Mrs. Serle stopped, for the footsteps were close, and she strove to thrust the forks into her pocket, but they got entangled with her dress, and would not go in. She was fain to make the best of it, and held them out before her, very consciously wishing Mr. Serle at York.

"Mrs. Serle; Lord Temple."

A tall, slender young man of distinguished bearing entered—a very aristocrat. His face was pale, and his features were almost delicately beautiful; his hair was dark, and his eyes were gray.

"What apology must I make for intruding upon you in this unceremonious manner?" he said, in a voice as pleasing as his air was frank. "Mr. Serle has been so kind as to say he will give me a bed to-night."

"I am most happy to see your lordship. I hope you will be able to make yourself at home with us; we are only plain people," was Mrs. Serle's confused reply, as she escaped from the room with the refractory forks.

Mr. Serle, apologising, also left it, and the Viscount remained alone. He sat tilting his chair, and stretching and yawning. The scrape he was in gave him some little concern, and he was sure this incarceration in his lawyer's house would prove "deuced slow." He had given his seat an extra tilt, and was in imminent danger of pitching over backwards, when the door opened, and a most beautiful girl appeared, quite as distinguished-looking as himself, her pink dress of rich and flowing material, and her necklace and bracelets of pearl.

Up rose Lord Temple, the finished gentleman. The young lady hesitated. He was a stranger, and she had believed the drawing-room to be empty.

"Allow me to give you a chair," he said. "I have the honour of speaking to Miss Serle?"

"No," she replied: "I am Miss Danesbury."

Charlotte Serle came in, and was soon followed by Louisa; for Louisa had declined her mamma's suggestion of coming in with the dessert. The Viscount scanned the dresses of the three, and suspected company. The next to appear was Mr. Serle, in orthodox dinner costume. Lord Temple looked down at his own frock-coat, and drew Mr. Serle outside the door.

"Have you visitors to-day?"

"Only a few, my lord."

"Then what am I to do? I am in morning dress. You said I should be quite *en famille*."

"Your lordship's dress is all-sufficient. We do not stand upon ceremony in our house, or our visitors either. They will not look at your coat, my lord, after they hear your name."

Mr. Serle spoke the last sentence in a joking tone; but he was always obsequious to rank—to be so was innate with him.

"Well, if Mrs. Serle will excuse it. I must wash my hands, and be obliged to you for combs and brushes, and such things. There is no time to send to my house."

"I will show your lordship to your room. It is ready."

"Who is that gentleman?" inquired Isabel Danesbury.

"Don't know him from Adam," was the response of Charlotte Serle.

"He is a stranger," resumed Isabel, "for he addressed me as Miss Serle."

"I never saw him before. He has on a curious dress if he is come to dinner. But he is evidently a gentleman."

"It is some grand client of papa's," interposed Louisa Serle. "Mamma came to me, all in a flurry, when I was in the nursery having my hair done, and wanted me not to go down to dinner. The idea! Some important client had dropped in, she said, and papa had asked him to dinner, and she did not like to have the table in a squeeze, and would not sit down thirteen. I told her there would be no squeezing at all, but plenty of room, and thirteen was as lucky as twelve. So I finished dressing and came down.

"I like his appearance very much," remarked Isabel.

"What is his name, Louy?" asked Charlotte.

"I forget. He is out of the common way. A duke, or a prince, or a something: at anyrate, a nobleman."

Charlotte laughed. "Louise is rather given to romancing, Isabel. We never have noblemen here."

As she was speaking, Mr. St. George entered. A little man, with a thin face, and keen, expressive, dark eyes.

"Walter," said his bride-elect, "who is this client come unexpectedly to dine with us?"

"Viscount Temple."

"A viscount! Louy's tale was not all romance, then."

The guests assembled. When dinner was announced, Lord Temple, who ought, in right of his rank, to have taken Mrs. Serle, drew back in all the humility of his frock-coat, and she was handed in by a big and burly Queen's Counsel. The Viscount looked amongst the young ladies, and offered his hand to Isabel.

So they sat together and conversed together, mutually pleased. Opposite to Isabel was her brother William, a remarkably handsome young man, though not quite so tall as Arthur. He had inherited his mother's soft dark eyes, and her beautiful cast of countenance, he had even her delicately-formed lips; but while hers had spoken of firmness, William's told of irresolution.

"Tell me who all these people are?" whispered Lord Temple to Isabel.

"I do not know the strangers," she replied. "Only the Serles, Mr. St. George, and my brother. That is my brother sitting opposite to me."

"A Mr. Serle, is he?"

"No," laughed Isabel, "I told you I was Miss Danesbury. He is William Danesbury."

"I really beg your pardon. Thrown amidst so many strange people at once, it has made me confuse names. St. George is to marry one of the Serles, is he not?"

"Yes; the one with dark hair, sitting next to him."

"You do not reside here?"

"I reside at Eastborough."

"Eastborough"—spoke Lord Temple half to himself—"Danesbury? Eastborough? why, you must be related to Arthur Danesbury?"

"He is my dear brother," answered Isabel.

"If we were not in a crowd, I should take both your hands and cordially shake them," exclaimed Lord Temple, his face, his eyes, his whole countenance lighting up with animation; "whatever you might think of me, I could not help doing it for Arthur's sake. We were together at Cambridge. You must have heard him speak of me."

Isabel reflected. "I do not remember that I have," she answered. "Your name appeared strange to me when it was mentioned this evening."

"Oh—I was not Lord Temple then. My father was alive. I was Mr. Dacre."

"You never can be Reginald Dacre!" uttered Isabel.

"Reginald Dacre is no other than my unworthy self. Very unworthy indeed, Miss Danesbury, if you knew all Arthur could tell you. He was a true friend to me, and saved me from many a pitfall. 'My good guardian,' I used to call him; and such he was."

"He is good to everyone," said Isabel.

"I am so glad to have met you," continued Lord Temple; "I have not seen Danesbury since we parted at Cambridge, though I have often thought, since my return from abroad, of looking him up. Arthur Danesbury is almost the only man I ever had a respect for."

"I hope not," remarked Isabel. "It does not say much for your circle of friends."

"He is, though. And now that I am told of the relationship, I can detect your likeness to him. You are very like him, Miss Danesbury. Your brother opposite is not."

"He is not, I think. I and Arthur resemble papa; and William, they say, is the very image of what poor mamma was."

"You have lost your mother?"

"When William was a baby."

"Now that I have heard of Arthur, I shall not rest till I pay him a visit. You will find me intruding some day upon you, Miss Danesbury."

"Danesbury House will be very pleased to welcome you. And if you respect and like Arthur, I am sure you will respect and like papa."

"I thought my sojourn in Bedford Row would have turned out unmitigatedly dull," candidly spoke the young nobleman, "but I need not fear that now, with you to talk to, and Arthur for the theme."

"Are you going to stay here?" she inquired in surprise.

"For a day or two. Serle & St. George are my solicitors, and are arranging some business matters for me. Will you introduce me to your brother William after dinner?"

"Certainly I will."

"You do not drink your wine," observed Lord Temple, perceiving that however often Isabel complied with the request to take wine, the quantity in her glass was never sensibly diminished, and the space to be filled up each time got less, instead of greater.

"Thank you: I do not like wine."

"Not like wine?"

"I never drink it by choice. At a dinner-table such as this, I sip it not to appear singular, but I do not like it well enough to do more than just put my lips to it."

"I never heard of such a thing as not liking wine," repeated Lord Temple. "What do you like?"

"Water."

"I wonder you can choose anything so insipid. Arthur never drank anything but water, I remember."

"Never. He is more particular than I. I almost call it one of the points in Arthur's religion, to drink simple water."

"But why?" inquired Lord Temple.

"For one thing, we were brought up to drink it; as children, neither beer nor wine was ever given to us; we were not suffered to know the taste of them. And," added Isabel, sinking her voice, "the very last words mamma ever said to Arthur, were an injunction not to drink anything but water."

"When she was dying?"

"Oh, no. She was quite well; as well as we are now, and had been dining at this very table, for we were here on a visit. But mamma received a hasty summons home, and she took leave of me and Arthur, and left us here, and started. Before she reached Eastborough, it had happened. The chaise was overturned, and mamma killed."

"How shocking! how distressing!" uttered Lord Temple, his countenance betraying its sad interest.

"We were only children," continued Isabel. "Mamma feared that in her absence Mr. and Mrs. Serle might be giving us wine and porter, and she whispered to Arthur, in the moment of her departure, not to touch either; and he promised. Those words, though only meant at the time she spoke them to apply to the period she expected to be away from us, Arthur has always regarded as a dying injunction, and he has never transgressed it. He is a strict water-drinker."

"And you and Arthur really like water better than anything stronger?"

Isabel smiled. "We like water much, and we do not like stronger things. The taste for water, which of course is born with everyone, mamma took care should be cultivated in our childhood. She deemed it most essential to bring children up to like water, and equally essential not to let them acquire a predilection for ale and wine."

"Well, all this sounds like a new theory to me," said Lord Temple, good-humouredly, though Isabel thought not altogether in belief. "I fancy it must be pleasant to like water as a beverage; convenient at times. But your brother, there, does not confine himself to water," he added, for he saw that William Danesbury drank as much wine as the rest of the table.

"No," replied Isabel. "Papa's second wife has had the bringing up of William, and she does not approve of the water-drinking system. She is Mrs. Serle's sister."

And thus they continued to converse upon one topic or another, until the ladies rose. It was Lord Temple who, oblivious of his frock-coat, held the door open for them as they filed out of the room.

"You very essence of flirtation!" uttered Charlotte to Isabel, when they reached the drawing-room. "Had you and Lord Temple been old friends, meeting after a long absence, or on the point of marriage, as I and Walter are, you could not have been more wrapt up in each other."

"A great deal less, before you all, had we been on the point of marriage," merrily laughed Isabel. "But we really did not seem unlike friends meeting after an absence, though I never saw him till this evening. Before we had spoken many words, he discovered that I was Arthur Danesbury's sister; and I, that he was the Reginald Dacre of Arthur's college days. They were close friends at Cambridge: Lord Temple says he never had so true a one."

"But you must have known that Reginald Dacre was Lord Temple's son," observed Mrs. Serle.

"Of course I knew it at the time," replied Isabel; "but the title had quite slipped from my memory."

"How singular!" exclaimed Mrs. Serle. "Such chance encounters do sometimes happen, though. Mr. Serle is as Lord Temple's right hand, and does everything for him," she added, for the benefit of her guests. "He has recently succeeded to the estates."

"Such estates as they are," spoke the Queen's Counsel's wife. "His father was a poor man—made himself poor; gamed, drank, and squandered his money. Lord Temple—the present Lord—was the only child, has come into a dilapidated purse; and is as careless and hare-brained as his father was before him."

"He seems a very delightful young man," quoth one of the ladies.

"Yes. But he made a hole in his manners to-day, coming to a dinner-party in a frock-coat."

"It was a—misapprehension," interposed Mrs. Serle, not choosing to be more explanatory. "He expected a quiet chop with Mr. Serle, and did not go home to dress. He talked about not appearing when he found we had friends, but Mr. Serle assured him—you know he is fond of a jest—that when the visitors had heard his name, they would not see his coat. Miss Danesbury, will you give us some music?"

Lord Temple did not leave Mr. Serle's at the end of a day or two. His affairs were in a more intricate state than Mr. Serle had supposed, and not until the eighth day was he at liberty to depart. He had not failed to improve his acquaintance with Isabel Danesbury. Indeed, it was no longer acquaintance, or friendship either, it had grown into love. Ay, love on both sides, short as the period had been.

But they had been very much together. Mrs. Serle and her daughters were fully engaged with the preparations for Charlotte's wedding; and Isabel was requested, as a great favour, to entertain the guest, that they might be more at liberty. She complied, nothing loth, for she had never met with anyone she liked so well as Lord Temple. She did not care to analyse her pleasant sensations; he did not think to analyse his. To analyse anything was not in Lord Temple's line. They only felt that the presence of the other was becoming strangely dear; and, by the time the eight days had gone by, too dear to be relinquished. The first use Lord Temple, impetuous in all he did, made of

"It was no longer acquaintance."

his liberty, was to hasten down to Eastborough, and lay his proposals for Isabel before Mr. Danesbury.

Arthur Danesbury was inexpressibly surprised: surprised at the sight of his former friend, and at his proposing for Isabel after so short a knowledge of her. Mr. Danesbury could say little for or against, Lord Temple being to him a complete stranger. He inquired privately of Arthur what character he bore at college, and what his principles were.

"He was no worse than many another at college," was Arthur's reply; "better than some. His chief fault lay in being so easily led away."

"Is he one to whom we ought to give Isabel?"

"As he was then, no; as he might have been, yes," replied Arthur. "His faults were not grievous ones. They were what are looked upon by the world with a lenient eye. Years have passed since then, and he had excellent seeds in his heart; quite sufficient to root out the tares."

Mr. Danesbury looked perplexed. "The question is, has he suffered the seeds to bear fruit," he gravely said, "or are the tares there still?"

"If they are there yet, the good must be well-nigh over-run," was Arthur's comment. "He has many good points, he is frank and truthful, and full of honour."

"I shall write and inquire of Serle what he knows of his private character," said Mr. Danesbury. "Lord Temple frankly states that his affairs are such that he cannot marry yet, for his father's death left all in confusion, and it will take time to get them even tolerably straight."

"He informs me that he has made himself answerable for some of his father's liabilities," observed Arthur. "He used to be generous to a fault. Suppose, sir, you accept him conditionally?"

"Yes, I think that must be it. I will tell him that if we hear nothing to his disadvantage, I will say yes, after a while. It is higher alliance than a Danesbury could have expected; but I look to Isabel's happiness, not to her grandeur."

Lord Temple went over the extensive works. He was pleased with all he saw. He appeared not to share in the popular prejudice which men of his rank hold against commerce. "I should think it an honour to be a second Danesbury," he remarked to Arthur, with whom he was alone, and very much in earnest he appeared when he spoke it: "and a lucky thing for me if it were so, for it would keep me out of idleness."

"Dacre," returned Arthur Danesbury, in a grave voice, "have you sown your wild oats? Answer me truly, because, if not, you know that you are no fit husband for my sister."

"I have sown most of them," replied Lord Temple, "and what few may cling to me still, a wife will, of necessity, dissipate."

"It is a serious thing to us, Dacre, to give away Isabel. Though pray forgive my still calling you 'Dacre,'" Arthur broke off to say; "I cannot rid my tongue and memory of the old familiar name. And were one to receive the gift who proved afterwards unworthy of it, it would break some of our hearts."

"She shall find me all she could wish," returned Lord Temple, in his impetuous fashion. "I would go through fire and water for her."

Arthur Danesbury doubted his lordship's being called upon to undergo the suggested ordeals. "Would you go through self-denial for her?" he asked.

"I would go through anything and everything for Isabel. Mr. Danesbury need not doubt me. She is the first woman who ever touched my heart, and I swear that I will do all in my power to make her happy."

Viscount Temple was soon back in London, whither Arthur accompanied him. He—her lover—informed Isabel that her father had no objection to him, and they plighted their troth. Mr. Serle had written word, in answer to Mr. Danesbury's application, that he knew nothing unfavourable of Lord Temple. The true fact was, that he knew nothing whatever of his private habits, except that he got out of money. And Isabel Danesbury returned home, after Charlotte Serle's marriage, an engaged girl.

But now, what was, in reality, the daily life of Lord Temple? He was an *idle* nobleman. Had he been trained to engage in any worthy pursuit, he would have been a different man. Want of occupation rendered him indolent, and an easily-swayed disposition led him into sin; few men but could resist temptation better than Viscount Temple. Let us glance at four-and-twenty hours of his life, and that will serve for an illustration of all.

A choice knot of young men had assembled to dine at the bachelor residence of Sir Robert Payn, a wealthy commoner of extensive purse, fastidious taste, and fast habits. The half-dozen guests collected, of whom Lord Temple made one, were all of fast habits likewise. Look at the preparations for the dinner—the costly table, with its costly appurtenances! Silver ornaments, silver dishes; brilliant glass, richly cut; superb china from the fair manufactories of Worcester, with damask linen of rare beauty! The preparation of wines was great. There was champagne, and there was sparkling Burgundy; Madeira, and golden sherry, and heady port; with the array of lighter wines from France, claret, Bordeaux—too many sorts to be named. Bottles of foaming ale were under the sideboard, and spirits stood on it in their handsome stands.

The dinner was most *recherché*—Sir Robert's entertainments always were—and the guests did it ample justice. They all drank deeply—not certainly to intoxication; that would have been a sin against good manners at that hour of the evening—and custom enabled them to drink much with impunity. After a potent cup of coffee and a glass of rich liqueur, they went out—to the opera, to the green room of a favoured theatre, or to look in for half an hour at some of the entertainments held that night by the noble and great. That over, the night work began—their clubs, their gaming-houses, their questionable saloons, and the supper, the finish-up. The less said about these suppers the better. It was a motley scene: gentlemen and ladies eating, laughing, and getting tipsy together; red and white wines, ales, spirits, and showers of brandy and champagne. Lord Temple's coroneted cab was waiting for him outside, amidst a crowd of other cabs, and wait it did till morning light. The grooms and servants in attendance on the cabs sometimes got loud and quarrelsome, for they also must while away the midnight hours in drink while waiting for their masters.

Daylight broke, and the lords came forth; some had to be helped into the cabs by their servants, little more sober than themselves. Lord Temple pitched into his, and was driven home. His valet assisted him to undress, and he got into bed at an hour when less exalted people were beginning their day. He awoke with aching head and fevered tongue. What was the time? Eleven. And he turned round and closed again his heavy eyes. Later, he struggled up, dressed, and went into the breakfast-room, not inclined to eat; on the contrary, shuddering at the displayed viands on the table. As he stood there, with his hands in his pockets, George Eden dropped in, one of the last night's party, with the same burning head and shaking frame. It was those cursed cigars made them ill; it was the adulterated wine; it was the impure brandy—the fellow at "The Finish" ought to have his licence stopped for supplying such. It was anything, in short, but the quantity they took, and of course it was not that. Certainly not; nobody ever acknowledged to such an imputation yet. What could they take now? A glass of hock, said George Eden; brandy and soda-water, said Lord Temple, and the servant supplied them. They were not fit for anything—they did confess that; and the horses were ordered round, that they might go for a long, bracing ride. The fresh air blew on their heated brows, and made other men of them; but they were awfully thirsty, and they called for some half-and-half at more than one roadside inn. They got back to town in time to pay some morning visits (morning, as they are called), and they looked in at the clubs for a gossip, and idled away an hour in the betting-rooms, leaving in time for the display in the park. Then came round the late dinner-hour, and they sat down to it, as on the previous evening, though not at Sir Robert Payn's, and afterwards finished up the night *selon les régles*.

Now this was a fair specimen of Lord Temple's days; and yet he told Arthur Danesbury that his wild oats were buried. Possibly Lord Temple believed they were. Possibly Lord Temple thought that when he married he should cut through his present habits, as effectually as a knife severs a cheese, and never return to them. Or he may have seen nothing to reprobate in this course of life, for example is fearfully infectious, and numbers, older and wiser and higher in the peerage than he, led it.

But what reckoning was it that he was laying up for himself? Time wasted, powers prostrated, talents thrown away! Lord Temple's intellect was fine, and his heart good, but what use was he making of them? He never cast a thought to the solemn warning, that "for all these things God would surely bring him to judgment."

CHAPTER X
LORD TEMPLE'S FOLLY

TIME went on. Time goes on with us all. Lord Temple paid occasional visits to Danesbury House, his conduct there being all that it ought to be, and Isabel's attachment to him grew deeper and deeper. Their marriage was not spoken of, even yet, as a speedy event, although they were both some years older than when first engaged, but his affairs did not get straight. Serle & St. George performed prodigies of wonder towards righting them, so the former assured Lord Temple; but the more they effected, the more his lordship spent. Every morning of his life did Lord Temple make a firm resolve that the morrow should see him begin a life of reformation, of saving, and every night saw his lordship spending as before.

Robert and Lionel Danesbury had been for some time resident in London. Robert's regiment, a foot regiment, was quartered there; and Lionel, who had done with Mr. Pratt, was with an eminent town practitioner, attending lectures, and walking the hospitals. William likewise remained in town. At the expiration of his articles, the firm had proposed to Mr. Danesbury that he should continue with them a few additional years, for he was clever in his profession, and of much use to them. William likewise urged it, "for improvement, and to gain experience," he said; but the unhappy truth was, that he was unable to tear himself from the fascinations of a London life. The three young men were in the first blush of manhood; William more than of age, Lionel approaching it. They were not very frequently together, for their pursuits lay in different spheres, and each had a separate lodging. Mr. Danesbury was startled at the frequent calls upon his purse, so much more than he had ever bargained for. All were ready with an excuse; Robert's, perhaps, the most plausible. He urged the expensive mess, the extravagant habits of his brother officers; and he must do as they did, unless he would like to be sent to Coventry. Mr. Danesbury believed that officers must be the greatest spendthrifts on the face of the earth; he made a handsome allowance to Robert, besides his pay; but the allowance and the pay seemed to be swallowed up, no one could tell how, and a vast deal beside it. He had left his ensigncy behind him, and was now lieutenant. William received a good salary from his employers, but he could not make it sufficient for his wants. Lionel was furnished with a liberal allowance, but it seemed as nothing to him. Mr. Danesbury consulted with Arthur, and grumbled, and wrote lectures to his sons; but Mrs. Danesbury made very light of it. Young men liked to see life before settling down, she said; but they would be all the steadier for it in the end.

But what was it that their London life was teaching them? Everything that was bad. Some things they learned need not be given in detail; but the worst habit that can possibly fall upon young men, they had rapidly acquired—to fritter away their hours in idleness, smoking, and drinking. We are speaking now more particularly of Robert and Lionel: William's days, till evening, were occupied in his business, therefore idleness could not be charged upon him. Robert's habits had grown bad, as well as alarmingly expensive: too many families remember now, with a sigh of agony, what were the lives led by the officers quartered in London during the long peace. Vanity, vice, betting, gambling, and—what this history has most to do with—drinking. All three were without control in that dangerous city; without a home, for the furnished lodgings of a young man cannot deserve the name. Lionel's companions were, of course, chiefly medical students of various ages; quite as notorious, in their way, as officers are in theirs; they were dissolute, idle, and irreligious, gentlemen though they called themselves. Robert and Lionel (do not forget that we are not much alluding to William, who was not quite so unsteady as his brothers) were not yet in the habit of *getting intoxicated*—that only happened to them occasionally: but, had they sat down and reflected on the immense quantity of drink they did consume in a day, it might have startled them. Lionel chiefly indulged in porter, medical student fashion; Robert in wine; and spirits came amiss to neither. Drinking begets drinking. Had anyone told them they were on the road to become men of habitual inebriation, they would have scoffed at the notion; yet had they recalled what had been their customary daily portion the previous year, and what the year before that, they would have been astonished to find how, with each year, the quantity had augmented. How could it increase? they would have asked themselves; they did not seem to take in one day more than in the preceding one. No, they did not *seem* to do so, taking one day with another, and yet the increase had been dreadful. Poor lads! the vice was insinuating itself imperceptibly upon them; they were thrown into its very midst; they did not wish, or intend, to do wrong; but they were unable to withstand the temptations that beset them, for London teemed then, as it teems now, with incentives to indulge in it.

A cab was dashing down Oxford Street into Holborn, a well-appointed cab, with a coronet on its panels. The refined features of its distinguished-looking driver bore the pale, jaded air, that tells too surely of a dissipated life; he seemed to urge his horse recklessly. Clearing all impediments, he was about to turn up Red Lion Street, when he checked his horse so suddenly that the animal was nearly pulled on his haunches.

"Holloa! Payn!" called out he; and Sir Robert Payn, who had been walking along in a brown study, regarding nobody, turned off the pavement, and went round to the driver's side of the cab.

"I say, Payn," cried he, stooping down and speaking in an undertone, "were you not in St. James's Street the night before last when I went in?"

"Yes," answered the baronet. "You had been in the sun, and no mistake."

"Did I play while you were there?"

"Not you. You were too far gone. You couldn't have held the cards. Why?"

"It seems I did get playing. And I thought if you had been there, Payn, you might have done me the service to pitch me out at the window, rather than suffer me to make a fool of myself, and ducks and drakes of my money."

"Do you mean to say you did do that?"

"Others say it; and there's no doubt I did."

"Much damage?"

"Pretty fair. What time did you leave?"

"What time did I leave?" pondered Sir Robert. "Let's see? After that, I looked in at Maggs's, and stopped about three-quarters of an hour, and I was at home and in bed before four. It must have been getting on for three when I left St. James's Street. Danesbury and Colonel Neeve went out when I did. You were fast asleep on the sofa then."

"Was Sandlin there?"

"No, Sandlin was gone. Whitehouse was there, and Georgy Eden; and those were about all, I think, except you and Anketel. There was nothing doing. Swallowtail was sitting by the fireplace, and Whitehouse and Georgy were flinging for sovereigns. Are you coming to Sandlin's to-night?"

"I don't know. I shall see. Good-day."

The cab sped on, up Red Lion Street, towards Bedford Row; and there it pulled up at the offices of Serle & St. George. The gentleman threw the reins to his groom, jumped out, went into the house, and opened the door of the front office.

"Mr. Serle in?"

"No, my lord. Mr. St. George is."

His lordship walked listlessly through the room. The clerks turned their heads after him. Scarcely a young clerk but gazed with a sigh of envy: his handsome person, his life of ease, his title, even his aristocratic cab at the door, with its blood horse, all presented, or seemed to present, food for envy. But had the breast of that nobleman been laid bare before them, they might have hesitated to exchange their own position for his, although they did have to scratch away from morning till night with a hard pen at a hard desk. The head clerk left his place, and held open the door of a very small room, the private room of Mr. St. George.

"Lord Temple, sir."

Mr. St. George rose. He had been sitting before a table covered with parchments and papers. "Serle's not in?" said Lord Temple, who was not only some years older than when we last saw him, but who looked it.

"No," replied Mr. St. George. "He is gone up west with Mr. Danesbury."

"With Mr. Danesbury! Is he in town?"

"He came up last night on unexpected business. Is it anything I can do, my lord?"

"I can speak to you, as well as to Serle; it is all the same, I daresay," said Lord Temple, throwing himself into the client's chair. "I want some money raised."

"Raised *again?*" echoed Mr. St. George, with an emphasis.

"And I must have it, too," added Lord Temple.

"I fear it will be difficult. The mortage on the Dacre estate—"

"I beg your pardon," interrupted Lord Temple. "I never go into these business details: Serle can tell you so. You and he must manage the practical part, but don't worry me with it. I must have three thousand pounds by the twenty-fifth."

Mr. St. George looked grave, and at length spoke hesitatingly.

"Lord Temple—"

"Well?"

"Will you pardon me if I am frank with you? Mr. Serle, I know, smooths matters over, and gives them a pleasant aspect. It is his way. So long as the evil day can be put off, he is sure to do it. I should like to be more honest with you."

"You would like to tell me that my estates are going to the deuce headlong, and the more money I raise, the quicker they'll be there," said his lordship, good-humouredly. "That's what you mean, is it not, St. George?"

"Part of it, my lord."

"Part of it! What's the other part?"

"I should like to ask how much longer you are going to play with Miss Danesbury," said the lawyer, in a low tone; "if I may dare to ask it?"

The colour rushed into the Viscount's face. He bit his lip.

"You will forgive my boldness, Lord Temple, when you remember that her mother was my near relative. I have long been pained to see your time, your fortune, your energies thrown away; pained for you, and pained for Miss Danesbury. You ought to give her up."

"Give her up!" echoed his lordship: *"give her up!* Never. She is dearer to me than my own life."

A contemptuous curl, suppressed instantly, rose to Mr. St. George's lip. "Is she dearer to you than your follies, my lord?"

The Viscount started from his seat in perturbation, angry, yet conscience-stricken. "You are the only man who should so speak to me, Mr. St. George. But, as you say, you were her mother's relative."

"It is time that someone should speak," returned Mr. St. George. "Mr. Danesbury, buried in the country, unsuspicious as his own honourable nature, believes that your affairs were so inextricably involved at your father's death, that it is taking all this time to get them straight. You know perfectly well they might have been set to rights twice over, had you been barely prudent—at least, sufficiently straight to allow of your marriage."

Lord Temple made no answer.

"You also must be aware that each year brings less chance of its being accomplished. Every sum of money you raise makes the prospect darker; while Mr. Danesbury—and no doubt his daughter also—is naturally looking, from one month to another, to receive news that the desired end is gained. Indeed, Lord Temple, you ought to give up Miss Danesbury."

"I will not give her up," was the answer, passionately uttered. "How dare you suggest so dishonourable an alternative?"

"My lord! Dishonourable! Whether would it be more honourable frankly to tell Mr. Danesbury that your circumstances bar you from marrying, or to waste Miss Danesbury's best years in a useless engagement which will never be fulfilled?"

His lordship turned his haughty face on Mr. St. George. It expressed the very essence of scorn.

"What are you saying, sir? That the engagement will never be fulfilled?"

Mr. St. George met the Viscount's anger equably. He was a plain-speaking, right-minded man, and had less reverence for rank (as rank alone) in his whole body, than Mr. Serle had in his little finger. It was with the senior partner that Lord Temple had hitherto consulted. But now that Mr. St. George had got him face to face, and broken through the official trammels of lawyer and client, the social trammels due to rank, he was determined to speak out his mind.

"My lord, I am saying nothing that the facts of the case will not justify. How can the engagement ever be fulfilled when you are daily putting it more and more out of your power to do so? When you were first engaged to Miss Danesbury, years ago, you were in a better position to marry than you are now."

Lord Temple could not gainsay it. "The fact is," said he, with a somewhat crestfallen expression, "I have been let unwittingly into expenses, one after another. But this shall not go on. I will begin the work of reformation, and get things straight."

"So you said then. I fear you will go on saying it to the end of time, but not acting. It is cruel behaviour towards Miss Danesbury. My lord, I must express it: cruel behaviour."

"I cannot control my circumstances, and convert shillings into pounds," cried Lord Temple, after an uncomfortable pause. He was provoked at the lawyer's manners, so cool, yet so evidently determined not to quarrel; he was provoked at his words, because they were true; and he was provoked at himself.

"But you can control yourself, and spend less," spoke Mr. St. George. "That, at least, is in your power. Lieutenant Danesbury was at my house the other night, and I gathered a hint of your extravagance from some words dropped by him. He said Lord Temple was 'going the pace,' even for a nobleman."

"*He* need not talk," returned Lord Temple, in a fiery tone. "There are not many men in this town, noble or simple, who go the pace quicker than Robert Danesbury."

"I believe that is unfortunately true. Mr. Danesbury's present visit to town is caused by some unpleasant extravagance of Robert's which must be looked into and provided for. But Robert Danesbury is not an engaged man."

"You harp so much upon my being engaged," peevishly cried Lord Temple. "I wish to my heart I was not engaged. I wish I was married. A single man—a man without home ties, as I am, cannot help getting into extravagance. I'll defy him. I am not a tenth part as extravagant as many of my order."

"Nor a fortieth part as wealthy to be extravagant upon," thought the lawyer. "I know what I should do in the dilemma," he added aloud. "I should marry."

"Marry!" echoed Lord Temple, in consternation.

"*I* should. I should lay a statement of facts before Mr. Danesbury, and say, 'Give me your daughter, sir, and save me from my follies, for I cannot save myself.' You would spend less as a married man, than you are spending now."

A rush of eager hope lighted Lord Temple's cheek, at the vista thus unexpectedly put before him. It was a way of solving the matter he had never thought of; for he had believed he must be a clear man before he could venture to become a married one. But the colour faded from his face again, faded with reflection. "No, no," he sadly said, "how is it likely that Mr. Danesbury would give her to me, trammelled as I am? I should blush to ask him."

"You can but try him," answered Mr. St George. "I think you should do that, or give her up. She is not looking well, and this uncertainty, this continued disappointment, is enough to break the spirit of any woman. 'Hope deferred maketh the heart sick,' Lord Temple."

"How do you know that she is not looking well?" demanded Lord Temple, catching at the words.

"I see that she is not. She and her stepmother accompanied Mr. Danesbury to town, and they are staying at my house."

"You cold, cruel man! Isabel at hand, and you could quietly keep it to yourself! Is she in now? Do you think she is in now?"

Lord Temple, in his eagerness, had approached close to the lawyer. His breath was hurried, his lips were apart with excitement.

"I cannot understand you," emphatically cried Mr. St. George, as he noticed the signs. "You are evidently deeply attached to Miss Danesbury, yet you will not relinquish your wild habits to obtain her. But my opinion is, that you and Miss Danesbury should not meet, unless things between you can go on more satisfactorily. I tell you, my lord, the engagement ought to cease."

"Perhaps you wish to prohibit my calling at your house to see her?" haughtily spoke Lord Temple.

"Pardon me, my lord. I hope you will never find me guilty of discourtesy; though I cannot shut my eyes to what is right and wrong, especially with regard to the interests of Miss Danesbury."

"If I could marry!" murmured his lordship. "But it is no use of dwelling on it. We could not live upon air."

Mr. St. George drew in his lips. "Do you live upon air now, Lord Temple?"

"No; of course I don't. But—to bring Isabel to an unsuitable home, a home unworthy of her! And you know things have come to such a pitch that the estates must be at nurse."

"I know they must. But a thousand or fifteen hundred a year can be managed out of them."

Lord Temple opened his eyes and his mouth. He doubted if he heard aright. "Marry upon that!" he uttered, "why, it would take as much nearly for Isabel's court-dress when she was presented! She should not go a fright, I can tell you, and disgrace her own noble beauty, and the coronet of Temple. And there would be the opera-box, and her own carriage and servants, and the re-setting of the family diamonds—for they have not been renovated since the time of my grandmother—besides the general expenses, housekeeping, and that. I don't see that ten thousand a year would go very far towards it all: and you talk of one!"

Mr. St. George, though considerably amused, felt angry. "We are speaking at cross purposes, Lord Temple," he said, taking out his watch, the lawyer's hint that a conference is up. "When I spoke of your marrying at once, I thought of your living retired for a time, as a private gentleman. I believe I said so. You, it appears, can only contemplate it in accordance with your rank as a peer. I confess that I see no probability of your being enabled to marry as such either now or later."

Lord Temple ruminated. "I would give all I am worth to have her," he said. "What is the smallest income I might ask for her upon, without an insult?"

Mr. St. George had grown as stiff as a poker. "Not any income that I shall suggest, Lord Temple. I have said all I have to say, and it has not found favour with you: were I to urge it further, you might deem that I, as a relative of Miss Danesbury, had a design to thrust her upon you."

"Now you are stupid!" retorted his lordship. "I only wish you could thrust her upon me. I should be too thankful. She is far superior to me, St. George."

"I think she is," was Mr. St. George's reply, as he drew up his little figure, and looked fearlessly in the peer's face. "Although you are my Lord Viscount Temple, and she is only plain Miss Danesbury, the daughter of Danesbury the ironmaster, I have long thought that you were not worthy of her. Now you have the truth."

Lord Temple played with his watch-chain. "My concern is for her, not for myself. If I were put in a first-floor lodging, or a cottage with two rooms, it would be as good to me as a palace, if she were but with me."

"Then why need you fear for Isabel? She has not been brought up to the luxuries of high life, and would not miss what she has scarcely been accustomed to."

"But she would be Lady Temple then."

"And could wait for her honours. However, do as you think best, my lord."

A clerk put in his head—" Captain Thomson's here, sir. He wanted Mr. Serle, but he'll see you instead. It's very important, he says."

"Ask him to wait a minute."

"I am going," said Lord Temple. "I expect you will enter this as a double conference, for I have kept you an unconscionable time," he laughed. "I have made up my mind to speak to Mr. Danesbury. But about that three thousand pounds, St. George. You will not forget to tell Serle?"

"I will tell him. Three thousand pounds—it is a large sum. It would have kept your married home for a year or two, if this plan be carried out."

"I suppose it would," answered Lord Temple, his brow contracting. "I won't get into such another mess, but this must be provided for."

"Was it play?"

Lord Temple nodded.

"I thought you had left off play?"

"You may depend I will leave it off," fiercely spoke his lordship. "They don't catch me losing three thousand pounds again. And I had left it off, that's more; and did not know anything about losing this. I should not have done it, had I been in my senses."

"I do not understand you," said Mr. St. George.

"It was that cursed drink," returned his lordship.

"Still, I do not understand."

"Why, it was in St. James's Street," explained Lord Temple, kicking the toe of his boot against the fender. "I went in with Anketel, the night before last, three parts gone, for I had been drinking wine freely, and I threw myself on a sofa, and to sleep I went. I declare that is all I remember of it. I no more knew that I woke up and sat down to play than you did, who were not there; and the next morning when Anketel called upon me, he began blowing me up for playing when I was not in a state to know one card from another. I was thunderstruck; told him it was a hoax; but he said I should find it no hoax when I came to pay. And I found I had lost three thousand pounds, and had given my I O U for it."

"Are you sure you gave it? Are you sure they were not hoaxing you after all?" asked Mr. St. George.

"I am sure I gave it. For I would not believe Anketel; and Swallowtail, who holds it, brought it to show me. It was my own writing, plain enough; rather shaky, but still mine."

"Swallowtail—Swallowtail?" said Mr. St. George. "Ah, he is much about gambling-houses now. The less you have to do with him the better."

"I don't like him myself; he is as keen as a razor. He is a lawyer, isn't he?"

"He was," replied Mr. St. George, emphasising the second word, "but his practice grew too sharp, and he was struck off the rolls."

"Oh, that's it, is it?" carelessly replied Lord Temple. "He has something to do with the establishment in St. James's Street, I think, for he is always there."

"Too much to do with it," muttered the lawyer. "Was it this man who won your money?"

"I suppose so. Or, *non compos* as I was, I should hardly have given him an acknowledgment. I have no more recollection of the transaction myself, than the child unborn."

"But you must surely remember the fact of playing, if you do not remember the details. And you could not give an acknowledgment in your own handwriting without retaining some conciousness of it."

"I assure you I am totally oblivious of the evening altogether. I have a faint recollection of going into the house, and of seeing Sandlin and Sir Robert Payn, and then, I think, somebody gave me some brandy and water, and I lay down on the sofa to sleep. I have no further consciousness of anything till I woke up next day in my own bed."

"It is very strange," exclaimed Mr. St. George.

"So it is," said his lordship; "but it's true."

"Who was in the room when you played?"

"How am I to know? I met Payn just now, and he says he left about three o'clock, with Colonel Neeve and Robert Danesbury. That I was asleep on the sofa then, with no play in me, and Whitehouse and Eden were tossing for sovs. I asked Anketel yesterday how on earth he could suffer me to play when in such a state, and he swears I woke up and would play, and there was no preventing me."

"I don't like Anketel," observed Mr. St. George.

"Oh, he is a good fellow enough, in the main: always at one's beck and call. Well, I don't get into such another pit. Tell Serle the money must be ready by the twenty-fifth, for that is the day I have promised it. Good-morning, St. George."

Lord Temple ascended to his cab, took the reins from his groom, touched his horse, and was whirled away towards Hyde Park Gardens, where Mr. St. George's residence was situated.

CHAPTER XI
THE DEMAND

NOT long had Lord Temple left Bedford Row, when Mr. Danesbury and Mr. Serle returned to it. The latter immediately closeted himself with Captain Thomson, and Mr. St. George obtained a moment's conversation with Mr. Danesbury. Mr. Danesbury was much altered: he was begining to look quite an old man. The courses pursued by his sons could no longer be concealed from him, apart from their expenditure, and they told upon his health and spirits.

"Lord Temple has just driven from here," observed Mr. St. George. "I expect he is gone to my house to see Isabel, by the pace at which his cab tore from the door. I fancy he will be making you a proposal to-day, sir."

"Of what nature?" inquired Mr. Danesbury.

"That he may be allowed to take Isabel at once, for better or for worse. He has been waiting all these years for his affairs to be set straight, with a miracle, I suppose, but they only get deeper involved."

"How is that?" said Mr. Danesbury.

"It is his own fault, sir. He spends ten times more than he ought, and makes no attempt at self-denial. But he associates with other men of his rank—which is but natural—and plunges into all their folly and improvidence. And plunge into it he must, he says, as long as he is a bachelor."

"I do not see the obligation," returned Mr. Danesbury.

"Neither do I. But it seems he does, or his want of resolution does for him. I told him to-day—for which interference I hope you will not be displeased with me—that he ought to resign Isabel, or else make arrangements so that he could marry her. He was ready to trample on me for hinting at such a thing as resigning her. I believe his attachment is fervent."

"Yes, I do think that," acquiesced Mr. Danesbury. "But there is a serious question in the midst of this, Walter. Are these habits of Lord Temple such as will cling to him after marriage?"

"I sincerely believe not. He has no domestic home in which to spend his evenings, and he goes out with those who have twenty times his rent-roll. Once let him be removed from the wild lot who beset him now, give his naturally good qualities fair-play, and he might become an ornament to his order. Isabel's daily influence would do much. I told him they might live upon a thousand a year, while the estates were righting themselves."

"What did he say?"

"Stared at me as though I had lost my senses, and wondered what would become of Isabel, restricted to a thousand a year. His notions extended to court-dresses for her, and re-set diamonds, and opera-boxes, and gilded carriages, and cauliflowered footmen. In short, he has as much notion of economy as my eldest son and heir has of a whipping, which his mother won't give him, or let anybody else. However, he came to the conclusion at last, that if you would entertain the proposal, and Isabel not think it 'an insult,' he should go wild with gratitude at its being adopted."

"If Isabel were restricted to a thousand a year all her life, she would not be much worse off than she has been," smiled Mr. Danesbury.

"I told him that, or something equivalent to it; but he has got a crotchet in his head, that though Miss Danesbury may pleasantly ruralise upon a thousand a year, such a calamity would be entirely out of place for the Lady Temple. He but judges according to the prejudices of his rank, sir."

"Isabel shall not marry without a settlement," said Mr. Danesbury.

"Most certainly not. That can be effected. A small one. And—pardon me—should Isabel inherit anything from you, it should also be settled on her."

Mr. Danesbury sighed deeply. "Isabel shall not suffer, whatever betide the rest of us," he said. "I set aside long ago, in my own determination, ten thousand pounds as my daughter's marriage portion, and she shall have it on her wedding day; but some of my sons are giving me great anxiety. I have serious calls on my purse now."

"I am sorry to hear it, sir."

"It appears to me that young men nowadays think of little besides pleasure and reprehensible pursuits. It was not so when I was young."

"These boys of yours have been less fortunately situated than you were, sir. You were sheltered in your paternal home, and did not leave it: they have been cast abroad in this city of evil, without the protection of one. Rely upon it, if we would keep a young man steady, we must give him a home that he can find pleasure in. We must compass him about and shield him, as it were, with home influence. The want of this has been Lord Temple's bane: he said so this very day."

"There is a great deal in it," observed Mr. Danesbury.

"There is everything in it," warmly returned Mr. St. George, "provided a young man has good principles. I believe that many a mother, if impressed with the influence it must exercise for good or for evil, would make home pleasanter than she does for her growing sons. A bright, pleasant evening home, where he will find amusement, merry society, and loving faces, is a young man's greatest safeguard."

A pang shot across the heart of Mr. Danesbury. His wife had *not* made home pleasant to their boys. "I can but hope and pray," he said aloud, as he rose, "that as my sons grow in years, they may grow in prudence and wisdom, and redeem what they are doing now."

"Are you going out again, sir?"

"To see William. I have not seen him yet."

"He returns home in autumn, I hear, for good."

"Yes," replied Mr. Danesbury, "he joins us in the works."

"You will ask them all three to come and dine with you to-day, sir. Mrs. St. George is expecting them."

"Thank you. I will tell William; but the question is, where I am to pick up Robert and Lionel. We have not long left Robert, but he may not be found again. Lionel I have called on twice, but have not seen him."

Mr. Danesbury was leaving the room when Mr. Serle came in, having got rid of Captain Thomson.

"Danesbury, my wife says you must all dine with us to-day."

"We are engaged to Mrs. St. George."

"That's not fair," returned Mr. Serle; "Charlotte had you last time. You must promise us for to-morrow."

"I hope to get this business arranged to-morrow, in time to go back to Eastborough."

"Not a bit of it," laughed Mr. Serle. "You don't know Knighton & Jukes, if you think they are going to get over business in that style. They are the slowest practitioners in London."

Mr. Danesbury went out. Mr. Serle stood with his back to the fireplace for a moment before returning to his own room, whilst his junior partner sat down to his writing-table.

"What a scamp that Robert Danesbury is getting!" uttered Mr. Serle.

Mr. St. George looked up.

"He has been signing bills wholesale. Must have done it when he was drunk, I say. He will be got out of this mess, but Danesbury will have future trouble with him, as sure as my name's Mat Serle."

"Does he drink much?"

"He must. His looks and his shaking hands bespeak it. Besides, he could not be squandering away the money that he is, unless drink played its full share. I smelled it strong this morning when we were speaking to him; I don't know whether Danesbury did. I think the very demon of mischief possesses the young men. There's Charlie got into a scrape at college, through some drunken bout, and a whole lot of money and worry it will take to get him straight."

"Your son Charles, do you mean?" questioned St. George, in surprise.

"He, and no other. I had letters from Oxford this morning, one from Mr. Charles and one from his tutor. A pretty parson he'll make! And the companions that help him out, pretty parsons they will make! I wonder the heads of the university don't find means to stop them from making animals of themselves. They ought. The colleges should be models of morality."

"There is as much drinking going on at Oxford and Cambridge as there is elsewhere," observed Mr. St. George.

"One may slave and slave for ever to little purpose," irritably continued the senior partner. "There's Danesbury, working and laying by in his line; and I am doing the same in mine. Where's the use? If our children are to spend faster than we gain, where's the profit?"

Mr. St. George was biting the end of a pen, listening, and ruminating. "I have begun to think lately," he observed, "that the most fortunate position a young man can be placed in is to have no expectations; no money to depend on; nothing but his own exertions. I had nothing else, and the knowledge kept me steady, and I got on. The Danesburys think that they have their father's money to fly to, your sons think the same: perhaps if they knew there was nothing, they would lead different lives."

Mr. Serle looked cross and vexed. His hands were in his pockets, and he was rattling the silver in them. His sons had given him some trouble, though not, as yet, to a great extent. "Has Cargill been here?" he suddenly asked.

"No; but Lord Temple has."

"What did he want?"

"The old errand. Money raised."

"I should like to know what upon," crabbedly retorted Mr. Serle. "He has pretty nearly drained himself dry."

"He wants three thousand pounds by the twenty-fifth of the month."

"How much?" was Mr. Serle's astonished rejoinder.

"Three thousand pounds."

"Why, what has he been at to want that?" he resumed, after a pause.

"Play," was the short answer.

"There's another nice specimen for you, his lordship of Temple," sarcastically cried Mr. Serle. "Money, money, money, nothing but money; have it, he will; and when he has got it, throws it away like water. Well, if he does choose to reduce himself to poverty, he must do it: it's no affair of mine. By when, do you say?"

"The twenty-fifth. Can it be raised?"

"Oh, it can be raised; this can: but I can tell him there will soon be nothing left to raise upon. What possessed him to be such a madman as to lose three thousand pounds at play?"

"He was drunk when he did it," returned Mr. St. George. "Drunk when he played, and drunk when he gave his acknowledgment of the debt."

"There it is again! there's the evil. Charles pleads drunkenness as the cause of his embarrassment; Robert Danesbury owes his to drink. I wish all the filthy liquor was at the bottom of the sea!" Probably Mr. Serle forgot, as he spoke, that he partook pretty plentifully himself, every day.

"It would be all the better for some people," acquiesced Mr. St. George, in his quiet tone.

"To go and lose three thousand pounds at play! He is mad."

"He says he was perfectly senseless. Knew nothing about it then, and remembers nothing now."

"Nonsense, St. George! If a man is sane enough to play, and sign for his losses, he is sane enough to remember it."

The same reflection had struck Mr. St. George. Yet Lord Temple's word was strictly honourable.

Mr. Serle nodded his head, several little nods successively, as if he were at a loss for words. "It is fine to be these noble blades.

What a way of getting out of money! Disgraceful! Who holds the acknowledgment?"

"Swallowtail."

"Who?" sharply repeated Mr. Serle.

"Swallowtail."

"Swallowtail!" uttered Mr. Serle. How can noblemen lower themselves to associate with such a man? He would not be tolerated at their houses. But he is a clever man! Ay, not a man in the profession, or out of it, has keener brains than he. If the money was lost to Swallowtail—'ware Temple, for he must pay it to the hour."

Later, as Mr. Danesbury was standing by Charing Cross, on his way from Parliament Street, Lord Temple and his cab came driving by. The young nobleman saw him, and pulled up.

"Whither are you bound?" he inquired, when salutations were over.

"To Bedford Row," replied Mr. Danesbury.

"Allow me to drive you," said Lord Temple. "Get up behind," he added to his servant. So the man got out of the cab, and Mr. Danesbury got in.

"I am delighted to have met you," exclaimed Lord Temple, slackening the reins. "I have a petition to prefer to you, though I fear you will not entertain it."

"What is it?" said Mr. Danesbury.

"I am ashamed to ask it," returned Lord Temple, with a heightened colour. "I had better bring it out without any softening," he added, in a sort of desperation. "The fact is, sir, I want you to give me Isabel at once, and I have nothing to keep her on."

A pause of some minutes. Lord Temple's whip gently played with his horse's ears. He was entrenched in all the pride and prejudices of his rank, as Mr. St. George had remarked, and really believed that it was little short of an insult to Isabel, to make her, at the present moment, Lady Temple.

"What do you call nothing?" asked Mr. Danesbury.

"A thousand or fifteen hundred a year, or so. It is all that can be screwed from my estates. Do you think Isabel would risk it?"

"Not if her heart be set upon opera-boxes and court diamonds."

The young nobleman looked round at Mr. Danesbury in surprise. "St. George has been talking to you, sir?"

"Yes, he has," replied Mr. Danesbury. "I went into Serle's just after you left, and St. George, in doubt, I believe, whether I should think he had done right, told me what he had been recommending."

Lord Temple scarcely breathed. "Do you approve of it?" he asked at length.

"I think it would be a far happier life, both for you and Isabel, than the one you are leading; and I should entirely approve of it, but for one thing."

"What is that, sir?"

"St. George spoke of your extravagant evening habits. He did not enter into them, but I can give a guess at what they are. Unfortunately, I am getting experienced in the evil indulgences of a London life. Are you sure, sure beyond doubt, that you can put these entirely and for ever aside? Morally sure in your own heart, resolutely sure in your own self-reliance, under help from, and trust in, your Creator? Unless you are, I will not consent to give you my daughter. My lord, I trust implicitly to your honour for a truthful answer."

Excitement flashed in the face of Lord Temple, eagerness to his eye, as he grasped the hand of Mr. Danesbury. "So long as I am alone," he said, "I must keep up, in some measure, my evening habits; but from the moment that I am a married man, I forswear them. Nothing, no temptation, were it likely that such could be then offered me, would induce me to rejoin my present wild companions; I would not so far wrong my wife and myself. On my honour, as a British nobleman, by my sacred word, sir, I tell you truth."

"Then, Lord Temple, you shall have Isabel."

They reached Bedford Row. Mr. Danesbury went in and Mr. St. George came out. "Has anything been done?" he whispered. "Have you said anything to Mr. Danesbury?"

"I have said all," was Lord Temple's answer, whilst a radiant expression sat upon his countenance; "and he thinks, as you do, that it will be the best thing. I shall be ever grateful to you, St. George, for suggesting it to me."

"I think you might have suggested it to yourself all these wasted years. But, Lord Temple, I have all but passed my word to Mr. Danesbury, that, with your marriage, your reckless habits shall cease."

Lord Temple bent his head forward, and looked full in the face of Mr. St. George. "I have *sworn* that they shall. Be easy."

"Good. Have you seen Isabel?"

"No; she was out. I am going up again. I suppose you will give your permission now," he added, with a merry glance.

Mr. St. George returned it. "I would say, come and dine with us to-day at six, only that there's sure to be a plain dinner: nothing fit to set before a viscount."

"Thank you," laughed Lord Temple; "I will be sure to come. Bread-and-cheese will do, if there's nothing else." And once more Lord Temple whirled away.

Some ladies were waiting in the front drawing-room of a handsome house, contiguous to Hyde Park, on that hot July evening. It was getting close to the dinner-hour. Mrs. St. George, grown into a perfect little dumpling since her marriage, sat on a low chair, nursing a young gentleman in long, white petticoats; another gentleman, in short, full, velvet ones, the very shape of a fan, was making himself troublesome in all parts of the room; and a little girl, in a pink embroidered frock, had seated herself on the carpet. Mrs. Danesbury, wearing a lavender muslin dress and a cross look, was at one of the windows, and Isabel had knelt to play with the little girl. Her form was elegant, her bearing stately, as of old, but a somewhat sad look had settled upon her lovely face. The light of the sun shone on the smooth bands of her chestnut hair, and her blue eyes were dancing with merriment at the little lady's queer attempts to talk. She wore a light blue silk dress with a gold chain and golden bracelets. They had been out shopping all the afternoon—Mrs. and Miss Danesbury's chief object in accompanying Mr. Danesbury to town.

"You look tired, Aunt Eliza," cried Mrs. St. George.

"I am vexed," peevishly returned Mrs. Danesbury. "I thought Robert and Lionel would have been here to see me before this."

"How do you know they may not have called while we were out, mamma?" interposed Isabel. "Have you inquired?"

"No," snappishly replied Mrs. Danesbury. "Had they called, I should have been told of it."

"Servants forget sometimes," observed Mrs. St. George. "Walter, darling, come and ring the bell."

"Shan't," was lisped from the far end of the room.

"Oh! come and ring it for mamma."

"No," responded Master Walter, who was at some mischief with the pedals of the piano.

Isabel laughed, rose, and rang it. And the servant, in answer to inquiries, said that none of the Messrs. Danesbury had called.

"Are you sure?" cried Mrs. Danesbury, turning sharply on the man.

"Quite sure, ma'am. No one has been but one gentleman, and he called twice. He asked for Miss Danesbury, and his cab had a coronet on it."

"No need to wonder who that was, Isabel," smiled Mrs. St. George, as the servant retired. "I am sorry you were out."

"Ugh!" grunted Mrs. Danesbury, "no great compliment. If he would fix the marriage, it would be more to the purpose. I know this, if a gentleman asked me to be his wife, and then kept shilly-shallying, off and on, for years, he might keep his calls to himself. His affection for Isabel looks more like moonshine than reality."

There was an awkward silence. Kind Mrs. St. George was wondering what she could say to soften down the speech, and Isabel's heart beat visibly, when Mr. St. George entered.

"Has Mr. Danesbury got back yet?" he asked.

"No, he hasn't," returned Mrs. Danesbury. "Have you seen Robert?"

"I have not. I believe he has."

"It is very strange the boys could not call here. Unless Mr. Danesbury, with his stupid memory, forgot to say that we had come to town with him."

Isabel looked quickly up, longing to say that her dear father's memory was not stupid. But she rarely cared to enter the contradiction lists with Mrs. Danesbury.

The children were pulling Mr. St. George about, screaming and talking. "That's just like you, Charlotte," cried he, "filling the room with these little brats, to deafen your visitors." But he nevertheless took up the "little brats," and kissed them fondly.

"Have you been whipped to-day, Walter?"

"No, pa."

"I shall never teach mamma what's good for you: I know you have deserved it. There, run along. Isabel, step into this room with me. None of you, remember. Charlotte, call the children. I want to talk secrets with Isabel."

The back drawing-room was empty, and he closed the door between the two rooms. "Isabel," he began, "have you seen Lord Temple?"

"No."

"Then what will you give me for some news?"

She made no reply.

"I have been talking with Lord Temple to-day. He had got it into his head that you would not marry him unless he had a nobleman's allowance—which is any sum you may please to mention from ten thousand a year upwards—and I told him I thought he was mistaken: that you did not consider an army of footmen essential, or a mansion in Grosvenor Square. So I believe—now do not look so scared and conscious, or I will not tell!—I believe he means to ask you to take him as he is."

Isabel did look very conscious, if not scared; but at that moment there was a thundering peal at the house door.

"I thought I would whisper it to you, for you have been kept in suspense long enough: much longer than you should have been, had I been your nearest relative. May Heaven bless you, Isabel, and render your wedded life happy; and more prolonged than was your poor mother's!"

Mr. St. George went out of the room by the door leading to the staircase, leaving Isabel in agitation. The news was indeed sudden, and her chest was heaving wildly. Mr. St. George encountered someone on the stairs, and then came back, as Isabel supposed, into the room. He closed the door and advanced to her, but she was leaning with her elbow on the mantelpiece, her fingers shading her eyes. In another moment, two white, aristocratic hands were laid on her shoulders, and she looked up. A faint cry of surprise, and Lord Temple clasped her to him.

"No, no; stay here. It will soon be your own legal resting-place. My dearest, this suspense is to end, for I am to have you, poor as I stand. Your father has consented. Will you consent?"

She did not answer. Only let fall a few happy tears, and remained passively where he had placed her.

"It is not as it ought to have been," he continued to whisper, "but they say you will be content to risk it, until things come round. What I cannot give in riches, I will make up in love, Isabel."

"Worth far more than the other," she murmured.

"My darling! may you ever think so!"

At this moment the door opened, and Mrs. St. George entered so quickly that Isabel had no time to draw away. Viscount Temple raised his face, placed her arm within his, and stood there with her, proud, calm, self-possessed. Mr. St. George came following his wife quickly.

"Now, Charlotte! what can you possibly want?"

"I—I thought it was only you," stammered Mrs. St. George. "I did not know Lord Temple was here."

"Did I not tell you I had secrets to discuss with Isabel?" remonstrated Mr. St. George, with mock seriousness, while his wife looked from one to the other, and Lord Temple laughed to see her bewilderment. "What is there for dinner to-day?" continued Mr. St. George.

"For dinner?" she echoed.

"Because Lord Temple will do us the honour to partake of it."

"Oh—if I had but known! Though, indeed, I am very proud and pleased to see your lordship," she added, in her good-natured way. "Only I would have had something better; something different, I mean."

"I bargained for bread-and-cheese," said Lord Temple, "so if there should be anything more substantial than that, it will come as a surprise."

"Bread-and-cheese!" repeated Mrs. St. George.

"*Is* it bread-and-cheese?" gravely questioned her husband.

"How stupid you are, Walter! But it is a very plain dinner. I wish I had known."

"Is it suet dumplings?" continued Mr. St. George.

"Walter, then! It is a salmon, and a piece of roast beef. Nothing else in the world, except some pastry."

"We shall not fast, it seems," said Lord Temple. "It is a dinner for a prince."

"You are both laughing," she returned. "You are also laughing, Isabel. You must all have some secret."

"Which you shall know very shortly, dear Mrs. St. George, and the world also," answered Lord Temple.

Mr. Danesbury and William arrived, and they sat down to dinner. When the cloth was removed, the troublesome Master Walter and his sister were brought in. Mrs. Danesbury took the boy on her knee, and after supplying him with fruit, and other good things from the dessert, held her glass of port wine to his lips, that he might sip it. Mr. St. George immediately placed his hand over the glass. "No wine for the child, Mrs. Danesbury."

"Just a little sip," said she. "That rich cake must have made him thirsty."

"No wine," repeated Mr. St. George, in an unmistakable tone, as he poured out some water and handed it to the boy. "My children do not drink it."

Isabel, who was on the other side of Mr. St. George, between him and Lord Temple, presently took occasion to whisper, "Have you adopted Arthur's theory?"

"I have adopted your mamma's," replied Mr. St. George. "The evening that I dined with her at Mr. Serle's, many years ago now, the fatal evening of the accident, I heard her speak of the *duty* a parent owes a child, to encourage in him the love of pure water. It made a strong impression on me, and I inwardly resolved, if ever I had children, that it should be carried out. That boy has never tasted wine or beer yet, and I do not intend that he shall. Charlotte will tell you the same."

"You are drinking wine yourself," said Isabel.

"Yes: I was not brought up to drink water," significantly responded Mr. St. George. "But I do not exceed, Isabel."

There was an interruption ere he had well spoken. Lionel Danesbury entered. A good-looking, pleasant young man, something like William—curious that it should be so, for William resembled chiefly his own mother. Lionel was not tall, scarcely reaching middle height. He was in high spirits, and seemed very well.

"A pretty dance I have had after you, Lionel," cried Mr. Danesbury. "Four times I was at your rooms to-day, and could not find you in."

"I was at the hospital, sir. Thank you, Mrs. St. George, I have dined. I did not get the note my father left till six o'clock, so I went and had a chop first, for I knew you would have finished. How well you are looking, Isabel!"

A remark that made Isabel colour very much. Lionel sat down by his mother, and Mr. St. George passed him the wine.

"Good gracious, Lionel," cried Mrs. Danesbury, in a whisper, "how you do smell of tobacco smoke! What can make you smoke so much?"

"Ah!" laughed he, good-humouredly, "put you in my place, mother, in the dissecting-room, and you'd smoke yourself. I don't wish to upset you over St. George's dinner-table; but I should, if I were to tell you of the work we have to do there. A medical student must smoke in self-defence."

"When shall you pass, Lionel?"

"In the spring. Pass the Royal College of Surgeons—not the Physicians, you know, yet."

"Of course not And where do you think of setting up?"

"In London, of course. I intend to be a great man before I die, mother; and I hope you'll live to see it. 'Sir Lionel Danesbury, Baronet, M.D., Physician to Her Majesty the Queen.' Nothing less than the top of the tree will content me. Especially when I get a peer for my brother-in-law."

"Well, Lionel, I see no reason why you should not rise to the top," returned Mrs. Danesbury, as she looked at the merry eyes that glanced at hers over the glass of wine which he was drinking. "You have every advantage: ten times more than most young medical men have. If you will but be steady."

"Oh, I shall be steady enough," laughed Lionel.

Later in the evening, it was nearly eleven o'clock, in fact, and when they had given up hopes of seeing Robert, they heard an arrival. Mrs. Danesbury's face lighted up.

"There's Robert!" she exclaimed. "It is sure to be he."

Voices were hushed, and eyes turned to the door in expectation; but no Robert appeared; neither he nor anybody else. The hum of talking recommenced, and Mrs. Danesbury had flung herself back in her chair in angry disappointment, when a servant threw wide the door.

"Mr. Robert Danesbury."

Something exceedingly brilliant loomed in, throwing the room and everybody in it into the shade. It was Robert in full regimentals. He had been attending an official dinner, from which he said he could not get away earlier. The delay in mounting the stairs had been occasioned by his stopping in the hall to take off his sword. He was the least good-looking of the four sons, for he inherited Mrs. Danesbury's cross look and her cold eyes, but he was nearly as tall as William, and made a fine, upright soldier. Dressed as he was now, people were apt to say, What a handsome man! Mrs. Danesbury's heart warmed to him, and a glow of pride ran through her veins and greeted the regimentals.

"But, Robert," she whispered, "what is this that we hear of you? That you are acquiring dreadful habits, and get out of money as if it were dross."

"Tush, mother! If you believe that, you'll believe anything," returned the lieutenant. "What dreadful habits, pray?"

"I'm sure I don't know," said Mrs. Danesbury. "But your father worries himself to fiddlestrings over it, and Arthur looks as glum as he can look. You and Lionel are ruining them, they say."

"Of course they must grumble: such staid old codgers always do. If I do exceed my allowance a little, I can't help it: I must be like my brother officers. And you know they make money wholesale at the works, so they need not grudge a tithe of it to me."

"You might be more careful, Robert."

Robert smiled. "So my father said to me to-day; made me promise it, in fact; so I suppose I must be. Don't let them frighten you, mother. I am all right; but gentlemen must live as gentlemen."

A very self-apparent axiom to the mind of Mrs. Danesbury. She looked at her two sons, at the splendid Robert, the merry-hearted Lionel, till all she possessed of maternal pride glowed within her—and it was no slight share. "I don't believe half the croaking tales told of them," she whispered to herself. "They would not look so well, and be so merry, if they were going the wrong way. Folks are envious of them, it's my belief. It's true they do get out of money, Robert sadly, but I daresay he can't help it, and these works are like a mine of wealth."

"Isabel, my child," whispered Mr. Danesbury, as he kissed her when the evening was over, "I consented, because I think it will be better and happier both for you and Lord Temple. I have done it for the best, and I pray that it may prove so in the end."

CHAPTER XII
MRS. DANESBURY — THE WEDDING

THE rich tints of autumn were already tinging the trees, for October had come in, and the ground trod crisply under Isabel Danesbury's feet, as she walked briskly along to the house of Mrs. Philip Danesbury, a compact white villa, standing in the midst of an ornamental garden. Isabel found the Misses Heber out, and her aunt alone.

"I will take off my shawl, aunt," she said; "I am come to stay the day with you. Things were cross at home."

"Meaning Mrs. Danesbury, Isabel?"

Isabel nodded. She sent her things away by a servant, and sat down by the fire, which began to look cheerful in the autumn weather. Mrs. Philip Danesbury thought that her face wore a peculiar look of sad care. Her marriage was drawing near, and would be celebrated ere the month was out.

William Danesbury had returned home in the beginning of September for good, and Lionel, who had come down for a few weeks' holiday, was also at home.

"Has Lord Temple left, Isabel?"

"He left after breakfast this morning. He comes down again for a day or two next week, and then not again until—"

Isabel had answered without looking up, in an abstracted sort of manner, her gaze fixed on the fire. She brought her sentence to an end without concluding it, and then burst into a sudden flood of tears. Mrs. Philip could scarcely speak for concern.

"Child, what is this? Is anything amiss between you and Lord Temple?"

"No, no, aunt. I believe it is the contrast my own individual happiness presents to other troubles, looming in the distance, that makes me so sad. Aunt, it is about the boys. I fear they are going all wrong; I fear both William and Lionel have taken to drink deeply. They drink a great deal at dinner: papa, you know, takes very little wine. Reginald takes more than papa, but not so much as they do; still, it is not what they take at dinner, if it ended there, but afterwards they go out, and I am sure they get more."

Mrs. Philip Danesbury mused. "What a pity that they go out after dinner! Why does not your mamma strive to give them some home attraction?"

"Oh, aunt, there it is! there is where I feel that all is wrong. They may have acquired the habit of taking too much in town, but we ought to try and prevent them doing so, now that they are at home. And, instead of being helped out of their bad ways, they are being driven on in them. They are indeed. Mamma *will not* make home sociable for them, ask her as we will. They have wished her three or four times to have friends in the evening, and she will not."

"Ah!" groaned Mrs. Philip, "if your own dear, judicious mother had but lived! Young men must have evening society, and young girls, too, and there's no earthly reason why they should not. How goes the old rhyme, Isabel?—'All work and no play makes Jack a dull boy.' Keep up your sons too strictly, deny them pleasant evening hours at home, and they will inevitably seek for such elsewhere. Then, in nine cases out of ten, they lose themselves. Mrs. Danesbury ought to see this."

"But she cannot; will not: she makes home a dull, miserable place. We never hear anything more cheerful in the house than complaints of her headaches, and orders that we should be still. I do not like to speak against Mrs. Danesbury, aunt, but I cannot but see that my brothers are not dealt with as they ought to be."

"Headaches!" contemptuously returned Mrs. Philip, "for headaches read a querulous temper, and ill-conditioned frame of mind. That is how it has been with Mrs. Danesbury."

Isabel need not have apologised for speaking her mind, for certainly Mrs. Danesbury was a most ill-judging woman. A few mornings before this conversation, Lionel had gone to her, and leaning over her chair in his good-tempered way, said he wanted to ask her a favour.

"Well, what is it?" she returned.

"I want you to have the Boyds and the Ropers this evening."

"How can you be so unreasonable?" retorted Mrs. Danesbury. "The house is upset with the fuss kept up for Lord Temple, without the trouble of bringing other people into it."

"It can all go into the same fuss," jokingly returned Lionel. "But where's the trouble of having half a dozen folks to tea, and giving them a sandwich after it and a glass of wine? If there is any trouble, hand it over to the servants, there are enough of them. Now do, there's a good mother: we never have a soul here, we might as well be shut up in a monastery. I'll go and secure them; I want something to do this morning."

"I tell you, Lionel, I can't have them, and I won't be teased," was the reply of Mrs. Danesbury. "Rubbish about a monastery! the least noise or excitement gives me the headache. I can't have visitors, and that's enough."

Lionel flew into a passion. Though naturally sweet-tempered, he could be provoked to passion on occasions. He flung a book, which he happened to be holding, on to a side table, where it upset, and broke a beautiful candlestick of Bohemian glass, and swore aloud as he banged the door to after him.

"If a fellow tries to keep on the square, she won't let him," muttered he, as he strode across the hall.

Significant words!

Scarcely had Lionel left the room when, strange to say, William entered it, with a somewhat similar petition, though he had known nothing of that just proffered by his brother. His request was that Mrs. Philip Danesbury and her two nieces might be asked to spend the evening with them.

Mrs. Danesbury felt provoked; she believed that William and Lionel must be in league together, and she gave him a most harsh and unqualified refusal, demanding, with a sneer, if they thought to take Danesbury House by storm. Isabel had been privy to this, and she now related it to Mrs. Philip. "That night," she concluded, sinking her voice, and pressing her handkerchief to her eyes, "that night they came home the—the—worse for what they had taken!"

"Both?" uttered Mrs. Philip Danesbury.

"They did, aunt. We were gone to bed, but it was spoken of in the house the next morning; and last night it was the same again! Lionel also was not himself on Sunday night. Sunday night!"

A pause ensued. Mrs. Philip broke out. "Mrs. Danesbury has much to answer for. Some day I shall be telling her so."

"Whether mamma was up last night watching for them, I cannot tell," resumed Isabel. "It was past twelve when they came in, and she darted out of her room in her dressing-gown and saw them both. William could not walk straight, and Lionel was worse. He could not get up to bed without assistance. They were both had into mamma's room this morning before papa left it. I don't know what transpired.

Mamma did not appear at breakfast: she only came down when Lord Temple was leaving. Since then, she has been quarrelling with everyone. She quarrelled with papa; she abused William shamefully; she tried to quarrel with me. Altogether, it was so uncomfortable that I came here to you."

"Mrs. Danesbury is out of her mind," said Mrs. Philip.

"When she gives way to these fits of temper she is almost like it. This unhappy conduct of the boys—especially of Lionel—augments her irritation, and renders it unbearable."

"Isabel, you may depend upon it that she is blaming herself in her heart of hearts. She was foolishly indulgent to Robert and Lionel, and, when they were grown into young men, supplied them with a ruinous quantity of pocket-money; yet was always thwarting them in trifles, through her own crabbed temper, and making their home miserable. Anything like self-control or self-reliance she never taught them. I repeat that she will have much to answer for. And where are the boys now?"

"William went off to the works before mamma's storm was over; and Lionel departed towards Brookhurst with his gun, and said he should not be home for a day or two. Of course, all this is hard for papa to bear. My heart aches for him. Do you not think him very much altered, aunt?"

"Yes," shortly replied Mrs. Philip. "But we will go to other topics, my dear, for talking of this unhappiness will not mend it. Is your wedding-day fixed?"

"Yes," answered Isabel, with a rosy blush; "it is to be very soon indeed."

"When, my dear?"

"On the eighteenth."

"Why, that will be in a fortnight!"

"Yes, I said very soon."

"Not any too soon, Isabel. I hope, my child, you will enter upon a happier home than you have had with Mrs. Danesbury. The more I see of Lord Temple, the more I like him."

"Reginald has been, as it were, an isolated man, and has had to look abroad for ties of interest. I do hope the future may be happier for both of us. His mother died when he was at Eton, and no one has supplied her place to him. He says he shall tell me all his wild feats when we are married," she added, smiling; "and that, when I hear them, I shall wonder he can be as good as he is. Louisa Serle is coming down to the wedding."

"Indeed! As bridesmaid, I suppose? Who proposed that?"

"I did. Mamma has been so—so—"

"So very cross-grained altogether, and so indignant that Mary and Anna Heber should be two of your bridesmaids, that you proposed her niece Louisa as a sop in the pan," interrupted Mrs. Philip. "I understand it all, my dear; just as well as you do. She took a prejudice against Mary and Anna before they ever came near the place, and she retains it. I have never been able to tell why, for more excellently good girls, gentle, loving, and lovely, it would be difficult to find. I conclude she dislikes them as belonging to me, and I know she has always hated me like poison."

Isabel laughed. "I do think she is only jealous of you, Aunt Philip."

"Jealous of what? She is more favourably placed than I am. Her house is finer, her income is larger; she has a good husband and children: I have neither. Her position is in all points superior to mine, save that she grunts and grumbles away her days, and makes herself and everybody about her uncomfortable; and I keep up a cheerful spirit, and try to make folks happy, and myself with them. What has she to be jealous of, Isabel?"

"Perhaps of the cheerful spirit," answered Isabel. "But—talking of marriage—has it ever struck you, aunt, that Arthur has any particular attachment?"

Mrs. Philip Danesbury looked at her niece—a peculiar look. "Has it occurred to you to think so, Isabel?"

"Not quite to think so, perhaps, but to doubt whether it is so or not. I allude to Mary Heber."

"Just so," said Mrs. Philip. "It has been my opinion for a long while past that they are attached to each other, but I am almost sure that Arthur has not spoken to her of it in words. She has liked Arthur from the first moment she ever saw him—admired, respected him, thought him worthy of esteem. It is curious to observe how she unconsciously adopts all Arthur's ideas and opinions. And I feel equally sure that Arthur likes and admires her beyond anyone."

"Then it is strange he should not speak out," observed Isabel. "Mary would make him a good wife."

"She would. Such a wife as your mother made Mr. Danesbury. Save in fortune, she is a fit wife for the first lord in the land. She is worthy of Arthur Danesbury; I cannot give her higher praise than that. Arthur is very dear to me—dearer than she is; many a time have I held him in my arms and cried over him, wishing he were mine. It was at the time I was hoping for children, and they never came. I think I will tell you a secret, Isabel. Mary has had two very desirable offers of marriage. One was from Thomas Boyd—but, of course, this is between ourselves. She refused them both; therefore I cannot help thinking that her heart must be filled with somebody else, and that somebody, Arthur Danesbury."

"I should like Mary to be Arthur's wife. Aunt Philip," resumed Isabel, after a pause, "William promised to spend the evening here: I asked him to come for me. I thought it might be keeping him from other temptations. Here come Mary and Anna: what glowing colours their walk has given them!"

They hastened in when they saw Isabel; lady-like, sweet-looking girls, with well-formed figures, and elastic steps.

"I hope you have come to spend the day," called out Mary, as she took Isabel's hand.

"The whole day, till nine or ten at night," said Isabel.

"Oh, that's delightful!" uttered Anna. "What a talk we can have about the wedding!"

And a "talk" they did have: trust young ladies for that, when a wedding is on foot. Dresses, bonnets, veils, wreaths, gloves, and etiquette; carriages and bouquets; breakfast and ceremony; and Mrs. Philip was as eager as they were.

William Danesbury came in to tea, and they went from talking to mirth. Laughter abounded—that sort of laughter which is contagious, irresistible, though nobody can tell precisely what has caused it. William related to them some ludicrous story current in the neighbourhood, and that set them on. Then they had music and singing; and William's flute, on which he played well, happened to be there. At half-past nine, they thought it must be half-past eight, so gaily had the time passed. Soon after, Isabel put her things on.

"Now, William, mind your evenings are spent here as often as you like," said Mrs. Philip. "Isabel will be gone, and Danesbury House may be dull. And bring Lionel with you, so long as he is at home."

"All right, aunt, I'll come. But I can't answer for Lionel."

They said good-night, and walked fast over the road. Isabel's heart was beating. She wanted to say something, yet did not know how.

"William, I am so sorry that I am going."

"Sorry? You ought to be glad. Why are you sorry?"

"To leave you. I think I could make—I should try, if I remained—to make things pleasant for you at home."

"My time will be mostly taken up in the works, Isabel."

"I mean your evenings. I wish," she added, in a lower voice, "I could leave you as securely as I can Arthur."

"Oh, I shall be all right."

"Dearest William," she whispered, "let me say a word of advice. If you were really to take to—to—that dreadful habit, I think I should almost die of grief and shame. I am sure papa would. Will you try and overcome it for my sake?"

He hesitated. He was evidently perturbed. "I was thrown amidst random fellows in London, Isabel, fast spirits, every one of them; of course, I got led away now and then, but there will not be the inducement to it down here."

"Then how was it—last night—" She stopped in distress.

"Ah! one cannot get out of fast habits and into slow ones all in a minute," was his reply. "But it shall come."

Her tears were dropping fast. "Will you make me a promise, William; here, as we stand alone in the still night, with those glowing stars above us—that you will overcome this miserable failing?"

He was silent.

"William, do you hear me?"

"Whatever may be my faults, I hold a promise very sacred, Isabel: my father taught me that in my childhood, and I cannot forget it. I never undertake a promise lightly. Do not distress yourself so."

"I will put it somewhat differently," she sighed. "Will you try to overcome it, William?"

A moment's hesitation, and then a clear, steady answer: "I will try."

When the hall door was thrown open for them, William took out his watch and looked at it by the light of the hall lamp. It was a quarter-past ten. He was then turning from the door, but Isabel turned with him.

"You are not going out again to-night?"

"Just for half an hour."

"Oh pray, pray do not!" she urged. "Come in, and play a game at chess with me."

"Will you try . . . for my sake?"

Whether it was that his conscience whispered of the promise he had just made, or that he marked her pained, eager countenance, certain it is, he entered with her.

"A pretty time to come home!" was Mrs. Danesbury's greeting. "What made you so late?"

"It is not late, mamma," returned Isabel, who was rushing off her things in a violent hurry, as if she feared William would be off unless she sat down to detain him. She then pulled forward the chess-table, and began setting out the men.

"You are not going to begin chess at this hour?"

"There is plenty of time for a game," exclaimed Isabel. "I have challenged William to play with me. It is only a quarter-past ten."

"There's not time, and I want to go to bed," retorted Mrs. Danesbury. "I was up half of last night; if you want to know the reason, ask William."

"I think," said William, chafing at the allusion, and at Mrs. Danesbury's words altogether, "I had better go back and spend my evening in the town. I had promised a friend to do so, only Isabel over-persuaded me."

"Go out and disgrace yourself, and come home as you did last night, is that what you mean?" cried Mrs. Danesbury. "I should fancy you want bed, and might be contented to go to it."

William turned on his heel and left the room. Isabel darted after him. He was striding along to the hall door. She grasped his arm.

"Oh, William, William! do not go! Do not heed her!"

"Not go! does she think to send me to bed at ten o'clock at night, like a baby? I would have passed a rational hour at home with you, Isabel, and not have gone out; I had made up my mind to do it, and she has stopped it. Let me go, my dear."

Her features were pale, her hands were trembling, but she would not loose her hold.

"For my sake," she implored, "for my sake. Stay in, and we will have our game of chess. I shall tell Mrs. Danesbury so in papa's presence. Come back with me! Dearest William, I shall soon be gone: I ask you for my sake."

He scowled, hesitated, and finally turned back with her. She took his arm, and thus they went into the drawing-room. "Mamma," she said, approaching Mrs. Danesbury, "my brothers must be allowed proper amusement in their own home. You will forgive me, if I say I must play the promised game of chess with William."

It is probable the speech took everybody by surprise. Arthur rose from his seat and finished placing the chess-men, which Isabel's sudden movement had interrupted. It was plain on which side *his* influence would be given. He then drew her chair forward, and looked to William and Isabel. All this without speaking.

Mrs. Danesbury was livid with anger. She rose up, and confronted her husband.

"Am I to be bearded in my own house by your children? Are you going to sit tamely by, and see me insulted, Mr. Danesbury?"

Mr. Danesbury was grievously annoyed and perplexed, but the principles of justice were strong within him. He was also keenly alive to the necessity of keeping William indoors, could it be effected. "You take things in a wrong light," said he to Mrs. Danesbury; "in a calmer moment you will see it, I have no doubt. It is not yet bed-time; if the children have a mind for a game of chess, surely they may be allowed to gratify it. It need not keep you up."

"And you will suffer them to insult me in my own home?" she repeated, with concentrated passion.

"I would not suffer them to act to you in any improper way whatever; you know I would not, and you know that they would not attempt to do so. As to the home, Eliza, you seem to forget that it is theirs as well as yours." Many a less calm man would have been tempted to add, "And was theirs before you came to it."

Mrs. Danesbury flung out of the room, pushing one chair here and another there, screaming all sorts of outrageous things, as an angry woman, unsubdued by a Christian spirit, will do. Isabel made things comfortable, and sat down to chess with William. At about twenty minutes to eleven, Mr. Danesbury rose, and said he should go to bed.

"I suppose you do not mean to be late, children?" he said, in a pleasant tone.

"The game promises to be a long one: I conclude you do not wish us to leave it unfinished," spoke William, with a touch of resentment in his voice, for his spirit was still smarting under the words of his stepmother.

"My son," said Mr. Danesbury, "I have never denied innocent gratification to my children, or placed an unnecessary check upon their wishes. You know that I should not wish you to leave the game unfinished; neither should I wish to drive you to bed before you care to go. I only wish you would spend your time thus every evening. Good-night, my boy," he added, holding out his hand.

William rose and grasped it. "Good-night, dear father," he warmly said, full of contrition for having momentarily pained so good a father.

Presently, William rang the bell. It was for hot water. He told the servant to put out the brandy.

"You will not take it, William," whispered Isabel, when the man was gone.

"I must have a glass, Isabel, and I shall. I cannot forego everything at once."

"Arthur," she said, "beg him not."

"I wish he was like me," said Arthur—"did not like it." But that was all the remonstrance he ventured on. Arthur knew that too much remonstrance might be worse than none: that no man can be *coerced* from evil to good.

"You foolish girl!" uttered William: "if I never do anything worse in an evening than play at chess and drink one glass of brandy and water, I should think even Mrs. Danesbury ought to find no room to grumble. I will only take one: I *promise* you," he somewhat significantly added.

He drank his glass of brandy and water, but he took no more. The chess-men were put away soon after eleven, and all three drew round the fire for a cheerful chat, going up to bed about half-past. Isabel went inside her brother William's room. He kissed her fervently.

"Not many could have influenced me as you have to-night, Isabel. God bless you, my dear sister."

"May He bless you, William," she returned, with streaming eyes, "and keep you from temptation when I am gone!"

And every night, save two, by hook or by crook, did Isabel contrive to appropriate the evenings of William and Lionel. Now at chess; now by the help of music and Louisa Serle, who came down from town; now by a few other friends, invited for the evening, which Isabel made her approaching departure the plea to Mrs. Danesbury for insisting upon; and now at Mrs. Philip Danesbury's. Those two evenings they went out, but did not come home the worse for liquor, so far as could be seen. Isabel's hopes rose high; she thought they had not fallen so low as she feared.

And thus the wedding-day came on, and brought grand doings at Danesbury. All the sons were at home for it, many friends gathered at the house, and the whole of the workmen were feasted. There was a long and elaborate breakfast, after which Lord and Lady Temple left, to proceed to Dover, for they purposed passing some months on the Continent; and there was an elaborate dinner in the evening. It all passed off well, and the guests departed, full of high spirits and good wishes, suspecting nothing amiss. Only to the household was it betrayed that Robert and Lionel had been carried up to bed helpless, on this, their sister's marriage day.

CHAPTER XIII
A DISCOVERY

LONDON was empty. The hot days of July had contributed to thin it. But now that August had come in, everybody was getting away. "Except myself and a few more drudges," thought Mr. St. George, as he stood at the window of the clerks' office, looking out on the hot and dusty road. It was close upon the Long Vacation. There was little doing, and even Mr. Serle had gone for a fortnight to his family, who were sojourning at Brighton. One of the clerks crossed the street, passed the window, and entered.

"Well?" said Mr. St. George to him. "Is the man in, all safe?"

"No, sir. The man's out. The money's paid."

"Paid!" echoed Mr. St. George, as though the information afforded him considerable surprise.

"I have got it here, sir, expenses and all."

Mr. St. George turned, went into his own room, and the clerk, first hanging up his hat, followed. He took from his pocket a fifty-pound note, and laid it before Mr. St. George. "I gave the change, sir, twenty-five shillings and ninepence."

"If the man—Pratt, or whatever his name is—had got the money, why did he give all this trouble?" exclaimed Mr. St. George.

"He had not got it, sir. It was his wife. When she saw the man was really in possession, she said she supposed there was nothing for it but to pay, for she could not have the children's beds taken from under them. So she went into the back room, and brought out this note. She cried, when she handed it to the man, and said she had had it by her ever since her husband gave it her, twelve months ago, and had kept it to apprentice out the eldest boy, but she must let it go now."

"Curious!" remarked Mr. St. George. "Did not her husband know that she had it?"

"No: I am sure he did not. He was as much astonished as I was. He said to her, perhaps, as she had got that, she had got another, and she sobbed bitterly, and said she had not another halfpenny in the world. She seemed quite a lady, though she was dressed poorly."

"It is a pity she did not produce it before, and save expense," remarked Mr. St. George, as the clerk retired. "I wish Serle would not meddle with these nasty, paltry things," he added to himself. "Taking children's beds from under them! I would not, if I were head of the firm. They turn in little profit and no credit. When people bring in this dirty sort of work, they should be sent away to find others to dabble in it for me. Holloa! what's this?"

Mr. St. George's eye had fallen on a name written on the back of the note, "Victor d'Entraigue."

There was nothing in the name itself, for he had never known anyone who owned it; but what had caused his exclamation, was a sudden conviction that that same note had passed through his hands before. He had a perfect recollection of the name, and also of the long, sprawling writing—the two words taking up two lines across the back of the note—from one side to the other.

"Now, where did we pay away that note, that it could come into the hands of such persons as these Pratts must be?" thought he. "Why! it was one of those handed by Lord Temple to Swallowtail, to liquidate that gambling debt of three thousand pounds."

Mr. St. George had never been satisfied, in his own mind, upon the circumstances of that loss. He had often ruminated over them, but could never solve the point of Lord Temple—or anyone else—having been able to play and sign away money in a state of utter unconsciousness. The engagement of Lord Temple to Isabel, and their subsequent marriage, had given him an interest in that nobleman beyond what he felt for the generality of clients. Lord and Lady Temple had just returned from the Continent; they were then in London, and he had been to see them only two evenings before. But of this more presently.

Mr. St. George leaned back in his chair and ruminated. He had a faint idea that this Pratt was connected with gamblers; but he knew nothing of him beyond what their client, who had given them instructions to proceed against him for a debt, had related. For twelve months the woman said she had had the money: it was rather more than twelve since the transaction between Swallowtail and Lord Temple; therefore, the inference to be drawn was that she had received it at the time. "Now," thought Mr. St. George, who was a long-headed man, with a remarkable facility for sifting details, "if Lord Temple lost that money to Swallowtail, why should fifty pounds of it be given to Pratt? It looks as if it had been a stop-gap."

Mr. St. George touched his bell. "Send Hadden to me," said he, as a clerk answered it.

The same man who had brought the money came in. "Hadden," cried Mr. St. George, "do you know anything of this Pratt, who and what he is?"

"I do not, sir. I never saw or heard of him till now; but the man whom Checkett sent in seemed to know him. He said, when we came away, that he was glad it was settled, for Pratt was not a bad fellow, and was nobody's enemy but his own. It is not often those sort of men find pleasure at such a termination."

"Did he say what Pratt was?"

"He said he once was very respectable, but had got down in the world, and was now a marker—or whatever they call it—at a gaming-house in St. James's Street."

"Ah," said Mr. St. George, in a tone as if he had expected the information. "I want to have a word with this Pratt," he continued. "Can you get him here?"

"I daresay I can, sir."

"Go and see."

Hadden was successful in his errand, and returned with Mr. Pratt: a thin, shabby-genteel man, with something of the gentleman about him still. He had a pale face, with hollow cheeks and hot lips. Mr. St. George pointed to a chair, and then took out the bank-note.

"A seizure was put into your rooms this morning, Mr. Pratt," he began, "and you settled it by means of this note. I want a little information about it. I have seen it before."

Pratt's face turned of a different white, more ghastly. "There—there's nothing wrong about the note, is there, sir? It is not a bad one?"

Mr. St. George locked up the note before he answered. He purposely abstained from relieving the man as to the false scent he had got upon. "Where did you get the note?" asked he. "I must know."

"Sir, if there's anything wrong about it, I never knew it. I am as innocent of it as I can be."

"Whatever there may be about it, wrong or right, I will hold you harmless, provided you tell me all you know of the transaction by which it came into your hands. Of that I pledge you my word."

"I got it a long while ago, sir."

"How long? What date?"

"I can't state it, for certain. It was last summer—in July or August, I think. I could tell, perhaps, by hunting up dates."

"How did you get it?"

"I got it paid me with another. The other was good, sir, I'll swear to it; for I changed it at the Bank of England."

"But I ask how you got them?"

"Somebody was owing me money, a hundred pounds, and paid me with these two notes."

"Mr. Pratt," said the lawyer, "it is of no use for you to beat about the bush. I told you I would hold you harmless of all consequences, provided you gave me the information I required. If you will not do that, say so. 'Somebody was owing me money,' won't do for me."

"Well, sir, I got them from Swallowtail. Lawyer Swallowtail, as he is sometimes called. He had to pay me one hundred pounds, and he did pay me with these two notes. In the flush of having the money, I went home and gave my wife one of them. When mine was spent, I asked her for the other, and she stood to it that she had spent it in paying debts, and buying things for the children; but it turns out now that she has kept it ever since, sewn up in her stays. Badly enough at times have we wanted money, but she never brought it forth. Our eldest boy possesses a wonderful talent for architecture; he has made drawings of all the public buildings, and beautiful structures, cathedrals, palaces, and things, out of his own head. His mother's heart is set, like his, upon his being placed with an architect, and she had kept the money to help him to one, and never brought it forth. But when she saw all the sticks and stones going this morning, out it came."

"Did Swallowtail lose it to you at play, at the gambling-house in St. James's Street?"

The man was surprised and looked up. Mr. St. George's keen dark eyes were fixed on him.

"Not at play, sir. Mr. Swallowtail calls himself one of the nobs, and I only hold a subordinate position there. He would not play with me."

"But, at anyrate, it was the proceeds of a gambling transaction; if not between you and Mr. Swallowtail, between Mr. Swallowtail and somebody else," calmly repeated Mr. St. George.

Pratt was silent.

"And the 'pull' out of the affair—that is the orthodox word, I believe—was three thousand pounds."

Mr. Pratt could not answer, he could only stare. "Do you know anything about it, sir?" he at length uttered.

"I know all about it," replied Mr. St. George, in a firm tone, "save some of the minor details, which you can supply. This money was chiselled out of Lord Temple when he was dead drunk."

No answer.

"In the presence of you, and Swallowtail, and Major Anketel," continued Mr. St. George, venturing on some guesses. "How many others were there?"

Mr. Pratt hesitated. "I should have no objection to answer your questions, sir; I thought it a shameful thing at the time—a dead robbery, many a poor fellow has been transported for less; but if it should come round to Swallowtail that I have spoken, it would be ruin to me."

"It shall not come round to anyone," said Mr. St. George, "your name shall never be mentioned by me in the business; and, indeed, I very much question whether your friend Swallowtail will ever know that the affair has been spoken of at all."

"Is the note a bad one?"

"There's nothing the matter with the note. I want to know how the money was drawn from Lord Temple. When he went into the gaming-house that night with Anketel, he was completely intoxicated, and lay on the sofa asleep. How was it he got playing? Earl Sandlin, Sir Robert Payn, young Eden, Lieutenant Danesbury, and others, were there."

"Several were there when Lord Temple and Anketel came in, but they left. By three o'clock all had gone, except Anketel and Lord Temple."

"And Swallowtail," interrupted Mr. St. George.

"And Swallowtail: but we look upon him as one of the establishment. Besides these, there was not a soul in the room but me, and I had sat down in the corner behind the refreshment table, wishing they would leave, that we might shut up for the night. Swallowtail and Anketel were whispering together over the fireplace, and presently they both came up to Lord Temple, pulled him off the sofa, and set him up in an arm-chair at the green table. Swallowtail got the cards to begin écarte. I think Lord Temple was worse than when he came in, more stupid. He could not hold the cards, but dropped them as fast as Anketel put them in his hands, and his head fell, unconscious. 'It's of no use,' said Swallowtail, 'he is too bad, he couldn't write. Could we guide his hand?' 'No,' answered Anketel, 'that would bear the marks of our handwriting, not his.' 'I'll tell you what, though,' cries Swallowtail, bringing his hand down on the board with such a thump that some dice sprung off it, 'I have got that I.O.U. for thirty pounds in my pocket, we can work the oracle with that.' 'Change the figures?' whispered Anketel. 'Add to the oughts,' said Swallowtail, 'and go snacks.' They helped Lord Temple back to the sofa," continued Pratt, "first of all trying to make him drink some brandy. A tumbler half-full of the neat spirit had been left on the mantelpiece, and they held it to his lips. I think he swallowed a little, but the rest went on to the front of his clothes. Beautiful diamond studs he had in his shirt that night!"

"But were you in the room during this?" cried Mr. St. George.

"I was in the seat that I tell you of, sir, and had not moved from it; and, from an angle, I could see most of what was going on. It is a crimson velvet chair, low and small, standing against the wall at the back of the refreshment-table, and anybody sitting in it would not be noticed by those at the play-tables. If you go to the place this very night, there you'll see the chair."

Mr. St. George thought that he would rather be excused the errand. "Proceed," said he.

"Major Anketel reached the pen and ink, and Swallowtail took a piece of paper from his pocket-book. 'I think the date will be just the ticket,' said Swallowtail, with that knowing wink he emits from his sharp, black eyes. 'It is dated the first, and this is the eleventh; if we add another one that will be right." 'Stop a bit,' said Anketel, snatching up the I.O.U., 'Temple will recognise this again, and know that it has been altered.' 'He'll no more recognise it than my grandmother will,' answered Swallowtail, 'he is entirely oblivious of having given it me. He was three parts gone then, or he would have written the amount in letters, instead of figures: though he could hold the cards, it was as much as the bargain.' 'That's the worst of Temple,' cried Anketel, 'so long as he keeps his noddle clear, there's no drawing him into play; it's not often he get's screwed tight enough to be of use to one. But is it safe he won't know this?' 'It's safe and certain,' said Swallowtail; 'he has no recollection such a thing is out. The other night, in this room, Groves was trying to reckon up how many of the sort he had got out, and Temple said he had none, thank the stars, he was clear, and intended to keep so. I had a great mind to produce it then, but thought another opportunity might be better.'"

"And so they altered Lord Temple's acknowledgment for thirty pounds into three thousand pounds!" exclaimed Mr. St. George. "They are nice jail-birds!"

"I did not know what they altered it into," returned Pratt; "all I heard was, that they would add to the oughts. But I heard Lord Temple's loss spoken of afterwards, over the tables, and found that it was three thousand pounds."

"Well—about your own share?"

"Swallowtail put up the memorandum, and Anketel said he would go, and he left. Then Swallowtail came to the refreshment table, and there he saw me. 'Holloa!' quoth he, 'are *you* here? What are you doing?' 'Nothing,' said I; 'only waiting to know if anybody's going to play again.' I never saw Swallowtail so taken to as he was then," continued Pratt. "You know him, of course, Mr. St. George, and must be aware that, for all his demure, quiet face, with its innocent-looking, turned-up nose, and his polished manners, there's not a more hardened or a deeper man going; but all the brass had gone out of him then. 'Pratt,' said he mildly, 'how's that clever boy of yours? Drawing still, and getting on?' 'He's drawing for ever,' I answered, 'but as for getting on, he wants instruction, and I can't afford it him.' 'I'll help you to afford it him,' said Swallowtail; 'I won't forget. What you told me has made me take an interest in him. Good-night, Pratt. See to his lordship.' I took that offer for what it was worth, sir," added Pratt, "never thinking it was worth anything, and Swallowtail went away. I called a man, and we got Lord Temple down to his cab, and hoisted him in. A week or two after that, Swallowtail called me aside, and gave me the two fifty-pound notes, saying they were to help the boy. Of course, I knew what that meant."

"And you accepted them, knowing, at the same time, that they were hush money, the proceeds of as nefarious a robbery as ever was perpetrated!" uttered Mr. St. George.

"When you are as low down in the world as I am, sir, which I hope will never be, you will not stop to look at how money's obtained when it's put into your hands," cried Mr. Pratt. "Low as I have fallen, badly off as my wife and family often are, I would not have joined those two fellows in doing it. But they did do it; and to split upon them would have been almost as much as my life was worth. Servants attached to gambling-houses may not tell the secrets enacted in them. They would make sober folks' hair stand on end. And, suppose I had refused the hundred pounds? it would have been doing Lord Temple no good; only adding to Swallowtail's booty. You need not reproach me, Mr. St. George: when the dark mood is upon me, I reproach myself keener than anybody else can do."

"What do you mean by the dark mood?"

"When I have got no drink in me, sir. I was brought up, you know, a gentleman—though you may not see much remains of it about me now—and the shame, the remorse, the physical depression that overwhelm me are so great, I must of compulsion drink to drown them, even if the habit were not upon me. But it is. I am obliged to be sober at night, for my work in St. James's Street, but I am rarely so at other times, unless money fails."

"What profession used you to follow? Any?"

"The medical," was the answer, after a slight pause of surprise. "I have not followed it much, for evil habits overtook me before I had well done walking the hospitals. I do not think any young men, as a class, are so much given to drink as medical students. A youngster, coming fresh among them, can hardly help falling into the habit: the example set him is too potent."

The remark made Mr. St. George's thoughts flow for the moment towards Lionel Danesbury.

"I half ruined my father, I completely tired out my other friends, and now I am attached to a gaming-house. I am ready to kill myself at times when I think of my wife and children. The little girl, thank Heaven, is at Eastborough. They have taken to her."

"Eastborough!" echoed Mr. St. George, in a startled tone, "you are surely not—not—you are no relation to Mr. Pratt, the surgeon, there?"

"Only his son. I thought you knew me, Mr. St. George. Is it possible you did not?"

"I am sorry for you!" uttered Mr. St. George, with deep feeling. "I did not recognise you. But you are yet a young man—so to say;

you are not forty. Surely you might, even now, reform, and become a respectable member of society, a protector to your children."

"Never," returned the unfortunate man. "I have tried in vain: the habit is too strong upon me. No; miserable and guilty as I am now, so I must go on to my grave; lost in this world, and, I suppose, lost in the next."

"And your only failing, a love of drink?"

"My only failing," he emphatically replied. "I was kind, just, honourable, well-intentioned. Whatever bad things drink has caused me to do, I should never have done them without it: now, it is excitement; now, it is despondency; both hard to bear, and both urging to sin."

"Are you very poor?"

"Mostly so. It is up and down with us. Sometimes my wife's relatives help us, and sometimes I have a slice of luck at the tables—not at the one in St. James's Street, I am only a servant there, but I frequent others in the day. We have managed to live. I thought that bill would have done us up, and turned us wanderers into the streets. Ah! that was another consequence of drink. I signed that bill for six-and-thirty pounds, at three months' date, when I was nearly as bad as Lord Temple was: a swindling fellow got hold of it: I was sued upon it, and the expenses mounted up. I never had the benefit of a sixpence from it, sir, never the value of a brass farthing."

"You say you want to place your son with an architect?"

"It will be of little use wanting. Even if his mother's friends would keep him in respectable clothes, which they have partly promised, I could never find the premium, and nobody will take him without, for I have no interest to get him in anywhere. Yet, it's a pity," added the unhappy man, with a sigh: "when a lad shows extraordinary genius for art, which of course must have been specially granted him, it's a pity it cannot be fostered and brought to fruit. He is near fourteen."

"Has he been educated?"

"Oh, yes. Not regularly, but he has had snatches of it; one quarter at school, and one away, and he's a clever boy, and has improved what he has had; he would not disgrace any office. He is a very steady boy, very good principled."

"I will think about it for you," said Mr. St. George. "A friend of mine is an architect, and I will inquire whether boys can get into an office without premium: perhaps he may be induced to take him, if his talent is so decided. I should tell my friend the circumstances," added Mr. St. George: "I could not in honour do otherwise: and, before speaking, I must see and converse with the boy myself. I was once, when a lad, laid up with an illness at Danesbury House, and your father brought me through it, and was very kind to me. I am sorry to meet you thus."

Mr. Pratt rose. He would have thanked Mr. St. George for the glimpse of hope for his son, but his voice was husky, and his eyes watered. Had that man always possessed the moral courage to eschew the dangerous vice, he would have been beloved and respected: as it was, he slunk through the clerks in the front office, self-ashamed and self-condemned.

In the course of the afternoon, Mr. St. George went up to Lord Temple's. He and Lady Temple were occupying temporary apartments in Brook Street. A slice of good fortune had befallen Lord Temple: which, indeed, had brought them to England somewhat quicker than they had contemplated. A great-aunt of Lord Temple's had died, and left him her town house, a small one, at Kensington, and fourteen thousand pounds. He had been previously thinking of turning his talents to political utility: his wife also wished it, she urged that his time was not given him to waste: and this house and legacy decided it. He determined to make it his residence, and become a useful man. The house was now being renovated and fitted up: some of Mrs. Dacre's old furniture was being disposed of, and new purchased in its place: and they intended soon to take possession.

When Mr. St. George had called in Brook Street two evenings before, Major Anketel was sitting there. Mr. St. George had not a good opinion of the Major, and was vexed to find Lord Temple again in contact with him. Isabel was well, and truly happy. She had found Lord Temple all she had thought him. Like many another man, like nearly all men, Lord Temple was only wild when led away by example: and, since his marriage, he had been subjected to nothing but good influence.

This afternoon, after the departure of Pratt, Mr. St. George proceeded to Lord Temple's, and he went there with one settled purpose—to put him on his guard against Major Anketel. Lady Temple was alone when he went in, and Mr. St. George thought he had never seen her look more lovely: she wore an elegant black silk dress, and small, white lace cap. Lord Temple soon entered. He was going down to Richmond with Lord Sandlin to dine. Mr. St George requested a private interview, and Lord Temple took him into another room.

"What dreadful plot have you to disclose," he laughed, "that you could not speak before Isabel? I have no secrets from her."

"My lord—about telling her, you can do as you please: but it would not have been proper for me to speak of it in her presence unsanctioned by you."

"How grave you are!" uttered Lord Temple.

"That three thousand pounds you lost at play to Swallowtail—which we had to raise for you—you remember?"

"Isabel knows of it," he eagerly answered. "I told her everything I had ever done, and assured her it lay with her to keep me right for the future. I told her I had been such a wicked fool as to get dead drunk, and then lose three thousand pounds."

"Then, as there is so much confidence between you, I might have spoken before her, and I hope you will let her hear the sequel. You never lost the money."

"Never lost it!" echoed Lord Temple. "What do you mean? I lost it, and paid it."

"You paid it, but you did not lose it. It has come to my knowledge—my positive knowledge, Lord Temple, though I cannot tell you in what way, for I am under a promise not to do so—that Major Anketel and that blackleg Swallowtail, concocted a plan to swindle you out of it."

"I do not understand," cried Lord Temple. "I remember nothing about playing, as I told you, or of giving the I.O.U., but there it was, in my own handwriting. They could not have swindled my writing out of me."

"I will explain. That transaction took place on the eleventh of July. On the first of the month, some days before, you had also been the worse for wine, had played with Swallowtail, lost, and given him an I.O.U. for the amount, thirty pounds."

"What!" said Lord Temple. "How many more I.O.U.'s will you say I gave?"

"My lord, you gave the one for thirty pounds, you did, indeed, though you might not and did not remember it. On the eleventh, all who had gone into the gambling-house left, except Anketel and Swallowtail. They dragged you up from the sofa and put you to the table, no doubt intending you to go through the farce of playing and losing, and then giving them a note of hand for the amount. But you were too far gone, you were nearly senseless, and could not hold the cards.

So they were baulked. But Swallowtail thought of a bright scheme. He had this I.O.U. for thirty pounds in his pocket; you had written the debt in figures, not in words; and he proposed to Anketel to add oughts to the thirty. And it was done."

The Viscount had gradually leaned forward over the table: his lips open, his eyes strained on Mr. St. George.

"Nothing else was wanted, save the alteration in the date. A 1 was added to the other 1, and eleven stood out complete. That was the three thousand pounds you paid."

"Can this be?" uttered Lord Temple.

"As truly as that you and I are sitting here, Lord Temple. I always suspected that Anketel was a bad man: we had to do with him a year or two ago, and found him anything but square. Besides, he has no income: how can he live? Swallowtail I need not enlarge upon: he is known. I came up this afternoon to tell you this, and to put you on your guard against Anketel. I saw him here the other night."

"You won't see him here again," cried the impetuous young nobleman. "If he enters a room where I am, I will leave it; or he shall. By Jove! I would rather associate with a Botany Bay convict."

"As to taking proceedings against them, I suppose it cannot be. In the first place, the evidence—"

"No, no," interrupted Lord Temple, "I will not rake up, and make public, a transaction so disgraceful to myself, even to punish them. I would not do it, for my wife's sake. They have got the money; and they spent it, no doubt, long ago: let them keep it, and I must put up with the theft—and serve me right for my pains! Thank you, St. George. That wretch Anketel came the other night to entice me out, and dared to affect a contemptuous surprise when I would not go. The villain; he wanted to try his hand again at making me forget myself."

"No doubt of it. The very night they robbed you, he openly lamented to Swallowtail, that you would not play unless you were 'screwed,' and that you got so too seldom."

Lord Temple rose in excitement, and paced the room. "And the worst of it is, that I must bury this in silence!" he chafed. "I cannot proclaim the fraud without proceeding against them."

"To bury it in silence will be the best plan in every way," said Mr. St. George. "There is no other alternative, but the one of proceeding against them, and that is not convenient. Only, keep clear of them for the future, Lord Temple."

"You need not tell me that, St. George," was the emphatic reply.

They returned to the presence of Lady Temple. Lord Sandlin was expected every moment, for he was to drive the Viscount to Richmond, to this all-important dinner.

"As Lord Temple will be out, why should you not come with me to see Charlotte, and take a plain dinner with us?" said Mr. St. George to Lady Temple.

"I do not know why," answered she; "I should very much like to see her and the children. She called here to-day, but I was out."

"Do, Isabel," cried her husband; "it will remove all the compunction I have in leaving you."

So Lady Temple put her things on, and, as she came back to the drawing-room from doing so, a servant entered, and said that Lord Sandlin waited. They all went downstairs together. "Good-bye, my dearest," whispered Lord Temple, shaking hands with his wife.

Lord Sandlin was in a—vehicle, half dog-cart, half commercial traveller's "trap," though he would probably fly into a rage did he hear it called so, for it had been built under his own special invention and superintendence. He was a short, sandy-haired man, very fat, with a profusion of whisker, and a face all one colour, and that scarlet. He tore off his hat when he caught sight of Lady Temple. The Viscount ascended to the seat beside him; and Mr. St. George could not help contrasting them as they sat side by side—the one all elegance, looking every inch a nobleman, the other like a young prize-fighter. The groom stepped up to his seat, which was placed back to back with the others, and they drove away, the lords once more raising their hats to Lady Temple.

CHAPTER XIV
A MAD ACT

AN all-important dinner was this dinner at "The Star and Garter" at Richmond, its anticipation having kept the partakers of it in town longer than they would otherwise have remained. It was the settlement of a bet which Lord Sandlin had lost to Sir Robert Payn. Of the twelve to assemble, one had been kept away by a death, and Lord Temple was invited to supply his place. They were all of the species denominated "fast," and not one but was a tolerably hard drinker. Had Lord Temple been solicited to join these men in a midnight revel, he might now possibly have declined, from fear of contagion; but to refuse on that score the dining with them in open daylight never entered his mind. It was a splendid feast, both as to wines and viands; and they all ate and drank well save one, and that one was—not Lord Temple.

It was Sir Robert Payn. He was suffering from illness, and took scarcely anything. The rest drank deeply—deeply even for them. After dinner (because they had not taken enough), they began upon cigars and punch and brandy—in short, upon anything that their hot throats fancied; and when they started for London they were gloriously uproarious, and terrified quiet dwellings as they passed by their noisy shouting.

Lord Temple had some very slight sense left in him, and told Earl Sandlin's groom, who then had the reins, to drive to his house. The earl whispered a contrary order, and the man of course obeyed his master. Lord Temple subsided into sleep; and when he woke he was stumbling up some stairs. He soon saw, though imperfectly, where he was—at the gaming-house in St. James's Street. Some half-dozen of the diners had agreed to resort thither. Lord Sandlin was one, and he had carried his friend with him.

"I must go home, Sandlin," hiccuped Lord Temple. "My wife is alone. I told you she'd be home early."

"She is not alone," returned the earl. "I sent to ask, and they said she was stopping for the night where she went to dinner."

"No!" uttered Lord Temple.

"Fact," stuttered the earl. "She stopped because she did not expect you back."

Of course this was an impromptu invention of the earl's; but Lord Temple, perfectly truthful himself, and most imperfectly in his faculties, took it in. Down he sat on a sofa. Somebody mixed him a glass of brandy and water. He drank it mechanically, simply because it was put into his hands, and in five minutes was asleep again. The others were helping themselves to brandy and water.

It was not very clear how long he remained there. Two or three hours. The room was in an uproar the whole of the time: laughing, talking, drinking, gambling, stupefying, and sleeping. Some went in, some went out; and Lord Temple slept through it.

He was aroused by someone roughly awaking him. He got his eyes open, after a struggle, his senses partially so, and looked up. It was Major Anketel. Lord Temple rose into a standing posture, cast aside the major's help with unmistakable scorn, and steadied himself on the arm of the sofa.

"S—S—Sandlin, is the ca—cab waiting? I'm going."

"Sit down again," said Lord Sandlin, "and don't bother."

"I—I—I'm going, I tell you, Sandlin. I can't sit down with blacklegs. There's one in the room." His lordship would probably have said "two," but his eye had not yet caught sight of Swallowtail.

A consternation. All turned round to gaze.

"You are dreaming," observed Lord Sandlin.

"Come along," said Major Anketel, in a coaxing tone, as he laid hold of Lord Temple. "I'll give you a hand at—"

"Off, sir!" shouted Lord Temple, livid with scorn and rage, in the midst of his brain's confusion, "how dare you touch me! Gentlemen," he stuttered, "this man, whom we have suffered so long to associate with us, is a cheat and a swindler, a man to herd with *roués* and felons. He gets his living by his tricks, and we suffer. Off, I say, fellow! Do not presume to touch me: I am a peer of the realm!"

Poor Lord Temple! had he been sober, he would have contented himself with walking out of the room as Major Anketel walked into it. Certainly, he never would have said the half or the quarter of what he did say, but for the demon he had imbibed into him: *that* spoke; he did not. What followed, none of them could have told distinctly afterwards: Anketel gave Lord Temple the lie, and the room was as a Bedlam; shouts, oaths, questions. Some espoused Lord Temple's part, one or two Major Anketel's. Lord Sandlin, thinking, as he said afterwards, that the Viscount had got a sudden attack of brain fever, dashed over his head a large decanter of water. As if feeling that water was what he wanted, Lord Temple seized another decanter, and drank glass after glass of it. And this partially sobered him. What was to be done?

He must either make good his charges, or go out with Major Anketel.

No, he would not. He, Lord Temple, go out with a blackleg!

"Will you go out with ME?" cried Colonel Groves. "I espouse Anketel's quarrel. I am no blackleg."

As he spoke, he struck Lord Temple on the cheek; his fist was keen, and the blood trickled down. The Colonel was a close and intimate friend of Anketel's. "Birds of a feather flock together." Not very long after this period, the two were caught out in a disreputable transaction—and then people remembered the words of Viscount Temple.

A hostile meeting was hastily arranged: they would go out with the first glimmer of the dawn, and fight it out. Sir Robert Payn was the only one cool enough to raise his remonstrance against it. Duels were no longer "in," he said; they had been put down by public opinion. Let them stop till to-morrow, when they should be calm, and no doubt Temple's words would be explained away. He was drunk, and not responsible for what he said. Would they go out like madmen, and shoot each other to blazes? Nobody did it now, but French students at St. Cyr, or Austrian gamblers.

Sir Robert Payn's words were wasted, his advice unheeded. All around were little better than what he said, madmen: their blood was fired. Earl Sandlin proposed to second Lord Temple; and the Honourable George Eden, Colonel Groves.

It was carried out. With the gray break of early morning they started: Lord Sandlin driving his friend, and somebody else driving Colonel Groves. Others followed in the rear; not many. Eager, frantic, as they had all been in urging it on, they were too wary to expose themselves to consequences, even as spectators.

Earl Sandlin, had, first of all, proceeded to his home, Lord Temple with him. There the former got his pistols, and each drank a cup of coffee, black with strength. The French call it *café noir*. As they were starting off in the dog-cart, Lord Sandlin exclaimed that they must take a surgeon.

"We shan't find one at this hour," cried Lord Temple, who was now three parts sobered. "Don't wait; let's get it over." It is probable that he would be glad to escape it now, for his wife's sake; but no possibility of escape presented itself; no alternative.

"I know a man who will do," returned the earl, "and we shall pass his rooms. He used to be attached to the —— regiment."

A little farther the earl pulled up. It was the place he spoke of. A loud alarum was sounded on the night-bell, which brought forth a face in a nightcap at the second-floor window.

"There he is; I could swear to him by his gray whiskers. Holloa, Moore! put that window up."

Accordingly, the window was put up, and the gray whiskers and the nightcap looked out.

"What's the matter, my lord?" was the demand, in a strong Irish accent.

"Dress yourself in a brace of shakes, and come down and see. A five-guinea job. Now, don't be an hour. He'd sell his mother for half-a-crown," added the Earl to Lord Temple, "so he won't wait to shave. He's often hard up for a sixpence: clever in his profession, but drinks like a fish. I say, Temple, shaking?"

"I am as cold as charity," explained Lord Temple. "The dawn is keen."

No more was said, at least by Lord Temple. The surgeon came out, took his seat by the side of the servant, and kept up a running fire of conversation with Lord Sandlin, as they sat back to back. The earl appeared to feel no more the awful nature of the errand they were bent on, than he would the going to a wedding; he was not of the feeling sort. What Lord Temple's reflections were, we cannot tell: but certainly not pleasant ones.

When the party had discussed the place of meeting, some proposed one place, some another. One suggested Scotland; another France; another Chalk Farm. Finally, Battersea Fields was decided on, Georgy Eden indicating a spot there "snug and safe." To Battersea Fields, therefore, Lord Sandlin drove, and found the others were there before him. They had brought another surgeon. No time was lost; the ground was chosen and measured; and while Lord Sandlin and Mr. Eden were conferring together, Viscount Temple looked round at the assembled faces. His eye rested on Sir Robert Payn's—on its severe expression, betraying discontent at the whole proceedings. He went up to him, and drew him aside.

"Payn, if I fall, will you undertake to break it to my wife? You will render me that service?"

"Yes. I hope it will not be necessary. This has no business to take place, Temple. It was in my mind, on the way down, to look out for a policeman, and have you all taken into custody. You were a fool to get into this for that beggar Anketel. But you had no right to say what you did."

"I do not remember what I did say; I was half asleep and half stupid; but I was enraged at the fellow's presuming to touch me. Whatever I may have said, let it be as bad as it will, he deserves it. Mind, Payn, I reiterate it, though they may be nearly the last words I utter; he is a gambler in the worst sense of the term, and a blackleg, and

Swallowtail is his confederate; and I have, unfortunately, good cause for the assertion."

"This may be so," returned Sir Robert; "but life is life, and yours ought not to be risked for them. There was no call whatever for your coming out: the age for duelling is over. It is not demanded now that a man should stand to be shot at. Anketel might have brought an action against you."

"I should not have come out with Anketel. Groves is different. And he struck me."

"You might have struck again. I should; and pummelled him till his chivalry was out of him. What need had he to take up other men's quarrels? Groves has the character for being a crack shot."

"Well—if I fall, you will soften the news in the telling to Lady Temple. Do not let her know the worst at once, Payn. It will break her heart, I fear, when she does know it."

"And if it turns out the other way, and you despatch Groves, shall you make yourself scarce for a time? Or you may both fall."

"Both cannot fall," said Lord Temple. "I shall fire in the air."

"What!"

"I shall. I have no quarrel with him; and, if I am to be sent out of the world myself, I will not go with murder on my hand."

"If there were time I'd fetch a policeman," muttered Sir Robert to himself.

But there was not time. The antagonists were immediately placed, and the pistols fired. Colonel Groves's as surely as if he had taken aim—Lord Temple's in the air. Lord Temple fell.

The ball had entered his chest. The blood was welling out, and he lay as one dead. Colonel Groves, his second, and one or two more disappeared. They probably deemed he was dead, and hastened to secure their own safety.

But Lord Temple was not gone; and the pulling him about by the surgeons awoke him to consciousness. They were both skilful men, and extracted the ball on the spot. The lovely morning sun was looking on them from the horizon, as they dressed the wound.

"Now, there are only two things to fear," cried Moore, when it was over: "one is internal hemorrhage, the other is the shock to the system. I don't think we shall have to look out for either. I believe he'll do well. Where's he to be moved to?"

Lord Temple opened his eyes. "Home."

"Too far, my lord."

"Home, home," he repeated; and the words, though faint, were eagerly uttered.

"It may be done with care," interrupted the other surgeon. "His mind seems set upon it."

Lord Temple made a movement as if he would have raised his head, and his eyes sought Sir Robert Payn's. The latter read their anxious expression. He leaned over him.

"I understand," he said. "I'll be off at once. Keep your mind easy: by the time you arrive at home, she will be expecting you. This will be all right, I can see: only keep tranquil."

Sir Robert Payn drove leisurely to Lady Temple's: he did not hurry, for he thought she would not be up, and did not care to disturb her earlier than was needful.

Lady Temple had not been in bed. Full of consternation, then of alarm, she had waited hour after hour for her husband's return. Now pacing the room with uneven steps, now leaning from the window, looking out for him in vain, now giving way to all the terrors of imaginative fear. With the gray dawn, just as *they* were starting on their sinful expedition, she dropped into a sleep in her bedroom, kneeling on the ground, her head resting on the sofa. The entrance of her maid aroused her, and she started up, alive with painful recollection.

"A gentleman is below, my lady, and wishes particularly to see you. He bade me give you this card."

Sir Robert Payn's. On it was written in pencil, "I am deeply sorry to disturb Lady Temple at this hour, but have brought a message to her from Lord Temple."

Isabel glanced at the glass. To smooth her hair and her cap was the work of an instant; and she shook out the flounces of her black silk dress, and went down with quivering lips and a sinking heart. She had never seen Sir Robert Payn, and Sir Robert Payn had never seen her; but ceremony in these sterner hours of life is forgotten.

She went up to him: she clasped his arm in her agony of suspense; her eager eyes were strained imploringly upon him, her pale lips drawn back. Sir Robert was grieved to see her—to witness her emotion; and he also saw that it was especially necessary he should be cautious not to alarm her more than was possible.

"What have you to tell me?" she murmured; "what is it that has happened?"

"A gentleman is below, my lady."

"Dear Lady Temple," he said, feelingly, leading her to an armchair and placing her in it, "it is not so bad as you are fearing. Compose yourself. A slight accident has happened to Lord Temple, but you need not fear."

"I have never been in bed all night," she returned; "I have passed it watching in the agony of suspense. Let me know the worst. Indeed, I can bear it; it will be less painful than the fears which have haunted me."

He hardly knew how to tell her; yet, told she must be, for her wounded husband was even then on his road home. He got through the task pretty well; making light of it. A mere flesh wound, he said.

She sat back in the chair, her head resting on it, her hands clasped on her chest, as if to still its heavings, and her face the hue of the grave.

"To fight a duel! to go out to fight a duel!" she wailed, in a low tone. "How could he be guilty of it? How could he be so led away?"

"I will go and watch for them, and come in with him," said Sir Robert; "perhaps I may be of use. You will calm yourself before him, Lady Temple: it is absolutely necessary. Were you to excite him, I cannot answer for the consequences."

"Yes, I will; I will control myself: can you doubt it? But it is hard to bear."

"Can I do anything for you? Summon any of your friends?"

A sudden thought struck her: she looked up. "If my brother could be got here, it would be a comfort to me, and I know it would be to my husband. The telegraph would apprise him."

"Give me the address," said Sir Robert. "I will despatch a message instantly."

The Danesbury family were at breakfast that same morning, when Mrs. Danesbury happened to raise her head. "Who is this coming to the house?" she exclaimed. "A man in a blue-and-red cap. He has got on a sort of uniform."

Arthur leaned forward and looked out. "It is a porter from the telegraph office," he observed. "He must be bringing a message."

"About that iron, no doubt," cried Mr. Danesbury. "But why do they send here, instead of to the factory?"

The servant entered with a despatch in his hand, and handed it according to its address—"Arthur Danesbury, Esq., Danesbury House, Eastborough."

"Now, I wonder what this is?" thought Arthur, as he rose. He signed the paper, and then went to the window to open the despatch, his back turned to the breakfast table. An unpleasant fear had crossed his mind that something was amiss with Robert. From fears of some kind or other relating to Robert he was rarely free.

LONDON, 8 o'clock, A.M.

"Sir Robert Payn to Arthur Danesbury, Esquire.

"An accident has happened to Lord Temple. Lady Temple wishes for you here. Lose no time."

"What in the world is it, Arthur?" called out William. "You are a long while studying it."

Arthur turned round, as if in a maze, keeping the despatch in his closed hand. Mr. Danesbury looked at him.

"It is unpleasant news, sir. Something is—"

"Unpleasant news!" shrieked out Mrs. Danesbury. "Robert is ill! I know he is! or else his regiment is ordered abroad!"

"It is nothing about Robert," answered Arthur to Mrs. Danesbury, again turning to address his father. "Something is amiss with Lord Temple. They wish me to go up."

"Does he telegraph?" asked Mr. Danesbury.

"He does not. Sir Robert Payn sends. There it is," he added, handing the ominous words to his father, now that he had in a degree prepared him.

"What can it be?" uttered Mr. Danesbury, in concern. "You will lose no time, of course, Arthur."

"I shall start immediately, by the express train."

When Arthur reached town, he made the very best speed to Lord Temple's that a London cab could make. Sir Robert Payn was leaving the house, when he saw a cab stop there, and a remarkably noble-looking man, with fine, fair features, and blue eyes that quite fixed attention by their intelligent beauty, alight from it. Sir Robert guessed who it was, and met him.

"I have the pleasure," he said, "of receiving Mr. Arthur Danesbury. You have lost no time in obeying my telegraphic summons. This is a shocking business."

"What is it?" inquired Arthur, knowing then that he spoke to Sir Robert Payn; "what has happened to Lord Temple?"

"He has been wounded in a duel. I trust we may not have to say killed. But symptoms, I hear, are less favourable than they were earlier in the day."

"A duel!" uttered Arthur, doubting whether he had heard aright. "A *duel*, did you say?"

"With Colonel Groves," returned Sir Robert. "A dispute occurred in the night, in a house where they were, and they went out at daybreak, and fought."

"A duel!" Arthur could not help repeating, unable to realise the extraordinary tidings. "Could Lord Temple have been in his senses?"

"Only partially so. He had taken too much wine. They all had, and there was a regular drunken brawl. Groves was cool and sober: he had not been of the drinking party."

"How is my sister? Do you know how she bears it?"

"Poor lady! my heart aches for her. She told me this morning, that she would be calm before her husband."

Arthur went in, and in a few minutes was standing over the bed. Lord Temple lay on it, panting, his sad, repentant eyes gazing upwards. His wife's hand was in his, but he loosed it for a moment to grasp Arthur's.

"Perfect quiet," whispered Isabel, as a caution to her brother, "perfect quiet. The medical men say it is the only chance."

"That I had been like you, Arthur!" he breathed; "that I had been like you, a water-drinker."

Lady Temple leaned over him, the tears falling. "Reginald, you know you must be silent."

"Had I not been full of wine this would never have occurred," he continued, unheeding the injunction. "Arthur, if I get well, I will forswear drink for ever."

"Be silent now," whispered Arthur, "that you may get well."

"Ay, ay; and, by God's help, redeem the past."

Then he lay without speaking, and they sat by him in silence. In a little while the medical men came in, two of the most eminent surgeons in London. Arthur followed them from the room when they went out again.

"Is there any chance of his life?" he inquired. "I beg you will tell me. I am the brother of Lady Temple."

"The chances are slight," was the answer. "We fear internal hemorrhage."

The day went on to the evening, and the ebbing of Viscount Temple's life went on with it. The doctors were in and out at intervals, but they could do nothing. Isabel had been reading to him out of St. John's Gospel, and he had listened with closed eyes and folded hands. When it grew dark, one of the attendants entered with a light, placed it on a table, and went out again.

"No—no," faintly cried Lord Temple.

His wife thought he meant to object to the light, as no doubt he did, and she took it herself from the room. In that moment he put out his hand: Arthur understood the movement, and bent over him.

"I—am—going, Arthur. I feel it. *Oh, my wasted life!* Thus to be cut off in its midst! Arthur, you will take care of her, and of her child. I leave them to you. If it be a boy, tell him his father's fate—that it may be a warning."

Arthur Danesbury did not answer, save by a deep pressure of the hand. It said all. His sister returned, and he moved lower, to give her her place by her husband. Lord Temple drew her face down that it might rest on his.

"Isabel—my darling!—it is nearly over."

She would not scream; she did not faint: but her heart beat wildly with the sickness of despair, and a cold perspiration broke out over her head and face.

"May we meet again!" he continued, but so low that she could scarcely catch the words. "All day long have I been inwardly praying that time here might be prolonged to me. But it will not be. May my sins be forgiven me! My wasted life! Christ died for sinners."

"Ay, for all; for you and for me," she murmured forth from her aching heart. "Reginald, how shall I live without you? Can I live?"

She turned her face aside, to hide its welling tears, but her husband drew it again to his, and kept it there. Oh! that last embrace between two young, loving hearts! Reader, may you never have cause to give or receive it! When the doctors next came in, a light was brought. "Good heavens!" exclaimed one of them, under his breath.

"Take her away, sir," he whispered to Arthur. "Her face is resting on the dead."

Isabel heard—raised her head—saw—comprehended; and, with a wild cry, she let it fall again on the pillow beside him. "O Reginald! Reginald!"

All around Lord Temple's bed believed that he had gone. Lady Temple was taken from the room in the belief, Arthur quitted it in the belief, the surgeons remained for some minutes in the belief; and it was only when the nurse came forward to commence what was necessary to be done, that a doubt arose. So prostrated was his state, so death-like his condition, that they held a looking-glass to his lips, and by that means alone found that he still breathed. Thus he lay for some time; but whether the inward hemorrhage had stopped, or that his constitution rallied, certain it is, a slight improvement began to be visible. From that time his progress, though very slow, was gradual. And Lord Temple did not die.

CHAPTER XV
A GRACELESS SON, AND AN EVENING IN A PALACE

THE following year was waning to its close, when certain unpleasant doubts and rumours which had reached Eastborough as to the further misdoings of Robert, Lieutenant Danesbury, reached their climax. But it may be better to relate first certain changes touching William and Lionel.

William Danesbury had married. As it had been at Danesbury House, the night the scene took place relative to the chess, so it continued, Mrs. Danesbury rendering the young men's home unpleasant to them—in fact, driving them from it. William, probably with a worthy motive—that of keeping from temptation, for which self-endeavour all honour should be accorded him—took to spend his evenings, or most of them, at his Aunt Philip's, and an attachment arose between him and Anna Heber. Mrs. Philip was made a confidante of by William, and she was the first to speak to Mr. Danesbury, and urge the marriage. She believed it might be the saving of William. Anna knew of the failing to which he was inclined, and she was willing to risk it. Mr. Danesbury acquiesced with pleasure; his only objection was that, in the altered state of their finances, and under the great demands of Robert, but a small income could be allowed them, three or four hundred a year. That should not hinder it, Mrs. Philip generously said; she had saved money, and would settle equivalent to two hundred a year upon Anna. Thus matters were arranged; a house was taken and furnished, and William married.

But what of Lionel? Why, Lionel was living at home. Lionel had fondly anticipated the setting up in London; but by the time Lionel was a qualified surgeon, his intemperate habits had become so confirmed that Mr. Danesbury did not dare to sanction his doing so. He judged—and very rightly—that Eastborough would be better for him than London. At Eastborough he would have a *home:* in London he had none; and Mr. Danesbury began casting his thoughts about to make arrangements. Mr. Pratt was looking out for a partner, a man younger than himself, who would take the hardest of the work, and Mr. Danesbury proposed Lionel. Lionel, at first—I use his own expressive phrase, not mine—kicked at it; but his father pointed out to him how necessary it was that he should, if possible, regain steady habits, and when that was done, he could take his degree as physician and establish himself in London. Lionel could not help being struck with the good sense of the proposition when he had allowed himself to digest it, and at length cheerfully acquiesced. It was not a bad plan, after all, he remarked, for he should be gaining ten times more experience with old Pratt than he would at first in London. So Lionel joined Mr. Pratt, making his home at Danesbury House.

Robert came down to the marriage of his brother William, and took the opportunity to press for more money for his extravagances; but Mr. Danesbury refused to supply it. He could no longer afford to do it, and peremptorily informed Robert that he must make his allowance and his pay—not a despicable income—suffice for the future. Robert returned to town; and there the infatuated man put false bills in circulation and obtained the proceeds, forging his father's business signature, "John Danesbury & Sons," and making them payable at their London banking-house, Robarts, Curtis, & Co.

The news came upon Mr. Danesbury like a thunderbolt. What he would be called upon to make good and save exposure, unless he suffered Robert to be prosecuted as a felon, amounted to a thousand pounds; but it was not the loss of the money that crushed him. The facts stood out, broad and hideous: a son of his had committed a crime for which he was liable to nearly the worst punishment of the law: but a few years previous, it would have been the worst. Many a man, for a far less offence in amount than this, had heard the awful sentence passed upon him, that he should be hanged by the neck until he was dead.

"Father," asked Arthur, when the first shock was over, "what is to be done?"

"The sorrows of my old age are telling upon me," wailed Mr. Danesbury, in a husky tone. "May they not become too heavy for me to bear!"

"We must seek out Robert."

"Seek him out, and bring him home. I question if he will allow you readily to find him."

"Bring him home, did you say?" returned Arthur.

"What else can be done with him?" asked Mr. Danesbury. "He cannot remain in the army to disgrace it. Were this to ooze out, think what his position would be with his brother officers! He must come home, Arthur. He may not be left amidst the evils of that great city—he might ruin himself and ruin us."

"I had better go to London at once, and see what I can do."

"Yes. Act as circumstances shall require. Do the best you can. I give you full authority. When you have arranged about his commission, bring him home."

"He may not be willing to come."

"He must come. Use any means. Threats of consequences, if persuasions fail. I was always against his joining the army: I knew it would lead *to* a life of idleness, probably of vice. It has done both."

Arthur Danesbury proceeded to London. His first visit was to Robarts's in Lombard Street; from thence he proceeded to the West End, to Robert's old lodgings. The people said Lieutenant Danesbury had left them some time, and they did not know where he now lived. Arthur expected this would be the probable answer, and he drove to the quarters of his regiment. Colonel Neeve stood at the entrance as Arthur was about to enter; they had a slight knowledge of each other, and shook hands.

"I am in search of my brother," said Arthur. "Does he happen to be here?"

"Here!" exclaimed Colonel Neeve. "No; he has never once condescended to pay us a visit since he left."

A puzzling speech to Arthur. "Is he absent?" he inquired.

"Absent from where?" asked the Colonel.

"From London. From his duty."

Colonel Neeve looked equally puzzled, and the two stood for a moment gazing at each other.

"I have come to London to see Robert," explained Arthur; "but the people where he used to lodge tell me he has left, so I came on here, hoping to catch him. Will he be at the mess this evening?"

"Is it possible you do not know that your brother has quitted the regiment?" exclaimed Colonel Neeve, in a tone of astonishment.

"Quitted the regiment!"

"He has sold out, this two months past."

Arthur Danesbury was perfectly confounded. He was quite unprepared for the intelligence. "What could have been his motive?" he resumed.

"Why, the fact is, he could scarcely do otherwise," cried the Colonel, dropping his voice to a confidential tone. "He was over head and ears in debt, and went in bodily fear of arrest. He wanted the proceeds of his commission to clear himself. Supplies from home were stopped, he said."

"He had been supplied too extensively from home," was the pained answer of Arthur. "Another year or two of his extravagance would have ruined us. When he was last down, I believe my father warned him that in future he would receive no more than his allowance."

"Ay, that's just what I understood. Lieutenant Danesbury was awfully fast; there's no denying it."

"And he has really sold out! And probably spent the money."

"That he has spent it you may be sure of. How is it you did not see it in the *Gazette*?"

"That portion of the *Gazette* does not interest us much, and often goes unread," replied Arthur. "Can you tell me where to look for him?"

"I am sorry that I cannot. He has never been here since. I have met him once or twice in an evening, but not very lately."

Arthur wished Colonel Neeve good-day, and left. He was at a loss what to do. It was absolutely necessary that he should find Robert; not only to get him away from London, and prevent further mischief, but to ascertain whether he had placed other false bills in circulation. He bent his steps to Bedford Row, and inquired of Mr. St. George if he knew anything of him.

"Not I," was Mr. St. George's answer. "I expect he is after no good. You astonish me by saying his family were left in ignorance of his selling out. I saw the announcement in the *Gazette*."

"I am very uneasy," observed Arthur. "I must see him."

"Did you come to town to see him?"

"Yes, I—" Arthur hesitated. But he found it would be better to tell the whole truth to Mr. St. George, and he disclosed the sad tale with shame.

"He is a wicked scamp," was the indignant comment of Mr. St. George.

"Sold out of the army, and entered on evil courses!" uttered Arthur. "What is to be his end?"

"Not 'entered' on them," said Mr. St. George. "Lieutenant Danesbury has been deep in them a long while. The kindest thing to him would be to prosecute. It would keep him from further crime."

"Impossible to prosecute him," returned Arthur. "It would bring public disgrace on us all, and sully the name of Danesbury."

"Well, I suppose it would not do. What a curse drink is, all over the world! It is that which has ruined Robert."

"Can you give me any track by which I may trace him out? You are so much better acquainted with the ways of London than I am."

Mr. St. George mused. "I wonder whether Pratt may not know something of him. He used to meet him sometimes in his night haunts."

"What Pratt?" inquired Arthur.

"That drunken son of Pratt's of Eastborough. There's another fine fellow ruined! he was made for better things than to lead a sinful life."

"He has been a great trouble to his father," remarked Arthur. "How does he get his living? Our old friend never speaks of him."

"Any way. Starves part of his time—from food, not from drink. He is attached to a fashionable gambling-house, and has some pay from it. By the by," cried Mr. St. George, with sudden emphasis, "what was the description Robarts's gave you to-day of the fellow who presented these bills for payment—a thin man, with a white face and scarlet lips? That is uncommonly like Pratt himself."

"Pratt had not a white face and scarlet lips," remarked Arthur.

"Ah!" quoth Mr. St. George. "How long is it since you saw him?"

"Ten or twelve years."

"And he has been drinking ever since. Quite enough to make his face white and his lips red."

"But," debated Arthur, "Pratt's son, whatever may be his faults, would not lend himself to crime."

"'Adversity makes us acquainted with strange bed-fellows,'" significantly remarked the lawyer, "and there's no adversity like a career of drunkenness. I'll send for him, and tax him with it."

"But you cannot accuse him of presenting these forged bills for payment, without first knowing that it was he," remonstrated Arthur Danesbury.

"Leave him to me, said Mr. St. George, carelessly. "If I were to accuse him of murder, he is too broken-spirited to retaliate; but the probability is, that he has been an innocent agent in the matter. Robert Danesbury may have made him his tool. Singularly enough, I sent for Pratt's son this morning, and am expecting him here. I told Pratt last year that I would get this lad, who is too good for such a father, into an architect's office, and I have just succeeded in doing so. My friend would not have anything to say to the boy till now; thought him too young."

As Mr. St. George spoke, he rang his bell, and a clerk entered.

"Is young Pratt come?"

"Yes, sir. He is waiting."

"Send him in."

A well-dressed boy, with a clear, bright eye, and capacious forehead, entered. He ought to have been there early in the day, but his new clothes had to be purchased, for which his mother's friends had supplied the means.

"Well," said Mr. St. George, "are you as anxious as ever to become an architect?"

"Oh, yes, indeed, sir," answered the lad, colouring with eagerness.

"A friend of mine is ready now to take you into his office, and try what stuff you are made of. Do you think you can be industrious and steady, and give satisfaction?"

"I hope so, sir. I'll do all I can. And I am very much obliged to you."

"Are you sure you feel obliged to me?"

The boy looked up. "Of course I do, sir, and so do my friends."

"Then you must repay the obligation by observing a certain rule which I wish to impose on you."

"What is it, sir?"

"That you never drink any sort of intoxicating liquor; neither wine, nor beer, nor spirits. You will be amongst young men who probably do drink such, and they will be for persuading you. Unless you can resolve to withstand that, and to abstain, you had better stay away altogether."

The boy's face became painfully suffused, for he knew why Mr. St. George thought it necessary to give him that caution. "Oh, sir," said he, "there will be no difficulty. I have promised the same to mamma, and I will keep my word. She has never yet permitted me to drink anything but water, and I never will."

"I will trust you," answered Mr. St. George. "Remember, I implicitly trust you. Before I give you directions where to go," he added, "I want you to step home and bring your father here. Tell him I wish to speak with him."

Young Pratt flew off, and soon returned with his father. The latter, a little the worse for liquor, had not stayed to dress himself, and he looked, as the saying runs, "seedy;" seedy in clothes, and very seedy in face and frame. He shrank into himself when he recognised Mr. Arthur Danesbury, ashamed that *he* should see him as he was. It proved that Mr. St. George was mistaken in his suspicions of Pratt's having been the man to present the bills at Robarts's. Pratt knew nothing whatever about them. Indeed, the probability was, that they had passed out of Robert Danesbury's hands three months before, into a discounter's. "There are plenty of men in London with white faces and inflamed lips," thought Mr. St. George to himself: "I was wrong."

"Do you happen to know where Mr. Robert Danesbury is now?" Arthur inquired of Pratt.

"No, sir. I have not seen the captain for some time—as we always call him amongst ourselves."

Not waiting to ask who "ourselves" might mean, though Mr. St. George well knew, Arthur Danesbury proceeded.

"Do you know where he removed to when he left his apartments in Bond Street?"

"He went to Arundel Street, in the Strand, and afterwards he left that place, and I don't know where he went to," was Pratt's reply. "He had a run of ill-luck, and since then he has not shown out much."

"What do you mean by ill-luck?"

"At the gaming-table, sir. And the captain was extravagant in other ways, and I expect he is keeping himself dark just now. I see him now and then at night; though I have not for the last week or two. His old night resorts are, I expect, too expensive for him at present, or else he is afraid to show himself at them, and I am not acquainted with his new ones. I shall see two or three people to-night that I can inquire of."

"I shall be obliged to you to do so," returned Arthur Danesbury.

"And come here to-morrow morning and report," said the lawyer sharply—"at eleven o'clock."

The following day, Saturday, Pratt made his appearance in Bedford Row at the appointed hour. Arthur Danesbury was waiting for him. He had not been able to see Captain Danesbury, he said, for it was as he thought; the captain was in hiding; but he had heard that he sometimes appeared at a certain tavern called "The Golden Eagle:" he "went there for his drink."

"Do you know what he is doing?" inquired Arthur.

"Not much, sir," replied Pratt. "He looks shabby now; though you may be slow to believe that of Captain Danesbury. He is hastening along the downward road that I have gone. Lately, I have never seen him but he has been half-screwed."

"Half what?" inquired Arthur.

"He means half-drunk," explained Mr. St. George. "It is one of our glorious town's fast expressions, and has not, I presume, travelled to Eastborough."

"Not to me," replied Arthur. "I will go at once to this 'Golden Eagle.'"

"It will be of no manner of use, sir," interrupted Pratt. "He never appears there till night; and then with caution. Your surest plan would be to watch the doors after dark, or go inside and wait."

Arthur Danesbury had plenty to occupy himself with that day, for he had business to attend to for the firm. He then went to his hotel and dined—"The Queen's," St. Martin's-le-Grand—and afterwards he went out to find "The Golden Eagle."

"The Golden Eagle" was situated in a low neighbourhood, near to Oxford Street. Arthur was somewhat puzzled with the courts and street; but on turning into the right one, there rose the structure before him. A magnificent white building—a gin-palace—imposing with pillars, and cornices, and balustrades, and ornamental architecture, all flooded with light. A "golden eagle," jetted with gas, spread its wings over the first-floor windows, and lamps with pretty devices on their variously-coloured glass, four in front and two on the side—for it was a corner house—raised themselves on pilasters from the pavement. But, glaring and brilliant as was the light without, it appeared to be eclipsed by that within.

Arthur took up his station at the corner. A most unenviable position; for the flood of gas streamed full upon and lighted him up, as if he had been placed there for show. But from no other point, or darker corner, could he see the two doors; and to watch only one was almost the same as watching neither. If that house was "The Golden Eagle," the one at the opposite corner of the narrow street might be called "The Golden Balls." It was a pawnbroker's shop. Do you ever see the two far apart? And many a one visited that before they visited "The Golden Eagle." Numbers were passing into it that Saturday night, carrying with them incongruous articles—flat-irons and children's clothes, pillows and time-pieces, wedding-rings and men's boots, Dutch ovens and chimney ornaments. Some pressed in there from sheer necessity, others, to obtain means of gratifying their fiery craving for drink. Arthur Danesbury was often jostled by the pestiferous crowd, who came too close to him with their poisonous breaths, their glassy eyes, and their tainted rags. They were swarming there in scores, for it was Saturday night with the drinkers as well as with the pawners; and, now and again, his view of the doors was baffled by the intervening mob, who stared at him standing there, as if he had been a wild animal, so entirely did he appear of a different species from themselves. He began to think he should be better off inside. It appeared a large place. Surely there might be a quiet corner where he could sit and wait: and he entered.

Several men, mostly young, and in shirt-sleeves, for it was hot within that reeking place, were serving behind the counter. It was the first time Arthur Danesbury had ever been inside a London gin-shop, and he stood in amazement. Lustrous mirrors in glittering gilt frames dazzled his sight, their costly plate-glass reflecting back the lights, as in countless numbers; massive pillars, all marble and burnished gold—at any rate to look at; showy time-pieces, and rich cut-glass chandeliers. Could this be a common gin-shop, where penny half-pints of porter and drains of gin were doled out. Ay, it was, indeed, and a luminous sight it was. The taps communicating with the spirit casks were of polished silver, or were silver-plated—it was impossible for the eye to tell which; farther on, a little space, were the beer-taps; and the beautiful shelves behind held bottles of various kinds and elegant ornament. They contained cordials and liqueurs whose very names were sufficient to tempt the unwary, as they gazed at them, ranged there before the plate-glass. No lack of good cheer was sold there, or what the infatuated crowd deemed such. Barclay, Perkins, & Co.'s entire, prime, double-stout, mild ale, best cordial gin, cream of the valley, Old Tom, pineapple rum, genuine Scotch whisky, best French brandy, rum-shrub, were some of the names that, amidst many other's, stared in Arthur's eyes. A little recovering from his astonishment, he approached a portly man who appeared to be the master. The latter gazed at him with surprise: his lofty form, his better than lofty countenance, his high breeding and affable tones, were such that had not often been seen at "The Golden Eagle."

Arthur courteously raised his hat: yes, even to a tavern-keeper, for he was a thorough gentleman at heart; and spoke in a low tone as he bent over the counter.

"Will you allow me the privilege of waiting here for half an hour? I wish to see a friend who occasionally comes here, perhaps he may do so to-night."

"Sir, with pleasure," respectfully answered the landlord. "Will you please to walk into our private parlour, sir?"

"Thank you, no. This gentleman may be in and gone in a minute, and I might miss him. I will stand aside and wait here."

The landlord bustled forward with a chair, and placed it at the corner of the counter. Arthur moved it back into the shade—if that term may be applied to any place so brilliant with light—somewhat out of the reach, and somewhat out of the gaze of the crowd. The landlord handed him a weekly newspaper, and he opened it, but his attention was much taken up by what was passing around him.

They were coming in, thick and threefold. Men, women, boys, girls; some old, some young; some "respectable," some the very dregs of the street. If ever Arthur Danesbury felt pre-eminently thankful for being a water-drinker, he felt so then. Repelling jokes met his ear, coarse conversation, profane swearing. Some were haggard with famine; some with long drinking; some were scarcely a day removed from their graves. One woman, pale and bloated, in a broken straw bonnet, came up to the counter, carrying a moaning infant. It did not seem to have strength to cry.

"Quartern o' prime Old Tom," she cried, putting down fivepence.

No sooner said, than the glass was handed to her with one hand, and the money swept away with the other. She drank it rather better than three parts, and the rest she poured down the throat of the infant, to dose it into quietness. Arthur Danesbury could not forbear an exclamation, but it was unheard in that Babel of sounds. As the woman turned from the counter, a young girl, in a green-and-red plaid shawl and tidy cotton gown, pushed her way into the place. She looked scarcely seventeen, yet the plague spot of intemperance had already set its mark upon her face. Thin and wan, and clammy in flesh and feature, it had the lack-lustre eye, and the hot, red lips. She fixed those poor eyes of hers upon the landlord, and spoke, with a pleading accent.

"Master, you'll just trust me with a half-quartern, won't ye?"

"Not if I know it, wench," roughly replied the same tongue which had been so civil to Arthur Danesbury.

"I'm dying for it," she went on. "I ha'nt had a taste in my lips this day, and I'm just fainting for the want of it. He ain't come out o' quod yet; when he does, I'll pay ye. Let's have it."

"Just take yourself off," returned the landlord; "you can't come the dodge over me."

She broke out into an oath: "Hear to him!" she shrilly cried, turning to the shopful. "He won't trust for a paltry half-quartern, and we have laid out pounds with him. You avaricious old Brimstone! I know who'll get his own some day."

The landlord did not reply. He nodded to two of his men in the shirt-sleeves, who emerged from behind the counter, and bundled the unhappy girl outside.

"We have rough customers here sometimes, sir," said the landlord, approaching Arthur, and speaking in a tone of apology; "and this is Saturday night: any other, it would not be so bad."

"Poor things!" returned Arthur Danesbury.

"Can I offer you a glass of anything, sir? I'm sure I should be proud to—if you'd please to name what. I have got as good a glass of port as ever was tasted."

Arthur shook his head. "You are very kind. I never drink."

"Never, sir? Not anything?"

"Except water."

"Law, sir! that's poor stuff to keep up a man's stamina."

"I don't know," returned Arthur, with an amused look. "If you contrast my 'stamina' with that of those I now see around, I think mine would not suffer in the comparison."

"Yes, sir," said the landlord; "but you must also contrast your position and advantages with theirs."

"It may be that some of those now present have had it in their power to attain to as good a position as mine," returned Arthur. "Two or three of them look as though they had been gentlemen once."

"Yes, I believe they have been, sir."

"Till ruined by the demon, drink," muttered Arthur to himself.

"Who is that sitting down in the bar?" demanded the smartly-attired landlady, when her husband went into their own parlour.

"I don't know who: some nob though. He's a real gentleman, whoever he may be; a lord, I shouldn't wonder. He took off his hat to me as stylish as if I had been a duke royal, and asked leave to wait to see a friend. But, I say, what d'ye think? he is one of them teetotalers."

"How do you know?"

"Because he said so. I asked him to take something—I'd have given one of my best beeswing ports to such a man as he, for that he was not one of the beer or gin customers, I could see with half an eye—and he said he never took anything but water."

"Perhaps he is one of those teetotal spies, come to show the trade up," suggested the landlady.

"No, that he is not. He has nothing of the spy about him. He carries the stamp of honour on his face. My belief is, he's a noble *incog.*"

"What made you give him that newspaper to read?"

"Because I thought he might like to amuse himself with it, while he waited."

"But that's an old one."

"An old one!" cried the landlord. "Ain't it to-night's?"

"No, last week's. Here's to-night's."

"Bless me," exclaimed the man. And, taking the fresh paper, damp from the press, he approached Arthur, with an apology for his remissness. The latter took it, but did not at the moment resign the other, for he was interested in something he was reading from it. Just then, there was a loud shout in the bar, causing Arthur to look up, and the landlord to step close to the counter. It seemed to speak of applause.

The young girl had come in again, and, flinging down a shilling on the counter, demanded a half-quarter of "mountain dew." The gin was served out to her and the eightpence change. She had taken off her cotton gown in the street, and pledged it for a shilling at the opposite pawnshop.

"Who says I am to be done?" cried she, when it was swallowed, turning round, and holding out her scant petticoat, as if she were prepared to dance a minuet. "Old Brimstone wouldn't trust me, so I went and popped it for a shilling. I think this is as handsome as that: at any rate, for his shop," she continued, still holding out the garment for exhibition, which, whether it was originally black or white, was of no colour but dirt now. "Ah! never say die!"

The applause was uproarious. Before half an hour had elapsed, she had spent the shilling in three half-quarters of mountain dew, and went reeling out Gin on an empty stomach: weak from long fasting!

Arthur's spirit was faint within him. In and out, in and out of the doors they poured—these poor, eager applicants, in all stages of misery, in all stages of disease, in all stages of intoxication. The doors were on the swing perpetually. Before one set had drained the poison that was destroying them, another was ready to fill up their places. What reward were they hastening on to in the next world? What were they hastening to only in this?

He sat till the house was ready to close, sat it out. Robert had not come in.

"May I trespass upon you again to-morrow night?" he inquired of the landlord. "I am from the country, and am unwilling to go back without seeing my friend. I do not know his address, but am informed he sometimes comes here at night."

"What is his name, sir?" asked the landlord.

"I question if you would know him by name. I believe not."

"Come to-morrow night, sir, and as many nights as you please. I am sorry it is so dull for you, sitting here, and watching others drink."

"I would rather watch them than drink myself," was Arthur Danesbury's answer. "What I have witnessed here to-night has not tended to increase my approval of it."

"Drink is not bad in itself, sir, when taken in moderation—only when swallowed in excess."

"But most of your customers do seem to take it in excess," was Arthur's rejoinder.

"A good many do; it can't be denied. But, sir, there are other things that do them harm as well as drink. Look at the low trash they are always reading, the bad, pernicious literature that they buy up and devour, the women especially. It's awfully demoralising, and destroys their minds faster than drink destroys their bodies. Goodnight to you, sir."

The landlord was not far wrong, for nothing can tend to demoralise the minds of the lower classes more than certain cheap and low publications, periodically poured forth with an unsparing hand in the British metropolis. Next to the unseemly indulgence in intoxicating liquors, they are the greatest bane that ever fell upon a nation's people.

CHAPTER XVI
MEETING OF OLD FRIENDS

SUNDAY morning rose. Arthur Danesbury attended divine service at St. Paul's, and then bent his course westward to Lord Temple's house at Kensington. The service at St. Paul's was over early, and Lord and Lady Temple had not returned from church. But they soon followed him in, and greeted him with glad surprise. He inquired, not without anxiety, after Lord Temple's health.

"I am getting strong again," was the reply. "When did you come to town?"

"On Friday morning. But I have been engaged, and could not get as far as this. I can stay with you to-day. How is my little godson?"

"You shall judge for yourself," answered Isabel. "You never saw such a lovely child as he grows, Arthur—and so good!"

"Never was such a child before—in his mother's eyes," cried Lord Temple.

"Now, Reginald! you know that he is lovely—and good."

"To be sure. Takes after his father in both respects," gravely responded Lord Temple.

They laughed at this. And Isabel quitted the room, laughing.

"I am glad to see you looking so much stronger," observed Arthur, when left alone with his brother-in-law. "I had grave fears that you would never be strong again. In the spring, when I was here at the child's christening, and you were, so to say, well—I had my doubts of you."

"Ay: my renewed life is a blessing I did not deserve."

"Have you persevered in your resolution of keeping to water?" inquired Arthur.

"Yes; thank God! And I will persevere by His help; persevere to the end. All that day, when I lay dying, as I and everybody thought, my inward prayer was, that God would mercifully renew my life to me—as He did to Hezekiah. Not for the sake of the life, the living longer in the world; it was not for that I so earnestly prayed, but that I might be enabled to atone for the past. Almost by a miracle I was raised up. The medical men said it was a miracle to them; and I am sure it was to me, for I had every sensation of a dying man. After mercy so great accorded me, so direct an answer to my earnest prayer, how could I relapse into a careless or evil life? It was prolonged to me to redeem it: to strive to please God; to be useful to my fellow-men: and my first resolution towards this was, that I would never drink anything but water so long as I should live. Wine and strong drink had led me on to most of the ill I had committed: they never shall again."

"Water is the only certain safeguard in such a case as yours," remarked Arthur.

"It is," assented the Viscount. "Some men, your father, for example, can take stronger drinks, and never exceed a harmless quantity; but, were I to return to them, I might take too much, as I often used to do: therefore, I keep the temptation at arm's length. Yet I have not escaped being tempted, even since my raising up—I shall never call it by any other name, Arthur."

"Tempted by your friends?"

"No. By my medical men. When I was growing better, they ordered me stout and wine; insisted on my taking it; told me I should never be well if I did not. But I kept my resolution. I was *helped* to keep it," added Lord Temple, reverently.

"Medical men little know the ill they do in pressing stimulants upon patients who are recovering from illness," cried Arthur Danesbury. "A man rises from his bed as you did, weak, emaciated, trembling, a living skeleton. He cannot yet take very substantial food, and his doctor immediately orders him port wine—a glass a day, or two glasses, or three, as the case may be, by way of getting up his strength. Many, many have become intemperate from only this slight beginning. They learn to like the wine, and to crave for it; they continue its use after health has returned, in gradually increasing quantities, and the rest is easy."

"I do believe you. I am convinced that it is so. Wanting the moral power to resist, and the better and higher safeguard, which I trust I have now within me, I should have been quite as ready to drink as my medical men were to order, and should have gone on from bad to worse. When Isabel was recovering, after the boy was born, they told her she must take double stout and port wine, that she *must*. After the first day or two she did not dispute the point with them, but quietly let them believe, if they chose, that she did take it."

"And drank only water?"

"Of course. You know Isabel never takes anything else. She got strong none the slower for it, and I am sure the child lost nothing by the bargain. He really is a beautiful boy, Arthur," added Lord Temple; "but if I were to admit it before Isabel, she'd be prouder of him than she already is, and be for showing him off to the public in a glass case."

"How do you manage to abstain from wine when dining with your friends?"

"Oh, I have put it hitherto on the score of my damaged inside, where the bullet went," laughed Lord Temple. "The time may come when I shall avow fearlessly my true reason, that water is better for the body, and better for the soul."

"I wish you would," earnestly spoke Arthur.

"It will come. Rome wasn't built in a day. Some of these nights, I may rise in my place in the House, and astonish the Lords by avowing that I have taken up the Temperance cause, and call upon them, as good men and true, to legislate for it."

"I pray that I may live to see the day," aspirated Arthur Danesbury. "Much depends on you of the higher orders; you make the laws, you are set in lofty places, you are the mighty counsellors of England's Queen. You might effect much, if you gave yourselves up, heart and spirit, to look into, and strive to check this monster evil."

"The Government might effect more than it does," said Lord Temple. "It might render the laws and the duty affecting spirits more stringent; it might close up some of the gin and beer shops; it might help in other ways. But, to suddenly convert the British community from a toping people into a sober people, is not in their power. Government cannot say to a man, 'I will not permit you to touch beer, spirits, or wine, for they are not good for you'; or, 'I will allow you but a moderate portion of each'; it is impossible. Such a change must come from a man's own will and heart."

"Undoubtedly it must. Still, much might be done towards it. The outward attractions of the gin-palaces, their floods of light, might be put down. Why should they display a nightly illumination more than other trades? If all shops were like them, we should require no street lamps. These flaring establishments are the worst temptation to the poor that ever were invented or permitted. It is all very plausible to say, man is a free agent, and need not enter them unless he choose: but it is man's nature to yield to temptation, especially when it is thrown attractively in his way, as are these gin-palaces. I was in one last night, Temple."

"You!"

"I, myself. I wanted to see a person on urgent business, and was told I might catch him there. I waited there for hours. And the scenes I witnessed kept me awake all night. I never closed my eyes till daylight. Misery, misery, nothing but misery. There lies an awful responsibility for guilt, somewhere."

"The question is, with whom does lie the responsibility?" remarked Lord Temple.

"It might do some good, Temple, if you would move that the House should cause a return to be made for one whole year, of all the crimes, accidents, and offences, committed by parties when under the influence of intoxication," said Arthur, after a pause. "It might be productive of more benefit than some of the parliamentary returns are, for I cannot but think it would startle the legislature into acting."

"You should get one of the Commons to do that," laughed Lord Temple. "It is in their department."

"If ever I enter Parliament, the prevalence of intemperance, and its possible remedy, shall be the first point to occupy my attention."

"Do you think of entering it? I wish you would."

"The thought has crossed my mind at times," replied Arthur. "I may, some day: as you observe of your rising in your place to astonish the peers. Have you learned yet to like the water?"

"A long while ago. If you put water and wine before me now, I would take the former from preference. I did not like it at first, I thought I never should; but, with the habit of drinking it, the liking came. I question whether I should have wholly recovered had I taken again to stimulants; perhaps, might not have lived many months. And I will tell you another thing it is benefiting, and that's my pocket. I shall have my affairs straight in half the time that we looked for."

"Have you seen Robert lately?"

"No. Isabel was wondering what had become of him. That was a mad trick of his, the selling out."

"Yes, it was," said Arthur, sadly. "We did not know of it at home. He is going all wrong, I fear."

"I fear so, too," said Lord Temple. "Drink again!"

At this moment, Isabel came in, tossing an infant of nine or ten months old. There was no mistake about his being a beautiful child, with his mother's clear, intelligent eyes, and his father's refined mouth. His white frock was tied up with blue ribbon, and his little fat arms were beating the air.

"There, Arthur," said his mother to him, "go to your namesake, and uncle, and god-papa."

Arthur Danesbury took him, awkwardly, it must be confessed, and little Master Arthur immediately rewarded him by seizing upon his whiskers. Arthur the elder cried out.

"Give him back; you are not a nurse at all," said Isabel; "you should see what a famous one Reginald is."

"He has been in practice," said Arthur; "I have not."

"Do you ever intend to be in practice?" returned Isabel, in a graver tone, which bore its own meaning, whilst Lord Temple carried the child across the room, playing with him.

"No one can answer for the future, Isabel."

"I once thought your choice of a wife would fall upon— Shall I say?"

"If you like."

"Mary Heber."

A slight colour flushed his face. He did not speak.

"Was I right or wrong, Arthur?" continued Lady Temple.

"Right: inasmuch as that, if I ever do marry, I would prefer her to all the world."

"Does Mary know it?"

"Not from me—in a direct manner."

"Indirectly, I presume. May I ask, Arthur, why you do not marry?"

"I have had too much anxiety and care upon me to think seriously of it," he said, in a low tone. "And I do not know that I could afford it."

"What!" she exclaimed, in astonishment. "Not afford it?"

"Things have been going backwards with us a long while, Isabel. Not with the business; but our expenses have so increased. They are a fearful drain."

"You mean the boys' expenses—their extravagance?"

"Yes. Robert's have been—I will not tell you what; and William's and Lionel's not despicable. Were I to inform my father now that I had resolved to marry, I candidly tell you that he would have difficulty in finding me a suitable allowance."

"But you are a partner. You have a share, to a certain extent," debated Isabel.

"But what I have accumulated I have been obliged to put back into the business: we could not have carried it on without; and for three years I have not drawn my full share."

"Is it possible? Arthur, you are sacrificing your prospects to the others."

"There has been no help for it. The liabilities they incurred in London had to be provided for to avoid disgrace. My visit to town now is caused by—by an act of Robert's"—he did not choose to speak more explicitly—"which will cost us a thousand pounds."

"How wrong! How wicked of him!"

"I would put up cheerfully with all we have lost if I could but see them renounce their habit of drinking. It grows upon them all."

"All! Even upon William?"

"Yes, upon William. He was decidedly better at the period of his marriage, but he is relapsing again. Lionel is much worse."

"What does Mrs. Danesbury say to this?"

"She is bitter against William, but ever ready to find excuses for Robert and Lionel; though William indulges, and has indulged, far less than either of them. I think this last exploit of Robert's will startle her."

"Why did he sell out, Arthur? He never comes here."

"We did not hear of it at Eastborough. I was going to ask you, why?"

"I do not know. He does not come here. A considerable time ago he called, and was closeted with Reginald. I found afterwards he had come to borrow money."

"Was it lent him?"

"Two hundred pounds. He has not been here since. What is he going to do with himself?"

"Lead an idle life at Eastborough, I expect. I have orders to carry him down with me. He must be got away from London, unless we wish to be quite ruined."

"Indeed, I would not have him at Eastborough, were I papa," exclaimed Lady Temple. "He should be left to himself, to take the consequences of his folly. Papa is not responsible for him as if he were a boy."

"The consequences might be more serious than you imagine, my dear," was the grave answer. "No; he must come home."

"Does mamma make the evening home more cheerful?"

"Quite the contrary. I frequently sit in my own room, or go to Mrs. Philip's: sometimes to William's."

"How hard it must be for Lionel! You say he grows worse, instead of better. Does he mean to take his degree?"

"Isabel, if he can only cure himself of his unhappy propensity, he will do that, and everything else that he ought. His wishes to do right are sincere, and he is clever in his profession; but he lets drink stupefy away his time and his energies."

"And what of William?"

"Well, I hardly know what to tell you. We had great hopes that his marriage was to do wonders; and, both before it and after it, he was quite steady. But, latterly, he has been out again in an evening, and has, to my knowledge, gone home intoxicated. It is a cruel thing so to speak of two brothers, but I fear that Lionel is just now William's evil genius."

"Lionel! In what way?"

"He is everlastingly after William, enticing him out and leading him to drink. As long as temptation is not thrown palpably in William's way, he keeps sober; but let anybody urge it on him, and he succumbs. I do not believe William is so much a slave to liquor in itself as to the inability to resist partaking of it when set before him. Lionel, on the contrary, is a slave to it—he loves it; and there lies the difference between them."

"Why does not papa forbid Lionel to go after William?"

"My dear, they are no longer boys, that they can be controlled," replied Arthur, "they are men. My father has spoken to him, and urged it upon his good feeling not to induce William to drink. Mrs. Philip met Lionel last week, and gave him a sound chastisement, so far as her tongue could do it."

"What did Lionel say?"

"Only laughed, in his easy, careless way, and said William was older than he, and it was hardly fair to blow him, Lionel, up for William's misdoings."

"There is a good deal in that," mused Isabel. "William is the elder of the two, and a married man. He ought to have the moral strength to resist any temptation that Lionel could bring upon him."

"*Ought!* there it all lies, Isabel. If we could but do as we ought, we should be good men. Lord Temple tells me that he still keeps to water: I think he is striving to do as he ought."

"Oh, yes, and he will do it," she said, with quiet happiness. "He is going the right way to work. He has found out WHERE to look for health and strength. That dreadful duel, which I really thought would have killed me at the time, has turned out to have been a blessing."

"'All things work together for good to them that love God,'" whispered Arthur, pressing his lips to her forehead. "Whatever sorrow may betide, remember that, my sister."

"No sorrow such as that was can ever befall me again, with reference to my husband," she answered, the tears standing in her eyes. "I am quite certain that in conduct he will keep right now: I have a positive, inward conviction of it, and so has he. And if death were to come to him, though very grievous for us, and for me hardly to be borne, we should only part in the sure hope of meeting and dwelling together hereafter. But oh, Arthur! that other death! when he was suddenly cut down in his sins! without having found Christ, or done a single thing to please God in all his life! I do believe it would have killed me had he died. He has gone with me to the Communion table," she added, sinking her voice still lower. "Only think of that! And he never went before in all his life, save the Sunday after he was confirmed, and then, he says, he should have been better away, for he went through the ceremony, *as* a ceremony, entirely in a matter-of-course sort of way. I used to ask him to go with me after our marriage, when we were staying in Paris and attended the Ambassador's Chapel, and he would laugh, and say he was not good enough. But he has been at last; he went of his own accord without my speaking of it; and I can see that in time he will go regularly. It has made me so happy, so thankful."

"How much longer am I to be nurse?" called out Lord Temple, from the opposite end of the room.

Isabel laughed. "Why do you not bring him here, Reginald? You have kept him yourself."

"But the young Turk has got his eyes and hands on this shining curtain bracket. If I take him away, he may deafen Arthur's ears with screams; and they are not used to the music."

Isabel rose, and took the baby. But if he had lost the curtain ornament, he had found his mother, and did not cry. She summoned the nurse, who carried away the child.

"I need not ask if you intend to make him a water-drinker," said Arthur.

"No, that you need not," heartily responded Lord Temple. "Neither he, nor any of his brothers and sisters who may come after him, shall ever touch aught but water while I control them. I don't know what they may do afterwards."

"'Train up a child in the way he should go, and when he is old, he will not depart from it.' That was spoken by a wiser man than either you or I, Temple," said Arthur Danesbury.

"Dinner, my lady," cried a servant, opening the door.

"We dine early on Sundays," remarked the Viscount, as he followed his wife and Arthur to the dining-room. "Isabel has got me into the habit—and we find it to be a good one: more particularly as regards the convenience of the servants. But—talking about getting into good habits—do you know that St. George has become a water-drinker?"

"Has he? St. George?"

"He dined here a fortnight ago, and wine was placed on the table as usual when we have anyone with us, for I don't force my temperate habits upon my guests," continued Lord Temple. "But St. George said I might order the wine off again; he had given up drinking it."

"Did he give his motive?"

"Simply that, seeing so much evil arising from indulgence in it, especially to young men, he had come to the determination to banish wine and beer from his own table, before his children should grow up. Of course, that could only be done by abjuring them himself; and he has done it."

"And his wife also," added Isabel.

Arthur looked up, amused. "His wife! Charlotte used to say that she loved her wine, and could not live without her porter. She was unappeasably offended with me once, for telling her that it was the drinking porter made her so fat."

"She did love her porter," resumed Isabel; "but she says she loves her children better, and therefore makes the sacrifice: and a real sacrifice I can readily imagine it to be to Charlotte."

"Ah," interposed Lord Temple, "if people were only brought up to drink water, as you two were, it is a sacrifice the world would know little of."

"Arthur . . . led him out."

CHAPTER XVII
A NICE YOUNG MAN

ARTHUR took leave of Lord and Lady Temple at the church door, as they were going in for evening service, and proceeded towards "The Golden Eagle." The shops were closed, every shop he passed; but the gin-shops were open and lighted up, outside and in. Ought this to be? he said to himself; ought this marked distinction to be permitted? The shops closely shut, in accordance with our professed religion, and with God's commandment that the Sabbath shall not be desecrated, while these flaunting liquor palaces, with their evil attractions, are staring boldly open! He recalled to mind what had been said by his brother-in-law that day: that the legislature might do more to crush—Arthur would have said, not encourage—the vice, than they were doing. It was self-evident.

He reached "The Golden Eagle." One of the first objects his eye encountered on entering was his brother Robert, in a state of semi-stupidity. He had been sitting, with other tipplers, for the last two or three hours in "The Golden Eagle's" public parlour, and was now reeling out of it into the bar, on his way to quit the house, having drank away his money. Arthur went up to him, and laid his hand upon his shoulder; and, partially intoxicated as Robert was, he was startled at the capture, and cowered visibly. He was dressed as Arthur had never yet seen him dressed, in a common gray suit of clothes; not at all like a gentleman's clothes, and not at all like Sunday ones.

Arthur tucked his arm within his own, and led him out. The landlord followed: he had caught a word of the recognition.

"Oh, sir," he said to Arthur Danesbury, "is *he* your brother?"

"He is."

"I couldn't have believed it. Why, sir, you and he are as opposite as light and dark."

"Ay," returned Arthur; "he has made a friend of wine, I of water. Good evening, my friend. I thank you for your courtesy."

"Sir, good evening to you," replied the landlord, and a bow of greater respect he had never made to anyone.

"Where are you lodging?" inquired Arthur of his brother.

"It's—it's—not far," hiccupped Robert. "I—can't take you there."

"Why not?"

"It's—it's a shabby place."

"Oh, never mind that. I have come on purpose to see it. Is this the way? Come, Robert."

His tone was decisive, his manner commanding, and the poor half-witted man yielded to it like a child. He led the way to a dirty house in the vicinity of Tottenham Court Road, the door of which stood open. Robert began stumbling up the dark staircase.

"Can I get a light from anywhere?" inquired Arthur, totally unable to see, and hesitating to follow him.

"I—I've not got a light, Arthur. I've not had a light for four nights. Once inside the room the street lamp shines in."

Just then the door of an apartment close to them was opened, and a woman burst out of it, holding a candle. She looked up the stairs contemptuously at Robert.

"So! you be in for it again, be you! You swore last night as you had no money to pay me; you have got some, it seems, to lay out in drink."

"Will you oblige me by letting me have the use of a light?" cried Arthur to her, in his courteous way.

The woman had not seen him, he had been in the shade cast by the open street door, and she turned round and stared at him. Her manner changed, and she dropped an involuntary curtsey.

"Did you please to want anything, sir?"

"I am with this gentleman." But Arthur Danesbury positively hesitated at the last word, so entirely unlike a gentleman was Robert then. "We will borrow your light, if you please."

"You are welcome, sir. 'Tain't as I've objected to lend him lights, but I can't be always a-supplying of him, and not get paid. Candles he have had; and three loaves, and a quarter of butter he have had; and a go of brandy, as I sent for for him, for he was a-praying and crying for it as if he'd die; and two quarterns and a half of gin; and a piece of soap; and a tumbler and plate he broke—he can't deny as he have had 'em, and owes me for 'em."

"How much is it in all?" inquired Arthur, putting his hand into his pocket.

"Well, sir, I know it's as much as four shillings, but I can't reckon it up in my head all in a moment. Oh, and there was the washing of his sheets; I forgot that. And there's the rent besides."

"How much?"

"Two weeks, sir, come to-morrow, at four-and-sixpence, making nine shillings. And if I says five for what he owes me, instead of four, I shan't be a gainer. A precious trouble my husband have had of him in his drunken bouts! That'll be fourteen shillings, sir, altogether."

Arthur placed a sovereign in her hand. "Is any notice requisite? because he will quit your house to-night."

"No, sir," answered the woman, who appeared to be a sufficiently honest one, whatever may have been her faults of manner. "He gave me notice a week ago, and though he was drunk when he said it, of course it was a notice. Six shillings: I'm feared as I've not enough change, sir, but I can run to the nearest public and get it."

"No, do not run there. You may keep the six shillings in recompense for any trouble he may have been to you."

"Well, sir, there ain't many like you!" exclaimed the gratified woman, after a pause of astonishment; "but you carries the gentleman in your face. Can I do anything else, sir? shall I run up and light a bit of fire in his grate? his room's chilly."

"Oh no. I shall want a cab brought presently, if you have anyone to send."

"Plenty, sir, if you wanted a dozen."

He took the candle from her hand, and followed Robert, who had disappeared upstairs. An open door guided him to the chamber. A cold-looking room it was, as the woman had said, and wretched enough. Robert had thrown himself on the bed, hat on, and was already slumbering. Arthur knew him of old; that he had naturally a sullen temper. Perfectly sober, they might try in vain to extract from him particulars of his condition and doings, present and past; the only plan was to take him now. When semi-intoxicated, Robert was voluble, and would answer what was demanded of him. Arthur roused him up, and he sat on the side of the bed.

"Now, Robert, I have a good deal to ask you, and you must answer me. You had brought sufficient trouble and sorrow upon us without this last act, which I believe will be the means of shortening your father's life. I speak of the forgery," he distinctly added. "Your forging our name, and getting a thousand pounds, and squandering it."

Robert burst into tears—a frequent habit of his when in this state—and howled and sobbed piteously.

"There, that will do. How did you so cleverly imitate your father's signature?"

"I was at my wits' end for money," sobbed Robert. "I was desperate. My father refused me more money, and I did not know what to do. If I could not have got money to meet some bills just then, I must have shot myself."

Arthur made no remonstrance to this. It would have been useless in his present maudlin humour. "Are there any more false bills out purporting to be ours?"

"Not one. I swear it. Those three were all. I never intended to rob my father," he went on, sobbing like a child. "I meant only to use the money in my exigency, and to take up the bills when they were due. I sold out to enable me to take them up. I did, Arthur."

"Then why did you not take them up?"

"Oh!" howled Robert, "don't ask me."

"But I do ask you, and I must have an answer. Do you hear, Robert?"

Robert sobbed away. "I went to—a—a place where they play, and I had it in my pocket, and I staked and lost it. I was drunk."

"As you are now," Arthur could not help saying, with contempt in his tone.

"And, since then, I have been in hiding, afraid of your finding me: and afraid of some others finding me."

"How did you so cleverly contrive to imitate our signature, I asked?" repeated Arthur.

"Oh, I practised it. I wish I could pay you back, but I never shall. I have not a shilling, Arthur; I have not a shilling or a shilling's worth left in the world; and I am next to starving."

Arthur looked round the room. It was devoid of luggage.

"Where are your regimentals?" he inquired.

"Sold."

"And your boxes?"

"Sold."

"And your ordinary clothes?"

"Pawned."

"Your linen, then?"

"Pawned."

"Your watch. Is that gone?"

"Pawned."

"This is a pretty state of things," thought Arthur. "I wonder he did not pawn himself." Robert sniffed and sobbed, and wiped his face with the sheet.

"Have you nothing but what you stand upright in? Am I to understand that?"

"That's all."

"You had a desk—you had many valuables, besides trifling articles: are they all parted with?"

"Pawned."

"Where are the pawn-tickets?"

"Sold."

"Sold!"

"Every one," sniffed Robert, in danger of choking. "I parted with the last to a fellow to-day for half-a-crown. Oh! I hope you'll forgive me! I did mean to place the money in Robarts's, to meet the bills. I hope you'll ask my father to forgive me! He will do anything you ask him, Arthur."

"You are without money, without food, without clothes. Had I not come here, what would have become of you? and what should you have done to-morrow?"

"Drowned myself."

Arthur paused. He was deliberating.

"She's a horrid woman, that one downstairs," said Robert, beginning to ramble on some domestic grievance. "Her name's Huff. She wouldn't make my bed yesterday."

Arthur went to the top of the stairs, and, calling to the woman, requested her to get a cab. When it came, he turned to his brother.

"Now, Robert, come down. You are sure you have nothing to remove from here but yourself?"

"No. Where are you going to take me to?"

"Home."

Robert started up. "Home! I won't go home. I won't, Arthur. How can you be so cruel? I will not face my father."

"You would rather do that than face the inside of Newgate," sternly returned Arthur. "It must be one or the other, by your father's orders."

"That woman won't let me go away. She's downstairs."

"Yes, she will, and be glad to get rid of you," replied Arthur. He put Robert's hat on his head, and conveyed him down to the cab,

Robert resisting as much as he dared. Mrs Huff officiously lighted them. There was some probability that the public house had been visited, and the sovereign changed, for her face was flushed now, and she smelled of gin.

"Had those 'palaces' been closed to-night, as other shops are," thought Arthur to himself, "she could not have procured it."

"Where to, sir?" asked the cabman, touching his hat.

"Holborn," he said to the man. "I will direct you further then."

His present destination was "The Queen's Hotel." Arrived there, he was somewhat puzzled: for he did not dare to leave Robert alone in the cab, lest he might attempt to escape. He caused a waiter to be called to him.

"I cannot alight," he said to the man. "Go into my room, put my shaving tackle and other things in the portmanteau, and bring it down. And my bill with it. We are in a hurry."

The waiter did as he was told. Arthur settled the bill, and ordered the driver to proceed to the railway station; and, by the first train that started, he and the disgraced Robert were being whirled to Eastborough. So Robert and Lionel Danesbury had returned to their father's home. Robert's disgraceful crime was not allowed to transpire beyond the family; he was supplied with suitable clothes, and it was supposed by the neighbourhood that he had only come home for a temporary sojourn. But that supposition was gradually dispelled.

What was to become of Robert? Who was to support him? Was he to live like a gentleman at home, upon the labours of others; or was he to go out into the world and starve? Of course, there was but the first alternative. He was unfit for everything; but, to keep him from idleness, or something worse, Mr. Danesbury assigned him some light employment in the works. Robert did not, for shame, object openly: he was conscious of his crime, and of the leniency which had been shown him: but when with his choice companions—and he was not long in finding such—he complained in a high and lofty strain of being forced to meddle with "trade"; of the degradation it was to him, Robert Danesbury, ex-lieutenant, an officer, and a gentleman!

CHAPTER XVIII
EVIL COURSES

THE months and the years went on, and the names of the young Danesburys became a byword in Eastborough. What was it that was blanching Mrs. Danesbury's cheeks, and rending their father's heart? "The boys have become confirmed drunkards!" they whispered to each other. It was so. Not occasional ones, as was the case when Robert first went home, but habitual. Night by night, sometimes early, sometimes not till morning, they would reel home partially intoxicated, or be brought in helpless.

One day a farmer, residing in the neighbourhood, met Thomas Harding, and stopped him. "What's going to become of those two young Danesburys?" abruptly inquired he. "They are carrying on their game."

Thomas Harding, a hale old man now, shook his head. "It is a sad thing. Mr. Robert never comes to the factory, and his father cannot get him to it."

"I would not keep him at home in idleness," cried the farmer, indignantly.

"Mr. Danesbury has no other resource. He cannot turn him out to beg, or starve."

"Wouldn't I though! He would look out for himself, if he were forced to it; and he won't have his father always here. I should send him back to London, and let him shift for himself."

Thomas Harding was silent. He knew what few others did.

"How much longer does Dr. Pratt intend to keep on the other? Mr. Lionel?"

"Keep him on!" echoed Thomas Harding. "He is a partner."

"Well, it is Pratt's own lookout," returned the farmer; "but if he retains Lionel Danesbury, he won't retain patients. The wife of our carter, Ann Jones, was taken ill yesterday afternoon. Dr. Pratt had notice to attend her, and was asked to come himself, for she was afraid of young Danesbury after what she saw of him when he came, half-seas over, to that boy who was caught in the threshing machine."

"I heard of that," interrupted Thomas Harding.

"So did all Eastborough, I should think: but let me go on. Pratt was sent for yesterday, but he was out, and young Danesbury came. He was all right, they say, except being a little shaky, and talked and cheered up Ann Jones so pleasantly, that she was pleased he had come instead of the old gentleman."

"I am glad he was all right!" again interrupted Thomas Harding.

"You have not heard the end," said the farmer, significantly. "My wife had been in to see Ann Jones, and made her a present of a bottle of brandy, knowing it's sometimes wanted, and had drawn the cork, for the Jones's don't possess a corkscrew, and had put it loosely in, and left the bottle on their kitchen mantelshelf. Ann Jones wasn't over quick; and Mr. Lionel was sometimes in her room and sometimes waiting in the kitchen. He spied out this brandy, and said to one of the women, that he would take a spoonful of it, for he was thirsty, and she brought him a glass and some cold water, and left him. An hour or so passed: they wondered he did not come back to the patient, who was getting very bad, and one of them went to call him. There he was, lolling on the bench, as drunk as a lord, and the brandy bottle three parts empty."

"Too far gone to be of use?" uttered Thomas Harding.

"Too far gone for anything. And who would trust to a drunken man? My wife happened to go there just as they found him, and she ran home again, and sent a messenger tearing off for Mr. Pratt. The old doctor was at home then, and made haste, and was not a minute too soon. But, suppose he had not been found, the woman might have lost her life."

"It is very distressing," exclaimed Thomas Harding.

"It is what we cannot put up with," returned the farmer. "Much as we all respect Mr. Danesbury, we cannot be expected to lose our lives at the pleasure of his son. So, in future, if old Dr. Pratt can't attend himself when anybody's ill, we shall call in the opposition doctor. I would not trust a cut finger to Lionel Danesbury."

The farmer's prophecy proved to be correct. Mr. Pratt was compelled to put away Lionel Danesbury. He dissolved the partnership, and took another gentleman in his place; so that Lionel, like Robert, was an idle vagabond on the face of the earth. Their evenings were, almost without exception, consumed in drinking, and their mornings were wasted in sleeping off the effects of the liquor. Their mother scolded, and implored, and wept; and their father reasoned, and persuaded, and threatened by turns. As for them, they would promise amendment in the light of the mid-day sun, when their heads were racked with pain, and their hearts softened by contrition. Mr. Danesbury repeated to them the question of others—what would they be fit for, what would become of them, if they continued these courses? Look at their already cloudy intellects and shaking frames! He would ask how it was that the dreadful habit was suffered to come upon them; to grow to such a height. They would reply, and with truth, that they could not tell; they never thought they were falling into habitual intemperance.

No. Few do. For it is the most insinuating vice that exists: no other evil, whether of crime or failing, steals so unconsciously over the victim it is fastening on. To what can its stealthy steps be compared? I am at a loss to say. Silently, as the darkness covers the light at the close of day; imperceptibly, as appears the first glimmer of morning; surely and quickly, as winter succeeds to summer, and summer to winter; or, step by step, unexpectedly and subtly, as glides on the approach of death? It is like unto all these; yet unlike: for, though the darkness of the coming night, the light of the early morning, the gliding away of the seasons, and the grasp of the grave, are things not in our own hands, or under our own power, and we could no more alter their order of working than we could alter the truths of Holy Writ; yet the other, the sin that creeps on us like unto these, *is* under our own control, and we might arrest its progress in the onset, and thrust it far away.

Robert and Lionel Danesbury could have done this. They would not now. Oh, no: it was scarcely still in their power. So long as the cup of liquor could be obtained, they flew to it: they could not abstain: it was like the *ignis fatuus* which allures a traveller to his destruction. A yearning for amendment would at chance periods come over them. They saw men around them, the playfellows of their childhood, the companions of their youth, who were fulfilling their appointed duties in the world, honoured and respected: but they knew it would be as easy to turn the sun from its course, as to turn them from the ruin they had entered upon.

They were not backward to declare that they would give over these practices and become steady men. Their mother would, over and over again, put trust in their word, and pity them, and carry them tea, or a mess of broth to their rooms in the morning, and urge them to partake of it, to "do them good." They did not turn angrily away from her, but they did from what she offered them—that was of no use to slake *their* thirst; they must have something else. Stealthily they would sup something else, of a different nature, and go downstairs, and—stealthily again, for they did not like their mother to see them drink it, in those moments of promised amendment—resort to the ale barrel, and consume long draughts of its contents. Ere half an hour elapsed, they would be as thirsty as before. A tumbler of brandy was what they longed for, but Mrs. Danesbury rigidly kept spirits and wine now under lock and key; though occasionally they would smuggle a bottle in, and hide it in their bedrooms. Failing brandy, they kept on at the ale, and, by the time evening came, where would be their good resolutions of the morning? Unheeded, uncared for: or, if thought of, their physical and moral strength were not equal to carry them out, for the temptations of the public-houses, and the fellowship of their boon companions were irresistible.

Mr. and Mrs. Danesbury became old, and gray, and broken. Mrs. Danesbury's very nature seemed changed. There was little anger or scolding now: tears in plenty, and midnight wailings. The dreadful habits her two sons had fallen into were no longer hidden from any: they could not be; and she was often tempted to speak of them to the servants, or to friends. Speak she must to someone, or her heart would break.

Bitter, bitter repentance had taken hold of Mrs. Danesbury. Her grief had led her to the only sure fountain of consolation, where she had never gone in a right way before; and her heart was softening, and things were becoming clear to her. She looked back on the past, and, in her self-reproach, almost feared that she could never be forgiven. She had loved her children, been proud of them, been vain of them, had indulged them reprehensibly, winked at their faults, joined them in deceiving their father in trifles, been anxious to further their worldly interests. But what else had she done? Striven untiringly to lead them to God, corrected their failings, trained them in strict habits of temperance, encouraged in them social virtues, shown them their duties, made them look on home as the dearest spot on earth? No; she had never done this. And, dreadful as were the present fruits, she knew that she was only reaping what she had sown. Often and often was the useless wish now wailed forth from her heart, that she had remained Miss St. George, or else been a childless wife.

But about this time there appeared to be a change for the better taking place in Lionel. A little for the better—not much. He less frequently forgot himself, came in earlier at night, and was more careful of his dress; for both he and Robert had fallen into slatternly habits in that respect. The change was hailed with thankfulness by Mrs. Danesbury, who looked upon it as a precursor to reformation. The real cause, however, came to light.

The inn chiefly frequented by Robert and Lionel was "The Wheatsheaf." It was kept by a man named Bing, and his wife, who had brought up their children in rather a superior manner. There were three of them, daughters, showy girls—too showy, the father thought, to wait upon his customers, so two of them had been sent from home to learn the dressmaking; the other, Katherine, an exceedingly well-conducted girl, remained with her mother. It began to be rumoured in Eastborough that Lionel Danesbury had latterly been seen walking with this girl; but, as is often the case, the last person to suspect it was Mrs. Bing, until one evening a gossip went into "The Wheatsheaf," and asked her if she knew where Kate was.

"She's upstairs," answered Mrs. Bing. "She went up after tea."

"Did she?" quoth the visitor, in a significant tone. "She's not there now, at anyrate. She's in the lane yonder, a-walking with young Mr. Danesbury; his arm round her waist, and her hand in his, as snug as two can be."

"With young Mr. Danesbury?" uttered the mother, appalled at the news, and then taking refuge in disbelief. "Your eyes must have deceived you. Katherine would not be walking like that with a Danesbury, nor with anybody else. She is a properly brought-up girl."

"Bless us, they are all alike. Girls are girls, and will have their sweethearts; and so did we, when we were young. But young Mr. Danesbury's not a suitable one for Kate Bing, and the town's talking about it. I said I knew you were not encouraging that."

The visitor left, and Mrs. Bing went to the side door and looked out, full of trouble. She remembered that Kate had latterly spent a good portion of her evening time away from her presence, but she had suspected nothing. It was a bright night, and Mrs. Bing presently saw Kate come flying along, round the corner of the lane, her cheeks crimson and her eyes bright.

"Where have you been?" demanded Mrs. Bing.

"I wanted a bit of ribbon, and I ran out to buy it," was the girl's evasive answer.

"Now, if you tell me another word of untruth, I'll send you off to your grandmother's to-morrow, and you shall never come back of one while," retorted Mrs. Bing. "You have been walking in the lane with young Mr. Danesbury."

Katherine hung her head, and the crimson of her cheeks spread over her face and neck.

"Katherine, *have* you been walking with him?"

"Oh, mother," she answered, throwing herself into her mother's arms, and hiding her face upon her neck; "he is so fond of me."

Mrs. Bing's heart went pit-a-pat. "Which of them is it?" she asked. "Mr. Robert, or Mr. Lionel?"

"Mr. Lionel."

"Child," she said, sitting down, "I had a great deal rather you had struck me a blow than told me this."

"Don't say so, mother. You would not, if you did but know the happiness it has brought to me! Everything in the world seems brighter and better since I had him to think of."

"How long have you been intimate with him? I mean, intimate enough to walk with him?"

"Not long."

"Is it a month? Or two?"

"No, I don't know that it is."

"Katherine," resumed Mrs. Bing, "it is just ruin, and nothing else."

Katherine stood up, her eye indignant. "Mother! don't say such a thing of me! I don't deserve it. Mr. Lionel wants to marry me."

"Marry the nonsense!" contemptuously uttered Mrs. Bing. "A Danesbury marry one of you! You had better not let such a speech get to Mrs. Danesbury's ears; she'd box yours. And if he did marry you, it would be ruin, for he is a dreadful drinker. You know he is, Katherine."

"He is leaving it off. He says he shall leave it off quite, and never take to it again."

"You leave off walking with him: that is all you need think about leaving off," retorted Mrs. Bing.

Katherine did not answer. She knew she would break her promise if she gave it; for she had become completely enthralled by Lionel Danesbury.

The news did reach the ears of Mrs. Danesbury, and she taxed Lionel with it. He answered, in a somewhat flippant manner, that he should walk with anyone he pleased.

"Your walking with Bing's girl will lead to no good, to you or to her," cried Mrs. Danesbury. "You cannot think to disgrace yourself and your family by marrying her."

"She is as good as I am," returned Lionel, "whether to walk with, or for a wife."

"Lionel," sternly interrupted his mother, "let us have no more of this absurdity. She is not as good as you are, and she is not a fit wife for you; and were you to stoop to marry such a person, the daughter of a common public-house keeper, you must give up your family, for they could not recognise you afterwards. But, before you talk of marrying any wife, just ask yourself how are you to keep one. You are living now upon us!"

Lionel stood by the window as his mother talked to him, drumming on one of its panes. He was still gentlemanly-looking in figure, more so than Robert, for Robert had grown bloated, but his once clear eyes were clouded, his fresh colour was gone, and his well-formed features were sunken. No lack of talents or of intellect had been granted to Lionel Danesbury, and how was he making use of them?

"Who told you anything about my walking with Kate Bing?" he resumed.

"The place is ringing with it, and crying shame."

"The place may be swallowed! Let people mind their own business: it's no concern of theirs. Here's my father coming in from the factory: I'll make myself scarce, or perhaps he will begin upon me."

Lionel might have spoken more civilly: but one great evil in such training as Mrs. Danesbury's had been is, that it causes children to forget their respect. As he went out, Mr. Danesbury came in.

"Have you heard the report about Lionel and that Bing girl?" Mrs. Danesbury immediately began.

"I heard it some days ago."

"You must speak to him."

"I did speak to him," replied Mr. Danesbury. "But it appears that it has had no effect; and the report is, that he means to marry her."

"What in the world can possess him?" uttered Mrs. Danesbury, in consternation. "Is he mad?"

"I have heard a curious version of what are said to be the facts," resumed Mr. Danesbury. "You remember that Lionel used to be forever with young Laughton, the solictor—who is another one going the way of drink."

"He has been less intimate with him latterly," remarked Mrs. Danesbury.

"Lionel often saw pretty Jane Laughton, he was nearly always there when presentable, and it seems he had grown very much attached to her. One day he told her so, and she answered him with undisguised scorn, reflecting on his habits. Lionel was half mad. The next day he was told that Jane Laughton was engaged to Thomas Boyd, and would be married shortly. He was in at "The Wheatsheaf," half tipsy, when he heard it, and he swore a fearful oath that he would make an offer to the first girl he met, and be married before Jane Laughton. As he was leaving "The Wheatsheaf," he met Bing's daughter coming in, and did make her an offer, and since then he has been much with her; and, they say, intends to marry her."

"Where did you hear this?"

"From William. He got it, he says, from a sure source, and thought it right to inform me."

If Mr. and Mrs. Danesbury were indignant at this proposed (though, whether in jest or earnest, they could not divine) marriage of Lionel's, Bing and his wife were equally alarmed. However they might be impressed by the honour done their daughter in the notice of a Danesbury, the unfortunate habits of Lionel were too notorious to admit of any chance of comfort for a wife. Kate was ordered to hold herself in readiness for a visit to her grandmother's; a sharp, active woman still, who had eyes on all sides of her where young girls were concerned, and farmed her late husband's bit of land just as well as he used to do.

Bing resolved to take her himself in the tax-cart. "No girl of mine shan't tie herself to a lazy, boozing vagabond of a gentleman," quoth he to some cronies, on the night previous to the expedition; "and that's what Mr. Lionel is: and I don't mean no offence to his respected father in saying it."

"Nor to Mr. Arthur," chimed in one.

"Nor to Mr. Arthur, nor to Mr. William," acquiesced the host. "But as to the other two, they are no credit to anybody."

"Mr. William's not a saint where a drop of good liquor's concerned. He don't spare it."

"And why should he spare it?" cried the landlord, indignant at the insinuation. "He takes his glass with any gentleman, but he keeps himself *as* a gentleman; he do. It the two young ones was like him, there wouldn't be no need of calling out."

Bing might have spared the projection of his journey in the taxcart, and his wife the trouble of writing to her mother to tell her to expect Kate, and to "keep her up tight," for, when the morning rose, Kate was missing. Lionel Danesbury was also missing: and when the two came back to Eastborough, they were man and wife.

Mrs. Danesbury's doors were haughtily closed against them; but Mr. Danesbury, ever merciful, ever considerate to his erring children, who were fast breaking his heart, could not let Lionel starve; and he was established in a small cottage residence, to get what practice he might—Mr. Danesbury being answerable for the rent, and allowing them twenty shillings a week to live upon. Kate's father was inveterate, and would not notice her.

"What a come down," quoth the gossips, "for one of the wealthy Danesburys!"

CHAPTER XIX
AN EVIL DEATH

DID Lionel Danesbury amend his ways and drink less now that he had assumed graver duties? Surely this marriage of his, this settling in a home of his own, might have proved a turning point. Far from any amendment resulting, he grew worse than before, and it was a rare thing now, morning, noon, or night, for him to be seen entirely sober. As to Robert—but the less that is said about him in detail the better.

As the months went on, and this change for the worse appeared in Lionel, Mrs. Danesbury thought it best to pocket her pride, and be reconciled. She fancied that her renewed favour and intercourse might be productive of some good effect upon him. She never could be cordial with his wife, not quite cordial; there must, and would, always be a reserve in her manner, as from a lady to an inferior. Poor Katherine Danesbury was sadly changed; her hopeful visions of her husband's reformation were worse than not realised. She was an excellent wife to him, a slave to him night and day, and Mr. Danesbury openly avowed his opinion, that she was a far better and more patient wife than Lionel deserved.

They had been married about ten months, when, one evening at dusk, Lionel's wife appeared at Danesbury House, sorrow in her eye and suffering in her pale cheek. If she had come to tell of trouble, she had not chosen an opportune time, for Robert had been causing an unpleasant scene. He had been demanding money of his father, and when Mr. Danesbury refused it, had broken out into a torrent of abuse, both of his father and mother, had dashed about the room, raving and swearing, and then rushed from the house. That he was so overcome as not to be fully aware of his words was no excuse. For the last three days he had not been for one minute sober, and his actions had partaken of insanity. They were sitting on each side the fire, Mr. and Mrs. Danesbury, and she was lamenting openly, weeping bitterly; his sorrows were buried in silence, but they were eating away his very heartstrings. While thus engaged, a servant opened the door and ushered in Lionel's wife.

"Well, Katherine," cried Mr. Danesbury, as he pointed to a chair beside him, and there was a painful amount of sadness and suffering in his subdued tone, "you look as if you had something bad to tell."

Katherine strove to speak, but, after a minute's struggle with herself, burst into tears. She had come to disclose a pitiful tale, and she was grieved and ashamed to be obliged to do it. Mr. Danesbury had given her the money for the rent, quarter by quarter—three quarters now—for his payments were always made to her, not to his son. She had handed it promptly to Lionel, who had always taken it, as she believed, to the landlord. It turned out now that he had never taken it, but had gone so perpetually with excuses, that the landlord, tired out, had that day put a man in possession.

"I am so ashamed to come, sir," she sobbed, "and tell you such a thing as this, after all your kindness to us. I went to try and get it from my mother, but I find she is gone out for a few days. And he has been so excited ever since the man came in, that I'm sure he must be got out to-night. He seems on the eve"—she lowered her voice—"of another of those dreadful attacks. His wrists and round his eyes are turning red, and his knees are shaking, and he is fancying he sees things."

"I gave the rent to you, Katherine," said Mr. Danesbury; "you should have paid it yourself."

"But, sir, he took it from me each time and said he would go up and pay it, and I never thought but what he did. He went out to do it, and came back and said he had. I asked him one day for the receipts, and he replied that he had given them to you. How could I suspect anything wrong?"

"I suppose he spent it on his drink?"

"I suppose he did," she sobbed. "He has taken such a horror of this man who is put in that it terrifies me. When these attacks are coming on he is not sane, and he might spring upon him and kill him. I did not know what to be at, sir. I was unwilling to come here to ask for the money, but Lionel raved out to me to come. I whispered to the man to be upon his guard."

"Swore at you, I suppose, Katherine?"

"Oh, sir, but it is only when he is like this that he swears. He is kind and good when he is well."

"Katherine," resumed Mr. Danesbury, sinking his voice, "I heard that he struck you this week: was it so?"

She shivered, and sobbed out a faltering excuse for Lionel—that he was "quite gone," and did not know what he did. "If he would but keep from drink!" she moaned; "if he would but keep from drink. This week he has taken enough to kill him."

Mrs. Danesbury listened, and a cold shiver passed over her frame, a sickness seized upon her breaking heart. "Oh!" she cried out in her anguish, "what infatuation is it that possesses my children?"

What could Mr. Danesbury do but relieve Lionel's house of its encumbrance? He wrote a word to the landlord, and the man was instantly withdrawn. But that same night Lionel had to be watched by two men in his dangerous delirium.

Mrs. Danesbury retired to rest, but not to sleep. Robert had come in, and was wandering about the house, pacing up and down the stairs incessantly, his mind unconscious; it appeared more with madness than with wine. What a sound for a mother! At length the noise ceased, Robert subsided into his room, and his mother sank to sleep. She was awake again with the first gray streak of dawn that glimmered in the east, awake to the new day and the pain it brought.

The terrible reality—stern, appalling, intense—rushed over the brain of Mrs. Danesbury, and she sprang from her bed with a suppressed cry, and paced the cold room with her hands to her temples, wondering that her senses did not quite leave her in these dreaded moments. There was no help on earth, and she sank on her knees and prayed that her sons' infatuating sin might yet be conquered; that it might not have laid hold of them past redemption. And yet she had so prayed for years, and amendment had not come to them; and she prayed as one who had no hope.

Mr. and Mrs. Danesbury rose as usual, and after breakfast the former went to the factory. He came back about mid-day, too ill to go out again. In the afternoon he was cowering over the fire in the dining-room, for he stood shivering and chill, when Robert came in, his dress loose, and his gait slouching. Though three o'clock, it was his first appearance that day. His eyes were bloodshot, and his countenance bore the marks of his evil life. His slippers were down at heel, his coat dirty and torn, his pantaloons unbraced, and he had no collar on. Mr. Danesbury looked up, and then averted his eyes with a suppressed groan. Robert held his hat, which he had carried on his head into his chamber the previous night; he now essayed to place it on the table, but his hand shook, and it slipped on the floor: Mrs. Danesbury, little less shaking than he, stooped and picked it up again. Yet Robert was sober then, perfectly sober, the drams he had been obliged to take ere he could dress himself not affecting him.

He was screwing his courage up to tell of his faults. Told they must be. In his excited mood of the previous night, he had demanded money; it was now his task to tell quietly why it must be supplied him. He had again got into debt, for the third or fourth time since he came home, and had drawn liabilities upon himself which must be discharged, or he dragged off to the county jail.

"You have brought me to the verge of ruin," gasped Mr. Danesbury, as he listened; "do you want to complete it? It is not eight months since I paid your debts. Then there was nothing but a jail before you, and I saved you from it."

Robert sat by, penitent and ill: he always felt penitent and ill when he was quite sober. He had nothing to answer.

"How many times have I paid your debts since you returned from London?" proceeded Mr. Danesbury. "Not one shilling of them had you any cause to contract. You have a good home here, with everything you can require, and you have a trifle to spend. What other father would keep you in idleness? You have squandered the money that I worked hard for. What will you do when I am gone?"

Robert had risen, and now stood leaning on the mantelpiece. He was intent on procuring what he wanted, and he began to offer some attempt at excuse.

"I cannot pay away much more," returned Mr. Danesbury. "I will not completely cripple the business, so that Arthur shall be unable to carry it on, and be left without resources. No! I have sacrificed enough to you and Lionel, but I will not entirely sacrifice your eldest brother, who never gave me an hour's grief in his life."

"And for William also, as well as for him and Lionel," somewhat sharply put in Mrs. Danesbury.

"Rather would I let want and poverty come upon me than ruin Arthur," proceeded the old man. "He has made unparalleled sacrifices for you of his own kind. He is a brother in a thousand. How much is this money that you are liable for?"

"It's—it's about two hundred pounds," hesitated Robert, ashamed of the confession. "It is not—"

"Two hundred pounds!" interrupted Mr. Danesbury. "What have you been doing to owe all that? I will not find it," he sternly added, "I cannot find it. You are reducing me to distress, sir, with your wicked habits. Would you wish your mother there to end her days in the workhouse? For myself," he continued, his voice broken with emotion, "I shall not long trouble any of you, and I care not how soon it may please the Almighty to remove me from a world which has been productive to me of so much suffering."

Mrs. Danesbury covered her face. Mr. Danesbury gradually changed his tone: his spirit was broken, his heart breaking, and he could not keep up anger long. He showed Robert how impossible it was that he could continue to supply means for this ruinous expenditure, and he enlarged upon his blamable course of life; the sin he was guilty of towards his parents, towards himself, and the far deeper sin he was guilty of towards God. Robert listened till he fell into a contrite spirit, and presently he burst into tears, openly lamented his conduct, and promised to amend. His father and mother seized upon the moment to implore him to reform, and Robert solemnly promised. He meant it, poor, deluded man, the sin of his daily life was pressing heavily upon his conscience; and, what with his sinking body and sinking spirits, it was impossible for any poor creature to feel more wretched. Mr. Danesbury would not advance the money which Robert demanded, he was firm in that, but he said the liabilities might be brought under his examination, and he would see if any arrangement could be effected towards paying them off by degrees, so as to release Robert from present fears. But he would only do this on condition that Robert entered into no further debts.

With this conciliation Robert was obliged to content himself, and very kind and fair it was; but the truth was, he wanted to get the money into his own fingers. He left the room, too physically miserable to stay in it; and what remedy did he resort to, to cheer himself? He went back to his bedroom, where he regularly kept spirits concealed now, and pouncing upon the brandy bottle, poured out a tumblerful, and drank it.

Do not ask where his promises of good resolution flew to. He did not stop at that little light draught; it was not enough for him; and, at the customary evening hour, having set his dress to rights, he slunk out, rather worse than usual for what he had taken.

It happened that Arthur had gone to spend that evening with his brother William. The clock struck ten, and Mrs. Danesbury retired, and for a few minutes Mr. Danesbury was alone. His head leaned on his hands, and he sat gazing abstractedly on the fire: he was thinking what a mercy it would have been had God seen fit to remove his two youngest boys in their infancy. Suddenly he heard the latchkey turn in the front door, turn and turn, as if he who held it were not in a state of competency; but, at length, it was pushed open with a burst, and Robert staggered across the hall, and came into the room. He reeled up to his father, his hair hanging about his countenance, and his attitude menacing. His words were indistinct, but, so far as Mr. Danesbury could gather, they were a demand for money.

"Are these your promises of amendment, Robert? Go to your room; go to your room, sir, and do not speak to me again until you are in a better state."

"I must and I will have money," screamed Robert. "What right have you to deny it to me? I will have it, I tell you."

Mr. Danesbury rose from his seat with dignity. "I do possess the right to deny it," he sadly answered; "and would that I had exercised that right years ago, my sons might have been more dutiful sons now."

He knew not what he did; it is to be hoped he knew not, that lost young man, for he cursed his father with a loud and grievous curse, and dealt him a blow on the temple. Mr. Danesbury fell to the ground, just as Mrs. Danesbury, her fears ever on the alert, ran in. She flew to her husband, she pushed Robert from her, she reproached him harshly in her shock of grief. He stood there raving, invoking imprecations on her, his mother, and then, with a shout and a crash, he swept the ornaments off the mantelpiece.

In rushed a man-servant, followed by Arthur, who had come home just in time to hear the noise. Arthur laid his powerful grasp upon the madman, whilst the man raised Mr. Danesbury to his chair. Mr. Danesbury's temple was bleeding, for it had struck against the fender as he fell, and as Mrs. Danesbury bathed it with water, she whispered to him, through her tears, not to be harsh with their poor mistaken boy.

"Harsh with him, no!" wailed Mr. Danesbury; "but let him take all, let him turn them out of house and home, rather than they should be cursed in their old age, by the child to whom they had given birth!"

Arthur and the man got Robert to his chamber, and undressed him, and placed him in bed. But there was no rest for the house that night, for he was out of his apartment again, as on the preceding one, stalking about, like a restless spirit, from room to room, and up the stairs and down. His state was akin to madness.

By the usual hour of the household's rising he was partially sobered, but the symptoms of insanity hung about him. His mother went to him once more, to coax, beg, entreat him to lie down and try and get some sleep. Yes, he would, he answered; and then he laid hold of her hands, and, melting into tears, whispered his contrition for what he did on the previous night. "Mother, I was mad with drink! I was mad with drink! Will you and my father forgive me?"

"Yes, yes, dear," she answered. "It is all forgiven: you were not conscious of your actions. Only go to bed quietly, and get to sleep. I will take you."

She passed on to his chamber, and he docilely followed her, muttering still, "I was mad with drink," and some other words which she could not catch, about the burthen of his bitter life.

He lay down quietly and they left the room, Arthur remaining for some moments to listen at the door. But it appeared that he did not move. Presently Arthur cautiously looked in. He was lying on the bed, with his eyes wide open.

"Did you call, Robert?" asked his brother, by way of excuse. "Do you want anything?"

"No. I'm going to get some sleep."

"Ay, do. It will do you good."

Arthur closed the door. Mrs. Danesbury was standing just outside her own chamber, and beckoned to him.

"Arthur," she whispered, "it appears to me that he is worse than I ever saw him: in a more strange sort of way. I think Dr. Pratt had better come and look at him."

"I am going for him now," replied Arthur. "If Robert cannot get to sleep, he will have an attack similar to Lionel's."

Mrs. Danesbury stole on tiptoe once or twice to the room door, but all was quiet within, and she hoped he was sleeping. In a short time Arthur returned with the surgeon. Mrs. Danesbury inquired if he had seen Lionel that morning; if he knew how he was.

"Yes, Lionel is better," replied Mr. Pratt. "He will get over this bout. But if he," nodding his head in the direction of Robert's chamber, "is in for it, we shall have some trouble. Lionel has made free enough, in all conscience, but he has made worse. To think of the evils wrought in this world by the influence of drink," uttered the old gentleman, who bore the appearance of a man of care. "My only son an alien from me! and yours more trouble than if they were aliens!"

He had gradually advanced to Robert's door as he spoke, opened it, and partially entered. But he drew back with a suppressed, hasty movement, closed the door, and kept the handle of it in his hand. Arthur and Mrs. Danesbury had followed him.

"Will you get me some vinegar?" he said to the latter. "Get it, and bring it yourself; there's a good lady."

As she turned away, Mr. Pratt looked at Arthur with a horror-stricken face. "I have sent her off purposely," he whispered. "I saw the inside of this chamber when I opened the door: it was no sight for any woman, least of all a mother. Can *you* bear it?"

A suspicion of his meaning dawned on the mind of Arthur Danesbury. "What has he done?" he asked, with blanched lips. "Surely he has not injured himself?"

"HE HAS COMMITTED SUICIDE," was the dread whisper. "May the Lord have mercy on his soul!"

They went in, Arthur nerving himself to it. The ill-fated maniac—let us call him so!—was lying on the bed in a pool of blood, the razor clasped in his right hand. He was not dead; but ere the lapse of many minutes he would no longer be numbered amongst the living.

Arthur went outside, awake, even in his despair and horror, to the humanity of keeping Mrs. Danesbury from the room. She was coming along the corridor with the vinegar-cruet in her hand. In spite of his efforts, he could not recall the colour to his face.

"Thank you," he said, offering to take it from her.

"No: I will go in with it myself," replied Mrs. Danesbury.

"Dr. Pratt—Dr. Pratt does not wish anyone to go in," rejoined Arthur.

"But I will go in. Why should I be kept out? Why are you looking so strange, so scared, Arthur? Oh!" she screamed, a fear flashing across her like lightning, "what has happened? What is amiss with my boy?"

She had the strength of a desperate woman, and struggled with him. He soothingly strove to lead her away, but she suddenly raised her foot and kicked open the door, and the scene within was disclosed to her. A long, shrill shriek rang through the house, and she fell back into Arthur's arms. It brought Mr. Danesbury out of his bedroom; and the frightened servants came running up.

What expression of horror was it that gleamed from the dying man's eye as he grasped the wrist of his father? Could it be that the accomplishments of his crime, or the close approach of death, had restored his powers of mind and memory? He appeared as conscious as he ever was before the fatal habit grew upon him; there was no mistaking the clear, sane expression of the eye. Who can imagine the awful tortures that were rending his soul?

That Robert Danesbury's intellect was clear and sane in those his dying moments was indisputable. He saw now all the inexpiable guilt of his past life: the talents he had misused, the parents whose hearts he had broken, the Heaven he had deserted. A little self-denial, a little strife and perseverance, a little help from above, and the victory would have been his. He saw it all now; but he had chosen to abandon his powers, both of mind and body, to the pursuit of a degrading vice, and at last he had rashly and impiously taken the life that was not his to take, and was winging his flight to the awful bar of an offended God. And so, amid piercing throes and mental torments, amid ineffectual efforts to give utterance to his remorse and anguish, he wrung his father's hands with a sharp pressure, and, with a last, wild cry, the spirit of Robert Danesbury passed away for ever.

"Oh, my son Robert," wailed out his anguished father, as did David of old. "My son, my son! would God I had died for thee, oh, Robert, my son, my son!"

CHAPTER XX
HOPES AND FEARS—AN UNEXPECTED EVENT

IT was autumn weather, and unusually cold; but the glow of a cheerful fire diffused its pleasant warmth over a commodious bed-chamber, and the gale outside was not felt within. A lady, young and fair, lay there on a sofa; her dark eyes were bent on the fire, as they had been for the last half-hour, as if she were in a reverie; and it would seem that it was not a pleasant one, for a contraction of pain flitted ever and anon over her brow. It was Anna Danesbury, William's wife.

In the adjoining room, the door opening between them, sat a woman before another fire, nursing an infant. It was three weeks old; and very precious was the little life to its mother, for she had not before had a child to live. Suddenly a visitor's knock resounded through the house, and the nurse arose and entered her mistress's chamber.

"Of course, ma'am, you will not see visitors this afternoon?" she said. "You are not strong enough for it."

Mrs. William Danesbury looked up. "I suppose not, nurse. And yet it seems to me that they could not do me much harm."

But instead of visitors, it proved to be Mrs. Philip Danesbury.

"Why did Mary not come with you?" demanded the invalid, as her aunt embraced her.

"Because I feared there might be too much chattering," replied Mrs. Philip. "I heard you were not so well as you might be. Mary will come and see you to-morrow. What has been the matter with you, my dear? Baby three weeks old, and you lying here!"

Anna did not answer at first. "I have had so much fever," she slowly said. "Aunt, I have wanted you at home."

"My dear, I did hope and intend to be back before your illness, but—"

"Not for that," interrupted Anna. "I did very well without you. Aunt," she repeated, in a whisper of emotion, her trembling hands seizing those of Mrs. Philip Danesbury, "my husband is going all wrong. It is that which makes me ill."

"Is he worse?"

"A great deal. Some one or other is always calling to induce him to go out in the evening. Sometimes it is Laughton, sometimes it is Lionel—when Lionel is in a fit state to call for anyone—sometimes it's others. Not one night since baby was born has he been in until the public-houses were closed; and almost always in a state that he cannot come to my room to say 'good-night.' Here I lie listening for him, waiting for him, unable to get to sleep, and when I hear him, he is not well enough to come and speak to me."

"I am truly grieved to hear this," exclaimed Mrs. Philip Danesbury. "But do not talk of it now, Anna."

"I must talk of it," she vehemently answered, whilst a burning, hectic spot appeared on her cheek. "Aunt, I have not spoken of it, and the silence is preying upon me: to tell you will be a relief."

"I thought William's resolutions were so good!" lamented Mrs. Philip Danesbury.

"He does make good resolutions, and sometimes he will keep them for ever so long. And then, again, he breaks out, and for several days will not be sober. Did you hear about the loss at the works, aunt?" she added, dropping her voice.

"No."

"It was all through William. Something in the making of the machinery. I do not understand it; for Mrs. Danesbury, who told me, did not enter into details—perhaps she did not know them herself—and I was too much annoyed to inquire. But it seems they had a great deal of valuable work in process, and William went in one day in an incapable state, gave wrong orders, and it was spoiled. The loss was some hundreds of pounds."

"Poor Mr. Danesbury! poor Mr. Danesbury!" uttered Mrs. Philip. "What sons! When will his cares end?"

"William came home almost like a madman. He was sobered then, and knew the mischief he had caused. I never saw him so cut up, so full of sorrow. I inquired what was amiss, but he would not tell me."

"And I suppose he drank more to drown it?"

"No, indeed, aunt. He did not touch a drop of anything for days afterwards. He is full of good hopes and resolves, if he had but strength to keep them."

"Do you know how the poor old gentleman is, Anna?"

"Much the same, I believe. He was here on Sunday, and I could scarcely keep my eyes from him, he looks so broken with care: every time I see him it strikes me more forcibly. Mrs. Danesbury is ill now. You are aware, perhaps, that the influenza has broken out at Eastborough?"

"It was the first news one of the servants received us with when we reached home to-day. She said it was raging badly, and two or three had died. I told her she was a Job's comforter, to give us that for welcome."

"Mrs. Danesbury was attacked with it some days ago," returned Anna, "and I hear she is very ill."

"She has never got over the shock of Robert's death last spring," observed Mrs. Philip Danesbury.

Anna clasped her hands together, as if her emotions were too much for her. "Aunt, when I think of Robert's fate, of Lionel's certain death—"

"Lionel is no better, I fear," interrupted Mrs. Philip.

"Better!" ejaculated Anna. "He cannot live long as he goes on now; or, if he does live, he will become insane. Mr. Pratt says his brain is softening rapidly. When I dwell upon Lionel's state, upon Robert's dreadful death, and remember that William may come to the same, my senses seem as though they would desert me."

"Now, do you know what?" exclaimed Mrs. Philip, in the peremptory tone we use to an offending child; "if you say another word upon this topic, I shall be gone. You are doing yourself incalculable harm."

"I am always dwelling upon it," was Anna's answer; "how can I help it?"

"You must try and help it. You will never get strong, if you don't," replied Mrs. Philip. "Nothing retards recovery so much as brooding over ills, real or imaginary."

She was resolute not to permit it, and Anna, perforce, was silent, and presently dropped into a doze. Mrs. Philip took the opportunity to leave, telling the nurse she would look in again in the evening.

William Danesbury came home at tea-time, and ran up to his wife's room. He was quite himself. He edged himself on to the sofa, and Anna drew his hand between hers, and held it there.

"Have tea in my room, William," she whispered. "Nurse will make it, and send it in for us."

"If you like," he cheerily answered. "When do you mean to get out of this room, Anna?"

"Soon. But I am not quite so strong as I might be. As I should be if—I——"

"If what?" he said, leaning over her.

She drew his face down, so that it rested on hers, and whispered, "If I were not so anxious about you."

He could not pretend to misunderstand her, but he strove to turn it off with some disjointed, careless words—that he was all right, and meant to keep so.

"Oh, that you would, William!" she murmured. "If not for my sake, for "—she pulled aside her shawl and disclosed a little red face nestled to her—"this child's."

"Do not fear, Anna. I know the responsibilty that is upon me. Nay, you must not cry. My dear wife, I will be all you wish me."

Thus, when himself, he was ever ready to say. A kind, loving husband, an attractive man was William Danesbury, so long as he kept his brain and mind clear.

Tea was over: the nurse had the baby in the other room, and William Danesbury was alone with his wife. He began to show symptoms of weariness; looked at his watch, walked about the room, and stirred the fire. His wife understood it all. She called him to her.

"William, you said, before tea, that you would be all you ought to be. Begin now: do not go out to-night."

He did not answer.

"Oh, William, for my sake, for your own sake! If you do not make the first effort, you will never carry out your resolve. Begin at once, do not go out to-night."

"Anna, I am sure it is not right for you to excite yourself like this."

"No, it is not; it is very bad for me. But how can I help it? If you would but stay with me this one evening?"

"Well, I will, Anna."

"You will! you mean it?" she eagerly asked.

"I will. I promise you."

"Oh, William! how happy you might make me!" she said, the anxious expression fading from her eyes. "See, my trouble is gone, and I am all at rest."

Scarcely had she so spoken, when a servant came in, and addressed her master.

"Mr. Laughton is waiting for you, sir."

Anna turned her large, yearning eyes upon him. The anxious look had come back again.

"Tell him," began William to the servant—" stay, I will go and speak to him."

"No! send the message. William, send the message," she broke forth, in terror.

"I will not go out, Anna. Have I not promised?" he answered.

He went downstairs. Soon Anna heard the front door close on Mr. Laughton, and her husband came back again. She took his hand and held it, by way of thanks.

"How dull you must be lying here all day!" he exclaimed.

"I read a good deal, and that passes the time. I wish I could see by candle-light to do so, but my eyes are not strong yet."

"Shall I read you something, Anna?"

"I was thinking how much I should like to hear *something* read. But perhaps you will not like to read that."

"Yes, I will. What is it?"

"A chapter in the Bible," she said, in a low tone.

William smiled. "I suppose you think that is not much in my line. It is more in Arthur's. I do believe he reads the Bible night and morning."

"As you will some time, William, I hope."

"Well, I will to-night," he said. "Where shall I find a Bible?"

She pointed to her own on the dressing-table, and he brought it forward. "Which chapter?" he asked.

She opened the book at the third chapter of Revelation. William Danesbury read it reverently. To him it was especially applicable: he felt it to be so, and knew why his wife had chosen it.

"'He that overcometh, the same shall be clothed in white raiment: and I will not blot out his name out of the book of life, but I will confess his name before My father, and before His angels.

"'Him that overcometh will I make a pillar in the temple of My God, and he shall go no more out: and I will write upon him the name of My God, and the name of the city of My God, which is New Jerusalem, which cometh down out of heaven from My God: and I will write upon him My new name.

"'To him that overcometh will I grant to sit with Me in My throne, even as I also overcame, and am set down with My father in His throne.'"

Those three verses were especially applicable. Would *he* overcome?

"William," she murmured, "we all have something to overcome, ere we can inherit; all, all. Christ Himself says, 'Even as I also overcame.' 'Because thou hast kept the word of My patience, I also will keep thee from the hour of temptation, which shall come upon all the world, to try them that dwell upon the earth.' William, those promises were not made for nothing."

William Danesbury was closing the book again, when the same servant appeared and called him out. He went downstairs. Anna wondered, for she had not heard anyone come to the house; but her attention had been occupied with other things. Immediately she caught the sound as of more than one going out, and the front door closed, and her husband did not return. She rang her bell, and her maid came up.

"Is Mr. Danesbury gone out?"

"Yes, ma'am."

"Gone out!" she could not help repeating.

"With Mr. Lionel," added the servant. "Master said I was to tell you, if you inquired, that he should not be long."

Her heart sickened within her. What! in the very face of his promise to the contrary: in the very echo of that warning chapter! Could he not "overcome" for that one night? She moaned aloud in her fulness of despair.

When Mrs. Philip Danesbury entered, she found her flushed and excited. "Not to stop in for this one night!" she reiterated. "After promising me! It is no use hoping, aunt: he is a lost man."

Two hours passed away, and William did not come in. Mrs. Philip was unwilling to leave her, she was so restless. Too ill to sit up, she yet would not go to bed. The nurse came in, and exerted her eloquence, but found it of no effect. Suddenly, they heard the church bell toll out.

"There's the passing-bell!" exclaimed Anna. "I wonder who is gone? Some one is released from a world of care and suffering." And she sighed so painfully, that it almost seemed to intimate a regret that *she* was not released.

"It's somebody of consequence, whoever it is," cried the nurse, having returned, "or they would not trouble themselves to ring it out so late as this."

Another half-hour, and then William Danesbury entered. They heard him go into the parlour.

"There!" exclaimed Anna to her aunt, "you hear! he does not come upstairs: that will tell you how he is."

"I will go down and see," said Mrs. Philip.

William was leaning over the fire when she entered, his elbow resting on the mantelpiece. His face looked pale and sad: not, Mrs. Philip thought, as that of a man in drink.

"Aunt, how do you do? I heard you were back. I am glad you came in: Anna is lonely alone."

Neither was his tone, neither was the expression of his eyes like that of a man in drink. Mrs. Philip looked keenly, and felt convinced that he was sober.

"Anna has been worrying herself much at your staying out," she said to him. "She is in so excited a state, thinking you have now come in from the—public-houses."

"No," he sighed, "I have come from a very different scene. Of course, you have not heard the tidings?"

"What tidings? we have heard nothing."

"Mrs. Danesbury is dead."

Mrs. Philip was shocked and startled. "Mrs. Danesbury dead!" she uttered, after a dread pause.

"Lionel came here, and said his mother was dying, and begged me to go to her without a moment's delay, for she had asked for me," resumed William. "I thought I should soon be home again, and I did not like to tell Anna the cause of my going out, lest it should alarm her."

"Then the passing-bell was for Mrs. Danesbury! What can have caused her sudden death?"

"She has died from this influenza that is going about," was William's answer. "She has been evidently sinking ever since Robert's death, and when this disease attacked her, she had no stamina wherewith to struggle against it. A physician was telegraphed for from town this morning, at five o'clock, and was here by ten, but he could do her no good. Poor thing! she was sensible, and took leave of us all. Aunt," he added, lowering his voice, "she asked me to pardon her for having forced me to drink wine and beer in my childhood."

"William! did she? She is another gone to her grave wishing that her life could be lived over again; that she might reject the evil, and choose the good."

"She held my hand and Arthur's, and begged us to forgive past unkindnesses. But the parting with Lionel—it was grievous to see."

"Robert and Lionel have sent her to her grave between them," impressively resumed Mrs. Philip Danesbury.

"Lionel is saying so. I took him home, and left him there in a state of excitement that you can scarcely imagine. Crying one minute, talking the next; and, should he fly to drink in the midst of it, he will inevitably bring on another of those dangerous attacks."

"William," spoke up Mrs. Philip, in a solemn tone, "all this ought to tell upon you as a warning. Will you not accept it?"

"Yes, I will."

"How does your father bear his loss?"

"Calmly. He has experienced too much sorrow for anything to affect him greatly now. My poor father will not be long after her," he added, with a sigh.

"Drink! drink! the evils of indulging in strong drink!" aspirated Mrs. Philip Danesbury.

William passed by the remark without observation. "May we tell Anna?" he asked. "Or will it excite her injuriously?"

"Tell her—oh, yes. Her fears and excitement all tend to one point, William."

He knew what that was.

Reader! how the close approach of death changes us. It was a strangely impressive scene that William had come from, one which might suffice for a whole life's lesson: Mrs. Danesbury lay on her bed, a dying woman; Lionel close to her, the others dispersed round her— her husband, Arthur, and William, and Mr. Pratt; the physician had returned to town again from his fruitless mission. Mrs. Danesbury had repented: her days had been one scene of bitter repentance ever since the death of Robert: *but remorse she never could put away from her; she could not recall the evil done.* If she had made her peace with God, so far as she herself went, she could not make it for the lost Robert: she could not make it for Lionel. She took William's hand in hers: "Forgive me, as I have asked God to forgive me, for having forced you to drink wine and beer in your childhood," she gasped. "William, be you warned while there is yet time; and put them from you. Do not let me have another lost soul upon my hands! It seems I would give my own soul if God would but grant me my existence over again, that I might bring up my children to strive for life everlasting. I brought them up for this world, not for the next; and I ruined them for both. Oh, Lionel, if I could but take your sins upon me, and bear them now before my Maker."

She spoke truth. She had ruined her sons, and they, in their turn, had sent her to her grave.

There was a deplorable scene enacted when she was being placed in it. Lionel was in a wretchedly nervous condition, and was obliged to take brandy ere he could venture to the funeral. As the mourners stood around the grave, Mr. Danesbury at their head, and the coffin was being lowered into it, Lionel seized one of the cords, and broke into a burst of sobbing and wailing, and, but for Arthur's firm grasp, who stood next him, he would have flung himself into the grave. Lionel had to be taken away ere the service could be concluded; and, that night, he was secured in a strait-waistcoat.

All this acted as a warning to William Danesbury, and he strove to master his baneful passion. For some time he kept sober. He stayed indoors in the evening, refused to join any loose friends, meaning those who were lovers of excess, and took only ale with his meals. He seemed quite resolved to put temptation from him. But, one Sunday—Anna had been downstairs some time then—the wine was on the table after dinner, and he finished nearly a bottle of port. He rose from his seat, and was about to decap another, when his wife glided up to him, and laid her hand upon his shoulder.

"William, do not."

He looked at her; looked at the wine: and then put the bottle back again upon the sideboard. There it remained; but ever and anon his eyes turned restlessly to it, as if they were fascinated.

Later in the evening, when Anna retired for the night, the struggle came to an end. He drew the cork, drank the whole of the wine, and then drew the cork of a bottle of brandy. At one o'clock in the morning he stumbled up to bed—as—as I hope you and I shall never stumble up.

CHAPTER XXI
ANOTHER DEATHBED

ONE evening in November, about two months after Mrs. Danesbury's death, William was on his way to Danesbury House. His road lay through the town. Eastborough had much increased of late years, especially in the matter of public-houses and beer-shops. For one that used to be in the place, three might be counted now. The chief object of attraction, however, lay in a showy gin-palace. A gin palace in the very heart of the long street, with a new stuccoed front, and illuminated lamps; and mirrors, and gas, and gilding inside. The other shops, and there was no lack of them, had not yet got into the fashion of glare and glitter; but so attractive was the novelty found, that it was crowded night and day.

William Danesbury passed, with an effort, these various houses of entertainment; really, with an effort, for sounds of revelry, mingled with the jingling of glasses, came from them pleasantly on his ear. The temptation to enter was very strong on William Danesbury then, but he resisted it and strode rapidly on. How strong it was, how the temptation, backed by the Evil One, was pulling at his heart-strings, he alone could tell; but he did *not* tell how he resisted it. In passing Lionel's cottage, he saw an old lady standing at the door. He stopped.

"If you want Mrs. Danesbury," she cried out before he could speak, "she's gone out for the doctor. And I am keeping the door for her, and am afraid for my very life."

"Is Lionel ill?" inquired William, guessing who she was.

"He's in the strangest way *I* ever saw," continued the old lady; "but, thank goodness, I have never been with such as him; he's fancying he sees cats and dogs. He has not been sober, I hear, since his mother died, two months ago; not to say sober for a day. The night before last he was dragged home by two men, his head hanging down, and his face purple and crimson. They threw him on the bed, and there he lay, like a clod, for seventeen hours! Beast!"

At that moment Lionel's wife hastened up. And then the old lady, her grandmother, who had come from her farm to stop a few days in Eastborough, found that the gentleman was Mr. William Danesbury, and she had been calling his brother "beast" to his face.

"Well, he is one," was her mental comment.

"I have been for Mr. Pratt, sir," Katherine said to William. "He is out: but they will send him when he returns."

She looked ill, thin, haggard. And no wonder: for, besides the anxiety, and the harassing life she led with her husband, she suffered from positive want of food. Lionel's habits ran away with the weekly pound, and, for days together, she had only dry bread to eat. A mixed feeling of shame, pride, and love to Lionel prevented her telling this, otherwise her mother would not have suffered her to want. Mr. Danesbury partially suspected it, though not to its extent, and many an extra half-crown, beyond the weekly allowance, did he slip into her hand, unsuspected by Lionel. Ah! there were not many like good Mr. Danesbury. A bad bargain had Katherine Bing in marrying his son.

It was thought that Lionel Danesbury would surely read a lesson from his brother's awful death. He did not. And yet, poor, infatuated man! the sight of that ghastly corpse, with its crimson gash, was never absent from his mind's eye.

"Lionel is ill again?" observed William.

"Very ill," answered Katherine. "Will you come up, sir, and see him?"

He followed her upstairs. Lionel was in the bedroom, in his night-shirt and boots, striding about, and looking wild and haggard. William saw what dreadful disorder was upon him again.

"I want my clothes," said Lionel. "She has got them." She had hid the boots.

"I did not dare to leave them in his way," whispered Katherine to William. "He would have been out, and over the town. Last night, at eleven o'clock, he stole out, and I was till three in the morning looking for him in all the rain. I found him at last on the bridge, wet through. I told grandmother to be sure and keep his boots from him, but I suppose she got afraid."

Lionel had fixed his gaze on the wall of the room, the pupils of his eyes dilating, and horror struggling into his countenance. He slowly backed as far from it as possible, and cowered against the opposite wall.

"Look there," he shivered to William.

"What?"

"See how black she is? That cat has been there twice before. Drive her away. Oh! William! drive her away!"

His voice had risen to a piteous scream. William went to the spot that appeared to excite his terror. "There is nothing here, Lionel; see"—kicking his feet against the wainscoting—"nothing at all. I will remove the chair. There; you see there's nothing."

Lionel's excited eyes were wandering round the room; under the bed, on the bed, along the walls, on the ceiling, just as if they were following the progress of some object.

"Lionel, you would be better in bed," cried his brother. "Come, get in; and I will go again and see after Pratt."

William laid hold of him. A peculiar tremor was running through all his limbs, the precursor of what was coming.

"Yes—yes," speaking in a wandering, abstracted tone, "yes, I'll get into bed; and you get Pratt here." But, instead of approaching the bed, he drew farther from it. William gently pulled him forward. Lionel suddenly stopped dead.

"There she is!" he whispered. "On the bed. Look! She has got spots on her coat now."

"Nonsense," said William, "there's nothing; you know it, Lionel. If you——"

With a spring, Lionel eluded William's grasp, and rushed to the head of the stairs. The old lady, who had stood on them, afraid to venture farther, set up a shrill scream, and dropped down them as if she had been shot. This arrested Lionel, and William drew him back towards the bed.

"I can't," he piteously said. "She's got inside, and some more with her. See how thick their tails are. There's one hanging out now. They are the imps, and more will be here presently."

"Come along," said William, cheerily; "I'll drive them all away for you."

Katherine turned the bedclothes down to the very bottom of the bed, and patted it with her hands. "You see," she said to her husband, "it is all your fancy."

He touched the bed himself, and looked wildly about the room again. And just then the surgeon came in.

"What is the matter here?" asked Mr. Pratt. "I have just met old grandmother Ducksworth flying down the street, as if she were flying for her life, afraid of stopping here, she said. Ill again?"

"More cats, sir, and other things," interposed Lionel's wife. "He is afraid now they are in the bed."

"Keep them away from me, Pratt, will you?" gasped Lionel.

"To be sure. Get into bed, and I'll see about it. Holloa! boots in bed! That will never do. Let me have those: we will send them after the cats."

Quiet as a lamb under Mr. Pratt's experienced eye, Lionel suffered his boots to be taken from him, and lay down in bed. The doctor administered some medicine he had brought with him, then tucked him up, and told him to be quiet and to sleep. As they were leaving the room, William looked back. There sat Lionel upright in bed, ready to spring out.

"I can't stop here," he shivered. "They are coming again. Don't leave me."

"No," answered Katherine, "I am going to stay with you. Lie down, and I will sit here upon the bed. The cats will not come where I am."

Mr. Pratt and William Danesbury went downstairs, the former carrying the boots. "I have told his wife never to let him have his boots in these attacks," he observed. "She knows they must be kept from him."

"Lionel found them, I believe, while she was gone for you."

"Not one in ten of these poor madmen will start out without their boots," remarked Mr. Pratt; "but let them put on their boots, and they'll watch an opportunity to be off, even if they be stark naked. Poor woman! she has a dreadful life with him. And this is going to be a bad attack."

"Do you fear so?" asked William.

"Ay. He has been drinking awfully lately. It will be worse than any he has had. His wife must have some men in the house, for before morning he will be outrageous. Mr. William, I will not answer for it that he'll get over this. I did not think he would the last time, when his mother died, you know. I'll look in at George Groat's," added Mr. Pratt, "and send up the men that were here before, if they are to be had."

"I will stay until someone comes," said William.

"Do so. It is not right that his wife should be left with him alone."

Quiet did Lionel lie while Mr. Pratt was in the house, but the moment he heard the door close on him, he was troublesome again. Who are more cunning than they? Katherine called out, and William ran up.

"I want my boots, William."

"Presently. What for?"

"Oh, they are round me, and I can't stop here. I must go out."

"Where to?"

"I—I want to see my father. Get my boots."

"Not to-night."

"Yes, I must. Get my boots."

"Very well. Presently," and down sat William.

Later, when the requisite help arrived, three men, William took his departure. When William entered Danesbury House, Arthur was sitting alone.

"Where is my father?" he asked.

"He is gone to bed ill," was Arthur's reply. "I do not think he will be here many weeks, William. If he is no better in the morning, I shall call Pratt in. He would not have him to-night."

"I have just been with Pratt at Lionel's," returned William. "He has got another attack. The old gentleman has sent three men in, so he anticipates mischief."

"Ah! I heard of his being carried home, unable to walk, the night before last."

"And last night he stole out, and his wife was for four hours looking for him, in the rain, and found him at last on the bridge."

"What a life for her!" uttered Arthur.

"Pratt says he may not get over this."

"Then it will be the death of our father!" sadly exclaimed Arthur.

William sat a little while, and then rose to go. His brother accompanied him through the hall to the door, and stood looking out into the night. "William," he said, laying his hand upon his shoulder with an impressive gesture, "go straight home."

"I will. I intend to." And he did so: bravely passing by the public-houses and liquor shops, as he had done in coming.

Lionel Danesbury had latterly been a burthen to himself and to all around him, but the end was come. The news spread in the town next day that Lionel was ill, dangerously ill. His aunt, Mrs. Philip Danesbury, went to see him, and entered the untidy, comfortless chamber.

The fire had been raked out of the grate, for the patient could not bear the heat, and a blanket, tossed off the bed, was lying on a chair. Two men sat in the room in readiness to act when they should be required, and a third was outside. This disease was overpowering him for the last time. He lay on the bed, his eyes rolling wildly; cloths steeped in vinegar were covering his head, and the burning fever of delirium was raging in his brain.

Need you be told the name of the malady he was stricken down with? Ask the surgeons what disease it is that they have most frequently to grapple with, amidst the miserable class who chiefly fall under their care; and they will tell you it is DELIRIUM TREMENS.

This was one of his quiet intervals; nevertheless, his whole frame, his legs, his body, his arms, his hands, shook to such a degree that the very floor of the room was agitated. Oh, it is a terrible disease! may we never encounter it in those who are near and dear to us!

Mrs. Philip Danesbury was awe-stricken. She remembered his once healthy form, his intellectual qualities, and she looked at what he was—the dying sinner. She advanced and took his hand; but an irrepressible terror came over her at the contact of that unnatural motion, which no human aid could stop or mitigate, and she dropped it again."

"Do you know me, Lionel? It is I; your aunt."

"They have been coming round the bed," he answered in a loud, important whisper, whilst his poor head turned incessantly from side to side, "millions of them."

Dr. Pratt, who was present, took hold of his wrists, and presently wrung some linen out of the vinegar basin, and exchanged it for that on his head. Lionel was conscious of this, for he raised his hand and pulled it lower on his forehead. "Ah! so! that's cool," he said, and then he turned again to Mrs. Philip Danesbury, looking calmly at her, and speaking in a tone perfectly rational.

"Do you know that William is dead? He'll be a great loss at the works. He went out, got in a street row, and they brought him in here, covered with wounds. His head was an awful sight. A great fool to get into it! However, he is dead."

Poor fellow! what was his brain working on?

"You never heard such a row," he continued, still so collectedly and rationally, that Mrs. Philip Danesbury was unpleasantly puzzled, and a stranger would have believed he was relating something he had actually witnessed. "The sounds came up here; I could not sleep for them. And," he added in a dread whisper, "he looked just like Robert did."

He stopped for the space of a minute, lay perfectly still, and then stealthily slid down the bed; and, with a spring so sudden that the attendants were unprepared, stood bolt upright on it, the raging madman.

Quick as thought they were upon him, the three men and Dr. Pratt, but the strength of these maniacs is almost supernatural. It was a fearful struggle, a fearful sight, that unhappy creature raving, struggling, and fighting with his opponents. If he should master!—and there almost seemed a doubt of it. All dangerous weapons, razors, knives, even the fire-irons, had been removed, and the windows were fastened down.

Mrs. Philip Danesbury hastened to descend the stairs. Katherine, ill and tearful, placed a chair for her.

"What did he mean when he spoke of his brother's having been killed?" she asked. "Has anything happened to him?"

"Oh, no, ma'am. Mr. William was here this morning. My poor husband has been going on like this all night, his mind wandering from one subject to another. It always does in these attacks."

Mrs. Philip wished Katherine good-day, and left the house, a conviction resting on her mind that she had seen Lionel for the last time.

That day passed, and the night, and in the course of the next day they had to strap him down to his bed. Now would be an interval of quietness, not rest; and now, one of outrageous madness.

Most men who have given themselves recklessly up to intemperance know that this disease will creep, or is creeping, upon them, that it will probably be their end; and yet they cannot bring themselves to abandon the courses which are inducing its approach. Lionel knew it. Faint hopes, half-formed resolves arose, that in time he would thrust from him this insidious vice, and embrace uprightness and peace. *In time,* take you notice; not at the present moment; at some future one.

Again dawned the morning light upon the patient. It was his last day of life, though he might know it not. The fits of delirium continued with unabated violence, broken, as before, by interludes of quiet—if it could be called quiet, when the whole frame was shaken as with a fierce ague. His mind wandered distressingly; yet in those wanderings might be traced a recollection of his present state, of the life he had led.

"They keep me here, you see," he exclaimed to Arthur, "and I want to be out. I want to——Father, is that you?"

It was Mr. Danesbury. Though very near the grave himself, he had insisted on being brought to Lionel's bedside. William was also present.

"That's good," continued Lionel; "I wanted to see you. I'm so hot, you know. They have been coming round, such a lot of them, millions and millions. Where's Robert?" With one hand he swept the cloths from his head, and Dr. Pratt, who had come in with Mr. Danesbury, though protesting against his old friend's visit, replaced them.

"Who says I am dying?" he shouted. "It is no business of theirs. Ah, is that you?" he cried, again momentarily recognising his father, and holding out his hand, which was vibrating like a pendulum. "You don't think I'm going, do you?"

Mr. Danesbury was taken by surprise; the question was put so rationally. He did not know what to answer.

"Oh, no, no!" reiterated Lionel, with a shriek of anguish that none present would ever forget; "not yet, in mercy! A little respite! A short period for reformation and redemption! Take away the drink; take it away, I say! I have led an evil life," he added, his mind a strange mixture of consciousness and insanity; "but I won't touch another drop: it's burning here." He pointed to his chest, and then lay still, recommencing, after a short pause.

"They came round me in the night, and told me I was dying; but it's not true. Hold me! hold me! at least till I have got through this multiplicity of work. Do you see all the duties that have accumulated? I have done nothing, you know—nothing but drink; but I *can* get through them."

"He has been raving all night about this accumulation of work and duties," whispered Katherine.

"It cannot be that I am dying! I must have the time I want first. Yes, I told you God would give it me. Katherine, my poor wife, you say you have been miserable, but we shall be happy now. You need not be afraid of me any longer: I'll keep my promises, and leave it off.

"William, is that you? Come here, closer. I have had such a horrid dream. I thought I was getting towards the prime of life, and that all the years given to me had been wasted, that I had been constantly drunk. Drunk! I thought—and it made me burn here," tossing the cloths from his brow—" that the time was come for me to die, and then I found that all these years had not been mine to waste. Who spoke then? It was none of you. Who says it's true? It is not true; I tell you it was a dream. Be off! be off! how dare you drive me mad? And if it were true, I am to have the time. What do you know about it? I say the time is mine. Who says I had it once, and threw it away? How dare you say it? Oh, mercy, mercy! A little time, for the love of mercy! I am not drunk now. Father, is that you? I have sworn not to touch another drop."

"My dear father," said Arthur, approaching Mr. Danesbury, "this is no place for you. Let me take you away."

"Arthur," said the old man, with quivering lips and trembling hands, as he grasped those of his eldest son, "there is no place for me much longer on earth. I question whether he or I shall go the quicker. My heart is broken. William," reaching out to take his hand, and bring him side by side with Arthur, "can you marvel at it? My son, can you marvel at it? Few and evil have the days of my old age been: my substance destroyed, my peace of mind wrecked. One of my children has gone before me; another—he, poor madman—is going with me, and I have no hope that I shall meet either of them hereafter. Do you act"—he wrung William's hand—"so as to come to me."

They took Mr. Danesbury from the room; they also took the unhappy wife, for Dr. Pratt saw that the end was at hand. In a paroxysm of violence, more acute than any which had gone before it, the troubled spirit of Lionel Danesbury flew away to Him who gave it.

Yes! he asked for time, in his half-conscious ravings; but time upon time had been vouchsafed him, and he had used it not! Was it not enough to break their father's heart? This is no imaginative history, it is taken from a family's life. The one son rushed into the next world, a suicide; the other was brought, in the early years of manhood, to his dreadful deathbed. Not one good action could they remember to have performed in their whole lives; not one hour, of the precious time granted them, had been used to good account. Their manly forms, their talents, their health and strength, had been offered up, and sacrificed, on the shrine of INTEMPERANCE.

"It's a good man gone home."

CHAPTER XXII
ONE MORE DEATH—ANXIOUS THOUGHT

THE church bell at Eastborough was solemnly tolling, as a funeral wound its way from Danesbury House. It was a long procession, all walking; for no carriages were used, by desire of the dead: and, indeed, the distance was but short. The officiating minister preceded the coffin, which was borne by eight of the Danesbury workmen, its pall being held by eight of the superior overlookers and foremen, Thomas Harding being one. The chief mourners were Arthur and William Danesbury, Viscount Temple, and Mr. St. George; but many others followed. Every house and shop in Eastborough had its shutters closed, to testify respect to him who was being carried past.

Stealing after it came groups of women, but, womanlike, they fell into gossip, though the tears were coursing down many of their cheeks.

"It's a good man gone home," said one. "We shall never see another like him."

"Yes, we shall. He has left one behind that will tread in his steps. Mr. Arthur will be his father over again. Only to think of it! but fifteen days, this very day, since poor, young Mr. Lionel was laid in the ground! It must have been sudden like; for Miss Isabel—Lady Temple, that is to say—was only sent for three days before the death."

"The poor old gentleman wanted to go to Mr. Lionel's funeral, but his sons and Mr. Pratt told him he was not equal to it, and at last he listened to them, and consented to stay at home. But when they got in again from the grave, there he was on the floor. It was not a fit; Mr. Pratt said he thought he was taken for death. After that he rallied for three or four days, and actually walked out into the garden and sat there, and then he was taken worse, and they telegraphed for Lady Temple."

"He was quite sensible up to the last minute, I heard, and had his speech and senses about him all clear."

"I heard another thing, I did: that when somebody asked old Pratt what he had died of, he said of a broken heart."

"Well, he has had enough to break it. He makes the fourth taken to the churchyard all within the year. What do you think?" added the woman, dropping her voice, "he is going to be laid by the side of the first Mrs. Danesbury, not the second."

"How do you know?"

"I do know. My husband heard old Green, the sexton, say so last night, in at 'The Cock-and-Bottle.' There was a vacant space left by the side of the first Mrs. Danesbury, which has never been filled up, and he is to lie there."

Yes. John Danesbury was gone! Gone from a world of care to his recompense above. He had learned in time to look to One who is a sure refuge.

The dark line wended its slow way along, past the public-houses—closed to-day—through the churchyard into the church. When it came out again, there was scarcely space left for it in the churchyard, or for the mourners to gather round the grave; and there was not a dry eye to be seen, there was not a heart but was lifted up in response to the words of the minister: "I heard a voice from heaven, saying unto me, Write, From henceforth blessed are the dead which die in the Lord: even so saith the Spirit; for they rest from their labours."

Back again at Danesbury House, the solicitor to the family marshalled all whom it might concern into the library, and produced the will. It was sealed with Mr. Danesbury's own private seal, and upon being opened, two letters fell out—one addressed to "My Son Arthur," the other to "My Son William," and were superscribed, "To be read before the will is read."

Each perused his letter in silence, Arthur's face flushing with surprise, William's with emotion. It was supposed by those around that the letters explained to each the motives which had dictated the will. After the death of Lionel, Mr. Danesbury had cancelled his previous will, and made this; and the letters bore the same date.

"Are you ready?" inquired Mr. Williams, the solicitor.

"Quite," they answered.

"First of all," premised Mr. Williams, "Mr. Danesbury wished me to declare publicly that he had had no adviser in the making of the will, and that no person whatever is privy to its contents, save himself and I, who wrote it." And he began to read.

The spectators listened in silence—some deeming it a strange will. It was found that the whole of the business and the capital occupied in it, was left exclusively to Arthur. A certain portion of its profits was to be paid yearly to William for five years. At the end of that period he was to be taken into partnership, and receive an equal share, *provided Arthur should deem it expedient.* If Arthur did not, things were to go on as before. There were a few trifling bequests and legacies; and to Katherine Danesbury was secured a suitable annuity, in accordance with her original position in life. Danesbury House, with its furniture, except the plate and pictures, was bequeathed to Arthur, and a sum of ready money to William. The plate was to be equally divided between Arthur and William, and of the pictures Lady Temple also took her share. They both understood, nay, they knew, the motives which had dictated the will—a doubt of what William's future conduct might be; and Mr. Danesbury, in making it, knew that the high honour, the exact justice of Arthur, needed no other guarantee for his performance of the contract, when the time came to fulfil it. Most earnestly did Arthur hope that William would act so as to enable him to perform it.

Earnestly, also, did William hope it; I am not sure but he prayed for it, as he walked home with his wife that evening. He was striving with all his might to overcome, and the strife was great, greater than he knew well how to battle with.

An afternoon or two before they were to quit Eastborough, Lord and Lady Temple were standing at the drawing-room window of Danesbury House. Isabel was talking, in a low, saddened tone, of many things connected with her old home and her late father. At length they began to speak of the will.

"Do you know, Isabel, I cannot yet understand it," he said: "so just, so good a man as your father, to leave his sons so differently provided for!—at anyrate, for five years."

"I can, unfortunately," replied Isabel. "It has proved to me what I have dreaded to ask—that William has not forsaken his old habit."

"Still, I cannot agree with the will," debated Lord Temple. "Suppose Arthur were not what he is, he might take advantage of William."

"But he *is* what he is," smiled Isabel, "and my dear father knew it. Otherwise he would never have left it so."

"It is a perfectly just will," called out a voice from the embrasure of the other window, "the will of a just and a good man."

"Who's that? William! is that you? We had no idea you were there."

William advanced. "I was here when you came in," he said, "and thought you saw me, but I was buried in unpleasant reveries, and did not interrupt your converse. My father could not have made any other will, Lord Temple," he continued. "Suppose he had constituted me an equal partner with Arthur; given me co-authority and co-ownership; and I were to squander my substance and his; run recklessly to work; go the way of Robert and Lionel? Arthur might be ruined long before the five years were up, the trade fallen through, and the works done away with."

"True, true," answered Lord Temple; "I did not look at it in that light."

"It was the kindest will to me that my father could have made. He had my true interest at heart; I know he had, and he told me so in the letter."

"Mr. Danesbury was a man who lived but for his children," said Lord Temple. "But, William, you are not going the way of Robert and Lionel?"

William heaved a deep sigh. "Sometimes I fear I shall have a difficulty to keep from it."

"But why? Do you doubt your resolution?"

"Yes, I do. I have resolved to be a sober man so many times now, and broken out again, that I begin to fear it."

"I have not seen you the worse for wine in the slightest degree this fortnight that we have been down," remarked Lord Temple, in a gentle tone of encouragement.

"No. I have not exceeded, neither did I for some little time before you came. But I have been cautious for as long as this before, and the temptation has overtaken me again. If I take but a glass of anything, I crave for more, with a longing positively painful in its intensity. One glass of wine, one glass of spirits, sets me on; and then the desire is almost irrepressible. I may almost add, one glass of beer."

"As it used to be with me," said Lord Temple. "You must do as I have done, William: confine yourself to water."

"But a single glass of anything cannot hurt a man!"

"Not a temperate one, who does not 'crave' for more; but it hurts us, because we do. Rely upon it, William, that for those who know not how to moderately use, and not abuse good gifts, water is the only safeguard. I remember Arthur making that remark to me years ago, as I now make it to you."

"Do you never take wine?"

"Never," replied Lord Temple. "Since I made my resolution, I have been enabled to keep it. I believe the chief help to my success was the abstaining absolutely: had I tampered with my resolve—'just one glass of wine,' 'just one glass of spirits'—I should probably have broken down. I could take a glass of wine now with impunity, if I chose, because I am become—both by inclination and habit—a sober man, and I know that I shall never relapse from it. But I do not choose. I like to set a good example: and I now prefer water."

"You really prefer it?"

"I do. I like it far better than wine or beer, or any other strong beverage you may please to think of. I like it for its own sake: use is second nature, you know."

"Ay," answered William; "there's a true proverb, 'Do what you should, that you may do what you like.' Many a time have I rued the day that took my mother from me, for she would have caused me to drink water, as she did Arthur. The last Mrs. Danesbury taught us to dislike it, and to love beer and wine. Poor Robert and Lionel!"

"You would soon get to like it," said Lord Temple. *"Your taste for wine and beer would die out*—as mine has done. Water, remember, is our natural beverage. Try it, William."

"Perhaps I may," he answered. "They will be 'bitter draughts' at first, though."

"Then fancy it bitter beer," laughed the Viscount. "Fancy goes a great way in this world."

Lord Temple left the room as he spoke, and Isabel moved close to her brother, and leaned upon his arm. Her tears were falling.

"Isabel! What is it?"

"Oh, William, I am overwhelmed with apprehension for you!" she said, laying her wet cheek against his. "Surely we have lost enough out of our family, and had enough misery. Let us who remain strive to live as we ought, that our days may be prolonged to the consolation of each other! We are but three now."

"Yes," he sadly answered, "we are but three. Seven once: three now."

"Promise me, William: promise me that you will throw off this dreadful fascination! Do as Reginald has done. Become what he and Arthur are: a temperate man, in the strict sense of the term."

He did not immediately speak.

"Once, near this house, years ago, it was just before I was leaving it, I prayed you to give me a promise: I now pray you again. Dearest William, for your own sake, I pray you."

"I cannot promise: I do not feel sure of myself, Isabel. I believe I said then I would try—and if I had not tried, and in some degree succeeded, I should, ere this, have been where our brothers are. I will say the same now. I will further try, earnestly try, to put a barrier between my inclination and this sin."

Lord and Lady Temple returned to London, and things went on as usual at Eastborough, Arthur, now Mr. Danesbury, quietly subsiding into his father's place, as the head of all things. The firm would remain as it always had done—"John Danesbury & Sons": he would not alter that.

On a bright, moonlight night, about a month subsequent to the burial of Mr. Danesbury, Arthur thought he should be the better for a walk, and strolled towards the town.

It was Saturday night. Into the public-houses streamed the people, in at the swinging doors of the gin-shop; men and boys rushing there to drink; while unhappy wives and mothers followed them, pleading for *some* of their wages, ere the provision shops should be shut. Mr. Danesbury stopped one man.

"Watts, how is it that you cannot make yourselves comfortable at home? It is bad for you in every way, this night-drinking; bad for your pocket, and bad for your health. You have a good home: surely you might be content to stay in it."

"Law, bless ye, sir! You just step and look at it, if I might make so bold. There's the wife all in a muddle, with a great tub afore the fire, a-washing of the children, and the children a-squalling, and the place all in a steam. After that, she sets on to wash the floor, and nobody won't be able to put a foot on it till it's dry. I can't stop in that mess. But I only take a glass or so, sir; I'm not one of the fast ones."

Arthur had nothing to reply. He went on his way, and the man entered "The Cock and Bottle." All throughout his walk he saw nothing else; men pouring into the public-houses till they were full of company, whose uproarious mirth reached his ears. He turned down the narrow, retired path which led to the churchyard, and halted at its gate. He opened the gate, and approached the large white marble tomb of the Danesburys, the two more recent deaths but just recorded on it.

His thoughts ran, naturally enough, upon the vice of intemperance, and its share in the death of those lying beneath him. Look at what it had done for them! His mother, recalled from her pleasant visit by the drunken mistake of Glisson, sent the same night to her death through the drunken agency of the turnpike man; Glisson herself, who also lay near, a victim to its effects; Robert, the next buried, what Arthur shuddered to think of, both in life and in death; Mrs. Danesbury, hastened thither by her sons' conduct; Lionel, just gone, a burden released from the world; and his father's broken heart, laid there before its time!

"If it has brought this amount of evil into one home," thought Arthur, "what must it bring to the world at large? Hundreds are dying daily of it, homes are rendered hells, families are scattered. This very night, in this town, close to me, it is raging unchecked. My own workmen are yielding to it now: making themselves into brutes, impoverishing their means, wronging their wives and children! How can it be dealt with?"

How, indeed? Many a one is asking the question as anxiously as did Arthur Danesbury. An earnest spirit has been abroad of late years, striving to grapple with the evil; and the busy and careless world, who give not their thoughts to these things, would be astonished to learn the good effected by it in connection with the exertions of the TEMPERANCE SOCIETIES. May they go on and prosper, and may they find their reward in the fruits they so largely bring forth!

But the good they have accomplished, though astonishingly great, is but little compared with what has yet to be done; and it equally behoves individuals, families, and communities, to give a helping hand.

All these, and many more such reflections, passed through the mind of Arthur Danesbury, as he stood there, leaning over the tomb. How should he deal with the evil; he in his little sphere at Eastborough? A responsibility was upon him, and was making itself heard: a large body of men were in his service, receiving fair wages in requital, it is true, but he felt that he was not the less responsible; that he might owe them something else. What to attempt, he knew not yet; sound deliberation must be given to dealing with the evil: to check it wholly, he feared he never should be able, but he might do something.

Circumstances were against him, and against the men, in the prevalence of beer-shops, and the low price of gin. The legislature allowed both. Liquor was plentiful everywhere; and, as to the places where it was sold, they would abound. If all the present distillers and large brewers shut up their concerns to-morrow, conscience-stricken at the nature of their trade, the source of their wealth, fresh ones would start the next day in their places. Under the present state of affairs, therefore, that was not the way in which Arthur Danesbury could deal with the eviL He knew also that it would be worse than useless to attempt a forced conversion. To say to the men, "You must leave off these debased habits, and take to better," would fall on inattentive ears—*the necessity for the conversion must previously be aroused in their own minds.* They must first find within themselves the higher motive for well-doing. Not only the more humble one of assuring peace in this, their transitory life: but peace also for the one above. They must be led to this gradually, perhaps insensibly, not by violent measures, but gently, step by step. Before anything could be done, it would be necessary to break through their present habits; to make them more moral, more thoughtful. Raise the mind, and in due time the spirit would follow.

Mr. Danesbury remained long in deep deliberation, pacing the churchyard. He was lost to outward things, when footsteps were heard in the lane, and he emerged from the gate. The footsteps proved to be old Thomas Harding's.

"Is it you, Harding? What brings you here?"

"I wanted to find you, sir, and was going the nearest way to Mrs. Philip Danesbury's; for I have been to your house, and they thought you might have gone there."

"What is it?" asked Mr. Danesbury.

"Brown has been to me again, sir," replied Harding; "he is at my house now, and I can't get rid of him, praying and entreating that he may be taken on once more. He says he'll never transgress again, but if he can't get an answer to-night, he'll be off with morning light, and enlist for a soldier. He says he is starving. I thought it right to come and mention it to you, sir, lest he should go. What is to be done?"

"His offence was very bad," said Mr. Danesbury; "but—he has a wife and child, poor things. Give him another chance, Harding. He may come on Monday morning."

"I thought perhaps you would, sir. I'm sure you are very lenient to them. Brown says he had been drinking when he did it, and was not in his senses."

"No doubt," cried Mr. Danesbury; "drink is the cause of most bad actions. Harding, my mind was directed to this very point when you came up. To-night, as I walked through the streets, the men—our men—were at the public-houses in swarms, drinking away their intellects and their wages. Something ought to be attempted to check it—something shall be."

"Who by, sir?"

"By me. I feel that the responsibility rests upon me."

"Nothing in the world can be done, sir, let your will be ever so good. There are the public-houses, and the men will go to them."

"Yes, I see great difficulties, even in the attempt."

"When a man has been at work all day, he wants some sort of amusement or recreation, sir," resumed Thomas Harding. "He can't get that at home—speaking of the generality of the men. Their wives are bad managers, the room is not comfortable, the fire's low, or out. There's no society for them there, except a scolding wife and crying children."

"Nearly the very words that Watts answered me with to-night," returned Mr. Danesbury. "I met him going into 'The Cock and Bottle,' and told him he would be better at home. Everything was uncomfortable there, he replied, and he was driven out."

"It is so," answered Thomas Harding. "Some few are differently situated, have superior women for wives, who make home a pleasant place for them to return to; and a sprinkling are gifted with intellect and thought beyond their station, and have their evening pursuits, their books, and their newspapers, and such like; but, take the workmen as a body, sir, their home is the public-house when the day's work is done. They have no resources within themselves—even if home were what it ought to be, they would be dull in it—out they must, and will go: and there's no hope but what they always will go out. They might be chained in, but they'll never stop in, otherwise; no, they would not for you, sir, much as they look up to you. Some of them, I truly believe, would lay down their lives to serve you, Mr. Arthur, but you'll never get them to stop indoors after work. Look at the Literary Institution that your good father gave himself such pains to set up, hoping it might keep the men from the tap-rooms. Who goes to it? There's a good room for them, well lighted and warmed in winter, books, and what not; but do they take advantage of it? No, sir; it's deserted; there's not half a dozen in it, I'll be bound to answer, any night all through the year, taking one night with another."

"If we could but close some of the public-houses!" exclaimed Mr. Danesbury. "Since I have sat on the bench, I have been chary of granting licenses; but my brother magistrates are less so, and my voice is only one amongst many. I wish I could shut up that gin-shop."

"Sir," said Harding—and his words only carried out some of his master's previous thoughts—"if you shut up that, another would open. I was talking last week to the man who keeps it, and told him it was doing harm, for its blaze of light enticed people in to drink. He answered—he is a civil, decent man in spite of his trade—that it was not the traffic he followed by choice; but that, if he gave it up, a hundred would be found ready to drop into it, so he might as well keep it himself, and pocket the profits: folks did drink, and would drink to the end of the chapter. And so they will, sir."

"Ay, although they know the curse it is to them."

"It is a curse both to rich and poor," returned Thomas Harding. "I saw Mr. William in one of the houses as I came along," added the old man, lowering his voice.

"No!" uttered Mr. Danesbury.

"I did, sir. I went to 'The Ram' to ask why my Saturday's paper had not been left, and the waiter opened the door of the gentlemen's parlour as I stood there, and I saw Mr. William inside, with a steaming glassful before him. My heart stood still: I could have found in it to go and pull him out: I have had such hopes of him lately."

Arthur could not answer; he was too pained to answer. He also had been cherishing hopes of his brother.

"Well, sir, I'll go back to Brown, and tell him," cried Harding. "Good-night, sir."

He turned to retrace his steps up the narrow lane towards the town: and Arthur Danesbury slowly pursued the path, which lay round and round the churchyard.

CHAPTER XXIII
OVERCOMING

WILLIAM DANESBURY was alone in his drawing-room, on the evening mentioned in the last chapter, when a servant opened the door to introduce a visitor.

"Mr. Bell, sir."

William had his head bent over some plans and drawings on the table, in which he was making corrections. He turned to receive his guest.

It was a large farmer, residing near Eastborough. The Danesburys were executing some orders of his, for agricultural implements, and he had come to inquire on what day one of the machines could be delivered to him. William did not know, but said the overlooker of the department might be able to tell.

"Where can I find him?" asked the farmer.

"He lives close by. I will go with you. Will you take anything first?"

"Well, I don't care if I do take a glass of brandy and water, to keep the cold out on my ride home," was Mr. Bell's answer.

William was vexed at this. Since the conversation with Lord Temple, now three weeks ago, he had *kept to water,* and did not much relish the temptation that brandy on his own table would induce. However, there was no help for it, and he went to the cellar and brought up a bottle of brandy, which happened to be the last he had in the house. The servant appeared with hot water and glasses.

"Hey! don't you drink yourself?" cried the farmer, perceiving that, though he was sipping his, William took none.

"You must excuse me to-night. I do not feel well."

William sat by, the fumes of the brandy under his nose, and his very lips watering for it. He took out his handkerchief and held it to his mouth, with his elbow on the table, his face resolutely turned from the bottle.

A perspiration broke out over his head and face. *Could* he hold out? "Lord, be Thou my helper!" he inwardly breathed, "for of my own strength I cannot withstand."

The farmer mixed another glass, and when he had finished it, rose, and said he was ready. William put the bottle on the sideboard, not having touched the brandy; and went out with Mr. Bell. So far, victory.

The overlooker was not at home; he was gone to "The Ram," to take his glass and smoke his pipe. Very much indeed did William Danesbury dislike to accompany Mr. Bell there: but it would have been neither courteous nor business-like to suffer him to proceed alone.

When he and Mr. Bell entered "The Ram," several gentlemen whom William knew were in the parlour; amongst them was Mr. Laughton, once poor Lionel's great friend.

"It's never you!" exclaimed Laughton, addressing William. "I heard you had joined the teetotalers, and were coming out in a medal and blue ribbon."

William winced: he was not yet sufficiently self-reliant to take these jokes with equanimity. He sat down in the midst of the temptation—the terrible temptation; that at home was nothing to it. Laughton gave a quiet order, and William saw a glass of brandy and water placed before him by the waiter.

"Now, if you have *not* signed the pledge, and cut us all dead, I recommend you to topple up that," said Laughton. "You never tasted better brandy than this. It's a fresh lot they have got in, direct from France—it has the true champagne flavour."

"Come, Mr. Danesbury," cried the farmer, "you shirked it at home, but you can't refuse to drink with a friend now. Take up your glass. Good health to you."

William Danesbury took up the glass, and drained it.

Then remorse set in. He saw himself what he was, a weak, guilty coward; a man without self-restraint; and yet a self-sufficient man, who had trusted to himself. Why had he not asked for AID to resist the temptation, as he had done in his own home? If self-torture ever overtook a man, it did William then. He rose from his seat, ready to curse himself.

"Danesbury, you are not going?"

"I must. I have an engagement."

That was so far true. For his wife was at a friend's, and he had promised to go and bring her home.

"Take another glass," cried Laughton.

"Not to-night. Good-evening, all."

William Danesbury went out into the moonlight; but hardly had he turned into the churchyard lane when he met Harding.

"Is it you, Mr. William? I am so glad!"

"It is more than I am," returned William. "Why are you glad?"

"Because I saw you in somewhere, Mr. William, and I thought you would be better away," he whispered; "and I am thankful you have come away. That's why, sir."

"I am a wicked idiot, Harding, and nothing else. So don't trouble yourself to be thankful about me."

"Perhaps you have been led to transgress to-night, Mr. William, and I know you have been striving against it lately. Forgive me, sir, but I was nearly an old man when you were a child, and I think if you were to fail at last it would break my heart."

"It is of no use striving," returned William, gloomily. "I have been striving, resolutely striving, and now a moment's temptation has upset it."

"Strive on, strive on, Mr. William; victory will be yours in the end. I *know it will,* if you only take the right means to help yourself."

"How can you say you know it, Harding, and assert it so impressively? I am no better than others. Worse."

"Sir," said Thomas Harding, the tears rolling down his cheeks, "I will tell you why I know you will be kept and preserved, if you only strive for it as you ought. I was in the chaise with your mother the night she died, when she was hastening home to you, a baby. At the moment of the accident, when the chaise was going over, and she saw her danger, and possibly foresaw her death—for when death comes to take the body, it is said to be visible to the living spirit—in that last moment she offered up a prayer: 'My Saviour, I can but commend my children to Thee. Do Thou make them Thine, and keep them from the evil!'

"Mr. William," added Thomas Harding, "no dying mother ever commended her children to Christ in vain. He *will* keep you from the evil, if you earnestly ask Him."

William was much affected. "Harding, I cannot do it of myself. All my efforts come to nought."

"No, sir, not of yourself; if we could do things of ourselves, Christ would not have told us to go to Him. He is waiting to give you aid, if you will only ask Him; you will not ask in vain. I have long wanted to say this to you, Mr. William, but I did not know how. Forgive me, sir."

William wrung Thomas Harding's hand with a grateful pressure, and continued his way towards the churchyard. Conspicuous amidst the white gravestones was the Danesbury tomb, and he stepped towards it. There she lay, his own mother; there was her name—"Isabel, the wife of John Danesbury." The words of Harding were ringing in his ears, and William's feelings overcame him; he bowed his head, and broke into a flood of passionate tears.

"My mother! do thou pray for me still, if it may be permitted thee. My Saviour, teach me to pray? Keep me from the evil, as she asked of Thee; teach and help me to overcome."

Exceedingly surprised he was to hear footsteps close to him, and more surprised still to find they were Arthur's. The latter linked his arm within his.

"I was near the gate, and saw you come in. William, what distresses you? Let me know it. We are alone in the world, save Isabel."

"I am so angry and vexed with myself! Arthur, I have been striving to do right, to abstain; for three weeks not a drop of liquor of any sort had passed my lips, and water was becoming palatable. To-night has undone it all."

"How was it?"

"Bell came to my house about his machines, and said he would have some brandy and water. I sat by while he drank it, taking none—though it was a sore temptation. Afterwards we had to go to 'The Ram' to find Sears. Laughton and some more of my old cronies were there; and I was such a weak fool as to be tempted to drink."

"Much?"

"One glass."

"I wish you had not. But, William, do not despair; if there were nothing to resist there would be no victory. Let the relapse serve to strengthen you for future fight. Seek aid where you know it may be found."

"I will seek it; I do," answered William; "but no one knows how hard the struggle is—the physical pain of abstaining—the inward, mental craving to fight against."

"HE knows, and He is all-sufficient. If you had nothing to overcome, where would be the reward? 'He that overcometh shall inherit all things; and I will be his God, and he shall be My son.' Oh, William, think of the glorious end! Persevere, and it will surely be yours."

William wrung his brother's hand, and departed to his home. He took a light, and went upstairs to his bedroom, shut himself in, and paced about, too uneasy to sit or rest. His mind was a chaos—self-reproach, self-anger, doubt, despondency, and hope. Yes, in the midst of it all, there was a little ray of hope, whispering him that, if he so willed it, the victory would be his.

William dropped his head upon his hands and *thought*. This little fleeting life, whose length, compared with eternity, was but as a grain of sand to the clouds of it on the sea-shore! *Eternity? for ever!—for ever!* He lost himself in striving to comprehend the depths of the word. All do. Robert and Lionel had entered on that "for ever." How? What was their state? What might be their remorse, their suffering at that very moment, then, when he was spared, in mercy, and could yet choose the good or the evil?

William shuddered, and, taking his wife's Bible from its accustomed place, opened it at the Book of Revelation. He was looking for the places, he knew there were several, which promised life to those who overcome; but, as he turned over the leaves, his eyes fell on some other words.

"And I saw the dead, small and great, stand before God; and the books were opened: and another book was opened, which is the book of life: and the dead were judged out of those things which were written in the books, according to their works."

According to their works!

"And whosoever was not found written in the book of life was cast into the lake of fire."

Then he found what he was looking for. And read the several verses fervently, with a yearning heart: a heart that felt its weakness and its need of God. The following were the two last his eyes fell on:—

"To him that overcometh will I give to eat of the hidden manna, and will give him a white stone, and in the stone a new name written, which no man knoweth saving he that receiveth it.

"To him that overcometh will I give to eat of the tree of life, which is in the midst of the paradise of God."

William Danesbury fell on his knees, and bowed his head on the book, and sobbed as he had sobbed in the churchyard. Earnestly he prayed; prayed that from that night henceforth, he might never return to his besetting sin, but might be kept in his recurring hours of temptation; and, in the end, so overcome, as to sit down with the redeemed in paradise.

He remembered that he had to go for his wife. Descending the stairs, and entering the sitting-room for his hat, which he had left there on coming in, his eyes fell on the brandy bottle. Without a moment's deliberation, he carried it outside the door and emptied its contents on the flower-bed. "May I ever be as resolute in rejecting it!" he aspirated.

His thoughts were still busy as he walked along the road. Strange to say, though he could scarcely account for the sensation, he felt a sense of happiness, of security, that he had never felt previously; as if he had entered on the right path to be reconciled to God.

When he reached the presence of his wife, she looked apprehensively at him. His face was pale, his eyes were red; as she advanced close to him, his breath gave forth an odour she knew too well, and her heart sank within her. They set out to return home. It was a silent walk, for her tears were nearly overflowing, and she dared not speak; and William seemed buried in a reverie. As they passed through their own garden, she exclaimed, suddenly, "What a strong smell of brandy!"

"Yes," he replied, "there is. Do you know what I have been doing to-night, Anna?"

"What you ought not," she faintly said. "William, William, will nothing avail with you?"

"It did not, to-night. I had to go on business to 'The Ram,' and there I broke through. The temptation was terrible," he murmured: "the desire for it burning me as a consuming fire; and I yielded."

She was weeping silently. He had halted with her at the flower-bed, in the midst of the grass-plot.

"So I came home, and I took a bottle of brandy, the last we had in the house, and which had been reached up, but not for me, and brought it out here, and emptied it on the earth. I trust—I think—that with this night my worst struggle is over. I believe that henceforth my strife will not be in vain. Anna! I have never said so much as that."

"You—will—strive—in earnest?" she slowly breathed, scarcely daring to admit the rush of joy which his words and manner brought her: "strive aright?"

"Ay. And overcome—by the help of God."

CHAPTER XXIV
ARTHUR DANESBURY— MURMURS

NOT for many a day had so great a commotion arisen in Eastborough. A commodious building in the heart of the town, belonging to Mr. Danesbury, was being repaired; to be rendered, so the report ran, as attractive as the gin-palace. A second gin-palace it was going to be, as was told throughout the place; and the commotion was caused by a rumour that these various alterations were being made for the landlord himself—Mr. Danesbury.

"Mr. Danesbury!" echoed the excited crowd. "He set up a gin-palace—that is, cause it to be set up—after all he has said and done!"

One who was in want of such a house applied to become its tenant; but Mr. Danesbury's reply was, that he required it for his own purposes. The commotion increased; but the doubt was set at rest, for one of the artisans respectfully put the question to Mr. Danesbury, "Was it really to be a house of entertainment for the men?"

"Yes, it is. I intend it in opposition to the public-houses, and especially to the gin-palace opposite," replied Mr. Danesbury. "My workmen must go out at night, it seems, and drink, so it occurred to me that I might as well derive some benefit from the habit, much as I disapprove of it. I hope, in a few weeks from this, it will be open and flourishing, and will have taken some custom from the other houses."

The questioner was confounded. "I beg your pardon, sir," he said.

"Why?"

"For asking, sir. I have heard that it was the master's, and was meant for a gin-shop, and it made me quite angry to hear it, because I did not believe it, and I thought I'd get your leave, sir, to contradict it."

"On the contrary," said Mr. Danesbury, "you may confirm it, that it is mine, and say that I hope they will give me their custom."

The man walked away like one in a dream. The more he reflected on it, the more he was puzzled; and he repeated the news, and thus set all doubts at rest.

A knot of tenant-wives in Prospect Row were standing before their doors, discussing the astounding fact just reported to them, that the proprietor of the new gin-palace *was* Mr. Danesbury.

"I wouldn't have believed it of him," resentfully cried Mrs. Gould; "and so I told Uncle Harding when the rumour first got wind. 'Mr. Arthur set up a new public, and put a man in to keep it? No!' said I, 'that he never will.'"

"All gas, and glare, and glitter, to 'tice our men in to drink, like t'other horrid place," chimed in another. "They wastes money enough as it is: what'll they do when the master hisself encourages them direct?"

"It's my certain conviction, and has been all along," said Mrs. Gould, "that the way in which Mr. Danesbury and Mr. Arthur set their faces against the liquor-shops, kept many a workman within bounds, who would not have been kept within them but for that. Mr. Arthur's turning round is a great misfortune upon us, and some of us will rue the day his place opens."

"'Cause we don't rue it enough as it is," called out a miserable woman with a torn cap and hanging hair. "How much d'ye suppose my brute of a fellow brought me home last Saturday night—or Sunday morning, for that's what it was? Six shillings."

"Shame!" was murmured around.

"He'll bring home three next, when he have got this shop of the master's to sot at. And the children in rags, and me famishing half my time. I wish I was dead, I do."

"I'd sooner have thought that Mr. Arthur would have finished those almshouses for the old, which his father began to build some years ago, and was forced to leave unfinished, through the expenses his sons brought upon him, than have turned his thoughts and his money to such a low-lived thing as this; low-lived for a Danesbury."

"Oh, I don't know about low-lived: some of the first gents owns publics and liquor shops, though they don't have anything to do with 'em personally, wouldn't set their proud feet inside one. But for them alms-houses, it was said in the factory lately, that now things was a-coming round a bit, and some of the pulls upon him was gone, the master meant to finish 'em."

"Yes, low-lived," persisted Mrs. Gould: "it is so, for Mr. Arthur Danesbury. He and his father have always been such respectable, lofty men: I don't mean lofty to us, or proud to us; we all know they are not that; but lofty in high and good things: for him thus to get up and start liquor-selling, is bringing him down dreadfully. Why, my husband, Richard, would never have kept as tolerably sober as he has, but for the fear of getting out of the good books of the masters."

"You know Tom Locke and his wife—who hurt himself in the machinery, and has never been able to do a good day's work since—well, it's them as the master is a-going to put in to keep it."

"What, Tom Locke? Why, he's one of they temperance lot: he can't a-bear his nose to come a-nigh liquor, he can't. Nor her neither."

"Who says it's going to be Tom Locke?" asked Jessy Gould.

"I says so; and says so 'cause I heard it. A rum lot he was, I thought at first, to put into a gin-shop, one as abominates the sight and smell of it, but it came into my head afterwards that that was the master's depth: if he had put in one that liked it, he'd have toped away some of the profits. So Tom Locke is just the right sort of man."

"Well, it's a new thing for us to be standing here abusing Mr. Danesbury," uttered Mrs. Gould. "It does not sound right: our best praises have never been good enough for him till now."

"But who was to think he would turn round like this? I say, did you hear of the row at 'The Pig and Whistle' last night?"

"Oh, yes, I heered on't. My husband was in it. They got fighting, some of 'em, and a heap of glasses was broke, which doubled the score. Wretches!"

As may be gathered from the above conversation, the female portion of the community did not view with favour Mr. Danesbury's new scheme. With the men it was, on the whole, popular, though the surprise amongst all classes was unbounded.

Mr. Danesbury was one evening coming out of the new place—palace, shop, or whatever it might be called—when he encountered Thomas Harding, who was passing. "Well," said he, cheerily, "we are getting on; we shall soon open."

"Are you, sir?"

"What say those most concerned?"

"The women are outrageous, sir," said Harding, with a merry twinkle in his eye. "Our relation, Jessy, one of the worst. They expect to be reduced to shorter commons than usual, now 'the master countenances the drink.' You have lost caste, sir, with them."

Mr. Danesbury laughed, and proceeded on his way.

He was going to Mrs. Philip Danesbury's. When he arrived there, Miss Heber was alone. Rather tall, slender and graceful, with clearly-cut, expressive features, and an earnest, thoughtful eye, she looked, in her way, as noble as did Arthur Danesbury.

She rose when he entered, and extended her hand. He took it and retained it, and they stood together before the window in the last rays of the setting sun.

"Did you ever see a more beautiful sunset?" exclaimed Miss Heber.

"I do not know that I have. I was thinking so as I came along."

"I am sorry my aunt is out. She——"

"I am glad of it," interrupted Arthur. "Because my visit this evening is to you."

Something in his tone caused the conscious colour to flush into Miss Heber's cheeks: possibly she had a foreshadowing of what was to come; and, in her maidenly reserve, she would have withdrawn her hand from his.

"No, Mary, suffer it to remain. I am going to ask you to give it me for my own. I have waited for you long: you know I have, Mary. For, though I would not speak until I saw my way clear, I am sure you have never mistaken me. Will you intrust your happiness to my keeping? Will you give yourself to me for all time?"

She burst into tears, and suffered him to draw her face to his breast, and hold it there.

Then—after a pause—they began to speak of details. He wished that they should be married with but little delay. She objected, saying that twelve months ought to elapse first from the period of Mr. Danesbury's death.

"Can you give me one good reason for that, Mary?" he returned. "Custom? Well, we can afford to dispense with custom. Do you think that I—or you—shall forget my dear father the sooner, or regret him one iota the less, because we become united together?"

"No. Oh, no."

"Then I know of no other point your objection can carry. Believe me, Mary, I should be the last to suggest anything that could imply disrespect to him. And were it possible that he could hear us now, I know he would judge my motives aright, and approve of what I urge."

A happy, reassured expression rose to her face, and she began to think her objection not insuperable.

"I am lonely at home: it is a large house for me to inhabit alone," he resumed, with a smile. "But that is not the chief argument. I want a helpmate in my new plans: a second self."

"With your workmen?" she asked, looking up.

"With my workmen; my poor, ignorant, improvident workmen. I want a lady—you, Mary; and if you never were to be anything to me, I can truthfully say I know of none more fit—to go to their homes, and try to talk, or beat, or soothe something better into the wives. You have learned my plans as to the men; but it will be of little use seeking to raise them from what they are so long as the women are dirty and careless, and make their houses everything they ought not to be. A man could not effect this: it must be a woman; one who will go amongst them, and take an interest in their cares and troubles, and show them how they may be made lighter. Now," he added, in a gayer tone, "it would not quite do for Miss Heber to go concerning herself with Mr. Danesbury's workpeople, but it will be the very thing for Mrs. Danesbury."

Her lips parted with a smile. She had no argument at hand to refute his words.

"And I want a counsellor, Mary: one to whom I can come for advice and help. I want you."

"Oh, Arthur!" she exclaimed, in surprise. *I* counsel *you!* I blush to think how very unworthy I am, compared with you."

"A kind, loving friend and counsellor," he whispered, "who will wait for me and welcome me when the bustle and cares of the day are over; who will listen to my schemes, and share my trials, and cheer on my hopes, whether of time or of eternity. My dearest! I know that you will be all this."

"I will be all I possibly can," she answered, the tears glistening in her eyes: tears of joy, not of grief, for none save herself knew how passionately, for years, she had loved Arthur Danesbury. "And I will do what I can for the workpeople. I used to think it wrong that Mrs. Danesbury did not take a personal interest in them."

"My own mother did. I have heard Harding say so many times. I have heard him say that, had she lived, the women never would have become the slatternly, quarrelsome scolds in their homes that they are. But she was removed early. The second Mrs. Danesbury would not notice them: I do not suppose she entered a single cottage the whole time that she was my father's wife. There is much to do, much to be effected."

"Will it be effected?" returned Miss Heber.

"Not, perhaps, as I could wish it to be—not as it might be, if the men and women were more enlightened; half of them are without any education whatever—cannot read or write. But a great deal may be done—I feel that it will; we shall both bring earnestness and hope to the rescue. Mary, I propose to devote, in a degree, my life to this object. Next to my own family—I mean to you, and—to"—(he momentarily hesitated, but continued, with a half-smile)—"those who may be born to us, I shall consider these poor dependants. Not only my energies shall be given to their service, to the raising them, bodies and souls, to a more healthy condition, but a great portion of my income must be spent in it. I warn you of this beforehand."

"Oh, yes, Arthur," she earnestly replied; "indeed, you will find me agree with you in all, and help you. When wealth is being accumulated by commerce, and no part of it, save their bare wages, is ever applied to benefit the poor, aiding operatives, I think a sin must lie at the rich man's door. It may be justice in the sight of man to pay them but their simple due, and leave them to make the best of it, in indifference and neglect; but it cannot be in the sight of God. Devote as much of yours as you will to the workmen, Arthur, I shall never say you nay."

"My darling," he murmured, bringing her face nearer to his, "I hope and trust we shall be able to do our duty to them, and to ourselves, and to Him who has placed us here to do it, and made us rich and them poor. Our probationary time on earth is but short at its best: may we always remember, in the great trials of life, and in its small, daily cares, in the pleasant social intercourse with friends, and in the dearer sunshine of our own home, that we are but travellers here, making our short journey to a better land!"

CHAPTER XXV
THE STAR OF HOPE

APRIL came in, and the new gin-palace was ready to be opened. But it lacked one thing: a sign. Not to have honoured the new place with any sign at all, gave considerable offence to numbers, who were already its warm partisans and supporters in prospective. Somebody ventured to name the omission to Mr. Danesbury.

"A sign, they want, do they?" said he. "I have not thought of one. Let them call it—call it—'The Star of Hope.' I hope it will prove one."

On the evening of the grand opening, Mr. Danesbury summoned all his operatives before him, of whatever degree, in the large machine-room of the factory, which had been cleared for the occasion. It was just before the hour for leaving work. He stood upon a raised platform, that all might see him as he addressed them.

"My friends, I have assembled you here, but not to keep you for many minutes, as it is but a few words I wish to say to you now; and the fewer I say the better pleased you will be, for I feel sure that you are on thorns to be off to that new place of mine. Is it not so?"

A murmur; then laughter; then a hearty cheer for their master.

"I shall be very happy to see you all there; but there are certain conditions attached to your entering, and it is to acquaint you with them that I have called you before me. Because," and here he spoke very slowly and distinctly, "unless you can take upon yourselves to observe them, you would be just as well away; at least, for the present."

"Let's have 'em, sir; we shan't objec' to 'em," called out a voice from the far end of the room.

"Was that you, Joe Smith?" cried Mr. Danesbury.

A roar of laughter against Joe Smith, who shrank into nothing.

"The first condition is, that whoever goes in to-night, must undertake to go in for a whole month, never omitting."

Oh, everybody would promise that.

"Stop a bit," said Mr. Danesbury, "don't promise anything till you have heard me further. The second condition is, that you must remain firm to my establishment for the whole month, and not enter any other during that period."

No danger they'd want to leave the master's.

"The third is, that for that month nobody pays for what they take. I stand treat for all."

A deafening roar: the huzzas seemed never to end,

"And the fourth is, that you must, during that period, endeavour to persuade yourselves—that you will *make an effort* to persuade yourselves—to continue in future to patronise my establishment, and not the one over the way."

Another roar; everybody's voice drowning everybody else's, in vows that they would do so.

"Stop a bit yet," said Mr. Danesbury. "You have heard the conditions of entrance: you must now hear a little of the rules and regulations. In the first place, no man drinks more than I choose."

A dead silence.

"In the second, no man must grumble at the liquor. It may be quite different from what he has been accustomed to; but, if he undertakes to go in, he must drink it, and not grumble."

That they'd promise.

"My friends, listen. You have been accustomed to drink beer that you think good; gin that you think good; but suppose in my establishment you meet with only bad beer and bad gin, next to undrinkable—you know I do not patronise either myself, and am no judge—what should you do, at being obliged to put up with them for a month? Would you do so, out of regard to your word passed to me?"

Yes, they would. Bless the master! 'twouldn't be his fault if the sellers imposed upon him.

"But suppose you should get neither beer nor gin, bad nor good? suppose the cheer you met with should be different from that which you are accustomed to take? *suppose it should be unpalatable?* You must still observe the condition of remaining your month."

Well—they'd do that.

"Finally, my men, understand fully, and then decide. If you go at all, you must go for the month, evening by evening; and you must abide by the cheer provided for you, even though it be not beer or spirits, or any drink of that sort. Joe Smith, could you manage to live without beer or spirits for a month?"

"I can't rightly say, sir," hesitated Joe.

"My friends, those of you who think they cannot, had better not subscribe to my conditions, or enter; for, understand me, the conditions and rules *must* be observed. But to you who do enter, I have a word more to say. Which of you ever found my father, or me, a hard master?"

Not one. Some looked ready to melt into tears. Mr. Danesbury and Mr. Arthur had been masters such as poor workmen did not often find.

"Then, if you have found us thus," Mr. Danesbury resumed, in a voice that could not altogether suppress its emotion, "you will not mind a little sacrifice by way of return. If the cheer provided for you be not quite to your minds, *put up with it; give it, for one month, a hearty trial*, in gratitude to my late father, your honoured master."

The words and the tone carried the room with enthusiasm, and nearly everyone bound himself in his own mind, and as fast as promises could do it, to stop out the month, at the new place, drink or no drink.

A ticket was now given to each man. They were differently numbered, up to three. The superior managers and overlookers were not included in the invitation, though Mr. Danesbury intimated that to see them there would give him pleasure. The foremen, such as Thomas Harding, had number one; the next grade below, had number two; and the last, number three. It was understood there were three reception rooms, and the ticket merely indicated which they were to enter, to prevent overcrowding and confusion. The men went out, after three times three for Mr. Danesbury.

"We will look in upon you in the course of the evening," said Mr. Danesbury to the men.

Curiosity was excited to the utmost to see the inside of the famous gin-palace, and they crowded in, but in an orderly manner, and were shown to their appointed room, each apartment being conspicuously numbered. No difference had been made in their fittings-up. The place was brilliant with gas, and with an immense fire in each room; tables and chairs and benches were scattered about; the better sort of the dear and the cheap periodicals, monthly and weekly; plenty of newspapers, and plenty of books, scientific, useful, entertaining, and amusing; also, there were several sets of chess and draughts men. A more complete picture of comfort the men had never entered on.

Might the men smoke? It was an anxious question. Oh yes; Mr. Danesbury knew that, to some of the men, tobacco was more than their daily food, and to strive to put away that, would have crushed the scheme in the onset. He did not find tobacco—the men had to bring that. When they had had time to settle themselves in their seats, and talk off some of their first wonder, a steaming cup of delicious coffee, such as some of them had never tasted, was brought for each man, with a substantial slice of bread-and-butter—really good bread-and-butter—not like what they got at home. A superior reader was appointed to each room to read aloud, if the men preferred it to conversation.

So! that was their master's gin-palace! A comfortable asylum, where they might enjoy each other's society, hear the news, and be well-lighted and warmed, all at his expense. "They might have knowed that *he* never would countenance a liquor traffic—where was their wits to have believed such a thing?"

"The coffee, too, that was at his expense. Well, it warn't bad."

"Bad! it were deadly good."

"Yes, it were; and so were the bread-and-butter. But about the beer?"

"And the gin?"

Nobody could say any more than that they had passed their word, and must put up with the evening coffee for a month.

"And at the end of the month we will talk again," said Mr. Danesbury, appearing just as the last words were spoken. "Perhaps we may enter on a fresh agreement then. Did you find the coffee to your liking?"

They had never tasted the like—for coffee.

Mr. Danesbury laughed. He sat down for a little while and conversed cheerfully with the men about indifferent topics of interest. After that, he passed into the other rooms successively.

"I think it will answer, William," he whispered, as they were crossing the well-lighted hall to leave.

"So do I," answered William. "I did not see a dissatisfied face amongst them."

"If, at the month's end, we have only gained over a few, it will be something effected; and we must hope on, and work on."

"It will come, it will come in time," said William. "Perhaps not with all of them, but with a great portion."

"The next step will be to try and induce them to leave off beer at home. Not yet: we must go to work gradually, little by little."

"If we can but do that," eagerly answered William, "that they may get out of liking the taste of it, and so out of the craving for it! You don't know, Arthur, how much lies in that; what a help it is."

"No: but you do, now."

"Yes, thank God."

What Arthur would have said more was arrested; for, on going out, they found themselves in the midst of a crowd of women.

News of the astounding truth had been carried to them that the new place was no drinking place, but one to keep their husbands and sons from drink, and the excited women had flown to the new place, and stood flocking round it, eager for more particular confirmation. Even Mrs. Gould had gone, and she was the first to address Mr. Danesbury.

"Oh, sir," she said, almost in impassioned tones, "I don't know how to forgive myself. I gave ear to the wicked, disreputable report that this was to be a gin-palace; and after watching your goodness, as I had, all through so many years! We shall never thank you enough, sir, for opening it what it is."

"We all joined in the delusion, sir, more shame to us for doubting you," cried another: "we never thought it was going to be nothing but a gin-palace."

"Yes," smiled Mr. Danesbury, "the report did get about. Not from me: I certainly never said it was going to be a gin-palace. But when I found you had picked up the notion, I did not contradict it."

"Well, sir, I suppose we jumped to the thought through seeing of it a-doing up so nice. I hope all the blessings in the world will rest upon you, sir, for trying to do something to reform our husbands."

"Perhaps I shall try to do something to reform you next," said Mr. Danesbury.

The crowd looked at him wonderingly.

"My good women," said he, in his low, clear, kindly tone, which reached the ears and the consciences of all, "how many of you have done anything to induce your husbands not to tope—except in the way of scolding and abuse? Have you—I speak to you all individually—made his home comfortable and peaceable? Have you kept it clean and cheerful? Have you ever met him with kind words? I fear not."

They were fearing not also, just then: and scarcely an eye dared to meet that of Mr. Danesbury.

"There have been faults on both sides," he resumed; "I am sure you are now feeling that there have been. I am trying what I can do to mend your husbands' faults; perhaps in a little time I may see what can be done towards mending yours. I speak in all kindness."

"Bless Mr. Danesbury! for ever bless Mr. Danesbury!" was echoed around, "we shall never know another gentleman like him."

Arthur raised his hat, and, passing his arm within his brother's, walked away.

CHAPTER XXVI
CONCLUSION

IT was a lovely day in June; the sun shone on the green trees, and the blue sky was without a cloud. All Eastborough, high and low, rich and poor, had gathered round the church, save those who had been able to get inside it, for it was the marriage day of Arthur Danesbury and Mary Heber. In deference to the recent melancholy deaths in the family, the wedding was as quiet as possible. No ceremonious breakfast was given, and Mary was plainly attired, for they were to go off from the church door.

They were in the church now, a small party only; and the officiating clergyman was Mary's brother, the Rev. Henry Heber.

"May all good luck and prosperity attend them!" ardently uttered old Mrs. Harding. "If any man ever deserved it in this world, it is Arthur Danesbury."

"He does that," acquiesced the listeners. "Only think of his having loved this young lady for years, yet he put aside his own wishes for the sake of his family."

"For them two good-for-nothings, poor, lost young fellows! It's not many as would consider his brothers before himself, and help them to the money he wanted to marry upon."

"Not more for their sakes than for his father's," rejoined Mrs. Harding. "Had he breathed a wish to marry, the old gentleman would have lived upon a crust himself, but what he should have been enabled to do it; and Mr. Arthur knew that, and kept it all locked up in his own breast. He deserves happiness now, for he has waited for it patiently, and done his duty by everybody before himself. Ay, and happiness will be his; he is one who may sit down under the shadow of his own vine and his own fig-tree, as was promised to the obedient under the Old Dispensation."

"Hush! here they corne! Look! they two first, she leaning on his arm. How pretty she looks, with her flushed rose cheeks, and her sweet, pleasant eyes. See! he walks bareheaded."

CONCLUSION

It was the bride and bridegroom, now Mr. and Mrs. Danesbury. The rest of the party followed, but nobody regarded them. Very good and noble did he look as he led her through the sea of faces to the chariot, placed her in, and took his seat beside her. The postboys touched their horses, but they could only move at a snail's pace, and the crowd burst into a simultaneous shout, men waved their hats, women shook their handkerchiefs. "Blessings on the future of Mr. and Mrs. Danesbury."

Mary sat back in the chariot, but he leaned forward and bowed around him; and the crowd shouted again, as they caught his genial smile.

And then, when the postboys had cleared the throng, and put their horses into a canter, a perfect shower of old shoes flew after the carriage for good luck; some alighting on it, some beside it, some amidst the horses; hundreds, they looked, whirling through the air.

Just as lovely a day, only hotter, arose a month later, in July. Preparations were making for a feast at Danesbury House. A large tent was erected in the adjacent field, and tables upon tables were set out in it, for all the workmen and their wives were to dine there, and spend a joyous holiday. Indoors, a table was laid for guests. Mr. and Mrs. Danesbury, who had just returned home, had some visitors staying with them; Lord and Lady Temple, their young children, and Mr. and Mrs. St. George. A few intimate friends were expected from the neighbourhood, and the first to enter was Mrs. Philip Danesbury. Following close upon her came William and his wife; and next arrived old Mr. Pratt, bringing with him a tall, gentlemanly young man, with a fresh colour and intelligent countenance. Mr. Danesbury, calm, noble, kind as ever, met them on the steps.

"May I introduce somebody else, as well as myself?" demanded the old doctor, in his quaint way, as he shook hands heartily with Arthur.

Arthur took the young man's hands. "It is not your grandson?"

"Yes, it is. He has come to stay a fortnight with me, out of the poisonous smoke and smells of London. He tells me he once saw Mr. Arthur Danesbury."

"Yes," replied Arthur; "it was in Mr. St. George's office, the day he was about to enter on his new employment. How have you got on?"

"Got on," interrupted old Mr. Pratt; "he is the right hand of his master, they tell me; never was such a head for construction, drawing, and the like. And, what's more, he is steady," he emphatically added.

Edmund Pratt stood listening with a pleasant smile. Arthur turned, and spoke in a low tone.

"I heard Mr. St. George make a bargain with you. Have you kept it?"

"Strictly, sir," was the ready answer, whilst his colour deepened. "I am, in the strict sense of the word, a water-drinker."

"Good. And how is your——" Mr. Danesbury hesitated. It was painful to ask after such a father.

"Don't inquire," cried the old surgeon; "don't mar our minds' peace on this day. It is down, down, and down with him: and it ever will be."

Mr. Danesbury turned away, for other guests were close upon them; and now they came rapidly.

When all had arrived, they sat down in the dining-room to a slight, mid-day meal, cold, with chocolate and coffee. Arthur presided. His fair wife, truly a helpmeet for him, both in person and mind, sat at his right hand, Lord Temple beyond her, and Isabel on the other side of Arthur. They were all anxious to know how the "scheme" worked, Mr. St. George being especially eager, not to say satirical, in his inquiries.

"Arthur's gin-palace," merrily put in Mrs. Philip Danesbury.

"You opened it in April," cried Mr. St. George. "How did it answer, and how has it progressed?"

Mr. Danesbury smiled. "I made use of a *ruse* to keep them for the first month," he began; "tricked them into it, as the men now, good-humouredly, say; and I think that was my strong point in the plan. Had they been at liberty to secede at pleasure, few would have remained beyond a night or two: when the novelty had worn off, away they would have gone again, to their dearly-loved beer-shops."

"Yes; undoubtedly Mr. Danesbury was wise enough to hit upon the right course when he bound the men to him for a whole month," interposed Squire Hanson, a neighbouring gentleman and a magistrate. "I had my doubts about its succeeding: I confess it; for I was in his confidence almost from the first: but I am rejoiced to be able to say that my doubts have been dispelled, and his hopes realised."

"All the men who had embraced the proposition to patronise my gin-shop," continued Arthur, laughing, "remained firm to their word passed to me, and came regularly."

"Then the whole of your operatives did not embrace it?" interrupted Mr. St. George.

"More than three-fourths of them did: the rest hesitated, alarmed at my conditions. At the month's end they had become, most of them, reconciled to the change: they could not fail to perceive the great benefit it was to their minds, their bodies, and their pockets. The public-house, intoxicating drinks, confusion, and expense: the master's house (for that is what they have taken to call it), clear heads, sociability, peace, and economy: besides, a few had actually begun to prefer the cup of coffee to the jugs of beer, and not a few were gathering a glimmering idea of the solemn fact, that they were different from the brute creation, and perhaps had not been sent into the world to live as such, and then die off and be forgotten."

Mr. Danesbury paused. But none interrupted him, and he resumed.

"At the month's end, I bargained with them for another month: I knew it was useless to demand, or attempt, too much at first; for our fellow-men must be led, not driven. I spoke to them, as I had spoken at the onset. After touching upon the advantages of the plan, which had then become obvious to themselves, I said, 'Will you be my guests for one more month, and oblige me? but, remember, if you enter upon the month, you must complete it.' Nearly all assented."

"Nearly all!"

"I think there were seven or eight only who did not. I suppose they had given way to the old longing for liquor, and could not, or would not, resist the returning to it. But, as a set-off against these deserters, four or five of the first refusers voluntarily joined us, and are with us still. At the end of the second month, the men spoke up, of themselves, and said they hoped to stay on at the master's house for good, and never to go from it again. I told them that nothing should be wanting on my part to induce them to patronise it: that fresh supplies of books, as they were required, should be furnished, with the daily and weekly newspapers; that I should be very frequently amongst them; and the light and warmth, the cup of coffee and bread-and-butter, should welcome them. I consider it a wonderful victory, and am thankful for it; I trust—I do trust"—here his voice trembled a little—"that, even in this short period, they and I are already beginning to reap the reward: and I feel within me a perfect conviction that a Higher Help than any poor efforts or plans of mine has been sending a blessing upon it."

What was the matter with Mrs. Danesbury? Her eyes were cast down, and the tears were dropping on her flushed cheeks. Arthur glanced at her, and knew that her emotion arose from love to him.

"I will say this," resumed Mr. Danesbury, "that since the men have been brought into contact with enlightened conversation and intelligence, their minds, short as the time is, have opened in a remarkable degree."

"Say, rather, since their leisure hours have not been rendered useless, and their senses stupefied, Arthur," interrupted Mrs. Philip Danesbury. "Formerly, it was work all day and drink all night; how could they grow out of their ignorance then?"

"I can tell you, better than anybody, how the scheme works in private," cried out old Mr. Pratt, "and that's first-rate. There have been no beatings of wives since the master's house was opened, or calls upon my sticking-plaster. Formerly, they used to sulk home, half-stupid, or reel home, swearing and abusive, all of which was vented on the unfortunate wives. Now they go home like cucumbers, cool and tranquil, upon good terms with themselves, and consequently upon good terms with others. Some of them are positively putting by money towards buying blankets for winter: a thing they never did before."

"But it bears better fruits than blankets," observed William Danesbury. "Many of them, after a three months' trial of coffee, do prefer it to beer or gin, as their evening beverage. You may not easily credit this," he added, lifting his eyes to the strangers present, "but, nevertheless, it is a fact. The next improvement we intend to have a try at, is to make them water drinkers in their own homes at mid-day."

"When my wife shall have persuaded the women into rendering their homes something like homes, which she will set about forthwith," interposed Mr. Danesbury.

"And not pigsties and scolding dens," put in the old surgeon.

"But do you consider that beer with their dinner can do workmen harm?" inquired a voice.

"It will do them no good," said Arthur Danesbury, "even if they should confine themselves to a moderate quantity. But you very rarely find a working man do this, whatever may be his grade. I pray you not to mistake me," he hastily added: "I do not imply that a steady working man takes too much with his dinner, in the meaning we give to the term 'too much'; but his taking it at dinner leads him to take it afterwards. Suggest to an artisan to leave off his beer. 'Leave off my beer!' he will answer you; 'I should never have strength to go through my day's work.' There lies the fallacy. It is a most mistaken conclusion. Beer gives a passing excitement, which lasts for the moment and appears like strength, but the effect goes speedily off, leaving the man weaker than he was before, and insupportably weary. Inquire of any workman whether, after drinking beer, he does not feel a lassitude creep over him at his work, an inclination to sit down and be idle. He does: and he believes he wants 'supporting,' and sends for another pint and drinks it, to give that support; and so it goes on, beer and lassitude, beer and lassitude, and beer again all the day through."

But allow me to put in a word myself, although it is interrupting Mr. Danesbury. Working men, you who read this, have you ever tried to do without beer at your dinner? Never: you have always believed it to be as necessary to you as the dinner itself. Oh, try it now! Substitute water: make the effort, and give it a fair trial. Do not drink the water for one solitary day: that would be of no use. For the first day and the second, and perhaps for five or six days you will make a wry face over the water, and gulp it down, as you will say, "against the grain," and protest that you dislike it, as compared to your much-relished beer. But persevere. If you had fought the battle for so long, you can fight it still, and you will find that you are losing your dislike to the water. Still a little longer, and there is no doubt about it, and you find your body is stronger for work, and your head clearer; no lassitude, or inertness, or disinclination for labour will creep over you now. And when the battle is won, and you find you *have* persevered, persevere on.

And now I will tell you another thing. Were it convenient for you to drink a small cup of coffee after your dinner, before leaving for work again, the support and energy it will give you, both mental and bodily, are wonderful. He who is here called Arthur Danesbury, one a vast deal wiser and better than I am, knew its invigorating properties: knew it by self-experience. In summer, when the mid-day fire is out, it can be made at breakfast-time, and taken cold: never mind the milk. And that's all I wished to say to you.

"One good result the plan has effected," resumed Squire Hanson, "is, that two public-houses and three beer-shops have been already obliged to shut up, lacking customers."

"I am glad to hear that," said Lady Temple. "There were so many."

"I have done what I can," said Arthur. "I will do what I can, so long as I am spared health and strength and means. I felt that it was incumbent on me to strive to raise my dependants out of the degraded habits they were pursuing; a positive duty laid in my path; a sin that would rest at my door, if I supinely neglected it."

There was a pause. It was broken by Mr. St. George.

"Now that Mr. Danesbury has had his say, I must have mine. Do you know, sir, that when the report of these doings, this wild scheme, reached town, you were looked upon by practical, matter-of-fact men, as being a little touched here?"

Mr. St. George tapped his forehead as he spoke, and his keen eyes twinkled with merriment.

"I daresay it was so," laughed Arthur. "I believe a debate took place in Eastborough, amongst my brother magistrates, whether it might not be prudent to send for a doctor and keeper from Bedlam."

"I assure you," resumed Mr. St. George, "I had my own doubts. Not as to your sanity: no, I don't say that; but as to whether you were not subsiding into a visionary; and the fear has chiefly brought me down to-day. 'You can't go,' said Serle to me, when the invitation came. 'I'll try,' said I, 'for it's right that somebody should see after Danesbury'; and, in spite of the law-courts, away I came."

"Walter! how can you utter such nonsense?" remonstrated his wife.

"Nonsense? Well, I'll go to sober fact then," said Mr. St. George, changing his tone to one of earnestness. "Danesbury, I don't know if there's another man living who would have thought of such a scheme; or would have dared to put it in practice, if he had thought of it. He would have feared ridicule."

Mr. Pratt put his hale old face across the table, and spoke meaningly. "Is there another man living such as Arthur Danesbury? And can ridicule approach *him?*"

"I can only say, then," said Arthur, in reply to Mr. St. George, "that if I have been the first to set the example, I hope others will follow it. But will you mention to me where lies, or may appear to lie, the insane points of the plan?"

Mr. St. George considered. "I suppose they lie in the supplying of coffee and bread-and-butter," quoth he, rubbing his nose. "Serle said, that was a proof which no lunacy commissioner would ever get over."

A general laugh went round. "That's the only part I deem to be extravagant," observed Lord Temple, when it had subsided. "It did certainly strike me as being so."

"Singular, not extravagant," returned Arthur. "Or—well—if you like—let us admit that the coffee point is extravagant—but there are two meanings to the word, you know. And, if you like, I will allow that my binding down the men from month to month, was also somewhat unusual; but what else is there to complain of?"

"Why—it's a completely Utopian scheme altogether, you know, Danesbury. There's so much of the ideal in it."

"The ideal!" repeated Arthur; "you must mean the real. Many and many a British master, employing numbers, has opened a place for his men in an evening, where they find lights, fires, and appropriate literature to while away the leisure hours. My father opened a reading room; but it did not take. In what does my plan differ? save that I take a personal interest in it, and give them coffee and bread-and-butter."

"Ah!" said Mr. St. George, shaking his head, "I fear it is that coffee that has done it."

"In two senses of the word," returned the magistrate, laughing. "Done the men out of their evening beer, and done Mr. Danesbury out of his reputation as a sane man."

"My poor operatives were going headlong on the downward road, as all must do who drink beyond their means," interposed the quiet voice of Arthur, "and I felt that I was, in a measure, answerable for them. Visionary again, you will say; but I am naturally of a thoughtful nature, possessing, I believe, a large share of the bump that phrenologists call conscientiousness; and past events in my family have tended to make me reflect deeply, more so than many do. I, gifted with a full portion of intellect, of intelligence, of means, was placed in authority over this body of *unthinking* men: I paid them fair wages for the work they did for me, and I often gave them good counsel; but the conviction arose, and pressed itself forcibly upon me, that our relations ought not to end there; that I ought to endeavour to help them out of their darkness. I determined to try some scheme: I formed my resolution——" Here his voice faltered in hesitation, but he rallied from it, and proceeded in a low, impressive tone—"as I stood over the tomb that contains my father, my mother, my brothers, and my father's second wife; all of these had strong drink, either through their own failing for it, or the failing of others, contributed to hasten to the grave. I was standing there without premeditation. I had been walking through Eastborough, a night walk, and had seen the men flocking into the public-houses, and there I made my resolve—to *try*—whether I should succeed or fail. A faint notion of the scheme I afterwards carried out, dawned then upon me. The difficulty was, *how* could I draw them from the public-houses? What possible inducement could I offer in their stead? What should you have done?"

"I!" cried Mr. St. George. "Don't ask me. The terrors of the law, a five-shillings fine, and the treadmill, are the only persuasions I understand."

Another smile went round; it would have been a laugh, but for Mr. Danesbury's solemn earnestness.

"I pondered over it long," he resumed. "I thought, 'if I am to wile away these men from one indulgence, I must substitute another, and I must see if I cannot bring them to like the substitute as well, in time, as the lost indulgence.' It is all very well to put a reflective man upon his own good sense; to impress upon him that to be temperate is a duty he may not transgress, unless he would offend God, and injure himself: my poor operatives had not attained to reflection, and I knew it would be of no use going to work in that way. Therefore, I hit upon the coffee scheme, and the binding down the men to it for a certain period. I could not think of anything better, and I honestly confess that, were it now to fail, I do not know that I could devise any better plan. It was an uncertain venture, but it was worth the risk."

"It will not fail now, Mr. Danesbury," said Squire Hanson.

"I don't fancy it will, squire," observed Mr. St. George. "The binding down the men to attend, that binding down accomplished the business. But this will be a pretty cost out of your pocket, yearly," he added, to Arthur."

"Not very much. Little, indeed, in comparison with the welfare of so many souls. Ought I to begrudge it to them from my ample means?"

"Mrs. Danesbury may be less generously inclined: and may let you know that she is, in sundry curtain lectures."

"Mrs. Danesbury married me with her eyes open, and my plans with me," returned Arthur, nodding to his wife, with a merry smile. "I expect she will be wanting her share of cost also, when she begins upon the wives, and the schools for the children."

"Your treasure will never weigh down your banker's chests, if you go on at many of these 'costs,'" said Mr. St. George.

"There is such a thing as another sort of treasure to be accumulated," answered Arthur, gently: "a Treasure that will stand us in good stead when that which we lodge at bankers' houses shall take to itself wings and flee away."

"Well," concluded Mr. St. George, breaking a pause of silence, "I shall convey word back to Serle that you are neither insane nor a visionary; but a man who has had the wisdom to look his responsibilities in the face, and the courage to act upon them. And, all I can say is, I hope your much-cared-for men will reap permanent benefit; and you, a rich reward."

"And when you hear my scheme laughed at for its extravagance, by those who, like myself, are placed in authority over the ignorant and the improvident, relate to them what mine is doing. Tell them that the extravagance consists only in the idea, not in the working, and that Arthur Danesbury hopes to see many others such, raised by the masters, in his native land."

When they rose from luncheon, Lord Temple linked his arm for a moment within that of William Danesbury.

"Let me have a word with you, William," he said. "Is it all serene? Isabel declares it is. She says she can read it in your face."

"Quite. For six months I have touched nothing. I begin to wonder now at my former marvellous infatuation, and at the difficulty I experienced in tearing myself from it. I can truly say I have conquered."

"It was difficult at first."

"Ay," answered William, with a deep breath, "it verily was difficult. But the difficulty is over. You might put wine, and beer, and spirits before me now, all poured out in glasses, and I should withstand them all. I *like* water now."

"As I told you you would. What a happy company we are to-day!" continued Lord Temple; "thinking, rational beings, aware of our responsibility—as St. George remarked with regard to Arthur—and striving to act up to it, firm in our self-reliance. God has been very merciful to us: you and I, William, have especial cause to say it."

"I thought the only face which bore a shade was that of Mrs. St. George."

"She was contrasting things here with her own family, I imagine. Her brothers are squandering their father's money, and one or two of them drinking wholesale. There goes Arthur: I never was so proud of him as I am to-day. Pratt is right in saying that there's hardly such another man on the face of the earth."

Arthur Danesbury had given his arm to his wife, and was proceeding to the tent. The guests followed. A hearty English dinner of roast beef and plum pudding had been disposed of by its occupants, but their drink was water, succeeded by a cup of coffee. Tea, with ample accompaniments, was to come in the evening. It was the first meeting of master and men since the former's return: they rose in a body, and their acclamations rent the air. Mr. Danesbury held up his hand for silence.

"My men, I am delighted to see you all again," he began, in his cheering way. "Have you relished your dinner?"

To assure him that they had was needless; and he made another motion for silence.

"I did not order you beer: I expressly desired that it should not be given to you. Not that I had any pleasure in depriving you to-day of your ordinary dinner drink, or that I hoped to force you suddenly to relinquish it. But I wished to afford you one self-convincing proof, how far more full of energy you will be this afternoon, how much lighter and pleasanter you will feel, although I daresay you have, some of you, eaten enough for six" (great laughter), "than you do when you drink the beer: in short, how far more capable you will find yourselves, whether for work or for enjoyment. You shall honestly tell me to-night if it be not so, and we will talk further, another time, about the expediency of your adopting it for your mid-day meal."

Symptoms of applause again, but Mr. Danesbury continued—

"I am truly gratified to hear that, during my month's absence, none of you have deserted to the opposition house over the way; but that two or three have voluntarily returned to mine. My men, what motive do you suppose I had in instituting this evening refuge, and in drawing you to it?"

"Our good," responded a voice.

"Just so. Your good, and that of your wives and families; your good in this world, and your good in the next. Oh, my friends, I have your welfare very much at heart; believe me, it causes me many a sleepless and anxious night. I have a duty to perform to you, as you have to me, a duty appointed by God; and in the next world, whither you and I are alike hastening, how shall we answer to Him, if we have neglected it? I want to lead you towards that better world; to show you how you may get there. So long as you were sunk in your previous bad and careless habits, you were not advancing to it. Were you?"

No. Conscience rose up before them, and they hung their heads sorrowfully.

"But I do think many of you are advancing now. A little bit; it cannot come all at once; there must be a beginning to all things. One of the greater of the prophets, in speaking of men who had erred 'through wine and strong drink,' says that, to those who would learn knowledge and understand doctrine, precept must be upon precept, line upon line, here a little, and there a little. And, by persevering on, step by step, a little and a little, it will come to you. I hope; I trust"— he looked from one table to another, affectionately—" that the time will come when you will all spend your evenings with me, without one exception. I say with me, because I shall often look in upon you. Some amongst you," he added, "still remember my mother. My good women, I speak now to you."

Yes, many did. They looked up eagerly.

"And you remember that she was all kindness to you; she would have been ever so, had she lived. But she is gone, and others have gone, and there is now another Mrs. Danesbury, my wife, whom I hold upon my arm. She will be to you and your families what my mother was. She is anxious to be so, to befriend and help you all; and I know that you will welcome her for my sake, until you have learnt to welcome and love her for her own."

A deeper shout than ever filled the tent, meant for Mrs. Danesbury, and Mary turned her hot face towards her husband, hoping to hide her raining tears.

"Courage, my darling," he whispered, fondly glancing down upon her. "Be not ashamed of their seeing your tears, Mary: tears are passports to hearts, you know."

And when the murmur had subsided, Mr. Danesbury resumed, to the men.

"You have been pleased to say that you have hitherto found me a considerate master: and you shall find me one. If you do as I wish you, and strive to be good men, single-hearted in the sight of your Maker, I will be more indulgent to you than I have yet been. Will you not strive to be so for your own sakes?"

"Ay, that they would!" Though some of them could scarcely promise it; for their hearts and eyes were full.

"Oh, my dear friends," concluded Arthur Danesbury, with solemn earnestness, "listen to my counsel, for it is born of anxiety for you. By the exercise of a little persevering self-denial, you will find great reward. I will do what I can to encourage you to exercise it. Your Saviour—your all-merciful Saviour—is looking down upon us; now, as I speak and you listen; He is waiting for you to choose the good and reject the evil; waiting to aid all who ask for His help. May you—and I—and all of us—be so strengthened in our labours here, that, when they are over, we may find Him waiting to receive us hereafter; waiting to welcome us with His own blessed words, 'Well done, thou good and faithful servant, enter thou into the joy of thy Lord!'"

"Amen, Amen!"

APPENDIX A
ELLEN WOOD: A CHRONOLOGY OF IMPORTANT DATES

1814 Born Ellen Price on January 17th in Worcester, England.

1827 (year is estimated) Develops scoliosis or spondytlitis causing permanent damage to her spine. This condition would stay with Wood for her lifetime. (Due to the severe curvature of her spine, she wrote many of her books with her pad in her lap. She would eventually have a special chair constructed so she could write at a desk).

1836 Ellen Price married Charles Wood. The couple moves to France for the next 20 years where they have four children: Henry, Arthur Edward, Charles William, and Ellen Mary. (Her first daughter, Ellen, died in infancy).

1851 Wood's first article, *Seven Years in the Wedded Life of a Roman Catholic* and her first ghost story, *Gina Montani*, are published in Ainsworth's New Monthly Magazine.

1856 The Wood family returns to England.

1860 Wood publishes *Danesbury House* and wins the Scottish Temperance League award.

1861 Publishes her blockbuster, *East Lynne* and secures her place as a prominent British author. With in the first six months of its publication, *East Lynne* would go through four editions. Countless editions and international pirated copies follow making her second novel an unprecedented literary achievement.

1862 Wood begins her most prosperous years as an author- writing up to four lengthy novels per year. Publishes *Mrs. Halliburton's Troubles* and *The Channings*.

1863 Publishes *The Shadow of Ashlydyat*, *Verner's Pride*, and *The Foggy Night at Offord*.

1864 Publishes *William Allair; or, Running Away to Sea* (a children's book), *Oswald Cray*, *Lord Oakburn's Daughters*, and *Trevlyn Hold*.

1865 Publishes *Mildred Arkell*.

1866	Wood's husband, Henry Wood, dies. Publishes *St. Martin's Eve* and *Elster's Folly*.
1867	Publishes *A Life's Secret*, *Orville College*, and *Lady Adelaide's Oath*.
1869	Publishes *Roland Yorke*.
1870	Publishes *Bessy Rane* and *George Canterbury's Will*.
1871	Publishes *Dene Hollow*.
1872	Publishes *Within the Maze*.
1873	Wood's health begins to decline affecting her publications. Publishes *The Master of Greylands*.
1874	Publishes *Johnny Ludlow*.
1875	Publishes *Told in the Twilight* and *Bessy Wells*.
1876	Publishes *Edina*, *Our Children*, *Adam Grainger*, and *Parkwater with Four Other Tales*.
1878	Publishes *Pommeroy Abbey*.
1881	Publishes *Court Netherleigh*.
1883	Wood sees the last book in her lifetime published, *About Ourselves*.
1887	Wood dies of heart failure on February 10th leaving behind several more unpublished books. *Lady Grace and Other Stories* is published. Wood leaves an estate valued at £36,393.13s5d, nearly three times the value of Wilkie Collins' estate.
1888	*The Story of Charles Strange* is published posthumously.
1889	*Featherston's Story* is published posthumously.
1890	*Edward Burton*, *The House of Halliwell*, and *The Unholy Wish* is published posthumously.
1894	Wood's son, publishes his biography of his mother, *Memorials of Mrs. Henry Wood*.

APPENDIX B:
INTRODUCTORY PREFACE AND *A TRIO OF FAMOUS WOMEN*

The following reprint, *Introductory Preface* and *A Trio of Famous Women*, is from Chicago's Rand, McNally 1892 edition of *Danesbury House*, written by Miss Frances Willard and Lady Henry Somerset of the Women's Christian Temperance League.

Introductory Preface
Nov. 14, 1892.

Perhaps the greatest difficulty known to us in the spread of the Temperance propaganda is the indifference of the great public outside our lines. Issuing from our publishing house one hundred and thirty-five millions of pages this year, the very existence of that house is unknown to the world at large. But here comes *Danesbury House*, a book written by one of the most famous novelists of our time, accredited by Christian pastors, and the Prize tale of a great Temperance Society. Its sales have already amounted to three hundred and four thousand copies in England, and you propose to put this fascinating and dramatic presentation of the theme to which we are devoted before the great world of American readers of fiction. For this we are grateful and glad. While our own lives are too thoroughly pre-occupied with temperance work for us to write stories, even had we the gift, or to read them to any extent after they are written, we are encouraged to hope that tens of thousands of young people will dwell on the attractive pages of this great story by a great author, and through its vivid lessons be led to shun the cup "that lures but to destroy."

Yours in this faith, and for the protection of everybody's home and loved ones from the curse of drink.

Frances Willard
  Pres. W. C. T. U. of America.
Lady Henry Somerset
  Pres. W. C. T. U. of Great Britain.

A Trio of Famous Women

ELLEN WOOD, one of the most justly celebrated British female novelists, and the author of this volume, was the eldest daughter of a Mr. Thomas Price, the head of one of the leading glove manufacturing firms in the city of Worcester, England. Born in 1820, and inheriting a literary talent from her father, himself a ripe classical scholar and an accomplished gentleman, the subject of this brief biographical sketch was married at an early age to Mr. Henry Wood, a prominent ship-owner. Commencing her literary career as a contributor to the New Monthly Magazine and Bentley's Miscellany, her first complete work (and by some even esteemed the finest production of her fertile pen) was this forceful temperance story, *Danesbury House*, which, published in 1860, gained a prize of £100 pounds ($500), offered by the Scottish Temperance League "for the best temperance tale illustrative of the injurious effects of intoxicating drinks, the advantages of personal abstinence, and the demoralizing operations of the liquor traffic." Issued by the league with the fervent hope and prayer that it might contribute largely to the temperance cause and kindred movements, this veritable "Uncle Tom's Cabin" of this righteous and rapidly growing cause, has well justified the propriety of the prize award made to its talented, and now, alas! lamented, author. Its success was phenomenal. Upward of three hundred and four thousand copies of this vivid picture of the vice of drunkenness have been sold and circulated in Great Britain alone; many copies of it being exported to America. In the years succeeding 1861, fecund indeed was the facile pen of the author of *Danesbury House*. *East Lynne*, the novel most frequently associated with her name, appeared in 1861, and, achieving a remarkable success, was, with some merit, dramatized by some seven or eight adapters; *The Channings*, *Mrs. Halliburton's Troubles*, *Verner's Pride*, *Lord Oakburn's Daughters*, and many other contributions of sterling worth to the literature of her country, and the moral amelioration of its inhabitants, does the nation owe to Mrs. Henry Wood. If, as according to Ben Jonson we learn, Shakespeare "never blotted a line," it can with equal credit be said of the author of *Danesbury House* that never a line from her pen required expunging. In every case, her portrayal of a character was to point a moral for the benefit of humanity, to lead to imitation of things noble or divine, or to warn, by a vivid picture, of the inevitable wages of sin. Of her works, the Saturday Review well said: "Mrs. Henry Wood has certain qualities which should have made her one of our best novel writers; popular is another word. No one lays out the plan of a story better than she does, and even Mr. Wilkie Collins himself, to whom construction is the Alpha and Omega of his craft, is not greater than she is in the cleverness with which she devises her puzzles and fits the parts together." Associated for many years with the editorship of the Mrs. Wood added to her honors as the author of those bright stories, *The Adventures of Johnny Ludlow*, and rapidly improved the contents and circulation of an excellent magazine. On the 10th of February, 1887, this first of a trio of noble and glorious women exchanged life's trials for an immortal crown of exceeding great joy.

Miss **FRANCES ELIZABETH WILLARD**, the second of this trio of celebrities, is the founder and for five years has been the president of the World's W. C. T. U., and now for twelve years president of the National W. C. T. U. She was born September 28, 1839, at Churchville, near Rochester, N.Y., and is the daughter of the Hon. Josiah F. and Mary Thompson Hill Willard. A graduate of the Northwestern University, Chicago; she took the degree of A. M. from Syracuse University. In 1862 she was professor of natural science at the Northwestern Female College, Evanston, Ill.; 1866-1867, she was preceptress of the Genesee Wesleyan Seminary, Lima, N. Y. ; 1868 to 1870 (about two years and a half), she traveled abroad—studying French, German, Italian, and the History of the Fine Arts; visited nearly every European capital; went to Greece, Egypt, and Palestine; 1871, she was president of the Women's College of Northwestern University, and professor of aesthetics there; 1874, corresponding secretary of the National Woman's Christian Temperance Union; 1877, was associated with D. L. Moody in revival work in Boston; 1878, president of the Woman's Christian Temperance Union of Illinois and editor of the Chicago Daily Post; 1879, president of the National Woman's Christian Temperance Union, the largest society ever organized, conducted, and controlled exclusively by women. In 1880 she was president of the American Commission, which placed the portrait of Mrs. President Hayes in the

White House as a testimonial to her example as a total abstainer. She made the tour of the Southern States in 1881-1883, and everywhere introduced the Woman's Christian Temperance Union, for the cause of gospel temperance, total abstinence, the prohibition of the sale of alcoholic drinks, and the ballot for women. She at that time traveled thirty thousand miles in the United States, visiting every State and Territory, accompanied by her private secretary, Miss Anna A. Gordon of Boston. Miss Willard gave to the National Woman's Christian Temperance Union its motto, "For God and Home and Native Land," and classified its forty departments of work under the heads of Preventive, Educational, Evangelistic, Social, Legal, and Organization. She is also founder of the World's W. C. T. U. (in 1883), and has served nearly two terms as president of that organization, 1888-1892. In 1884 she helped to establish the Home Protection Party, and was a member of its executive committee which nominated Gov. John St. John of Kansas for President of the United States at the National Prohibition Convention, Pittsburg, Pa. In 1887, Miss Willard was elected president of the Woman's Council of the United States, formed from the confederated societies of women; in the same year she was elected to the General Conference of the Methodist Episcopal Church, which represents one hundred annual conferences and two million church members, and in 1889 she was elected to the Ecumenical Conference of the same church by the Rock River Conference; but previous to said Council her name was thrown out by the board of control because she was a woman. She is the originator of the great petition against the alcohol and opium trade (two million names being now secured), which is to be presented to all governments by a commission of women. She is likewise the author of the *Home Protection Movement*, to give women in America the ballot on all temperance questions, and of the following works: *Nineteen Beautiful Years*, or sketches of a girl's life, written by her sister, 1863; *Hints and Helps in Temperance Work*, 1875; *Woman and Temperance*, 1883; *How to Win*, 1886; *Woman in the Pulpit*, 1888; *Glimpses of Fifty Years, the Autobiography of an American Woman*, 1889; and in 1891, *A Classic Town—The history of Evanston—The Mecca of Methodists*. Of her autobiography, 50,000 copies have been sold. Miss Willard is one of the editors of The Union Signal, the official organ of the World's and National Woman's Christian Temperance

Union, is associated with Joseph Cook as editor of Our Day (Boston), and is one of the Board of Directors of the Woman's National Temperance Hospital, Chicago, and of the Woman's Temperance Temple, Chicago, the chief room in which is called Willard Hall. Her birthday (September 28) is celebrated by Children's Temperance societies throughout the United States as a "Harvest Home." Miss Willard is also at the head of the Purity work of the World's and National Woman's Christian Temperance unions, which has secured from National and State legislatures, laws for the better protection of women, and which advocates the scientific education of the people in habits of personal purity. Miss Willard has been made chairman of the Woman's Temperance Committee of the Columbian Exposition, Archbishop Ireland, who is at the head of the men's committee (with which this is correlated), having requested that she represent the women. A World's Temperance Congress, under the charge of these committees, is to be held at Chicago in 1893. A recent and most interesting character sketch in the Review of Reviews, styles her, with more than accuracy and considerable art, "The Uncrowned Queen of American Democracy." It is from the able pen of Mr. W. T. Stead, the celebrated English journalist.

ISABEL, LADY HENRY SOMERSET, not the least in this grand trio, was born in 1851; she is the eldest daughter of Earl and Countess Somers of Eastnor Castle, Ledbury, in Herefordshire, England. Ledbury is a quaint old market town where John B. Gough spoke for temperance thirty years ago, and where now a strong branch of the white-ribbon movement flourishes under the presidency of Lady Elizabeth Biddulph. Three miles from this railway station is Eastnor Castle, on the River Wye, and on the western side of the Malvern Hills. It is beautiful in situation, majestic in character, and historic in surroundings. In sight is the Herefordshire Beacon, the highest point on the Malvern Range, one of the strongest hill fortresses in Britain. For ages the same summit of this hill has been used for beacon fires, whose heats hare charred its ranges. At the approach of the Spanish Armada, Twelve counties saw the blaze On Malveru's lonely height. Thus, Eastnor Castle is the home of one who to-day stands as a beacon-light, not only for England, but for the world. Having no brothers, Lady Henry Somerset succeeded to the vast estates of her father. The

Somers family had been long land-owners in County Kent, certainly as far back as the thirteenth century, numbering many illustrious men and women in its line of succession; among them Lord Keeper Somers, of whom Macaulay said, "In some respects he was the greatest man of his age, uniting all the qualities of a great will—an intellect comprehensive, quick, and acute—with diligence, patience, and suavity." Born thus to an inheritance of culture, refinement, and wealth, married in 1872 to Lord Henry Somerset, the second son of the Duke of Beaufort, receiving the crown of motherhood in 1874 by the birth of her only child, Lady Henry Somerset seemed to have all that the world could give. Her life was passed in the gayest of England's most aristocratic society, and with it she seemed content until 1885. What heavenly breezes swept her soul then we do not know, but the result is manifest. In 1885, in the little village of Ledbury, at her castle gates, she signed the pledge with forty of her tenants. She had large possessions in the east of London, as well as in the beautiful Weald of Kent, her tenants in the city numbering nearly one hundred thousand. Over these she felt her heart stirring like that of a mother, and she who had been the light of the West End drawing-rooms now went to the London missions to seek and save those who were lost. Lady Henry became one of the chief supporters of the great work undertaken by Rev. Hugh Price Hughes in St. James Hall. She went to him and offered to receive into her country home some of the destitute souls in the slums of Soho; she gave fêtes to probably ten thousand poor people at a time; so Eastnor Castle had new visitors. Mrs. Hannah Whitall Smith seems to have been the connecting link between Lady Henry Somerset and the British Women's Temperance Association, of which she is president (and, therefore, vice-president of the World's Women's Christian Temperance Union). They had never met until Mrs. Smith went to Ledbury, a year or two ago, to give a series of Bible readings. Here they communed concerning the things of the kingdom, and each discovered in the other a kindred spirit. Lady Henry Somerset does not shrink from bringing temperance into politics by laying the responsibility upon the consciences of the voters. She said at Eastnor Castle, recently, to the thousands assembled: "When the political struggle is hot, and your opinions run high in favor of this party and that, consecrate that vote of yours to this one great temperance question, and the riddle will be solved that includes many others. My friends, in this great cause we want God's honor remembered at the ballot-box, and we need not be afraid that He will not watch over the best interests of our nation." Like her two compeers, she is also an author, as a beautiful series of sketches of English life appeared from her pen, in 1884, entitled "Our Village Life."

APPENDIX C
FATHER DEAR FATHER

This song was written by Henry Clay Work in 1864 and was included in the dramatization of the temperance novel *Ten Nights in a Barroom*. As she stands in the door to the bar, ten-year-old Mary sings to her drunken father, Joe Morgan. At the song's conclusion, a bar fight breaks out and she is hit a fatal blow in the head by a stray bottle.

> Father, dear father, come home with me now,
> The clock in the steeple strikes one;
> You said you were coming right home from the shop
> As soon as your day's work was done;
> Our fire has gone out, our house is all dark,
> And mother's been watching since tea,
> With poor brother Benny so sick in her arms
> And no one to help her but me,
> Come home! come home! come home!
> Please father, dear father, come home.
>
> *Chorus*:
> Hear the sweet voice of the child,
> Which the night-winds repeat as they roam;
> Oh who could resist this most plaintive of prayers
>
> "Please father, dear father, come home."
>   Father, dear father, come home with me now,
> The clock in the steeple strikes two;
> The night has grown colder, and Benny is worse
> But he has been calling for you:
> Indeed he is worse, ma says he will die—
> Perhaps before morning shall dawn;
> And this is the message she sent me to bring
> "Come quickly, or he will be gone."
> Come home! come home! come home!
> Please father, dear father, come home.

Chorus:

Father, dear father, come home with me now,
The clock in the steeple strikes three;
The house is so lonely, the hours are so long,
For poor weeping mother and me;
Yes, we are alone, poor Benny is dead,
And gone with the angels of light;
And these were the very last words that he said
"I want to kiss papa good-night."
Come home! come home! come home!
Please father, dear father, come home.

APPENDIX D
REVIEWS OF *DANESBURY HOUSE*

From *The Athenaeum*, March 24, 1860.

It is the story which was successful in obtaining the £100 prize which had been offered by the Society for the best tale "illustrative of the injurious effects of intoxicating drinks, the advantages of personal abstinence, and the demoralising operations of the Liquor Traffic." A tale written on these conditions would naturally be under difficulties, which might well quench the "genial current" of the most vivid imagination...'Danesbury House' gets over the natural difficulties of the task extremely well; the story, as a mere story, is interesting, and there are occasional spirited delineations of life and character, which indicate that the authoress might write a very good novel if left to follow what whist-players call an "original lead".

The sketch of Lord Temple is about the best in the book, and the account of his life and embarrassments and good resolves, and how he happens to break them without intending any harm, is given in a human, natural way, as though the authoress had sought to be true rather than didactic...

The style is hard and not pleasing, but the story has the aspect of truthfulness and reality, which give it the air of being, in many particulars, a real narrative:—things do not fall so smooth and easy as in tales they often do. It is a good, wholesome story to put into the hands of a young man or boy, and the maxims and examples about temperance arise naturally, and as they would be likely to do in actual life.

From *The Critic*, July 7, 1860.

We are informed by the preface that this is the result of a competition incited by an offer of £100 for the "best temperance tale, illustrative of the injurious effects of intoxicating drinks, the advantages of personal abstinence, and the demoralising operations of the liquor traffic." It is cleverly written, and is constructed with as much ability as works produced under such inspiration usually are. The misfortune, however, is, that such works do no good, for the simple reason that they are liked only by those who do not need to be convinced; whilst to those who require conversion they convey no faith. To take individual cases showing the evil effects of the abuse of liquor, and lay then before a drunkard, is to tell him nothing he is not already acquainted with. None knows better than he the horrors of the pit into which he is plunged, and for every harrowing tale you can lay before him his own heart will supply fifty personal experiences more agonising to him, because closer to him...

From *Meliora: A Quarterly Review of Social Science*, Vol III, 1861.

The prize of 100£ was given [to *Danesbury House*] which is "illustrative of the injurious effects of intoxicating drinks, the advantages of personal abstinence, and the demoralizing operations of the liquor traffic." These themes are strikingly portrayed in a well-told tale. The drunken cases introduced are decidedly bad; but they can easily be paralleled from real life. There is good writing, lively description, and fine delineation of character, with a wholesome moral in *Danesbury House*.

From *The London Quarterly Review*, Vol XXII, 1864.

Mrs. Wood is a writer who puzzles us. Some of her stories are as pure, as free from anything that could offend, as earnest in their inculcation of virtue, as any writings of their class. On the other hand, others are just as unhealthy in their tone and as questionable in their principles. Perhaps, in all there is too much straining after effect. Even *Danesbury House*, which obtained the prize offered by the Scottish Temperance League, and first won her a name, is, to a very glairing extent, disfigured by this fault. Of course, it is the desire of those who instituted the competition that the story should represent drunkenness as the parent of all vice and misery; but it must have required strong digestion even for a teetotaler to swallow all of the horrors that Mrs. Wood has crowded into the narrow compass of her tale. It may be that the adjudicators had nothing better offered them; but, believing that the moral effect of the book is utterly destroyed by its exaggeration, we have always regretted their decision, and viewed it as one evidence of that growing appetite for sensation which is the course of our literature. We object, too, to the general moral of Mrs. Wood's good books, in which virtue is always rewarded, and vice always punished. This may be poetic justice, but it is not that which marks God's dealings with men in the present life; and it certainly rests the appeal on behalf of goodness on the lowest possible ground. ... Mrs. Wood is capable of better things; we trust she will yet perform them, and that she will live to blot out the memory of the errors committed in the worst class of her novels by the abler and more ennobling books of a brighter future. If she would write better, she should write less, and should eschew every temptation to pander to a depraved appetite, and to purchase a present and unworthy popularity by the loss of a more endearing and nobler fame.

From *The Medical Age: A Semi-Monthly Journal of Medicine and Surgery*, Vol XV, 1897.

[*Danesbury House*], a well known classical bit of fiction, emanates from one of the ablest women authors of Great Britain, and this work is contemporary with *East Lynne*. No one can lay out the plan of a story better than Mrs. Wood, and not even Wilkie Collins, to whom construction is the Alpha and Omega of his craft, is superior in cleverness with which puzzles are devised and the parts fitted together. To attempt to review the tale itself would be to spoil it for the reader. It is one of the most fascinating of nineteenth century novels.

APPENDIX E
LETTER TO GEORGE BENTLEY, PUBLISHER, AUGUST 8, 1861[6]

In this selection from a letter Ellen Wood wrote to her publisher, George Bentley, she reveals her keen marketing insight.

One of my sons tells me that he saw *East Lynne* advertised today in the Times "By the author of *Ashley*." I do not think you do well to advertise it "by the author of *Ashley*." *Ashley* is no book. It has never been before the general public, it was the name of one short paper in Colburn's New Monthly – years ago, and my papers since in the magazine have been headed "By the author of *Ashley*." In short, it is a nom de plume for the New Monthly and that is all. What I mean to imply is, that the word *Ashley* will not strike upon the ear or memory of the reading public, only the readers of the New Monthly and *East Lynne* will be enough for them. Personally, I have no objection to *Ashley* appearing only I do not know it will enhance the success of *East Lynne*. People who see *East Lynne* advertised "By the author of *Ashley*" may go to the library (for I speak chiefly of ladies) and ask "Have you a book called *Ashley*?" The answer, probably would be "No; we have never heard of it" and the conclusion come to might be that Ashley was a venture which had died away without sale. This would give an unfortunate impression of *East Lynne*. At least, it strikes me in that light.

You might advertise if you please "By the author of *Danesbury House*." *Danesbury House* is a class book, but it has had an immense sale, and I believe it is in most libraries, though it was not intended as a library book. I think Mudie took it but am not sure. If you advertise *East Lynne* in Scotland, in any of the large towns "By the author of *Danesbury House*" it will be read by hundreds and hundreds..... If you choose to advertise "By the author of *Ashley* and *Danesbury House*" you could do so; as the one is well known, though the other is not. I have written in a great hurry, for I am very busy, and I would not have troubled you, but I think a vast deal lies in an advertisement.

... On the title page of the book I must request you to put "By Mrs. Henry Wood, Author of *Danesbury House*." Be particular that the Christian name (Henry) is inserted.

---

[6] From Maunders, Andrew, ed. *East Lynn*. Peterborough: Broadview Press, 2000. 693. Courtesy of Broadview Press.